Whales for the Wizard

D0774476

For Cathy

Whales for the Wizard

Malcolm Archibald

Polygon

First published in Great Britain in 2005 by
Polygon, an imprint of Birlinn Ltd
West Newington House
10 Newington Road
Edinburgh
EH9 1QS

www.birlinn.co.uk

ISBN 1 904598 40 4
ISBN 13: 978 1 904598 40 4

The publishers acknowledge subsidy from

Scottish
Arts Council

towards the publication of this volume

British Library Cataloguing-in-Publication Data
A catalogue record for this book is available on request from the British
Library

Typeset by HewerText, Edinburgh

Printed by Bell & Bain Ltd., Glasgow

The grinding of reinforced oak against ice woke the man and he lifted one hand to rub his eyes. Frost had already formed on his mitten, glistening in the deep trench beside the thumb and across the rope-work pattern on the back. He forced himself upright, breaking the film of ice that threatened to attach him to the soiled pine planking. He looked around the foc'sle, seeing the piled bodies of his shipmates, their eyes glaring from deep sockets, beards already white with frost.

'Hello!' The creaking of wood on wood accentuated the hollow echo of his voice. 'Hello! Can anybody hear me?'

A lantern swayed slowly with the movement of the ship, its wick long since burned out, and its reservoir empty of oil. The man stilled the trembling of his legs as he pushed open the door and hauled himself on to the deck, where a single eider duck rose slowly into the air. There were two more bodies sprawled across the planking. 'Oh, Jesus!'

Mollies hopped before him, their bright eyes predatory but beaks not yet busy. They fled on frantic wings when he shouted at them.

Ice glistened from canvas boat covers, from spars that spiralled a slow salute to the sky, from the hand-lines that were intended to keep men safe in foul weather. There was no ice on the great funnel. Instead, smoke spread a smutty stain over the stationary vessel. All around was ice, with the bows thrusting deep into a blue-tinted berg and loose floes clinking against the hull. Unless he shut off the engines, the ship would blow herself up.

Swearing softly, he staggered down to the engine-room, but only dead men lay there. Two firemen stared at him through wide eyes, their faces white beneath the coal-dust. He shouted louder as he fought his fear, but the returning echoes drove him on deck again, where the wind cut like Neptune's trident.

'Ahoy! Is there anybody left alive?'

Nothing human replied, only the noises of a wooden ship and the endless chattering of the mollies that hunted for scraps.

'Sweet Jesus,' he whispered, 'am I alone on board?'

He looked to starboard, where brash-ice sat soft on the surface of the sea, and saw, far in the distance, the raised sail of a whaling-boat.

'Ahoy! Over here!'

Stumbling aft, he clutched at the speaking-trumpet that the Master always kept in brackets hard by the wheel. He wasted precious seconds opening his knife to hack away the seal of ice, then lifted the trumpet.

'Ahoy!' His voice sounded harshly metallic as it bounced across the ice. 'Ahoy! It's Jimmy Gordon! Don't leave me here!'

The boat did not deviate from her course. He felt fear rise within him. Lifting the trumpet high, he dashed it against the mizzenmast, hoping to make a loud enough noise, but still she sailed away. As he watched, a fresh breeze filled the lugsail and she altered course, to slide out of view behind a pyramid-shaped iceberg.

'Come back!' he shouted, waving the trumpet, nearly crying in his fear and frustration. 'Don't leave me here alone!'

Every breath a bright agony in his chest, he stumbled to the nearest whaleboat, which swung on its davits above the slowly heaving sea. Swearing, he began to work the mechanism, hoping to lower the boat into the water.

'I'll catch you,' he muttered. 'I'll get you. You can't leave me here.'

A shaft of sunlight shone on the stern of the whaleboat, catching the brave name *Ivanhoe*. He swore more loudly when one of the blocks jammed. He looked upward to see the source of the blockage, but stopped as a shadow passed over the deck.

'Who's that?' The hope in his voice faltered as he saw who moved towards him: strangers, wearing the thick furs of the Innuit. 'Oh, Jesus, no!' He thrust his knife towards the three men. '*No!* You don't belong on this ship! Get away from me!'

The nearest man moved closer and lifted his spear.

Dundee, February 1860

'Hard times, I see.' The speaker slipped out of a doorway and walked beside Douglas. 'Home from the wars?'

Douglas nodded. His jacket, patched and faded until the original scarlet was nearly gone, proclaimed that he had been a soldier. He sucked his empty pipe and bent his head against the icy drizzle.

'And searching for a job, no doubt?' The speaker was as slim as the ebony cane he carried, a head taller than Douglas's five foot eight and dressed in a tightly fitting black coat. He wore his lum hat at a rakish angle.

'I have been,' Douglas admitted. Experience had taught him to be wary of sudden friendships.

'I am John Wyllie,' the slim man said. 'And you are?'

'Robert Douglas, late sergeant in the Seventy-Third Foot.' He moved aside to allow a group of spinners to pass.

Though obviously in a hurry, they paused long enough to voice their opinion of a soldier on their street. 'Oughtn't be allowed,' one said, 'letting them mingle with respectable people.' She looked only about seventeen, but long working hours had already carved deep grooves round her eyes. 'Bloody redcoats! All they're good for is drinking.'

'Walk with me, Mr Douglas,' Wyllie ordered easily, swinging his cane to clear the spinners from his path. 'Have you had much success in obtaining a position?'

Douglas shook his head. He had been little more than a boy when, eighteen years earlier, he had accepted the Queen's fatal shilling, hoping for excitement, adventure and glory. Instead he had found sordid hardship, hunger and misery which only comradeship had alleviated. For much of those eighteen years he had dreamed of returning home, only to find that the reality did not match his expectation. 'Not much.'

'No?' Wyllie rattled his cane along the dull sandstone wall of Campbell's Crown Hotel. A fisherwoman, one of the many who walked from Auchmithie and Arbroath to sell fish in Dundee, glowered at him. The wickerwork ripp on her back overflowed with line-caught haddock. 'And yet the city is booming.' He flourished the cane, pointing to the tall stacks of factory chimneys that rose above the many-windowed tenements of the Greenmarket. 'You see? Mills and factories at every corner, shipping increasing every year, an expanding population. We live in changing times, Mr Douglas.'

'Indeed,' Douglas agreed. 'But we live in times when there are few jobs for men in Dundee.' He had spent the past few weeks knocking at doors and presenting himself before a succession of avaricious-eyed men. Each interview had been a copy of the last, with a catalogue of questions, a firm shake of the interviewer's head, and a shamefaced return to the streets. There was no place for a man in his thirties with neither experience nor a trade, particularly when he wore the Queen's scarlet.

'Perhaps I can alter that, Mr Douglas. Walk this way, if you please.' Obviously educated, Wyllie had a pleasing tone and dressed like a gentleman. Raising his hat to a passing lady, he led Douglas down to Dock Street, where the masts of ships blocked the sky and seamen spilled from the riverside public houses. 'Do you ever come this way, Mr Douglas?'

Again Douglas nodded. He sought employment at the docks every morning, hoping for even a few hours' pay to supplement his steadily diminishing capital. However, it seemed that dockers were careful in their choice of fellow workers.

'A fascinating place, the docks.' Wyllie took a deep inhalation of salt air mingled with the rich scents of tar, whale oil and effluvia. 'The very life-blood of Britain.'

A pool of prostitutes had gathered outside the Castle Bar to watch a grimy collier brig manoeuvre round a fleet of sprat fishing boats. The two men stepped round them and walked on.

As they passed the Royal Arch, the vast gothic monument erected to commemorate Queen Victoria's visit to the city, a group of women came slowly towards them. Most wore sombre clothes, with black veils and gloves, but one walked straight-backed and proud in her bottle-green coat.

Working men fell silent, or made sympathetic comments as the women passed. A carter reached out and patted a woman's shoulder, while a shipwright touched a hand to his cap. A flight of pigeons erupted from the ornate carvings of the Arch and fluttered over the long warehouses beside the dock.

'Who are those women?' Douglas asked quietly. 'They seem to be here every time the tide is suitable for ships to berth.'

Wyllie raised his hat in salute. 'They are the *Ivanhoe* widows.'

Douglas shook his head. 'I'm sorry, but that means nothing to me.'

'*Ivanhoe* was a whaler. She was lost with all hands last season up in the ice.' Wyllie replaced his hat, jamming it on his head with some finality. 'Those women are the crew's widows. They spend half their lives at the dock, weeping. All except that one.' He pointed his cane at the woman in the green coat. 'She still expects her man to come strolling through the Arch with his wages in his pocket. Look at her, walking proud as Lucifer, and her with the patches coming away from her coat. She should be ashamed of herself!'

'Why is that?' Douglas felt a quickening of interest as he looked at the green-coated woman. 'What has she done?'

'It isn't what she's done, though I suspect that's plenty.' Wyllie's face darkened into a scowl. 'You know what whaler's women are like. No, no, it's what she's not doing. She should accept the will of the Lord as the other women have, mourn for her lost husband – if he was her husband – then find another man.'

6

While the black-dressed widows huddled in a dejected group, the green-coated woman questioned every seaman she could. One by one they shook their heads, some with an expression of sympathy, one or two with an attempt at intimacy. Her large eyes accentuated her high cheekbones as she looked across at Douglas, and she nervously gripped the dark tartan shawl spread across her shoulders.

She stepped closer. 'I can see you're not a seafaring man.' Her accent was pure Dundee and she enunciated her words with an obvious attempt at respectability. 'But you may have heard aught of my Jim. James Gordon. He's the carpenter in *Ivanhoe*, which has not yet returned from the whaling.' Her voice lifted appealingly at the end of each sentence. 'Have you seen him, sir? He's not a tall man, but well made, and he's late home.'

Douglas shook his head. 'I'm sorry, I haven't.' As she turned away, he reached into his pocket and withdrew a silver three-penny bit. 'Here, this might help until your man comes back.'

She looked at the coin. 'I can manage,' she said, stepping backward. When she looked up at him, her wide eyes were murky green and shadowed with hardship. 'Jimmy never lets me go without.'

Wyllie smiled as Douglas replaced the coin. 'She would only drink it, Mr Douglas. You were merely casting pearls before swine.'

'Or mammon before a pearl, perhaps.' Douglas watched Mrs Gordon approach another seaman, saw the quick shake of the man's head and momentarily shared her disappointment. 'Jimmy Gordon has a good wife there. I hope he appreciates her.'

'He was a whaler: he probably lifted the skirts of half the women in Dundee.' Wyllie flicked his cane through the air again. 'But come, Mr Douglas, you have seen the results of unemployment now, the numb hopelessness of these poor widows. Are you to join them, or will you listen to my offer of employment?'

'I will listen to any offer of employment.' Douglas resolutely turned his mind away from Mrs Gordon's hopeless task. He had witnessed too much suffering already.

'I need a runner, Mr Douglas. Could you be my runner? Indeed, do you even know what a runner, a leg-man, is?'

'Not exactly, but I presume that it's somebody who runs with something. Messages, perhaps?' Paddy McBride had often spoken of soldiers who had left the army to become messengers. 'Penny-letter boys', he'd called them, men whose desperation knew no shame. 'It's not the job for me, Douglas, not for me. I'm going to open a pub in Draperstown, with the Sperrins for a backdrop and my own good Irish whiskey from the hills.' He never had, though.

Wyllie strode under the arch and turned left, past the Earl Grey Dock. 'Splendid! You have understood. A runner is somebody who runs. Did you do much running for the Queen?'

'Running?' Douglas shook his head. 'I did a lot of marching.'

Marching? Aye, he had marched. Marched until his feet bled and his knees jarred with every step. Colonel Eyre had temporarily discarded their scarlet serge, dressed them in grey canvas and marched them so fast they earned the sobriquet of 'the Cape Greyhounds'. He remembered all too well the monotonous rhythm of boots on the hard brown veldt of Africa, with the dust rising behind them. Umkye of the Gaikas in his leopard-skin kaross; struggling across the flooded Keiskama river with a train of wagons; the hiss of spears in the Chumie ambush when Paddy McBride saved his life; the secret staircase to Macomos Den. Then back to scarlet jackets and India, the slaughter at Seria Ghat. Sweat and flies and confusion beneath the burning sun while the acrid reek of powder mingled with the raw salt of blood. But, above all, the trust in a girl's eyes as he promised to protect her.

'Indeed. But could you run for me?' Wyllie gestured expansively. 'I will give you Dundee as your domain, Dundee and the surrounding area. I would give you a fine new uniform, with boots that do not let in water' – his cane tapped the cracked boots that squeaked damply with every step Douglas took – 'and a coat without patches' – the emerald in his ring gleamed as he prodded the darn on the elbow of Douglas's tunic. 'You will become an officer, so to speak, rather than a sergeant. I would pay you enough money to fill your belly with food and sample the best beer on a Saturday night.'

The cane rapped on the ground. 'But man cannot live by bread and beer alone. Women, such as work in there' – the cane jabbed at the factory chimneys that punctured the skyline – 'would be eager to spend time with a gentleman like you, if you worked for me.'

Douglas nodded. He felt blisters forming where his feet rasped against the damp leather of his broken boots. 'Maybe so, Mr Wyllie, but I'm not sure that I would be eager to spend time with them.'

Wyllie adjusted the rake of his hat. 'Just so, Mr Douglas, just so. And very commendable, too. Very.'

Neither spoke for a minute as a train rattled out of Dundee East station on its way to Newtyle, leaving the street shaking and a gaggle of urchins running in its wake. 'You may take it, Mr Douglas, that I pay good wages for good work. If you do as I say, you will rise in my estimation – and in your chosen profession, I dare say.'

'My chosen profession?'

'As a runner, Mr Douglas. You will run for me and do as I bid. In return, I will pay you.' Wyllie took out a gold pocket-watch. 'Nearly two of the clock, Mr Douglas. Time for a comforting repast and something to drink, would you not agree?'

Douglas nodded. It was a long time since he had enjoyed something to drink. 'If you think so, Mr Wyllie.'

'Indeed. And when you work for me, you, too, can have a comfortable repast at two of the clock.' Wyllie replaced his watch. 'Meet me tomorrow, Mr Douglas, at ten sharp, in front

9

of the Old Steeple. I shall have work for you.' With a parting flourish of his cane, Wyllie strode away, his boot-heels clicking confidently on the grey paving-stones.

Work! The word rebounded around Douglas's head. This time tomorrow he would have his self-respect again, would be earning a wage, holding his head up. He would be a runner, whatever that was, working for Mr Wyllie, whoever he was. He felt new energy as he tramped up the open stairway to his rented room in the steaming squalor of the Overgate. He pushed aside the doubt he had felt when Mr Wyllie appeared. Where employment was concerned, there was no room for doubt. This was a matter of trust.

'Robert!' Mrs Sturrock was waiting for him in the dim common hallway, her plump face animated. 'Have you seen this?' She held up a newspaper.

'No, Mrs Sturrock, I haven't.' Douglas always made it a point to be polite to his landlady, particularly when he had no money for the rent.

'Come in, come in.' Grasping his arm, Mrs Sturrock guided him through the low door. The building being overshadowed by the tall tenement next door, little light seeped through the small window, so Mrs Sturrock lit the oil-lamp in the corner of the room. Douglas allowed himself to be ushered into the only seat, and waited patiently while Mrs Sturrock folded the newspaper for him and indicated the relevant paragraph.

'Sit down, Robert, and read this.' She paused for a significant second. 'You are a scholar? You can read?'

'I can, thank you kindly for asking.' Her breath was hot on his neck as she leaned over him, her softness pressing maternally against his shoulder. 'It's an advertisement.'

The Managing Owner of the Waverley Whale-Fishing Company wishes to engage a Personal Assistant. The most Suitable Candidate will be of a Capable Disposition, with Experience of Life, and an Ability to Use his Mind as well as his Hands. He will be a man of

Sobriety and Honesty, Discretion and complete Loyalty. Some security work may be required. Application should be made in person to Mr George Gilbride at the Offices of the Waverley Whale-Fishing Company, Dock Street, Dundee, at eight a.m. prompt, 21 January 1860.

'That's tomorrow,' Mrs Sturrock told him helpfully, 'and it's just the position for you. You are a capable man, and sober – I've never seen you drunk once in all the days you've been here. You're honest, discreet and loyal, I know you are. I say that you're the most suitable man, and with experience of life.' She patted his arm fondly, as if the matter was already settled. 'There, now. You see Mr Gilbride tomorrow morning at eight, and you'll be all settled in. How's that now, Robert?'

Douglas looked over the advertisement again. 'Yes, Mrs Sturrock, it reads very well, but I'm already meeting a Mr Wyllie tomorrow, about a job as a runner.'

'Mr Wyllie! And a runner!' Mrs Sturrock exhaled noisily. 'Why now, Robert, Mr Gilbride is a far finer gentleman than Mr Wyllie, and his Personal Assistant far more important than a runner – a bookie's runner, I expect. When you could be working for the Waverley Whale-Fishing Company, I'm surprised that you should even consider such a thing.'

Douglas smiled. Mrs Sturrock had never mentioned his pecuniary misfortunes, and he appreciated her help. 'I tell you what I'll do, Mrs Sturrock. I'll knock at Mr Gilbride's door tomorrow morning at eight, and meet Mr Wyllie at ten. Then I'll decide which position is preferable – if, indeed, either of them requires me.'

'Mr Gilbride requires you.' Mrs Sturrock pointed a plump finger at the advertisement. 'Experience of life, honesty, sober, good with his hands and mind.' She stepped back from the table, scrutinising him. There was a new edge to her voice when she spoke. 'But you're not going like that, Robert. You'll be as clean and tidy as I can make you. After we've eaten, we'll get to work.'

Douglas looked down at the battered remains of his clothing and shook his head. 'You're right. I shall hardly make a good impression dressed like this, but I've nothing better.'

Mrs Sturrock smiled. 'We'll see what we can do.' She hovered over Douglas while he ate, then pounced. 'Right, off with your clothes!'

'What?' Douglas instinctively fastened his jacket. 'That's indecent!'

'Maybe so. It's also sensible. Do you want to be employed?'

'Of course.'

'Then you'll do as I say.' Mrs Sturrock put her hands on her hips. 'I'm waiting.'

It was not the smile on her lips that worried Douglas, but the sudden light that had appeared behind her eyes. He sighed, remembering Paddy's advice: when besieging a fortress, lesser dangers had to be endured for the sake of the greater prize. In this case the fortress of employment necessitated enduring the dangers of Mrs Sturrock's loneliness. He slipped off his jacket and handed it over.

Like many Dundee women, Mrs Sturrock was short in stature but able to exert complete control over a man. Tutting at the patched elbows, she bent her head over the frayed cuffs. The few grey hairs amid the brown glistened in the light. 'You need a good woman to look after you, Robert. I suppose you had a servant when you were in India?'

Douglas shook his head. 'I wasn't in India long enough. I saw most of my service in Africa.'

'I see.' She was already busy with needle and thread. 'This needs washing, too. And I'll have your trousers – they're in an even worse state.' She looked up and laughed. 'Don't look so shocked. I've buried three husbands, and I won't swoon at the sight of another man. I don't suppose that you're made all that different.' That possessive look was back on her face when she took his trousers, very gently, from his hands, and barely smiled as he pulled the tails of his shirt down over his thighs. 'Don't feel too safe, now, for that shirt must be washed, too, and everything beneath it. I'm not having a man from this house walking dirty into the office of a gentleman like Mr Gilbride.'

When Robert Douglas rapped on the door of the Waverley Whale-Fishing Company, his jacket was patched and clean, his trousers washed and pressed, even his boots were oiled, with the soles carefully glued back in place and a cunningly fashioned piece of paper disguising the hole.

The clerk raised a supercilious eyebrow and ushered him into the office of Mr George Gilbride where Douglas stood, automatically at attention, in front of a desk swamped by a pyramid of paper. A marble bust stood on a plinth in the corner of the room, its sightless stare a contrast to the gentle eyes of the lady in the portrait that hung over the fireplace. A clock ticked away the seconds while Douglas waited for the large man behind the desk to speak.

The man looked up and studied Douglas for a few minutes before he said, 'Good morning. I am George Gilbride, managing owner of the Waverley Whale-Fishing Company. I expect that you have come to apply for the position of Personal Assistant?'

'Yes, sir.'

'Then tell me about yourself.' Gilbride leaned back, his brown eyes studying Douglas intently. The ticking of the clock dominated the room.

'My name is Robert Douglas, sir, and I have recently completed eighteen years with the Seventy-Third Foot, mainly in Africa, but also helping to quell the late uprising in India. I was latterly a sergeant.' He stopped, unsure what else to say.

'Eighteen years? Why did you leave?' Gilbride sounded more curious than interrogative.

'I was invalided out, sir.' Douglas caught himself staring into the gentle eyes of the portrait. 'I took a fever in India, and they sent me home and discharged me.'

'With a pension?'

'No, sir.'

'I see.' Gilbride turned and addressed the marble bust in the corner. 'And this is the way we treat the guardians of our Empire, the Quentin Durwards of our day. Do you wonder that the beggars cry havoc in the streets and the French lay siege to our seas?'

'I beg pardon, sir?'

'Quentin Durward, Mr Douglas. He was a soldier of the fifteenth century. Have you read the novels of Sir Walter Scott?'

'No, sir.'

'Then you should, Mr Douglas, particularly as you have such a famous name. You can read?'

'Yes, sir.' Douglas recognised the first question of an interrogation which would drag out all his weaknesses.

'That is well. And can you write?'

'Yes, sir.'

'That is also well. Tell me about your regiment, the Seventy-Third. Not the most illustrious, I fear.' Gilbride cocked his head to one side, brown eyes shrewd, mouth slightly smiling.

Douglas felt a surge of anger, which he could not altogether conceal. 'The Seventy-Third, sir, is the finest regiment in the British Army. No, more than that, it is the finest regiment that has ever existed in any army, and it is greatly renowned for its deeds, from the storming of Seringapatam to the men's heroism during the loss of the troopship *Birkenhead* in the year 'fifty-two!' He stopped, appalled at how his voice had risen. It was not a good idea to shout at his prospective employer.

'Excellent, Sergeant Douglas. We can certainly add loyalty to your list of attributes.'

Douglas felt some relief when he saw the humour twinkling in Gilbride's eyes. This was a cunning man.

'You are wearing a much-patched and -darned uniform, Mr Douglas. No suit of new clothes for you. Did you gamble away the loot you found in India? The gold from Lucknow? The jewelled crown of the Rani of Jhansi?'

Douglas shook his head. 'I could not gamble away what I never had, Mr Gilbride. There was nothing in Africa but hard knocks, dust and flies, and I was in India to fight, not to loot.'

Africa had also held tragedy, betrayal and death. The image returned, as it so often did: the fire and the horror, the hand at the edge of the ashes, the smiling brown doll, the sick knowledge of a failed trust.

'And would you have looted, given the chance?' The humour was gone from Gilbride's eyes but the shrewdness remained.

'Any man would have, given the chance,' Douglas answered. 'Only an angel could resist temptation like that.'

'And you are no angel?' Was that mockery in Gilbride's tone?

'I am not.'

Gilbride nodded. 'That's an honest answer, Mr Douglas, and another virtue to add to your formidable list.' Gilbride contemplated the bust, as if for guidance. 'Well, sir, now that I have learned a little about you, it is time that I told you what this position entails.' There was a few seconds' silence as Gilbride settled his bulk on the padded seat of the chair. 'What I want is a man in whom I can place complete trust, a man who can work well in an office or outside, who can mingle with people or enjoy solitude. I want a man who can use his head and work at his own discretion, but who never loses sight of his ultimate loyalty to me. Do you think you might be that man, Mr Douglas?'

Douglas nodded. 'I believe I might.'

'And I believe you might be the man for me.' Gilbride tapped his fingers on the paper-strewn desk, his eyes suddenly sharp. 'No time-wasting, now, Mr Douglas. Are you interested in this position? Tell me yes or no.'

'I am indeed interested, Mr Gilbride, but I have also been

offered a position as a runner for a Mr Wyllie. I am to meet him at ten this morning.'

'Mr Wyllie?' Gilbride looked momentarily troubled. 'Then, Mr Douglas, I will detain you no further. It is now ten minutes short of ten. If you have arranged a meeting, you must go.'

'But this position, sir?' Douglas could see his job slipping away.

'Remains open for seven days. I believe that you would be suitable. The stripes on your sleeve indicate that you are a man who has known authority. You appear to have a deal of integrity and you have certainly had experience of life. Good qualities, Mr Douglas, unusual qualities, which I should like to foster.' Gilbride began to shuffle through the papers on his desk. 'If I do not hear from you within seven days, Mr Douglas, I shall assume that you prefer the employment offered by Mr Wyllie. Good day to you, sir.'

Douglas rose. 'You are more than fair, sir. I shall let you know my decision as soon as possible.'

'Within seven days, I trust.'

Dundee, February 1860

Frost crisped the indentation that each step left on the grass, and Douglas's breath hung in damp clouds around his face. The steep path was hard underfoot, with frozen puddles between the shin-high ruts. He moved quickly, leaning forwards, alert for any unusual noise or movement. Dawn had come sharp to the rolling countryside west of Dundee, starkly silhouetting the trees of Balgay Hill against a pale sky. In front, stretching to the Bay of Invergowrie and beyond to the Carse were fields bleak and bare and bitter.

So this was what a runner did. He ran with messages from place to place, from door to door in the crowded streets of the town, between the clattering mills on the Scouring Burn and up to the massed tenements and unnamed wynds of the Hilltown and Bonnetmaker Row. He had knocked on a hundred doors, entered a score of public houses, left the same message with faces expectant and predatory, hopeful and desperate.

'Wednesday, noon, at the Myrekirk Stones.'

There had been nods and grunts, rapid understanding or requests for more information, dumb acceptance from broken men and blatant offers from women careless of lust but desperate for food. And still Douglas had run, run with the message from one address in his list to the next. He, who had worn the scarlet coat of honour, was now running errands.

Mr Wyllie had promised that he would be an officer, with a new suit of clothes and boots that did not leak. But Douglas had learned that an officer was a man who carried this private information to the Fancy, and the new clothes came only after

17

the money had been earned. He had run where the raw factories accepted healthy young humans and discharged debilitated children with deformed bodies and women with harsh voices and haggard faces. He had run to the quarries of Lochee, where bhoys from Slieve Aught swore in a brogue achingly familiar to any man who had served the Queen. He had run to the long sands of Broughty, where weary fishwives waded shoulder-deep in surf to drag their men's boats ashore. He had run to the Dens Road mills, where women laboured long, hard hours to produce canvas for the sails of Royal Navy ships.

'Wednesday, noon, at the Myrekirk Stones.'

He was still running. It was Wednesday morning, and he had been sent on his last mission, to the settlement of Kingoodie where the quarrymen toiled within sound of the whispering Tay. He had people to contact in Invergowrie of the historic church, then he was to return to the Stones and prepare for noon. Time was passing.

A long skein of geese rose from the sandbanks of the Tay, calling mournfully as they winged overhead on their passage to the fields of Angus and the despair of the farmers. Not all made the flight, for there were wildfowlers among the reeds and the pop-pop-popping of flintlock muskets echoed in the bright bowl of morning.

There was a man slouched over the tail of a cart hard by the firth. 'Noon, today, at the Stones.'

And on again, running, running until his legs were slack and weary, running until the breath burned in his chest, running until the message was passed from person to person, from merchant prince to pauper to lord of a thousand fertile acres. Until it was ten in the morning and the Sidlaw Ridge ran sharp in the bright, brittle air and the ground was frozen hard and unforgiving around the Stones.

Already the people were beginning to gather, from unemployed men, who at twenty were too old for the mills, to farmers in their broadcloth and to the idle rich. Prizefighting being illegal, lookouts were posted all round the farm, perched in trees or on high ground.

Douglas was not idle. The running might be finished, but Mr Wyllie ensured that there was always work. There were corner-posts to place and a double barrier of rope to erect between the Fancy and the contestants. There were directions to give and a couple of drunkards to hustle away.

Douglas lit his pipe and leaned against the largest of the ten standing stones that gave the site its name. Local tradition held that Druids had performed strange ceremonies here, but Douglas cared only for today's spectacle. The crowd was thicker now as the Fancy arrived at the Stones. Some came in carts, some on foot, and the gentry in closed and shining carriages. People had come by steam-paddle ferry from Ferryport on Craig, passing over the winter Tay in their eagerness for blood and gore and the thrill of a gamble. The poorest were barefoot, the workers watchful while the sporting gentlemen stroked their Dundreary whiskers and doffed their white top hats to overdressed women who responded with replies too bold for respectability. Snippets of conversation drifted to Douglas: the betting odds; disputes over the shocking price of flax since the Crimea business; the high cost of labour, which was crippling the textile industry. One man gripped his silver-topped Malacca cane and addressed a young woman who thrust her head from the open window of her carriage, until she tipped her broad hat forward in a gesture which surely bade him a fast farewell.

Douglas found himself looking at the woman, whose laugh ran freely above the crowd. Her face was elfin in its purity of complexion, with almond eyes above a chiselled nose and a mouth which spoke and laughed constantly. As she stepped lightly to the ground, she handed something to her maid, waved her light-blue parasol like a sergeant's swagger-stick and exchanged a few words with the coachman. Her crinoline was fashionably wide, but the ivory and peach pattern was distinctly out of place in this rutted field.

'Here, Mr Sergeant.' Wyllie dropped his languid pose as he shouted orders to the dozen men under his command. 'Tell the lookouts to make sure that there are no bluebottles around.'

The lookouts nodded or grinned to Douglas, but none reported worrying activity. By the time Douglas returned to the Stones it was a quarter before twelve and the crowd was thick and boisterous. The great days of prizefighting were long gone, and today there were no giants like Mendoza or Tom Cribb. Nevertheless, despite the disapproval of the Righteous, the taverns rang with talk about the proposed fight between the English champion, Tom Sawyers the bricklayer, and Bernicia Boy John Heenan of the United States. John Wyllie had tapped into the interest in the Golden Ring by arranging a more local competition.

'Douglas, make sure that the Diamond Squad have the best view.' Wyllie indicated the coaches of the gentry, imposingly parked along the south-facing side of the square. 'That's where the money is. The rest only add farthings to the purse.' A contemptuous sweep of his hand took in the masses who crammed the remaining three sides of the ring. 'And keep your peepers open for the magistrates and their blasted bluebottles!'

Douglas had only a limited knowledge of pugilism, but he realised that Wyllie liked to use the cant of the ring, probably culled from the book he had been languidly reading. The title, *Life in London*, was known to Douglas, for Major Donnachie, one of the older officers in his regiment, had been a prizefighting enthusiast and owned both that book and *Boxiana* by Pierce Egan. The Major had laced his speech with pugilistic terms, one or two of which Douglas still remembered.

Bookmakers slid through the crowd, accepting bets with a smile, handing out the fatal slips of paper that could give a man enough money for a week's debauchery or enslave him in debt and despair. There were beer-sellers doing a rattling trade, spirits vendors selling clear and caustic whisky which had been carried on ponies from the glens of Angus, and there were pickpockets who had travelled from Edinburgh. There were fortune-tellers whose claims of gypsy blood were as spurious as the charms they hawked, and brown-faced labouring men whose cravats concealed the lack of a shirt. All had come to the Stones at twelve noon on that Wednesday.

The crowd's murmuring swelled to a roar as Mr Wyllie strolled into the centre of the square, swinging his ebony cane, then subsided when he raised his hands high above his head.

'Ladies, gentlemen and fellow peasants!' He had obviously expected the appreciation, and waited until the cheers and catcalls had faded away. 'We are here because we follow the noble art, the true mark of a man, that most British of institutions, the bare-knuckle prizefight. Whosoever does not thrill to the sight of flowing claret, let him or her' – he bowed to the elfin-faced lady, who was seated on a folding chair in the centre of the front row of spectators – 'leave now. I give you fair warning, ladies and gentlemen, for this will be a bloodstained and an exciting spectacle.'

There were no withdrawals from the crowd, only a murmur of impatience, which Wyllie rode expertly. 'I see that you are all eager to begin, and no wonder. This will be a day to remember, a day when fighters to rank with Tom Sawyers and Bendingo Thompson will battle for supremacy. Without further ado, therefore, permit me to introduce the two combatants, the gladiators of the square, the proud exponents of the noble art!' The crowd cheered at that, some throwing their hats in the air, others tipping their bottles skyward as they emptied the contents down thirsty throats.

There was a commotion to Douglas's left, and three men entered the ring, one large and muscled, obviously a prizefighter, the other two his seconds.

'Here is one of the heroes now!' Wyllie bellowed. 'Let us all welcome David Anderson, the Carnoustie Carter!' There was a rising round of applause as Anderson lifted two massive arms to the crowd.

'And, opposing him, our own William Houston, the Dundee Destroyer!' This applause was louder, with even the Diamond Squad rising from their seats and the commonality from Dundee stamping out a ground-vibrating drumbeat. The Dundee Destroyer, dark-haired, tattooed and unsmiling, acknowledged the crowd with a straight-backed hornpipe round his opponent.

The referee, a stout ex-pugilist with enormous side-whiskers, called the fighters to the mark and ordered them to strip. Shirtless, both men looked bigger, the Carter perhaps slightly the heavier and the Destroyer's muscles gleaming in the cold winter sun. The referee looked small compared to them, and the embroidered snake that coiled round his red shirt looked worn and out-of-date. His orders were brusque and professional. The Carnoustie Carter looked a little awed by the occasion, whereas the Dundee Destroyer only looked impatient, glowering at the crowd and occasionally touching the brass ring that dangled from his left ear.

Running an experienced eye over both men, the referee shouted their weight to an uncaring crowd and, after a brief word about not gouging or stamping, ordered them to shake hands.

Both pugilists looked toward Wyllie as the timekeeper rang his bell to signal the start of the contest. During eighteen years in the army, Douglas had seen scores of fights, from redcoats brawling with belt-buckle and bottle to full-scale battles between armies of thousands, so he watched with professional interest as the two men squared up to each other.

It was immediately obvious that, despite their descriptive epithets, neither man was a trained prizefighter; both relied on brawn and aggression rather than skill. Yells of 'Give him toco, Carter!' came from the section of the crowd that had travelled from Carnoustie, to be followed by catcalls and hoots from the Dundee majority.

The first round was an affair of wild rushes by the Carter,

each met by bludgeoning fists from the Destroyer, so that the audience enjoyed the sight of blood early in the contest.

'That's your claret tapped, Carter!' called one of the gentry, an elderly man with distinguished white whiskers, as blood flowed from the fighter's nose.

When a particularly brutal blow on the chest knocked the Carter flat, the timekeeper sounded the bell and the Carter's seconds dragged him back for resuscitation and advice.

Wyllie beckoned Douglas over. 'It's going quite well,' he said in an undertone, 'but it may be over too quickly. The crowd likes early blood, but there's more money in a long contest. Run over to the Destroyer and tell him to pull his punches a little.'

'Is that sporting?' In the 73rd Foot, fights were conducted on a strictly fair basis: the best man won as quickly as he could and then everybody retired to the nearest source of drink.

'It's as sporting as your job's worth, Mr Sergeant, so jump to it,' and Wyllie jerked a thumb toward the Dundee Destroyer.

A thickset man with a sinister bulge in his yellow waistcoat cast poisonous eyes at Douglas from a few feet away. When a second man slid a sandbag from his sleeve, Douglas realised that they were Wyllie's bodyguards. They looked the sort of men who would enjoy administering a savage beating, and he was not inclined to indulge their pleasures.

While the audience continued to yell their delight and the Diamond Squad tapped their canes on the floor of their couches, Douglas trotted round the ropes to where the Destroyer was drinking from a bottle of water.

Close to, the prizefighter looked even bigger, with a gin-trap mouth and a developing bruise around his left eye where one of the Carter's wild swings had taken effect. His face and neck were deeply weather-beaten, as if he had lived out of doors most of his life, but from the neck downward his skin was soft and white under curling black body hair.

'Mr Wyllie says you are to pull your punches. You're not to win too easily.'

The Destroyer glowered at him. 'Tell Mr Wyllie that I'm here to win a fight. If his man can't look after himself, that's his concern.' One of his seconds whispered something in his ear, and the Destroyer's look grew even darker. 'I'm not his bloody servant!' He stood up as the bell sounded again. 'And you can tell *Mr* Wyllie that, too!'

The second round was a repetition of the first, with the Carter making extravagant rushes and the Destroyer landing monstrous blows which would have chopped teak. There was more blood on the frosted grass, more yells of delight from the crowd. The elfin-faced girl was leaning forward eagerly, shouting advice to both pugilists.

The roar grew louder when the Destroyer for once over-reached himself and the Carter trapped his neck under the crook of a thick left arm while punching furiously with his right. The Fancy enjoyed the sight, and the gentry led a chant of 'Blood! Blood! Blood!'

Breaking free, the Destroyer landed a chest-blow which knocked the breath from the Carter, then threw him over his hip. Only when he began to kick the prostrate body did Wyllie's guards interfere, with the Carter's seconds adding their weight.

'Tut tut!' Wyllie was watching the crowd as much as the contest. 'Not allowed to kick. Very unsportsmanlike.' His voice sharpened and he pointed with his cane. 'There's a young woman over there who seems to be causing a disturbance, Mr Sergeant. Remove her.'

Douglas saw a tall woman in a poke bonnet who appeared to be selling newspapers. Shrugging, he plunged back into the crowd. The shouts behind him subsided as the pugilists returned to their corners, but the betting was as brisk as ever.

'A shilling on the Carter. That last round must have weakened the Destroyer.'

'Sixpence on the Destroyer. He cracked the Carter's ribs then.'

'Look at the Destroyer's face. He'll no' see a thing now.'

'He doesn't need to see. He's got the Carter beat.'

'More ale here, Jennie, lass – my throat's as parched as parish charity.'

'You'll get your ale when I get your money, Archie Nicol.'

'You come here, my lass, and I'll give you something better than money.'

The woman with the newspapers did not seem to belong amid the raucously bantering Fancy. Respectably dressed in a sober brown skirt which brushed the ground and an austerely cut brown jacket with a high collar, she looked like a Sunday-school teacher, an impression strengthened by the tracts she was distributing.

'Repent! Repent and come to the Lord, who will forgive your sins!' There was space around her as the Fancy backed away from repentance and salvation. 'You, sir.' She approached Douglas. 'You're a military man. You've seen death and destruction at Sevastopol and the vengeance of the Lord in Hindustan! Will you be eternally damned for your sins? Or take the path to temperance, redemption, and the Lord?'

Douglas relaxed a little. He had met evangelicals before: many of the Boers in South Africa had been devout Christians, and there had even been one or two in the army. 'Maybe I will, miss, but first you'd better take the path to Dundee, for it's not safe for you here.'

She faced him squarely, brown eyes level in a determined face. 'Everywhere is safe for a servant of the Lord. Even if the hordes of the Philistines smite me with fire, I will be safe in His keeping.'

'No doubt, miss, but I'd prefer a servant of the Lord to be elsewhere than in this pit of Satan.'

She thrust a tract at him. 'You recognise this place for what it is, Sergeant? You can see that Satan's work is being done here?' Her eyes were dark and intense.

'Indeed I can, miss, perhaps more than do you.' Douglas

25

searched for words that might appeal to a religious woman. 'I think it would be best if you were to leave. Sow your seeds in more fertile ground, for the soil is stony here and the weeds would choke your precious words.'

'You will take a tract, Sergeant, for I see that the Lord is already at work within you.' Earnestly, she pressed one into Douglas's hand. 'Read it, Sergeant, and repent.' The words came in an urgent whisper which supported those forceful eyes.

'Thank you.' Douglas tucked the pamphlet into his hip pocket. 'But now you really should leave, miss.'

'Throw her out, Sergeant. We don't want the likes of her here.'

With the prizefight temporarily halted to revive the prostrate Carter, the crowd sought other diversions. 'Get rid of her!' Predatory faces and ragged, unwashed bodies began to move closer.

The woman held up her tracts, as if in defence. 'Seek the Lord and he will save you!'

'I'll have one of them,' a sturdy woman with a red-veined nose demanded. There was rough laughter as she snatched a tract and made a circular gesture behind her back to demonstrate the use to which she would put it.

When the evangelist recoiled, a thin man with a narrow face and a battered peaked cap clutched at her. 'Come here, you. I'm Lord Peter. Come here and I'll demonstrate the love of the Lord!' He clawed at her jacket.

Douglas brushed him aside and shouted, 'Move back, all of you! Get back!' Thrusting an elbow into the throat of a drunken quarryman, he bent suddenly, set his shoulder against the woman's waist and straightened up. She screamed and kicked furiously as she was lifted, her fists pounding Douglas's back.

'Keep quiet,' he hissed, 'and keep still!' Ignoring the jeers of the crowd, he pushed through them, heading away from the ring.

26

'Stop the sojer!' yelled the thin man. 'He wants the woman for himself!'

Douglas avoided the man's grab, then cursed as a gaggle of screaming women slashed at his face with hooked fingers. Still gripping the evangelist, he landed one solid blow with his left fist and grunted with satisfaction as a putrid-mouthed harridan spat out blood and rotten teeth. He pushed on, ducking as a bottle cartwheeled past his head.

'Put me down! You've no right! I demand that you put me down!' Frightened though she obviously was, the woman had not lost her spirit: she was still flailing her feet and arms.

Douglas walked a good hundred yards clear of the crowd before gently lowering her to her feet.

'You're no gentleman!' Red-faced with indignation, she straightened her clothing with quick, jerky gestures. 'You're . . .' She sought for a telling phrase. 'You're a cad, nothing but a cad!'

'No doubt, miss,' said Douglas, 'but you're safer with this cad than with your parishioners back there.' He heard the crowd roar again and guessed that the fight had been renewed.

Throwing him a look fit to curdle milk, the woman turned away and strode off towards Dundee. Douglas watched for a few minutes; she had a long walk in front of her and he wondered if he should escort her. Deciding that, with most of the undesirables watching the fight, she would be safe once she reached the turnpike, he returned to the bout. He took up his position beside Mr Wyllie just in time to see the Destroyer raise the Carter clean over his head and throw him in a heap on the ground.

The Carter tried to rise, scrabbling feebly at the grass, but the Destroyer lifted him by one arm, reared back and butted him in the face with such force that Douglas heard the hollow crack of breaking teeth.

Wyllie jabbed his cane into the ground in frustration. 'I thought he had been told to go easy. This is only the third round. Somebody will pay for this – and I shall take good care it is not me.'

The guards closed round him, shoving aside a group of sportsmen who shouted that the fight was a cross, and gestured to the Destroyer to stop.

Blood streaming down his face and his eyes unfocused, the Destroyer stepped closer, his fists clenched and his chest gleaming with sweat. Wyllie held his cane in front of him, and his bodyguards moved forward.

The man with the poisonous eyes pulled out a short cosh. 'Step back, Houston. Back!'

'Was this fight crossed? I said, was it a cross?' The referee bounced from Wyllie to the battered Destroyer. 'I want no hand in a crossed mill – I've my reputation to consider.'

A gentleman of the Diamond Squad, red-faced in anger, his mutton-chop whiskers bristling, waved a riding-crop at Mr Wyllie. 'That was a travesty, sir, not a fight. A gross mismatch! You won't get a penny from me, sir, no, nor even a farthing.'

As Douglas hesitated, wondering if he should help his employer, a shrill cry pierced the crowd's din: 'Bluebottles! The bluebottles are coming!'

At once there was pandemonium. The man with the riding-crop retreated rapidly to his coach. 'Drive like the devil,' he ordered the coachman, 'and don't stop for anything.' The coachman, his vivid blue livery spattered with mud, cracked his whip and turned the two horses in a tight circle before heading directly for the group in the centre of the ring. The guards pushed Wyllie to safety, but the rear offside wheel caught one of the Destroyer's seconds and tumbled him to the ground. Other carriages whirled past, the coachmen showing a fine lack of concern whether their whips cracked over the backs of the horses or the heads of the Fancy.

Douglas heard high-pitched laughter and saw the elfin-faced girl leaning out of the window of her carriage, waving her blue parasol to the crowd. The less affluent members of the Fancy scattered on foot, though a few of them stood their ground and shook fists, sticks and bottles at the police now visible in the distance.

'My carriage, quickly!' At that crucial moment Wyllie did not lose control. Tossing a small bag to the referee, he shouted, 'There's your fee. I'd advise you to make haste lest you are hauled before the magistrates. Destroyer, I'll speak to you later. After a performance like that, don't expect much charity from me.' He sneered at the battered Carter, who scowled through the blood that masked his face. 'And that goes for you too, fellow. You fought like an old woman. Mr Sergeant! Here's your pay,' and he passed Douglas a crown piece. 'I hold court in Mother Scott's. I expect to see you there tomorrow.' He leaned close and winked. 'You've taken my crown, Douglas, five times the value of the Queen's shilling. You're my man now. Don't forget it.'

Douglas stared for a second, then laughed. 'A fair day's work, Mr Wyllie, for a fair day's pay. And that's an end to it. You'd better be off before the magistrates arrive.'

The field around the Stones, so busy a few minutes before, was now nearly deserted, whereas the tracks to Dundee and Invergowrie were congested with carriages, and the surrounding fields were rampant with running men. The men who had been shouting defiance realised that they were unsupported and began to slink away, singly or in little groups.

A line of policemen crested the ridge from Dundee, with a horseman on either flank. To Douglas's astonishment, in the centre of the line there was a woman. Then he recognised the brown skirt and neat jacket: evidently, it was the evangelist who had alerted the police.

Slipping off his scarlet jacket, Douglas began to run inland, towards the distant Sidlaw Hills. After his years of skirmishing with the Gaikas and Basutos, he had no fear that a handful of

Dundee bluebottles could catch him, even if they were mounted. However, he had not greatly enjoyed his day acting as a runner for Mr Wyllie. It was time to pay a visit to Mr Gilbride.

Dundee, February—March 1860

Mr Gilbride took an ivory holder from his jacket pocket and lit one of the new-fangled cigarettes that the army had brought in from the Crimea. Douglas had tried them, but had not liked them much; when he could afford the tobacco, he much preferred his pipe.

Mr Gilbride blew out a stream of smoke. 'As my Personal Assistant, Mr Douglas, you would be working for me rather than for the Waverley Whale-Fishing Company. Is that clear?'

'Yes, sir.' Douglas nodded.

'So that if I should need you to work outside the company – in my house, say, or in any of the other concerns in which I have an interest – you would be obliged to do so. You understand?'

'I do, sir.'

'Good. Now that we're clear on that point, I may tell you that it is my initial intention to employ you in the Waverley Company itself.'

'Yes, sir, but . . .' Douglas hesitated. He had intimate knowledge of the frontiers of Empire, places which respectable people such as Mr Gilbride would never see. He knew the Great Karoo and the soaring Drakensberg, the tangled bush of the Keiskama and the stinking splendour of Lucknow, but his knowledge of the sea was confined to the cramped lower decks of a troopship. He said, 'I know nothing the sea or about whale-fishing.'

'I don't want you to go to sea, Mr Douglas. I am not seeking a harpooner, I am seeking an explanation.'

'An explanation of what, sir?'

Abruptly rising, Mr Gilbride strode to the window. He gestured to Douglas to join him, and together they looked out across Dock Street to the bustle of Earl Grey Dock, where a uniformed fishery officer was supervising the loading of herring into a brig. Further along the quay, passengers hurried aboard an elegant Dundee, Perth and London vessel which contrasted with the grimy black-hulled Baltic barque that was being refitted in one of the shipbuilding yards across the dock.

'Busy scene, isn't it?' He lit another cigarette. 'Plenty of ships, plenty of seamen, plenty of work. Quite a change from the hungry 'forties, eh?'

'Yes, sir.' As a youth, Douglas had seen paupers crowding the wynds, and Chartists mustering on Magdalen Green. 'Hunger drove men to desperate acts then.'

'Indeed.' Gilbride faced him for a moment, new interest on his face. 'Was it poverty that made you take the Queen's shilling?'

'Partly that, partly other things.' Douglas well remembered the emptiness gnawing his stomach, the sodden march to Forfar behind the brave Chartist banner. He remembered men collapsing beside the road from exhaustion and hunger, and the taste of the unripe turnip that he'd pulled from a field. He did not know whether his thoughts were reflected on his face, but he strove to push away the memories.

'Much better now, then. Two job opportunities in a day, eh?'

'Yes, sir.'

'One would think that, with conditions so much better, men would be happy to work, would one not?' said Gilbride, indicating the bustling docks. 'Trade is the lifeblood of Britain and the future of Dundee. Flax from the Baltic made into linen for the finest sailcloth in the world; machinery exports and jute, too, since the Russian war. What do you know about jute, Mr Douglas?'

'Jute, sir?' Douglas stared out of the window, hoping for inspiration. A long, sleek, red-hulled clipper was being guided into port by a pilot boat, her crew working diligently on deck and in her rigging. Large bales were piled high behind them, ready to be loaded on to carts as soon as she docked. 'I've seen it in Hindustan, being loaded on to ships like that one.'

'Exactly like that one. Jute can be made into a useful rough cloth, perfect for sandbags, wagon-covers, tarpaulins and sacks, commodities for which demand is great in these unsettled times. War fuels the jute trade, Mr Douglas.' He pointed to the clipper's cargo. 'That is raw jute, which is very hard to work until it is softened. The best thing in the world to soften jute is whale-oil. Did you know that?'

Douglas shook his head.

Mr Gilbride let a trickle of smoke escape from his mouth. 'So long as the Dundee manufacturers work with jute, they will need whale oil. Already the price of oil has risen, and it looks set to continue. There are more jute mills being built, so they will need more oil, and heightened demand creates a seller's market. The Waverley Company hopes to supply that oil, Mr Douglas, but as things stand, we cannot.' He walked heavily back to his desk and leaned against it.

Douglas decided to ask the obvious question: 'Why is that, sir?'

'Because I cannot raise a crew for *Redgauntlet*,' said Gilbride simply, as if everything were now explained.

'Please tell me more,' said Douglas. 'I have not been back in Dundee long enough to recognise ships' names.'

'*Redgauntlet* is the finest of vessels, Mr Douglas. She was launched only last year, and returned safely from the fishing-grounds. She is the most modern of all the Dundee whaling-fleet, with iron tanks rather than casks for the blubber, and the most comfortable accommodation for the men. Even better, she has a steam engine, to lessen the time crossing the Atlantic, and make it easier to break through ice. She even has a steam launch on deck, in case she ever goes sealing at St John's.' Gilbride smiled. 'The anchorage at St John's is many miles from the town, you see, so the launch will make it easier for the master to buy stores, and for my men to visit.'

'She sounds a fine ship, sir.' Recalling the vermin that had crawled from the bedding and woodwork of troopships on their interminable passage through tropic calms, Douglas felt a pang of envy for the whaling men.

'I oversaw her design and fittings myself, and my elder daughter was to have performed the ceremony of launching her, but alas I was unwell and she was nursing me and could not. You recognise the ship's name, of course?' Before Douglas could admit his ignorance, Gilbride continued, 'Sir Edward Redgauntlet was a Jacobite, dedicated to the Bonnie Prince. The Forty-Five was over, but he did not surrender; he tried all he could for a lost cause.' Gilbride went over to the marble bust in the corner and gazed at it. 'That is true loyalty, Mr Douglas. That's a quality I like in a man, and that's what you showed when you defended your regiment.'

'Is that the bust of Redgauntlet, sir?'

The only other bust that Douglas had ever seen was of Napoleon Bonaparte. The pugilistic Major Donnachie had used it as a resting-place for his hat, and some of the younger officers occasionally decorated it with items of female underwear.

For a moment Gilbride looked shocked, then he smiled. 'Good heavens no, Mr Douglas. Redgauntlet was a character in a book. This man' – he patted the bust – 'is the book's author. This is Sir Walter Scott.' Now the brown eyes were challenging. 'You have heard of Scott?'

'Indeed, sir.' Douglas relaxed a little. Sir Walter Scott was the favourite author of half the literate world. Every bookshop stocked the works of the man who had worked himself to death to pay off debts incurred not by himself but by his business associates, and even Queen Victoria read his words. Scott's fame had outlived him. 'He wrote the Waverley novels, sir.' In a burst of inspiration he added, 'And you named your shipping line for them.'

'Quite right.' Gilbride's eyes were friendly again as he burst into unembarrassed poetry.

> ' "He came not from where Ancram Moor
> Ran red with English blood,
> Where the Douglas true and the bold Buccleuch
> Gainst keen Lord Evers stood." '

' "The Douglas true": that's what Scott wrote about your clan, Mr Douglas. I hope I can count upon you as "the bold Buccleuch" could upon them.' The expressive brown eyes were suddenly fierce, then in an instant softened again as he laid a hand on the brow of the bust. 'Scott was known as "the Wizard of the North", true Mr Douglas, as once they called me "the Wizard of Dundee". Whereas Scott wove spells with his words, I worked magic with enterprise and progress – you may perhaps have heard me called the Wizard out in the streets of Dundee?'

Diplomatically, Douglas agreed. 'I believe I have heard the name used, sir.'

'Yes, but not for much longer.' Gilbride sighed and removed his hand from Sir Walter's brow. 'There have been a couple of experimental steam ships used for whaling, sailing-ships converted by adding an engine, a hybrid breed – no doubt you have heard of the Dundee ship *Tay*? No? You surprise me. Like every other whale-ship owner, I observed their progress. Since they were moderately successful, last season I had two ships built, *Ivanhoe* and *Redgauntlet*, for the whaling. If they succeeded, they would change the face of whaling for ever. If they failed, the Waverley Company and my fortune would fail with them. For that reason I built the best. My ships are prime ships, sister ships indeed, with not a whit of difference save for the figureheads.' For a second Gilbride looked embarrassed. 'Despite my position, Mr Douglas, I am a romantic, and I like a ship of mine to have a figurehead. It gives her character, personality, makes her instantly recognisable.

'But fortune has not favoured my fine new ships thus far. *Ivanhoe* and all her crew but the mate were lost when she exploded up there in the ice – on the thirteenth of July, of all dates, my birthday – and the sailors think *Redgauntlet* is also an unlucky ship. Unfortunately, the newspapers reported that two men died building her, and when she was being launched a drunken woman – a spinner, I believe – was taking snuff and sneezed so hard that she fell right in the path of the ship. She was killed, of course, and from that time on the men have believed that *Redgauntlet* is cursed.'

'Yes, sir. Have you tried to alleviate the curse?'

A look of annoyance crossed Mr Gilbride's face. 'Indeed I have. I had the incident investigated, and Simpson, my clerk, gave me a full report. It was the spinner's own fault, of course, and he paid the family twenty pounds of my money in compensation. Damned waste of money, if you ask me, and not a whisper of gratitude did I receive.'

'Yes sir.' Douglas thought it best to agree.

'I put a great deal of my own capital into those two vessels, Mr Douglas, I owned twenty shares in *Ivanhoe*, and I own forty-two – that's more than half – in *Redgauntlet*. I believe, very firmly, that there is a future for whaling in this city, but only if we modernise. If my ships are more successful than the other Dundee vessels, and I get the oil back to the city, the Wizard will have returned. It is therefore imperative that *Redgauntlet* should succeed. But to sail her I need men, and there are none forthcoming.'

Gilbride drew on his long ivory holder until the end of the cigarette glowed red. 'I can only assume that they are afraid of her unlucky reputation. All nonsense, of course, but you know how superstitious seamen are.' The brown eyes were dark now. 'I want you, Mr Douglas, to go out and find me a crew.'

'Yes, sir.' Used to obeying orders without question, Douglas nodded. 'I'll report to you as soon as I can.'

Gilbride handed him a small purse. 'You may need this, but I expect you to keep an account of every penny you spend. If your expenditure is excessive, the balance will be taken from your wages.' He looked at the bust of Scott again. 'If you fail, I shall raise a crew by more forceful means.'

'Yes, sir.' Douglas felt the coins shift in the purse as he gripped it. Mr Gilbride was testing his honesty with regard to money.

Sir Walter gazed unseeingly across the paper-strewn desk, but the lady in the portrait above the fireplace was smiling. Douglas had never seen such encouraging eyes in his life.

Dundee was truly maritime: the sounds and scents of the sea penetrated to the city's commercial and residential heart. Ships of all kinds, from the Tay ferries to the Baltic traders or the three-masted jute clippers, thrust their bowsprits toward the taverns and tenements of the town. His battered uniform discarded, and wearing clothes purchased from a slop-shop, Douglas began his investigations. The best place to find seafaring men would be either at the docks or in the dockside taverns, so he picked the public house nearest to the Earl Grey Dock and positioned himself beside the door.

It was a small place, brightly lit to attract custom, and fairly clean. All the men who drifted in were willing to accept the drink that Douglas offered, and most were willing to talk of *Redgauntlet*. The stories varied in detail, but had the same theme: *Redgauntlet* was cursed. There had been strange noises on her return voyage from the ice last season, and one of the crew had seen a spectral figure gliding along the deck in the dark hours of the middle watch. Some said that it was the spirit of a long-dead whaling man who had boarded when *Redgauntlet* was stuck in the ice; others said the ghost had come aboard when the surgeon shot a seagull which had held the spirit of a drowned mariner. Most, however, thought it was the ghost of the spinner killed when the ship was launched. Not one was willing to sail in her.

'Sign articles in *Redgauntlet*? No' me. I've got myself a secure berth with the Eastern Company.'

'I'm a Baltic man. Once the ice melts, I'm for the Kattegat.'

'Ask me when my money runs out. Until then I'm happy in the beer shop.'

'I'm not long back from Hindustan, mister. You'll not catch me with the Greenlandmen – they're all crazy!'

Many seamen appeared to share this view. The Greenlandmen, as they called the whalers, had a reputation for truculence, superstition and violence, which deterred men from other seafaring trades from signing on whaling-vessels.

Douglas persisted until early evening, then made his way across the crowded room to the street door and went out, ignoring the muttered oaths of a ragged man in a brown cloth cap who was huddled in the doorway recess outside. He had been given much food for thought. He had hoped that persuasion would suffice to obtain a crew for *Redgauntlet*, but he had not reckoned with the cross-grained nature of seafarers: deepwatermen despised short-haulers, and South-Spainers affected disgust at the behaviour of those who sailed on collier brigs.

On impulse, he turned in through the dockyard gates and walked slowly past the berthed ships. *Redgauntlet* lay forlorn in the far corner of King William IV Dock, sheltering beneath the vats of the Waverley Boiling Yard, the great fist of her figurehead punching frustration at the darkening sky.

The watchman raised a suspicious head when Douglas asked permission to board, and asked, 'Why?'

'Mr Gilbride sent me to have a look.'

'Horse Gilbride?' The watchman muttered an obscenity. 'You'd better come aboard, then.'

Douglas's footsteps rang hollowly on the gangplank and the

wooden deck. He stared around. He had shared his last ship with four hundred other men, sick and dying and crippled redcoats returning from saving the Indian Empire. The stench belowdecks had been foul, the hammocks crammed, the air full of creaks and groans and muttered oaths. He preferred *Redgauntlet* as he found her, empty and quiet and lonely, with the breeze moaning through her standing rigging.

'Was there anything in particular that Mr Gilbride wanted?' the watchman asked.

'Aye. He wanted me to have a look over the ship.' Douglas could feel the man's scrutiny, and was sorely aware that his slop-bought clothes did not proclaim authority. 'I'm told she's been cursed. What do you think?'

The watchman grinned. 'Your breech is cursed, man!' He spat over the stern. 'Greenlandmen would believe fresh air was cursed if somebody told them.'

'So you have seen nothing you shouldn't see? No ghosts or bogles?'

'No, nor fairy queens, neither!' He rapped dirty knuckles on the taffrail. 'She's a fine ship, mister, but the tales of a curse make my job easier, for nobody comes aboard. Would you like to see below, maybe? I'm sure Horse wouldn't object.'

'Horse?'

'Horse Gilbride. That's what he's known as.'

'I see.' Not 'the Wizard', Douglas noted.

The flickering flame of the watchman's lantern cast long shadows as they descended, exploring the vast coal hold. A solitary rat scampered from the light, its long tail whipping behind it.

The hold was almost empty, so Douglas wondered why Mr Gilbride should go to the expense of keeping a watchman aboard.

'Each ship is allocated only so much duty-free coal,' the man explained, 'and on all the rest the full tax is paid. Part of my job is to make sure nobody steals what's left aboard her.'

'That's an important job,' Douglas acknowleged, hoping the man would be flattered. His voice echoed and re-echoed, and he looked along the hold. There was only coal and deep shadows, the solid timber of the bulkheads and the faint hiss of the lantern.

The engine-room was more interesting, with the massive machine imposing its seventy horsepower on a myriad supporting pipes and levers, the function of which Douglas could only wonder at. Everything was so modern and impressive that he could not imagine a ghost wanting to stay here: it was just not eerie enough.

'Have you ever heard anything unusual?' he asked. 'Anything at all?'

'Nary a thing. Quiet as the grave.'

They moved on to the cargo hold. As Mr Gilbride had said, whereas the old-time whalers stored the blubber in casks packed into the hold, *Redgauntlet* had massive iron tanks with an access hole. There was also an inspection hatch, down which Douglas peered, lowering the lantern on a pole the watchman provided. Even now, when the tanks were empty and had been cleaned, the stench of blubber was powerful, and he tried not to imagine how it would be with a full cargo. He swung the lantern back and forth, seeing only alternate darkness and light, nothing untoward.

'No bogles down there, either,' said the watchman, grinning again. 'They'd die anew of the stink.'

'Storerooms next, then the crew's quarters,' Douglas said. 'I want to make a thorough tour of her.'

'As you wish, Cap'n, but you're wasting your time, I tell you.'

The storerooms were empty: the racks for the harpoons and flensing-knives offered only scarred wood, while the huge compartments that could hold enough food for a six-month voyage were bare and forlorn. Douglas inspected the quarters for the forty-eight men of the crew, with their box beds to give extra warmth against the Arctic chill, and a discarded blanket scuffed into a corner. A name was hacked into the bulkhead by one of the cots: 'Davey'.

The half-deck, where the specialists lived and worked, was so quiet that his footsteps echoed; and the shadows cast by the lantern danced darkly on wooden bulkheads. A sailmaker's bench lay tidy beneath an empty hook. The captain's cabin was locked, but the mate's was open and still, as were the quarters of the whaling specialists and the carpenter and his mate. Unsure for what he was searching, Douglas looked closely at everything, but found nothing save a strange loneliness, as if *Redgauntlet* were waiting for her crew to return. He led the way back on deck.

Sitting snug under padlocked tarpaulins was the steam-launch, a tribute to Gilbride's thought for his men – or an expense which detracted from the company's profits. All the whaling-boats had been removed from the ship and lay up-turned in the company's yards, awaiting the next season. Without them the deck seemed spacious, dominated by the tall masts and the tubular funnel bearing the company's crest of a *W* pierced by a quill.

'Still no ghosts, Cap'n?' asked the watchman, amused.

'Not this time.'

'Maybe next time, then. Have you tried another ship?' He gestured across the dock. 'Maybe *Pride of the Tay* there, just returned from Bengal, or *Charleston* – she'd be a good ship to explore, another whaler, but owned by the Eastern Sealing and Whaling Company. That's a new company, formed just before the flax trade slumped during the late war with Russia. I've heard rumours of a new partner buying lots of shares, if you're interested.'

'Thank you, no. I'm only interested in *Redgauntlet*.'

'All right, Cap'n, only trying to help.' The watchman's derisive chuckle followed him out of the ship.

Douglas noted the ragged man with the brown cap at the

41

dock gates, realised that he had seen him recently but dismissed him as no more important than the blatant invitation of the prostitute who followed him into Fish Street. His thoughts were on the task entrusted to him, and he was determined not to fail.

He spent the next three days visiting the dockside taverns and ale-houses, talking to the seamen and, alas, getting the same answers.

'I hear *Regauntlet*'s an unlucky ship.'

'A man told me she's haunted.'

'They say she's death to sailormen.'

'*Redgauntlet*? Don't ship on her if you want to come back. Haven't you heard the stories?'

Douglas had indeed heard the stories. He had heard about ghosts on deck, about strange sounds in the foc'sle, about crewmen who had disappeared. Yet when he inquired further, nobody could offer proof of what they said. Not one of the men had actually sailed on *Redgauntlet;* they were only repeating what they had been told.

When he took his findings to Mr Gilbride, the latter shook his head and looked across at Sir Walter, as if hoping for inspiration. 'I've no explanation, Mr Douglas,' he said. 'I cannot fathom it. I've offered double the wages for this voyage but still the men will not sign. However, on the credit side, I have signed a good surgeon whom I've used before, and one of the toughest mates in the trade.'

'And have you a Captain, sir?'

'Adam Fairweather. He's an old ice-master, twenty years' experience, solid as a rock. He sailed with the Eastern Sealing and Whaling Company for a season but he's come back to us. The officers are no difficulty, only the crew.' Gilbride's hand was unsteady as he lit another cigarette.

'What about last season's men?'

'Some of the specialists – the harpooners and so on – have signed articles, but none of the common mariners.' Gilbride produced a sheet of foolscap from the papers on his desk. 'Here are the names and addresses of *Redgauntlet*'s crew for last season. Some of these men have sailed with the company for voyage after voyage. Not one has engaged himself this season. Not one. It's as if they were terrified.'

'May I have a copy of the list, sir?'

'Of course.' Raising his voice, Mr Gilbride called in his clerk. 'Copy out this list, Simpson, and bring it to me. Sharp, now.'

After some minutes, Simpson returned and handed the copy to his master.

'What do you intend doing with it?' Gilbride asked, waving dismissal to Simpson.

'I'll speak to the men, try to persuade them to change their minds.'

'If you can persuade even ten, we'll be all right. We'll pick up the rest at Shetland – good seamen there, and we pay them less.'

'I'll do my best, sir,' Douglas promised.

'I'm relying on you, Mr Douglas. As I said before, I could use more forceful methods, but I prefer a willing crew.' He shrugged. 'What was it Bonaparte said? You can't make an omelette without breaking eggs. In this case we may not be able to make a whaling voyage without breaking heads.'

'Yes, sir,' Douglas answered automatically.

He went to the door and opened it, nearly falling over Simpson, who was standing immediately outside. The clerk apologised profusely and withdrew.

The list told Douglas nothing of significance. Names like Rougvie, Pert, Strachan and Ogilvie would fill any crew in any port from Wick to Berwick. Five of the addresses were in Fife, one in Arbroath and one in Westhaven. The other men lived in Dundee or in the fishing-village of Broughty Ferry, a couple of miles to the east. Douglas resolved to check the Dundee seamen first.

When he reached his lodgings, Mrs Sturrock was waiting for

him. 'And how did you fare today?' she asked immediately. 'Was Mr Gilbride pleased with your work?'

She nodded encouragingly when Douglas told her how he intended to proceed, patted his arm reassuringly when he mentioned his lack of success, and looked over the list with him.

'I'm sorry, Robert, but I don't know any of these men. If I did I would order them to sign on again.' Her laughter was a tonic and Douglas smiled in return. 'Now you sit there and I'll make a nice pot of tea for us both.' Her shoes clicked comfortably on the scrubbed floorboards.

Early next morning, Douglas went to the first address. He frowned as a man scurried away from the door and round the nearest corner, for that was the third time he had seen that brown cap. A quick trot to the corner revealed only an empty street, but Douglas was slightly wary as he knocked on the door.

At his third knock a woman appeared, bleary-eyed and tousle-haired.

Douglas was glad he had been able to purchase a more respectable set of clothes. 'Good morning. Are you Agnes Robertson, wife of Thomas Brown?'

She nodded.

'My name is Douglas. Mr Gilbride employs me and he would like you to know that he is offering double wages to any mariner who signs articles on *Redgauntlet*.'

'Why?' Mrs Robertson was obviously a woman of few words.

'Mr Gilbride told me that your husband is a good seaman, who would be an asset on *Redgauntlet*.'

'No.' Mrs Robertson began to push the door shut, but Douglas blocked it with his foot.

'Double wages,' he repeated, 'with an assured position and oil-money. Those are good benefits for a seaman.'

The door opened very slightly. 'You'll not get my man back on that ship. Tell Horse Gilbride that.'

'May I ask why not?'

'No.' The door slammed against Douglas's foot. 'Move your foot or I'll smash it with a hammer!'

There was no reply at the next three addresses, so Douglas decided to try his luck at Broughty Ferry. When he arrived the tide was out, the yellow sands stretching to distant surf. There was a score of sails on the firth as the local fishermen hunted the herring and two colliers carrying coal from Ferryport on Craig in Fife to Dundee. Broughty Ferry consisted of a handful of thatched fishermen's cottages by the shore and a scattering of buildings inland. The sea dominated the place. It was a village of mariners to which few strangers apparently came: the people stared at him suspiciously.

At the first address on his list the door was answered by a compact, muscular man with calm eyes.

'I'm looking for Tam Wilson,' said Douglas.

'You've found him.'

'I've been sent by Mr Gilbride to—'

'To offer me double wages and a secure position if I sign aboard *Redgauntlet*. I know.' Wilson shook his head. 'You're wasting your time. Nobody will sign articles for that ship. Not now.'

'Why not? Do you believe that she's cursed?'

'Don't you?' Wilson countered. Stepping outside the low door of his cottage, he leaned against the wall. A weak sun highlighted the rope-like muscles of his folded arms. 'Or don't you believe in such things?'

Douglas was about to say that he did not; but then he remembered the fear that witch doctors created among African warriors who were otherwise as brave as any men in the world. He recalled a strapping young giant who had died because he had been told he was cursed. He recalled the 'smelling-out' ceremonies at which the chief mustered his people and the small, ugly witches shuffled along the ranks, deciding who was or was not possessed of an evil spirit. There had been horror on

45

the victims' faces as they were dragged to a painful death, but none had protested.

He said, 'I believe it might be possible.'

'And do you believe that's why Horse Gilbride can't raise a crew? There's worse things than curses to scare a Greenland-man, Mr Douglas.'

'How do you know my name?'

'The same way I knew why you were here, and what you were going to say: I was told, as was every other man of *Redgauntlet*'s crew. You'll get the same answer from them.'

'Tam?' A young woman, fair-haired, anxious and heavily pregnant, emerged from the cottage. 'Who's this now?'

'Nobody for you to worry about.'

'Is that the man from Mr Gilbride?' She laid a protective hand on Wilson's arm and challenged Douglas with a stare. 'He'll not go, sir. You can't take my man.'

'Mr Gilbride is offering double wages. I am sure the extra money would be welcome.' Douglas forced a smile. 'And with the new steam-engine the voyage will be faster – and safer.'

'Like it was for *Ivanhoe*?' Wilson's wife was quick with her tongue. 'She blew up, didn't she? Only one of her crew survived – and only for a little while. Tam'll not sail on that steam-kettle.'

Douglas sighed. 'I can see that your minds are made up, so I won't trouble you any further. I wish you well, ma'am. And the offer stands, for the present.'

Mrs Wilson did not relent. 'And will it still stand when *Redgauntlet* goes bang, too? We'd rather starve ashore than have my Tam die like that. Pieces of wood all over the ice, men scalded, the poor engineer half roasted and floating on a cask until he froze to death. I know exactly what happened.'

'So it appears. I'll bid you both good day, then.'

'Besides,' she said triumphantly, 'Tam's been offered another position. We're going to take that one, aren't we, Tam?'

Wilson put an arm round her. 'If that's what you want, lass, we'll do it.'

Resignedly, Douglas turned away and began the walk back to Dundee. He had not gone far when he became aware that the ragged man in the brown cap was following him.

Dundee, March—April 1860

It should have been a pleasant, albeit cold, walk back to Dundee, with the surf sounding softly beyond the railway line to his left and the magnificent new mansions of West Ferry on his right, but Douglas was too aware of being followed. He had seen the shabbily dressed man outside the door of the ale-house where he had spoken to the sailors, and then at the dock gates when he looked over *Redgauntlet*. Who was he and what did he want? Douglas slowed down, hoping the man would approach him, but instead he stopped, pretending to admire the view over to Fife.

Douglas drew a deep breath. So far, this job had brought him nothing but frustration. Glancing behind to check the man's position, he crossed the road and began to hurry inland. A track took him between small fields, some ploughed, others used as pasture. In the window of a steading which stood among sheltering trees, a candle gleamed.

As Douglas had expected, his pursuer moved swiftly to lessen the distance between them. Douglas scrambled a dry-stane dyke and lengthened his stride so that the man had to run to keep him in sight. Vaulting the next wall, Douglas ran for twenty paces, then rolled into a fold of ground and crawled until he was out of sight. Damp soil stained his fingers, and a flight of partridges whirred from the shelter of the wall and over the field, plump silhouettes against the sinking sun.

There was a soft scrape and a subdued curse as the man upset a coping-stone while scrambling over the dyke near Douglas, then he looked both ways before setting off across the field. He stumbled in the soft earth and swore again, vividly. Douglas took three long strides and dived at the man's legs. There was a yell as his quarry overbalanced, arms flailing.

'Got you!' Douglas caught the fellow's arms and held him face down on the ground. 'Time we had a wee chat, I think.' He twisted one arm. 'Name?' There was no reply, so he twisted harder. 'Name?' The man merely cursed him.

'Let's try something else, then. It'll soon be dark so nobody will see you, and we're too far from anywhere for your screams to be heard.' Setting his knee in the middle of the man's back, Douglas pressed down firmly and this time twisted both arms. 'What will happen first, do you think? Will I pull your arms from their sockets, or break your spine? Let us see.'

'Peebles – I'm Samuel Peebles. You're breaking my bloody arms!'

'Samuel Peebles, eh?' Douglas eased his grip for a moment, then said, 'No, I don't think that's your real name. Try again,' and increased the pressure anew.

'No, please!' The man tried to wriggle free but Douglas held on grimly. 'That *is* my name – Peebles!'

'All right.' Douglas let Peebles recover a little. Despite his threats, he was very aware of the nearby steading, and hoped that the gathering dark would shield them. 'Why have you been following me?'

'I wasn't – that is, I mean, I was told to.'

'Told by whom?' Douglas applied a little pressure, and Peebles flinched. 'I think I'll dislocate the left arm first, then the right.'

Peebles screamed, and a second light appeared at a window of the farm. There was movement, the bang of a door, and voices came on the breeze. Peebles yelled. 'Murder! Help! I'm being murdered by a madman!'

'Told by whom?' Douglas twisted harder, feeling the give of muscles and sinew in Peebles's left shoulder. 'Tell me or I'll leave you crippled for life.'

49

'I don't know his name.'

'Describe him.'

There was more movement from the farm, the barking of a dog, a flicker as somebody passed in front of the window. Light gleamed yellow through the trees: someone had come outside with a lantern.

Douglas twisted the arm again. 'Now!'

The dog's bark became insistent. A man shouted a challenge across the fields, and second light and a third light appeared in the trees. A woman called, 'Be careful, Sandy! Take your gun!' and another dog bayed loudly.

Cursing, Douglas leaned low and hissed in Peebles's ear, 'Describe him!'

'Ugly . . . a heavy man. He wore a bright waistcoat.'

'That is true of half the men in Dundee. Tell me more.' The dogs were at the edge of the field, and the voices were clearer: the men must have emerged from the trees. 'Why did he tell you to follow me?'

'I don't know. He just told me to see where you went and who you spoke to.' Peebles yelled again, louder than before, 'For God's sake, help! He's murdering me!'

'Hey! What's happening over there?' The people from the farm came slowly nearer, their swinging lanterns casting circles of yellow light, beyond which the dark seemed denser, more threatening. Their dogs barked around them.

Giving Peebles' arm a final, malicious twist, Douglas released him. 'Go! Get away before I do indeed murder you! Run!' He kicked at the departing man, watched the farm dogs bound after him, and lay back in his fold of ground. A few moments later there was a loud yell, then raised and excited voices, and shortly afterwards the farmer shouted at the dogs, calling them off. The farm party withdrew, grumbling, to the house. Douglas got to his feet and concentrated on following as Peebles limped away.

Peebles jinked and dodged, doubled back and changed his

pace, but his limp slowed him and always Douglas was able to keep him in sight, drawing closer as the night grew darker.

When they reached the outskirts of Dundee Douglas dropped back somewhat, so that his quarry would think himself safe. He saw him stop and look back searchingly. Douglas immediately turned away slightly, and made play of lighting his pipe, shielding his face from the flare of the lucifer, and all the time watching Peebles out of the corner of his eye. Eventually, evidently satisfied that he had shaken off his pursuer, Peebles slid from the Murraygate down Horse Wynd. Douglas hurried after him, and paused on the corner.

Like most back streets in central Dundee, the wynd was packed with people, some returning from work, others standing outside their squalid homes. Children played beside the open gutters that carried raw sewage down the centre of the wynd, while their mothers formed a forbidding gaggle, gossiping or trying to prevent their husbands from drinking away their wages.

Peebles looked back again, briefly, then went into an alehouse. The sign above the door said '*The Merchants' Arms*' and below that '*The Best Beers and Ales and Quality Spirits*'. This had once been one of the better areas of Dundee, but now it was in decline as the richer people moved away from the noise and stink. Murraygate was a thriving street but its wynds and closes no longer housed shipmasters and flax merchants.

Douglas waited a minute or two, to give Peebles time to settle, then squeezed past the jabbering women, and slipped into the Merchant's Arms. The oil-fuelled glow from frosted globes was reflected in the bottles behind the wooden-topped bar, where three barmen served their thirsty customers. On the floor stood a fine selection of brightly gilded spirit casks, each carrying a number indicating the number of gallons of 'Old-Tom' or 'Mother's Blessing' or other euphemism for the kill-me-deadly contents. Twin mirrors on the back wall exaggerated the size of the establishment and allowed the bar manager to see into every corner. Stained sawdust soaked up the spilled drinks of the inebriated.

This was not by any means the worst class of public house. The drinkers were a mixture of lower-grade clerks, struggling artisans and the omnipresent millworkers. Nursing a tankard of beer, Douglas looked around. Peebles was in a corner seat, speaking with a burly, powerful-looking man wearing a yellow waistcoat. Douglas had seen him before, somewhere.

Tankard in hand, Douglas strode over to them. 'Peebles, I've not finished with you yet.'

Most of the customers shrank away, but Peebles's companion merely slipped a hand inside his waistcoat and sat back, saying nothing.

Douglas threw himself into the unoccupied seat beside Peebles and banged his tankard down on the table. 'We have a conversation to finish.'

'Mr Sergeant, you will take one of these and save your soul.' The voice was loud, clear and feminine.

Startled, Douglas looked up.

The young evangelist from the prizefight marched up to him, a leaflet in her outstretched hand. 'You obviously have need of being saved if you frequent places such as this.'

Aware of movement beside him, Douglas slammed Peebles back in his seat. 'I'm sorry, miss, but I'm busy. I have no time to talk.'

'No, you're too busy drinking to spend even a few minutes with the Lord.' She slapped a leaflet on to the table. Somebody laughed; Peebles began to wriggle free. 'I insist that you read this and give one to your friends, too. If you can't read,' she said, her voice a little gentler, 'I will read it to you. I can even arrange lessons if you wish.' Her voice rose again. 'That goes for all of you! The Good Lord did not intend mankind to live in ignorance and sin. He wants you to prosper and live in His grace! Come to the Mission Hall and—'

Douglas did not hear the rest of the sentence, for Peebles

slipped free, dived across the table and flung the evangelist aside. Instinctively, Douglas caught her arm to prevent her falling, but Peebles's companion pulled a knife from beneath his waistcoat and slashed wickedly. Douglas flinched as the blade tore the flesh of his arm, swore once and smashed a backhanded blow to the man's face. He felt the satisfying shock of contact, but Peebles slipped away, thrusting an elbow into his kidneys in passing and hissing, 'I shall see you again, Mr Sergeant!'

His companion followed, lashing out again with his knife. The evangelist gasped and jerked back. She slipped on the wet sawdust and would have fallen had Douglas not put a steadying arm round her waist. He felt the give of firm flesh rather than the rigidity of whalebone stays.

And then it was over. By the time the evangelist had recovered her balance, Peebles and his colleague were out of the door. At this hour of a winter night, there was no point in attempting to follow through the myriad wynds and alleys.

When Douglas cursed in frustration the evangelist glared at him. 'Those are fine terms to use in front of a lady, Mr Sergeant.'

The tone of voice, rather than the words, silenced him. He snatched his hand away from her waist and apologised. She merely shook her head, entirely composed. Stooping, she lifted Douglas's tankard from the floor, turned it upside down so the last dregs drained out, and put it neatly in the centre of the table. She hummed a psalm as she replaced the chairs. 'I had better look at that arm of yours, sir.'

'My arm?' Douglas realised that blood was flowing freely from the wound. He shrugged. 'It's nothing, miss. I'll bandage it when I get home.'

'Indeed? And then it will no doubt putrefy and you'll lose your arm and be unable to work. Come with me and I will dress it properly.' There was almost a smile on her face as she laid one of her tracts on the table. 'The Lord works in mysterious ways His wonders to perform.' She looked into his eyes; her own were deep brown, with only the slightest flecking of hazel reflecting the light from the lamps. 'Thank you for your help, Mr Sergeant. It would not have been dignified to fall in a place such as this.'

She led Douglas along the Seagate to where a solitary lantern burned unevenly at the low doorway of what was obviously an ancient building. Above the door a notice announced, '*Christian Mission. God Loves a Sinner Come to Redemption*'. Pushing open the door, she showed him into a large stone-floored chamber with a groined ceiling. It smelled of damp and mould and disinfectant.

'At one time,' she said, 'when Dundee had a large wine trade with France, this was a wine-cellar. Now we use it for more Godly purposes.'

Only three lamps illuminated the stark interior, which contained a handful of empty beds, a table upon which a black leather bag reposed, and an overflowing bookcase. A drunken woman sprawled across one of the half-dozen hard chairs, while another sang a soft psalm somewhere in the shadows. A notice on the wall informed Douglas that '*The Eyes of the Lord are in Every Place.*'

'Sit down here,' ordered his guide, 'and let me examine your arm.' She lifted a chair over to the table and obliged Douglas to sit down. 'Mrs Sturrock!' she called. 'A moment of your time, if you please. And bring a basin of warm water and a clean cloth.'

'Mrs Sturrock?' Douglas looked round in astonishment as his landlady bustled up, as neat and clean as if she had been in the kirk.

'Oh, Mr Douglas,' she cried when she saw the blood dripping from his arm, 'whatever have you been doing?'

Before he could reply, the evanglist said tartly, 'A drunken brawl, I regret to say, Mrs Sturrock, in a low public house.' Lifting her skirt from the knees, she knelt beside him, pursing her lips as she did so. 'But he did prevent me from falling so there is some hope of redemption. Please remove your jacket, Mr Sergeant. Or is it Mr Douglas? Have you two names?'

'Robert Douglas, ma'am. I used to be a sergeant in the Seventy-Third Foot.' He slipped off his jacket; his shirt-sleeve was sodden with blood. 'But Mrs Sturrock, I didn't know you worked in a place like th—'

'How do you know him?' interrupted the evangelist.

'Mr Douglas is a tenant of mine, Miss Gilbride.' Mrs Sturrock set a wooden basin on the stone-flagged floor. 'He works for your father. Robert, this is Miss Ellen Gilbride.'

Douglas gaped at her. This young lady was the elder daughter Mr Gilbride had mentioned? Well, he thought ruefully, certainly she seemed as formidable as her father, and every whit as capable.

'Works for my father?' There was real anger in Miss Gilbride's voice. 'Not for much longer, if I have my way. He frequents prizefights and low public houses.'

'As do you, ma'am,' Douglas pointed out.

'I was there on the Lord's work.' Miss Gilbride sounded quite composed.

'And I was there on your father's, ma'am.'

She ignored his words and ordered him to lean forward. He obeyed, and with surprising deftness she removed his shirt. The wound at once began to bleed more freely. Despite her severity, Miss Gilbride's hands were gentle as she washed it with warm water.

'Now this will sting. Prepare yourself.'

Douglas thought he detected a note of satisfaction in her voice. She took up a small bottle and poured some of the contents on to the open wound. It did indeed sting, but he would not give her the satisfaction of seeing him wince.

Her eyes slid across him with perhaps more than professional interest. 'I see this not the first time you have been wounded.' She pointed to the long, ragged white scar that ran across his ribs.

'A Kaffir spear . . .'

*   *   *

55

A hot day by a nameless African river and the butterflies bright around the sweating faces of the men. Major Donnachie leading as they escorted a wagon-train to Greytown, the tall wheels crunching over the hard red earth and the colonists muttering a mixture of prayers and doubts. Thunderhead clouds gathered on the horizon and the wait-a-bit thorns snagged the grey canvas uniforms that Colonel Eyre had insisted they wear. Jerking his chin, the Major sent them to patrol across the river. Great green-bodied flies arose in masses when they probed into the bush on either side of the track.

Then the drumming started.

'Keep by me, Rab, me boy.' Paddy lifted his eyes to the trees. 'It's Donnybrook time.'

With high-pitched yells that raised the hairs on the back of Douglas's scalp, the near-naked Kaffirs burst out of ambush. There was the double crack of musketry, the flicker of a dozen thrown spears, the roar as he aimed and fired, then the flaring pain as the assegai ripped across his side. A moment of confusion as the warriors leaped in among them, the gasp and roar of combat and the sound of a falling body. Paddy was there, standing over Douglas; his long Irish face was concerned and his bayonet greasy with blood. The dying Kaffir thrashed on the ground at his feet.

'Rest easy, Rab. We'll soon have you out of here.'

'. . . a long time ago.' Douglas came back to the present. He looked at his arm and shrugged. With the blood washed away, he could see that it was only a small gash.

Miss Gilbride was still examining his ribs, her fingers cool and soft. 'The Lord kept you safe. This was an honourable wound in the service of your country – unlike the scar you will have from brawling while in drink.' She opened the black bag on the table and produced a needle and thread. 'I'll stitch you up now. Keep still; or Mrs Sturrock can hold you, if you prefer.'

He shook his head. 'I can keep still.'

There was intent concentration on Miss Gilbride's face as she worked, pushing the needle through his flesh and laying a neat row of stitches across his arm. Her eyes were narrowed, with the hazel seemingly contesting the brown for dominance. The eyelashes were long, and curled at the ends.

Douglas asked, 'What made you take up this work, ma'am?'

'We are all the Lord's children, Mr Douglas, and I serve Him in the best way I can. If dealing with these unfortunates is my lot, I will soldier on as bravely as I am able.'

'Miss Gilbride volunteered for Miss Nightingale's nurses,' Mrs Sturrock explained. 'She has a calling to spread God's Word and help the less fortunate.'

Douglas thought that admirable. 'Volunteered? And did you serve in the Crimea, Miss Gilbride?'

The needle jabbed deeper, drawing fresh blood as Miss Gilbride threw Mrs Sturrock a look that could have curdled milk. 'Miss Nightingale did not accept me. She said I was not suitable. Indeed, she said that I was a "prim little body but too pretentious to be a nurse". She meant that I was not so malleable as her other volunteers.'

Douglas smiled. He could not imagine the intense Miss Gilbride being in the least bit malleable, and, if what he had heard of Miss Nightingale was correct, that lady demanded instant obedience.

'Does something amuse you, sir?' Miss Gilbride turned her milk-curdling look upon him. There was no hazel in her eyes now, only a brown so dark that it was almost black.

'Oh no, ma'am,' he said hastily. 'I was thinking how useful your skills would have been in Africa. Unlike the Crimea, our campaigns did not attract Russell of the Thunderer, so ladies such as Miss Nightingale did not flock to nurse our sick and wounded.'

'I see.' Miss Gilbride's sewing did not falter a second time; each stitch was as precise as the last. She motioned to Mrs Sturrock to wipe away the blood. 'I intend to enlarge this

Mission, and to encourage ladies of sense and breeding to help the unfortunate. Once we are properly established I shall advertise in the newspapers.' She glanced up at him. 'Now tell me, Mr Douglas, in what capacity does my father employ you?'

Trying to keep the pride from his voice, Douglas explained his position and what he had been doing in the public house.

Miss Gilbride was expressionless as she listened, nodding occasionally. 'I see. So you entered that iniquitous place as part of your work. Of course, I shall check that what you say is correct. But, Mr Douglas, are you not aware that your body is a temple of God?' She finished her sewing and examined her handiwork critically before jabbing a finger at him. 'By defacing yourself you are breaking God's law.' As she leaned closer to examine the tattoos that adorned his arm a loose wisp of her brown hair brushed his chest. 'What is that? A beehive? And these smudged words, what do they say?'

'Yes, a beehive. I had it done in Cape Town. The other is crossed muskets and "Great Mars the God of War did never see such men before", with "Seventy-Third" beneath. It's the words of a song.' Paddy had taught him the words as they lay in the sweating 'tween deck of the troopship to Cape Town. And he recalled the men bellowing it in mingled fear and defiance as they waited for the Gaikas to erupt from the forest . . .

The drumming echoed through the bush, augmenting the Gaikas' war cries. The handful of redcoats checked their weapons and loosened the bayonets in their scabbards.

Paddy nudged Douglas. 'Noisy buggers, aren't they? But look at the Major. He's ready for them.'

Major Donnachie had removed his tunic and was swinging his fists as if preparing for a prizefight. 'Time for a song, McBride!' And the Major lifted his head and roared out the 73rd's answer to the drummers' challenge:

'Great Mars the God of War
Did never see such men before,
Nor Alexander fight like us at Mangalore.
At Serangipatam we fought and Tipoo Sahib we slew.
'Twas there we showed the dog what the Seventy-Third can
    do.'

Minutes later, the attack came in.

It was Douglas's first experience of fighting. He still remembered the fear and elation and carnage. He had shot two men
that day, brave warriors fighting for what they believed to be
their land and freedom.

'. . . A regimental song, ma'am. It meant a lot to me, once.'

'Perhaps so, sir, but you really should not paint your body
like that, especially with the names of pagan gods.'

Douglas shifted his arm so that Miss Gilbride could wrap a
clean linen bandage round his wound. From the corner of his
eye he glimpsed Mrs Sturrock watching him, and he asked her
for his shirt.

'Not until it's washed and mended,' she told him primly.
'Until then you must wear something else.'

It was Miss Gilbride who helped Douglas slip on a worn but
clean shirt from some secret store, and Miss Gilbride who took
away his bloodstained one, but Mrs Sturrock who guided him
to the door.

'You be careful walking home, now,' she said softly. 'Not all
the bees make it safely to the hive.' Her eyes were bright and
wise and terribly knowing.

Douglas spent the next few weeks around the docks, speaking
with the crew of every ship that called. Most knew about
Redgauntlet's ill reputation, for the fraternity of seamen passed
information with a speed and accuracy which would have
shamed the Secret Service. Of the scores of men Douglas

interviewed, only one agreed to sign articles on her, and his companions looked on him as feeble-minded.

When he was not attempting to recruit, Douglas asked questions about Peebles and his yellow-waistcoated companion. Many men knew Peebles as a shiftless character who would oblige anybody for a free drink, but no one knew his whereabouts – until his corpse was discovered one morning on the Arbroath railway line. The newspapers reported his death as suicide. Douglas was not convinced, but when he voiced his doubts to the police, Inspector Murdoch shook his head.

'Maybe it was murder, and maybe it was not. Either way, we're well rid of a scoundrel. Let it rest.'

Douglas had little time to pursue the matter, for *Redgauntlet*'s due date of sailing was drawing alarmingly close and still he had been unable to raise a crew for her. As the days passed he met Mr Gilbride more often. He reported his lack of progress, and his suspicion that Peebles's death was in some way related to *Redgauntlet*, but Mr Gilbride did not seem as worried as perhaps he should have. He spoke again of 'more forceful' ways to raise a crew and suggested that Douglas should search for the man in the yellow waistcoat.

'I agree, sir,' Douglas said, 'for I believe that there is more than *Redgauntlet*'s reputation at stake. Almost every man I spoke to gave one of two reasons for not coming. They said either that the ship is unlucky or that she might blow up.' He leaned forward over the desk. 'I think they were told what to say. I believe that they were scared off.'

There was resolution in Mr Gilbride's face when he looked up. 'Then we have them, we have them indeed. The Merchant Shipping Acts of 'fifty and 'fifty-four state clearly that it is illegal to incite seamen to refuse to sail. Frightening off a crew would certainly be within the meaning of the Act, and would attract a heavy penalty.'

'I do believe it, sir. I also believe that the person who ordered

Peebles to follow me and the person who told the seamen not to sign on *Redgauntlet* are one and the same.'

Mr Gilbride shook his head. 'It seems I have an enemy, then, someone who is resolved that *Redgauntlet* shall not sail. Now, Mr Douglas, do you think you can discover who and why?'

Douglas looked up at the lady's portrait, and again drew encouragement from her serene eyes. 'Yes, sir,' he said.

He left the office musing over a theory which he had no evidence to support. The only lead he had was the man in the yellow waistcoat, who seemed to have disappeared.

Douglas asked questions in the Merchants' Arms every evening, but all the drinkers claimed to have been elsewhere on the night when he had been wounded. Even the barmen said they had been relieving themselves at the time. There were so many negative responses that Douglas wondered if only the deaf and the blind drank there.

It was a relief to return home after each frustrating day. Mrs Sturrock was always pleased to see him and, when she listened to his dispiriting news, always nodded in the right places and patted his arm when he needed reassurance. She seemed to have his welfare at heart, for she even advised him to buy a decent set of clothing for his next meeting with Mr Gilbride.

One evening, as soon as he crossed the threshold she handed him a note and said, 'A Mr Simpson gave me this for you.'

'*Mr Douglas,*' it read, in a slightly crabbed copperplate hand, '*one of my poor unfortunates was in the public house on the night you were wounded, and he has informed me that your attacker works at an establishment called Mother Scott's. It might be to your benefit to visit that place. Ellen Gilbride.*'

Dundee, March 1860

'I fear I must hurry out again, Mrs Sturrock.'

Mrs Sturrock frowned and shook her head. 'You'll not hurry anywhere without a good meal inside you, Robert, nor until I've changed the dressing on your arm. I suppose this is more tomfoolery for Mr Gilbride?'

Douglas grinned. 'Just doing my job, Mrs Sturrock – the job you found for me.'

'I thought you would be working in the office, not gallivanting around all the ale-shops in Dundee.' She took Miss Gilbride's letter from him and read it, then snorted in a most unladylike manner. 'Mother Scott's, of all places! You know that it's not even real Highland whisky that they sell there? It's kill-me-deadly, made from methylated spirits and water, sweetened with sugar and prune juice.'

'I can imagine it, but I hardly ever drink spirits.' Douglas knew about the rotgut arrack sold to the soldiers in Cape Town and Calcutta. He had seen strong men reduced to mumbling cripples unable to move, and had even seen men die after one night's over-indulgence.

'I'm glad to hear it.' Mrs Sturrock's severe tone moderated and she began to bustle about with pots and plates. 'All I can say is thank the Lord for the Forbes Mackenzie Act. At least that gives us one day a week free of drunken sots, and a fixed time for closing these places of the devil.'

Douglas had learned that it was best to agree with Mrs Sturrock when she was on one of her verbal crusades. Leaving her to pour forth her wisdom, he withdrew into his tiny room and made ready for the evening. He read the note again, then tucked it beneath the straw mattress of his bed. In his search for crewmen he had learned something of Dundee's public houses, and Ma Scott's was one of the lowest, a combination of a lodging-house for the riff-raff of the seas, a brothel and a thieves' kitchen. Seamen who frequented the place would hardly be suitable for work on a whaler, so he had given it a wide berth. Now, however, Miss Gilbride required him to visit it.

Experience had taught Douglas to carry a weapon when entering low drinking-dens, so he tucked a length of blackthorn up his sleeve. Only a year ago he had been the sergeant of thirty battle-hardened soldiers. He had led them through ambush and escort, across kloofs and riverbeds, and over the plains of India. He could depend on their skill, courage and loyalty to back him in any situation; now he was reduced to defending himself with a stick.

Douglas scowled at his reflection in the scrap of mirror that covered a hole in the plastered wall. He saw a man of thirty-two, deeply tanned, wiry rather than muscular, with eyes that never varied: whether he smiled or frowned, they were steady, dark as his hair and cynical as a huckster's promise. He was not tall, but his straight-backed military carriage gave him presence. The sailor's garb he affected would have to serve as a disguise.

Mrs Sturrock put her head round the door and asked, 'Are you ready, Robert? Your soup is waiting for you.'

He was not sure if that was amusement in her eyes, or compassion. Angry at his moment of vanity, he turned abruptly away from the mirror.

The faded board above the door of Mother Scott's carried the official name of '*The Crossover Inn*', a reminder that the place had once served as a staging-post for passengers crossing the Tay. It squatted between a shipyard and the reeking boiling-house of the Eastern Sealing and Whaling Company, the only buildings remaining on a peninsula which the Arbroath Railway had cut off on its coastal drive to Dundee.

If the Crossover had had an architect, he must have had an eye for the picturesque, for it was a strange-looking place. The middle level was built of ordinary poor-quality Dundee stone, the lowest part seemingly carved out of the coastal rock, and the top patched on with planking salvaged from wrecked ships or looted from the timber yards along the foreshore. At high tide the waves battered against the seaward wall; at low tide the foundations clung on to smeared mud; the whole place reeked of rotted seaweed, sewage and stale alcohol.

It had been busy once, with accommodation for pilgrims heading to St Andrews, but recent years had brought gradual decay. Now the door hung half open on a broken hinge, and a shivering whore in a tartan shawl touted for business on the undrained ground outside. Rumour had it that a network of tunnels and passages wove through its cellars, where desperate mariners had hidden from the press-gang half a century and more before, but Douglas doubted that the proprietors' charity would have extended so far.

He pushed through the broken door, and descended three stone steps into a gloomy chamber. A single lantern hung from the vaulted stone ceiling, which was half hidden by a haze of tobacco smoke through which Neanderthal shapes dimly moved.

'What'll it be, sailor? A shakedown for the night, a dram or something else?' The young woman behind the bar granted Douglas a professional smile.

He estimated that she was around twenty-five, certainly no older, and far too young to be Mother Scott. Despite her surroundings, she had an aura of friendliness which made Douglas like her immediately. Her clear blue eyes were attractive, and both her fair hair and the mob cap above them were clean.

'Just beer, thank you,' he said. 'And perhaps a little help – I'm looking for somebody.'

Her smile broadened, showing surprisingly white teeth behind soft lips. 'Half the world passes through Ma Scott's, sailor, and the other half pretends places like this don't exist. Who've you lost? Or who do you want to see again?'

'I'm not sure of his name, but I was told that he works here.' Douglas described the man who had cut him.

She listened carefully, nodding occasionally as she poured beer into a battered tankard. 'I think I know who you mean – he does work here sometimes.' She pushed the tankard towards him. 'That's Peter Williamson.' She glanced around the room and lowered her voice. 'Ma Scott employs him in case any of the customers get too rowdy.'

'That is work he finds congenial, no doubt.' Douglas tasted the beer, guessed that it was constituted of slops and rainwater, and set it back on the counter. 'Would you care for a drink yourself?'

'Of course I would.' Golden curls bounced prettily as she threw her head back to laugh. 'It's almost the only pleasure this job offers! Now, pray don't misunderstand me. If it's a woman you're after, they're through there,' jerking her thumb at a green-baize-covered door in the far wall. 'I am not on the market.'

'I didn't for a moment think you were,' said Douglas hastily. 'It's plain that you're not of that sort.' It sounded clumsy but she seemed pleased. The blue eyes met his and crinkled at the corners in a smile. Their owner produced a bottle from beneath the counter and poured herself a small drink.

'Is Peter Williamson expected in tonight?' he asked. 'I very much wish to see him.'

'Is he a friend of yours?' The blue eyes narrowed thoughtfully. 'No. If he were, you'd know his name. So either you owe him money, or he owes you something.' She leaned across the bar, exuding a faint waft of perfume. 'And if you owed him money, he'd be breaking down your door at this very moment. So you want something from him. Am I right?'

'You're not far wrong.'

'Well, as you seem too nice a fellow to be in a place like this, I'll give you some free advice.' She patted his arm with a small hand on which a ring glittered brightly. 'Turn round, go out of that door and never come back. Forget whatever Peter Williamson owes you because you'll not see it again. Forget Peter Williamson, too.' She leaned closer and her perfume caught at the back of Douglas's throat. For a brief second her breasts brushed against his arm. 'For your own sake, hurry away now.'

Douglas pretended to consider, then shook his head. 'No, I fear I cannot do that. It's a personal matter.' He attempted the beer again. 'If you know Williamson, perhaps you also know a friend of his, a man called Peebles, Sam Peebles?'

She shrugged and drew back. 'Everyone knows Sam Peebles. He did half the world's dirty work.'

'Including Williamson's?'

'Including everybody's. Anyway, if you've any sense, you'll go home. If you insist on seeing Williamson, he'll be in there later tonight.' She jerked a pointed chin towards the green door. 'I've got customers to serve.' Once again she leaned across the counter and gave that bright smile. 'At least the drink's better through there.'

So was the light. The door led into an even lower room, where oil-filled lamps glimmered enticingly in a place of comfortable furniture, wood-panelled walls and bright rugs over polished floorboards. There was quiet music from a duo of violinists sitting in one corner, and warmth from the fire that filled the huge fireplace. For a moment Douglas thought that Mother Scott's evil reputation was undeserved, but then he saw the company.

If any of the men who slouched along the bar or sprawled on the seats had entered the 73rd Foot, Douglas would have immediately marked him down as a troublemaker. The women, in dresses cut too low and skirts too short for any semblance of decency, wore scents so powerful that they nearly masked the stench of sweat and unwashed bodies. Powder concealed the pits of disease on faces which were shockingly young, prematurely aged, or bitter and predatory.

Nevertheless, the service was quick and the beer palatable. Douglas chose an unoccupied table, waving away an approaching harridan who looked fifty but was probably nearer thirty; she swore fluently as she swayed away. Two other women watched from a nearby table, smiling whenever he glanced in their direction and making repeated gestures to the empty glasses in front of them.

Douglas tried not to watch the customers paw each other unimaginatively, but listened when a man stood up to sing. Weather-browned and lanky, he wore the brass earring of a seaman. When two of the women joined in the chorus, Douglas guessed that he was a regular. The song was of a whaling-ship called *Diamond* which brought a full catch to Peterhead – Douglas wondered if the Diamonds had squandered their wages in places like Mother Scott's. Suddenly he felt very sad for all these wasted lives; he wondered if these broken people had possessed dreams and hopes and ambitions before they descended the ladder.

It was a relief when the young woman from the neighbouring bar joined him.

'Peter Williamson will be here soon,' she said, sliding gracefully into the seat beside him. 'Are you sure you won't leave?'

There was no comparison between this woman and the others. She was neat and clean, with frank, open eyes and a complexion unmarred by disease or cosmetics. She held out her hand in a gesture which was both unwomanly and very appealing. 'My name is Lucy.'

Douglas accepted the hand. 'And mine is Robert Douglas.' He met her smile.

Lucy kept hold of his hand. 'You are no seaman, Robert

Douglas. Seamen have callused hands from hauling on ropes.' She laughed at his expression and released his hand. 'In this trade you soon learn to read people, the bad, the terrible and the plain unfortunate. But I'm not certain about you.' She put her head to one side; a strand of blond hair escaped from beneath her cap and coiled round her ear. 'Perhaps you are a searcher, a man looking for something. Is that right?'

As she patted his arm her ring sparkled anew. It looked too expensive for a barmaid, and Douglas wondered which fortunate seaman had exchanged the wages from a long voyage for a night with Lucy.

'Well,' she said, 'I hope you find it, if it's right for you.' Her smile faltered, as if something were troubling her. 'But I don't think you'll find it here. I think you'd be well advised to forget all about Peter Williamson.'

'I cannot do that,' Douglas repeated.

She dropped her eyes and sighed.

The seaman brought his song to and end with a flourish and looked over to her, smiling. Her presence seemed to alter the whole character of the place. Douglas understood whence came the attempt at wholesomeness, the bright colours, and even the better quality of the drink, but there was something else about her, too. Paddy would have warned him to turn and run, for women like this were always trouble.

'Will you take another drink?' he asked.

Lucy smiled, shaking her head. 'You seem resolved to waste your money, Robert Douglas.' She leaned forward again. Though decorously covered, her breasts were infinitely more alluring than those so blatantly offered by the other women. 'It's beer you drink, isn't it? Then you shall have some good beer. Tell Emily – the dark-haired barmaid – to give you a glass of Lucy's special brew. That'll set you up for Peter Williamson, all right.'

'And yourself?'

She patted his shoulder. 'Oh . . . anything. Tell Emily my usual. She knows.'

Like most British soldiers, Douglas had forced just about everything down his throat, but he appreciated quality when it was offered. Lucy's special beer was different, dark, with a distinctive taste and a bite like a bayonet.

'You don't belong in a place like this,' he told her as he sat down again. 'I'm sure you could find something better.'

Lucy laughed. 'Something respectable you mean? Working sixteen-hour shifts in a mill and ending up worn out before I'm thirty? Or perhaps working in a shop, on my feet from dawn to midnight for a pittance? Or being a servant in one of the big houses at West Ferry, fondled by his factory-ownership and treated like stour by his wife?' She gestured around the bar. 'Nobody belongs in a place like this, not even these human wrecks. But what I have here frees me from slavery.' Regret shadowed her summer-blue eyes. She touched his cheekbone, gently running her hand down to his chin. 'Unfortunately, Robert Douglas, there is a price to pay for everything in this world, and tonight it is you who must pay it.'

Douglas blinked; Lucy's face was slowly altering, as if he was seeing her in a distorting mirrors at a fairground.

Her smile vanished. 'Beginning to work now, is it? And just in time for Peter Williamson.' She stood up, allowing her hand to slide on to his shoulder, and spoke without raising her voice. 'Over here, Peter. This is the man.'

'What?' It took a great effort for Douglas to move. He tried to rise, fighting the lethargy that swept over him in increasingly powerful waves. He saw the broad, ugly face of Peter Williamson coming closer, saw the bulge in the yellow waistcoat.

'I remember you now,' Douglas said, his speech as slurred as if he were drunk. 'You were at the prizefight. You were one of Wyllie's guards.'

An unappealing grin spread across Williamson's face. 'That's right. You turned down a job from Mr Wyllie. Right disappointed, he was. He said to make you regret it before you died.'

The words seemed to come from a great distance, yet

Douglas understood them perfectly. He felt himself being dragged off the seat, but the fist he swung arced feebly through empty air.

'How long will it last?' Williamson asked.

Lucy was watching, her arms folded across her chest. 'I gave him four drops of laudanum. He'll be out for about twelve hours.' She leaned closer to Douglas, pressing her breasts against him; so close that Douglas saw his reflection in her innocent blue eyes. 'I'm surprised he's still conscious. He must have the constitution of an ox.'

Williamson backhanded Douglas across the face. 'I'll put him out now, if you like. Soften him up a bit.'

'No need. He's harmless enough.'

Another face appeared. Douglas concentrated hard and made out Mr Wyllie.

'Ah, Mr Sergeant, I warned you, didn't I? Hold him, Williamson, I want to check something.' Douglas's arms were pinned to his side and he heard the ripping of cloth as Wyllie tore open his shirt-sleeve. 'It's true, then. The vanity of the tattoo betrays your secret, Mr Sergeant. But it will not be a secret for much longer, you'll be sorry to hear.'

Douglas closed his eyes to welcome the sweet sleep that would release him from Limbo, but inside his head he could still hear the purr of Wyllie's voice.

'You see, Mr Sergeant, I know the meaning of that symbol and the letters around it, the beehive and the letters "T. P. C." – The People's Charter. You were a Chartist, Mr Sergeant, a member of the Jacobin horde that wanted to bring bloody revolution to our fair country.'

He knelt beside Douglas, his eyes as blue as Lucy's, but not as innocent. 'I know all out about you, Mr Sergeant. You and your father participated in the Chartist march in 'forty-two. You were both convicted of theft – stealing turnips from a field on the road to Forfar. Your father was jailed but the magistrate was kind to you, because of your youth, and allowed you to join the army instead. I wonder, does Mr Gilbride know that he employed a convicted thief? That his Personal Assistant is a revolutionary?'

Douglas looked up, saw the faces of Lucy and Wyllie intermingle as if they were one, but whereas Wyllie was gloating Lucy looked troubled. She opened her mouth to speak, but her words merged with the background noise to become meaningless sounds.

Wyllie was still speaking, his mouth opening very wide and moving very slowly. 'I shall tell Horse Gilbride what I have discovered. So you should return from where you're going, which I very much doubt, you won't have a job. Think of that, Mr Sergeant, as you suffer. Good evening to you.' He stood up and adjusted his hat. 'Put him with the others.'

Douglas tried to struggle as he was dragged away, but Williamson punched him hard in the stomach and he fell to the ground. Williamson kicked him, swearing, until Lucy stopped him with a quiet word. After that Douglas could see only the ceiling as he was dragged backward, through another door. There was a flight of stairs, then the sound of something – water, he decided, lapping on stone – and the stench of rotting seaweed. He felt a heave, and he was lying in a boat with a heap of unconscious men.

Fighting the drug-induced weariness, he thought he saw Lucy in the boat, thought he felt a farewell kiss, then there was a blast of chill air and the boat was rising to the first swelling wave of the Tay. He closed his eyes at last.

German Ocean, Spring 1860

At first Douglas thought he was back in the army, with the harsh sun of Africa beating on his unprotected head and the bloody flux rampant inside him. His head ached as if he had been on a three-day drinking-spree, and there was a terrible nausea in the pit of his stomach. He felt Paddy's weight lying across his chest, and the cart on which he lay was swaying from side to side, yet forward and back at the same time. Turning his head, Douglas vomited.

There were sounds he recognised: a creaking which had haunted his nightmares and the subdued hushing of surf on a distant beach; the smell was familiar, too. Douglas realised he was still in the troopship bound for Calcutta. He groaned, then grinned sourly, expecting Paddy McBride to make a joke about the lack of women aboard, but Paddy was dead, killed by a sniper while charging toward an obscure up-country village. He remembered the swaying silvery grass, and the hard red earth spurting as the Pandy's bullets kicked in. He remembered Paddy staggering as the first ball found him, yelling an Irish slogan as the second ripped into his stomach. He remembered Paddy rising again, the pink intestines sliding from his belly to the ground, but still moving forward one slow step at a time.

Douglas closed his eyes to force away the memory, but it was too strong. He remembered screaming in anguish as he ran forward, bayonet jab-jab-jabbing at everybody in his path. 'Paddy!' He had marched a long road with Paddy, and now Paddy was dead.

Douglas opened his eyes, aware of the swaying and the smell, of the whispers and mutterings of men and the incessant creaking that filled the air. There was something carved on the wooden wall in front of him. He squinted at the badly formed letters. There was a 'D' and an 'a' and . . . 'Davey'. He had seen that before somewhere, long ago, when he could think clearly and his head was not full of wool and his throat was not stuffed with powdered glass. 'Davey'. It had been on a ship – it had been on *Redgauntlet*. The memory returned slowly and he smiled at the coincidence that that name should be carved in the same way on two different ships.

Somebody swore behind him, then swore again. The sound echoed in the confined space.

'Where in God's name am I?'

The voice was confused, but Douglas could not explain that they were on a troopship because he was no longer certain. Paddy McBride had been killed in India, so they could not be on the troopship sailing to India. This must be later, after the voyage. After the campaign, too.

Douglas sat up, pushing away the man who lay sprawled across his chest. 'We're on *Redgauntlet*,' he said. 'But I'm not sure how.'

'*Redgauntlet* be buggered!' The voice was angry. 'I've signed articles for *Charleston!*'

Other voices joined in as men began to stir: guttural, sleep-slurred, disjointed voices. There was a retching and somebody was violently sick, then swore in a low, continuous monotone; somebody else giggled in high-pitched hysterics. Other bodies lay supine, a heap of ragged humanity which Douglas could barely see in the dim light of the single, guttering lantern that swayed dizzily from a hook in the ceiling.

'Can anybody find a way out of here?' Douglas called over the babble. 'We might get back on shore before we sail.'

'Door's locked,' said the first voice, 'and bolted from the outside, by the feel of it.' The man began to hammer on the wood, shouting, and all the others joined in, kicking the door or the bulkheads in an effort to attract attention. The noise made the pain in Douglas's head infinitely worse, and he was glad when the men grew tired and ceased. The swaying continued, but now he could hear a battery of creaks and groans as the fabric of the ship moved with the sea.

'*Redgauntlet,* you say?' The *Charleston* seaman shoved his way closer to Douglas. 'Are you sure of that?'

'Sure as I can be,' Douglas replied.

The man sucked in his breath. 'Aye. We all knew that Horse Gilbride couldn't raise a crew, but I didn't think he would stoop to using a crimp. Do you know how much blood-money Ma Scott will get for us? Five pound a head. Yes, five pound – and it'll come out of our wages.' He sat on the bunk next to Douglas. 'My wife will be worried to death, and her with a bairn due, too.'

The voice was familiar and when Douglas squinted at its owner through the dim he remembered the young couple at Broughty Ferry. 'You're Tam Wilson, aren't you?'

'How do you know that?' Wilson eyed him suspiciously. 'You seem to know a hell of a lot for a man who's been crimped. You know my name and you know what ship we're on. Who are you?' His tone brought a couple of other men towards them. They stank of stale alcohol and foulness.

'I'm Robert Douglas. I was in Mother Scott's and woke up here. I worked for Mr Gilbride.'

'You still work for Gilbride – we all do now.' Wilson sounded bitter. 'I remember you now. You were asking questions at my house. No, no you weren't, you were trying to get me to sign on this ship.' Although his voice raised only slightly, there was no mistaking his anger. 'Now you've got your wish – you set me up nicely, you bastard!'

Douglas shook his head. 'Not me. I was crimped, too, remember? I'm locked in here as securely as you are – and I'm no seaman.'

Wilson grunted, clearly unconvinced. He looked away.

74

'We'll see about that later. But you're right about one thing, we're all aboard the jinx ship.' He raised his voice so everyone could hear. 'We're on the steam-kettle, boys, so don't expect to get back to bonnie Dundee. It's the *Ivanhoe* treatment for us.'

'What's the *Ivanhoe* treatment?' asked a voice out of the gloom.

'Take us up to the ice, blow up the ship and claim the insurance.' Wilson's sardonic laughter was cut short as *Redgauntlet* shuddered and a low rumble ran through her hull. 'Jesus, that must be the engine. We're moving, boys.'

Men ran to the door, yelling to be released. Despite their frantic noise, their repeated kicks and howls, there was no response. The vibration increased and the ship began to pitch and roll more heavily, so that some of the men lost their balance and were thrown against the bulkheads. There was a long wail from a ragged-looking fellow, and more retching as the movement upset stomachs made queasy by alcohol and opiates.

'We might only move into the roads and lie to for a while,' Wilson said hopefully.

But the engine continued and the lantern jerked in short arcs which cast ugly shadows around the cabin. It seemed that *Redgauntlet* was sailing directly out of the Tay.

Douglas lay quiet, trying to control the pounding in his head and wondering why he was here. Was Wyllie gaining revenge for his supposed disloyalty, or was it just coincidence that had brought them together in Mother Scott's? Perhaps he had been crimped by chance. Douglas swore silently, trying to fight off the dark possibility that Miss Gilbride had been involved. Her letter had directed him to Mother Scott's. Had she deliberately sent him to *Redgauntlet*? Douglas pictured her expressive eyes, recalled her intense religious belief, and slid away from the idea.

He felt the vibration increase and guessed that *Redgauntlet* was moving faster, further and further from Dundee. How long did whaling voyages last?

*   *   *

'So here you are, then, young fella.' The tall man grinned lopsidedly at him, his thumbs hooked in the waistband of his trousers and his muscles writhing beneath the tanned skin of his arms. 'Gone for a soldier, eh?'

Douglas, short and scrawny for his fifteen years, stared upward. 'Yes, sir,' he whispered.

'Och, I'm not a sir, nor ever will be.' The tall man extended a broad hand. 'I'm just a man from the hungry country. Paddy McBride, they call me, out of Draperstown in the Sperrins.' The brogue was soft and comfortable and the smile infectious as Paddy sat down. 'I was not much older than you when I took the Queen's tarnished shilling, and for the same reason, too. You joined over a turnip or two, and I joined when a landlord's rick caught fire.'

Douglas felt badly in need of friendship. He made space on the deck at his side for the Irishman to sit down, and asked, 'How long will the voyage take?'

'Weeks or months, young fella, and maybe a bit longer than that.' Paddy produced a small plug of tobacco, broke it into two and gave half to Douglas. 'But the longer we're on the ship, the less time we'll be getting shot at by whoever we're being sent to fight. We'll survive, you and me, as long as we stick together.'

Douglas began to chew the tobacco. His father had smoked dried weeds, because what little money he had earned was given to his wife, until she died of fever. Then his father still smoked weeds, and spent his wages on his children. Until the job had ended and there was no money at all. He shook the memories away. 'We'll stick together.'

'That's the way,' said Paddy, nodding. 'We'll be like brothers, young fella. We'll look out for one another, but we must have trust. Do you trust me?'

At that moment Douglas's need of a friend rose to desperation. 'Aye, I trust you.'

'Then we'll get through this.' For a second the dancing eyes were old and terrible as Paddy stared along the steaming troopdeck.

Douglas gritted his teeth. He would get through this and return to Dundee with a hatful of gold. His father would be able to smoke real tobacco every day of his life, once Douglas got back. He only had to survive, and trust.

By the time the door was opened, Douglas, like most of the other men, was fighting seasickness. It was Tam who heard the noise of footsteps and waited, fists clenched, to rush whoever first appeared. The others watched, or swore, or cowered against the bulkhead to be out of the way. The door slammed open, a blinding light glared into their eyes and a figure seemed to fill all the space.

'Right, you scum, you've skulked down here long enough. Time you did some work.'

Despite their angry words of only a few moments before, none of the men moved.

The huge figure spoke more loudly: 'Come out, you lubbers, or I'll come and get you. Look lively, now. I swear to God that I'll knock the bloody face off the first man who doesn't jump to it.'

'You bastard!' Tam launched himself forward but the man in the door shot out a massive fist. There was the crack of knuckles on bone and Tam sprawled on the deck.

'Any more?'

There was no response.

Weak from the effects of laudanum and seasickness, Douglas did not try to offer resistance. It would be better to bide his time and see what transpired.

'Then pick him up and get on deck.' The giant man's face was hidden in the gloom, but his shoulders filled the doorway. He spoke in an intimidating roar and his words were followed by a flailing boot and a string of blasphemies.

Douglas stooped and hoisted Tam over his shoulder. It was bitterly ironic: he had helped break in Johnny Raws in much the same manner in the Seventy-Third. Now he was back in the position of recruit, but eighteen years older and without Paddy to ease his passage.

He staggered as he reached the heaving deck. The wind moaned through the rigging as if it shared the anguish of the crimped crew, while dirty black smoke belched from *Redgauntlet*'s funnel. They huddled round the mizzenmast. The gusty wind kept shifting, first covering them with soot and smuts, then flicking the smoke in the opposite direction so that everything was fresh and clean.

Blinking in the daylight, which seemed too bright after hours locked in the gloom of the foc'sle, Douglas instinctively measured the distance to the coastline away to the left, the brown fields of early spring, a church spire pointing to the sky. How far? Two miles, perhaps, across a sea of grey waves which frothed with foam around the ship. Too far to swim.

Four shouting men herded the unwilling recruits to the stern, where a fifth man, squat, bearded and dressed in a crumpled blue uniform, regarded them impassively. Douglas lowered Tam gently to the deck. There was an ugly bruise already developing on his chin, but he was beginning to stir, his eyes flickering open.

'Lie still just now,' Douglas advised. 'We're up on deck.'

He looked around, and recognised some of the faces from Mother Scott's. The seaman who had sung of the bonnie *Diamond* winked at him, but the expressions of the others did nothing to bolster his confidence. Showing dissipation, fear and nausea, they huddled in a dispirited group, round-shouldered, pigeon-chested, cowering, licking dry lips. Did the master really expect to sail *Redgauntlet* to the whaling-grounds with such poor creatures? A sudden lurch dipped the bows into the sea and brought a mass of cold water surging aft, soaking everybody. The men wailed. One began to sob.

'Listen, you vermin!' the big man roared. Douglas looked up

– and instantly wished he had not, for the man was none other than the Dundee Destroyer, who glared down at him like a living nightmare.

'These are the facts, for good or ill. You're aboard *Redgauntlet*, bound for the Davis Strait whaling-grounds under the command of Captain Adam Fairweather.' He indicated the uniformed man, who nodded slowly, surveying each man in turn. 'Some of you are seamen; I shall soon discover which ones. The remainder will be mustered as Greenmen, and paid as such. My name is William Houston, and I am mate of this vessel. That means that I am second in line from Lord God Almighty.' He paused for a second, allowing his words to sink in. 'However, as the Lord is not here and I am, whenever I speak you will act as if all the angels of Creation were prodding their flaming swords into your arse.'

Houston ran his eye over the men, who either glared back sullenly or kept their heads down. 'I know that none of you want to be here – that is why we had to tear you from the arms of your poxed-up lovers. But you are aboard this ship now, and will remain aboard until we return to Dundee. Those of you who are seamen, I'm sorry, but you know how it is. As for the rest of you, you've got a lot of work to do. If you don't know what work is, you're going to learn. Most of you don't know a bowsprit from a bowline, and probably don't care, but by God I'll teach you.'

Houston stepped aside and Captain Fairweather took his place. In a surprisingly hoarse voice, he said, 'Now, men, this is a fine ship, and if we work together we'll have a fine crew. Just remember that there is neither justice nor injustice aboard a ship. There are only two things, duty and mutiny. All that you are ordered to do is duty. All that you refuse to do is mutiny. Follow that rule and you can't go far wrong.' The bearded face broke into a sudden and unexpectedly friendly smile. 'But come, cheer up, boys. We've plenty of spirits aboard and the finest of food. The best of you will earn oil-money and fast-boat money, and the lucky ones might even have a ride in our very own steam-launch.'

Houston had been walking around the mustered men, peering into a face here, prodding a reluctant body into attentiveness there. 'You will listen for my commands. When I give a command, you will not walk, and you will not run. When I give a command you will fly, you idle lubbers! Fly!'

Douglas heard Tam groan at his feet, and somebody vomited green bile upon the deck. Then Houston was looming a full head above Douglas, pointing a finger the size of a musket-barrel. 'You, I remember you. You were the runner, one of Mr Wyllie's flunkeys. On board to spy on me, are you?' A massive hand grabbed Douglas by his collar and lifted him two inches off the deck. 'Well, runner, *Mister* Wyllie may be a big man on shore, but at sea I'm the man to watch out for. Do you hear me?'

'I hear you,' Douglas said. 'But I don't work for Wyllie.'

'That's right. You work for me now, and by God, I'll see that you do work!'

Houston was a man of his word. Once *Redgauntlet* was clear of the coast, the engines were shut down and the sails hoisted, and she made her way north by wind and canvas alone. It was then that Douglas learned just how much power the mate of a whaling-ship had. While the Captain made the decisions about navigation, Houston controlled the day-to-day working of the ship and the hour-by-hour lives of the seamen. During the first hectic days, as *Redgauntlet* battered her way through the German Ocean, he hazed the mariners with obscene abuse and a weighty fist. Whenever Douglas looked up, the mate's bitter eyes were upon him and the wide mouth was open in a roar of anger.

Douglas soon learned that Greenmen were placed on a whaling-ship solely for the purpose of getting under the feet of real sailormen. Some of the more experienced crew tried to add their own abuse to Houston's, but Douglas, though he could not oppose the mate's lawful authority, refused to submit to bullying by his own kind. After two bruising encounters in one morning, even the more loud-mouthed of the Greenland-men learned to avoid the man with the level eyes.

His experience in the army had taught Douglas how to endure discipline, so when Houston roared he kept his head down, did exactly as he was told and did not complain. He knew Houston was trying to mould the rag-tag men into an efficient crew, but the knowledge did not make his position any more comfortable. When he could snatch a minute to think, he wondered whether he still held his position as Personal Assistant to Mr Gilbride, and whether Miss Gilbride had betrayed him, but neither thought was helpful as *Redgauntlet* heaved and rolled her way northward.

The seasickness soon passed, for Douglas had voyaged before, from England to Cape Town, across the Indian Ocean to Calcutta and back again. The steep chops and sudden squalls of the German Ocean were wicked, but no worse than the slow-building storms of the tropics, and not as bad as the Cape Buster that had battered his first vessel on to her beam-ends and split her mainsail. Douglas was naturally fit, and as strong as the army could make him, so the physical work was not over-taxing, although the ropes rasped the skin from his hands before the calluses began to form. He learned his way from the taffrail to the bowsprit, and from pump duty at the bilges to the lower crosstrees of the mainmast, although he was never as agile aloft as Tam Wilson and the other seamen.

As he struggled around the ship, Douglas also learned something about how she was manned. As well as the Captain, the mate and a quiet man named Cargill who doubled as second mate and harpooner, there were a handful of specialists, such as the carpenter, cook and surgeon, who lived in the half-deck. There were eighteen veteran whalers, who were divided into the three categories of harpooner, line-manager and boat-header, and a small, confident man known as the spektioneer.

Beneath them were the seamen or common mariners, and right at the bottom of the pile were the apprentices and Greenmen.

On the second day Tam told him that they would first call at Shetland.

'Why?' wondered Douglas. He could feel the sharp twist of another blister on the palm of his hand as he hauled on a rope.

'To pick up stores and seamen. Real seamen,' Tam grunted, 'not longshore rubbish like you lot. After that it's a wee trip across the Atlantic to the whaling-grounds. He glanced aloft before adding gloomily, 'Although, in a jinx ship like *Redgauntlet*, we might not get that far.' He jerked his chin towards Houston. 'Especially with him on board.'

'Houston? Why him in particular?'

'That's Bully Houston,' Tam said. 'He was the mate of *Ivanhoe* and the only man to survive – he wasn't aboard when she blew up.' He looked up and shouted, 'Haul away, lads! She's not up yet!' then continued, 'One thing's for certain. If anybody aboard this steam-kettle ever gets home again, it'll be Bully Houston.'

On the morning of the third day the surgeon summoned the crew for a medical inspection. Dr Michie was a young, fussy man, who seemed conscientious, judging by the time he took to examine each man. Douglas waited his turn in the line, watching those ahead of him shuffle one by one through the surgeon's cabin door. Surprisingly, Captain Fairweather was present, walking along the line with a bottle of rum, from which he poured a generous tot for each man.

The surgeon emerged, with one arm round the shoulders of a man who was so thin that Douglas could count his ribs through the holes in his shirt. 'Captain Fairweather,' Dr Michie said, so gently that the sparse moustache that covered his upper lip barely moved, 'this man is not fit enough to serve.' He patted the man's arm reassuringly. 'He has consumption, poor fellow. He'll have to be paid off at Shetland.'

'Shetland it is,' the master agreed, 'for sick men are no good to me.'

'There,' said the surgeon, giving the rejected mariner a gentle push on the back, 'you're done with. Next man, please.'

Douglas followed him into the cabin, which was not only tidy but scrupulously clean.

'Shut the door, please, and strip naked.' Dr Michie tutted at the tattoos on Douglas's arm and said disapprovingly, 'You should not desecrate your body. You should keep it in its original beauty.'

Miss Gilbride had said something similar.

Remembering the short and brutal inspection by the army surgeon, Douglas was surprised at the gentleness with which Michie conducted even the most intimate part of his examination.

'No piles, ruptures or varicose veins; you'll make a fine seaman. You're fit as a horse!' The gentle hand patted Douglas's arm as a signal that the interview was terminated. 'Next man, please.'

'You passed too, then?' The speaker was was the singing seaman from Mother Scott's, whose name Douglas had learned was Scrymgeour. 'That's the first time I've known a ship's surgeon be so thorough. Normally it's just "Cough" and "Lay off the grog".' He grinned. 'This one didn't mention grog at all, so I must be getting better!'

'Better?' Houston had overheard him. 'I'll make you better! Better at splicing the anchor cable rather than splicing the mainbrace. Get to work, you lazy, drunken fool.'

'He knows me. Two days in the ship and he knows me already.' Scrymgeour grinned at Douglas again. 'What a man.'

Douglas's days passed in a blur of effort, and Houston's face and ranting haunted his exhausted few hours of rest in the foc'sle.

'Move, you pox-blasted soldier! I'll teach you, by God!' The words echoed round his head. 'So Wyllie sent you to spy on me, did he? You can spy at the pump now double watch for you!'

Everybody hated working the pump, thrusting at the great handle to ensure that *Redgauntlet* was comparatively free of water. Douglas found himself there for eight hours at a time, bending, pushing, gasping, hating the ship, hating Houston, knowing he must survive. But for what? Once Mr Gilbride learned about his Chartist connections, he would be unemployed again. Pump, pump, pump, while the muscles of his shoulders screamed and his back ached and burned with fatigue. Pump, pump, pump, while he wondered why an accomplished seaman like Houston should work as a prizefighter. Pump, pump, pump, while speculating what the connection between Houston and Wyllie might be; obviously not one born of loyalty and mutual respect. Pump, pump, pump, and try to forget the subtle flecks of hazel in the brown eyes, and try to forget that Miss Gilbride might have betrayed him.

Douglas decided that he would use some of his precious free time below decks to write to Mr Gilbride and explain what had happened. He would not mention his Chartist background and, until he heard otherwise, he would continue to act as Mr Gilbride's Personal Assistant aboard *Redgauntlet*. He might even find out who was acting against the Waverley Company.

Wyllie had been present when he was crimped, and so presumably had been involved in the crimping of other seamen. Wyllie, indeed, seemed to have a finger in many sordid little Dundee pies. Pump, pump, pump, while the muscles in his arms screamed for release and his head thumped from the foul air. Wyllie had given orders to Bully Houston at the prizefight, and now Houston was mate of *Redgauntlet*. Was that another coincidence? Or had Wyllie contrived the mate's appointment?

Mr Gilbride had threatened to use 'more forceful methods' to man the ship, which Douglas thought must have meant using crimps. Resting for a second to catch his breath, he listened to the sounds of the ship working around him. Presumably Mr Gilbride had not intended to crimp him, but somebody else had. Wyllie? Miss Gilbride? Peter Williamson? No, not Williamson: he was only Wyllie's bruiser.

Pump, pump, pump, and ignore the roaring in his ears, the thought that these were but the opening days of a voyage which would last for months. Work and survive. It was common knowledge that desperate shipmasters used crimps to obtain crews, but he had not known the practice was current in Dundee, where there was always a surplus of mariners.

As the thoughts whirled around in his head, the rational part of Douglas was able to disregard the weariness and resentment and loathing to form a definite idea. Mr Gilbride had given him three distinct duties. His first had been to discover why men refused to sign on *Redgauntlet*; his second had been to help recruit a crew. He had succeeded in the first, but failed in the second. While he was at sea it was unlikely that he could complete his third duty by discovering who had tried to stop *Redgauntlet* sailing. However, he might be able to perform a different service. He might have the chance to remove *Redgauntlet*'s reputation for ill luck. He must ensure that she returned safely, and with a full cargo of blubber and whalemeat. To do that, he would have to learn as much as he could about seamanship and whale-catching, which, he realised, would in any case help him to survive aboard. If he succeeded, Mr Gilbride might forgive his Chartist past.

And Miss Gilbride? Douglas closed his eyes again and pumped mechanically, like an automaton. She was the daughter of a ship-owner and businessman. She was also a devout Christian, who willingly gave her time to work with the less fortunate. She would hardly concern herself with a former redcoat like himself. She could not have been involved.

Paddy McBride had stood at his side as the troopship steered into Cape Town harbour, with the white tablecloth slithering down the mountain and the breeze still fresh after the Cape buster.

'Here we go, then, Robert, your first campaign.' He tapped

Douglas's shoulder. 'Now, listen to the advice of an old soldier. Obey the orders you're given, but don't forget that you're also a man. Trust your instinct and you'll live longer. If you think there's danger, there probably is.'

Now Douglas's instinct told him that Miss Gilbride was not a source of danger. That left Wyllie, and Bully Houston.

They steered north and east, with the crimped crew grousing and *Redgauntlet* apparently dogged by misfortune. It always took immense effort to get the ship to perform any manoeuvre. Despite Houston's oaths and ranting, there seemed always to be a rope breaking, or a sail escaping from its earing cringle. At each setback, the men shook their heads and muttered about the curse.

During one period of fine weather, Houston ordered that kites should be set.

'What's a kite?' Douglas asked Tam Wilson.

'An extra sail. He must be dissatisfied with our speed.'

'He's dissatisfied with everything, it seems, on this voyage.' Douglas eyed the mainmast, which soared aloft in a series of mighty steps.

'Stow your gab and get aloft!' Houston's bellow was nearly enough to fill the sails on its own.

Tam hesitated for only a second. 'God! I hate going aloft on this devil ship!' Glancing upward, he began to climb so rapidly that Douglas felt cumbersome.

From *Redgauntlet*'s gyrating deck, the waves seemed much larger than they had from the shore. Each one was distinct, a phenomenon with its own individual identity, yet still only one wave in a never-ending sequence which rose and hissed and burst against the reinforced hull. Spindrift spattered Douglas's face as he peered towards the west, where the granite bulk of Scotland could be felt, if no longer seen. There was sanity on land, a security which was wholly lacking in this constantly changing world of water and noise and frantic, muscle-tearing work.

As they passed Kinnaird Head blustery squalls had Houston bellowing to the crew to furl the sails again, with the usual quota of small incidents. When the flying-jib halyard worked loose, Houston worked himself into a frenzy. 'God damn you all for a set of one-legged farmers! Can't you do any God-damned thing right? You' – he pointed at the nearest man – 'get out there and secure that before it shakes loose. What am I running here, a ship or a bloody brothel?'

The man selected was an eager-to-please youngster who darted forward at once, balancing on the bowsprit, to tighten the halyard, both hands on the rope and his feet gripping the rounded wood of the bowsprit. As if by intention, *Redgauntlet* suddenly dipped her bows under, throwing hundreds of gallons of seawater over the bows. When *Redgauntlet* rose again, shaking herself free of the water, the bowsprit was empty.

'Man overboard!' Douglas ran to the foc'sle head. Leaning over the low rail, he looked over the side. The sea was churning grey-green, with white froth hissing and bubbling on top. There was something round and black bobbing in the water about half a cable's length to starboard. 'Throw a line! I'll go for him!' Balancing on the rail, he prepared to jump, but a mighty arm swept him back.

'Don't be a bloody fool! The man's gone.' Houston's glare was venomous. 'The sea's taken him.'

'I saw his head! I'll get him!' Douglas pushed past the mate, who again thrust out his hand.

'Obey orders! Stay inboard.' Houston's grip did not falter. 'He's lost.'

Houston was right. *Redgauntlet* had surged past the spot where the youngster had been washed overboard. When Douglas looked back there was no head bobbing. There were only the waves, ugly and insensible.

There were renewed mutterings after that, with more than one man blaming the mate for the death. 'Houston should never have sent him there in this weather. He murdered that laddie, sure as if he'd plunged a knife into his belly.' Tam curled in his bunk with his head buried deep in his arms. 'We're all going to die, Rab, all of us on this damned ship. We're all going to die.' Tam's voice was hoarse.

Douglas sat beside him. 'Not if we pull together. We'll get you back to your wife.'

'That's just it.' Tam looked up. 'We can't pull together, not with Bully Houston there. I was behind you with a lifeline when he stopped you saving that boy. We abandoned him. Houston killed him twice. I saw his head in the water, and his arm, waving for help.'

Scrymgeour, who had been quietly sipping from a secret bottle of rum, shook his head. 'I didn't. I only saw a seal.' He grinned drunkenly and burst into song:

> I'll tell you boys, 'tis hot in hell,
> An' I should know the place damn well –
> Whisky O, Johnnie O,
> Rise me up from down below!

The following night, stories of the ghost began to circulate.

The maritime day was divided into six watches of four hours, marked by the sounding of the ship's bell. The middle watch lasted from midnight until four in the morning and was disturbed twice on *Redgauntlet's* third night at sea.

'There was a half-moon reflecting on the sea last night, and the ship kicking up a haze of spray that seemed to drop exactly on my station.' Although Scrymgeour had been crimped in Mother Scott's, he was an experienced Greenlandman. 'I've no idea why Houston wants us to spend our watch on deck – we're just tiring ourselves out.' He shrugged. 'Anyway, I was sheltering in the lee of the funnel when I heard a sort of scurrying sound, like rats in a barrel.'

The seamen in the foc'sle listened intently to his story. Some looked scared.

'I thought it might be Bully Houston prowling around, so I tried to look busy.' Scrymgeour's eyes widened. 'But it wasn't the mate that came across the deck. It was something that walked like a dog, except it was shimmering and green, with little sparklets of light on its head. I watched it for a minute and then it headed slowly aft, as if it was looking for somebody.'

'What was it?' asked one of the Greenmen. 'A sea-monster?'

'No.' Scrymgeour shook his head firmly. 'I've seen plenty of them. Sea-serpents, mermaids, sharks, unicorns, walrus, I've seen them all, but never anything like this before.'

Douglas had moved closer. 'So it was something green and shimmering, with four legs and sparklets of light on its head.'

'That's right.' Scrymgeour nodded. He rolled his eyes back in his head. 'It's the ghost of that spinner who was killed when *Redgauntlet* was launched. She's coming to blow us up, like *Ivanhoe* was blown up.'

'Oh? Was she on *Ivanhoe*, too?' Douglas asked. He laughed. 'A spritely ghost this one, moving from ship to ship! Are you sure it was not shadows you saw? Could it have been a shadow from the funnel's smoke?'

'Green smoke?' Scrymgeour shook his head, his eyes serious. 'Anyway, we're under sail, man. No, I've been a seaman for years, and I'm telling you that I've never seen the like before.'

There was a whimper from one of the crimped men. 'We're on a jinxed ship – we'll never get back to Dundee again!'

'I'll get home,' came Tam's voice out of the gloom, 'I'm jumping ship in Shetland. I'll not be going to the Arctic to get blown to pieces.'

'If we ever get as far as Shetland.' The words came in a low mutter as a shag-haired fellow thrust his head up from his box-bunk Douglas recognised another of the men from Mother Scott's. 'I saw that green thing, too, and I heard it. I was at the heads when it crawled past me, talking to itself.'

'What did it say?' asked Tam.

'It had a woman's voice, no error, and it was saying, "Food, food, food," as if it was hunting for somebody to eat.'

'God save us!' a tall man said quietly.

'So much for your green shadows, then,' Scrymgeour jeered at Douglas, but there was more fear than malice in his voice.

Somewhere in the darkness, a man began to sob. 'We'll never get home alive.'

Lerwick, Spring 1860

The smoke in the low-ceilinged bothy was so dense that Douglas felt he could cut it into chunks, and the noise was an unending roar as men sang and drank and danced with their women. Sitting in a corner beside the fierce peat fire, he watched the crowd and slowly sipped the fiery island whisky. *Redgauntlet* had made the voyage to Shetland with no further incident except two more sightings of the ghost. Almost as soon as they anchored in Bressay Sound a whole fleet of small, finely shaped boats had rowed out, filled with islanders intent on bartering fresh food and fine knitting for whatever the Greenlandmen had to offer.

Feeling themselves veteran seamen, the crew lined the bulwarks, shouting cheerful abuse down to the islanders, who replied with a wit which more than matched the Greenlandmen's. Douglas watched, gauging the temper of the crew, seeing relief on some faces, calculation on others. Most, however, spoke only of drink and women. The first part of the voyage was over; now they would enjoy life for a day or two and forget that there were hardships ahead.

From *Redgauntlet*'s deck, the little town of Lerwick looked grey and mysterious and picturesque, with the private piers and stone houses of the merchants dipping their feet in the sea.

'I've never been so far north before,' Douglas said. He shivered involuntarily.

'You'll be further north yet before we've done,' Tam warned. 'You'd better draw warm clothing from the slops.' He gestured around. 'It's a lively harbour, though.'

The broad sweep of Bressay Bay was alive with vessels, from the dozen or so whaling-ships to the coastal traders and timber-vessels from Norway. There were half a dozen Faroese cod-smacks tied up at Morrison's pier, waiting for the season to start, a paddle-steamer which churned up the water as she began the journey to Leith, and a flitboat, full of cattle, which headed for the Gas Pier.

Beyond the smoke-sheathed town, fields stretched up to bleak hills still streaked with snow, while scattered cottages squatted amidst smears of mist. Stacks of peat were everywhere in the treeless landscape, a reminder of the ferocity of the climate in these islands. Lerwick was small compared to Cape Town or Calcutta, but it was as exotic in its own way. More importantly, it was a town with good communications, so Douglas would be able to send his letter to Mr Gilbride.

When Captain Fairweather allowed his crew to swarm ashore, the picturesque became tangible, the mysterious solid; and the people of Shetland turned out to be scarcely different from those of Dundee or Greytown or Allahabad.

'Whisky!' Scrymgeour shouted as he stepped out of the shore-boat and on to the pier. 'Find me whisky!'

Tam nudged Douglas. 'Whisky it is, Scrimmy, whisky fit for seamen, and we'll have a fiddler or two and dance the day away. We'll lift the roofs off Lerwick tonight, boys. They'll know that the lads from *Old Fisty* were here.'

Douglas was not surprised that the Greenlandmen had re-christened *Redgauntlet Old Fisty*, for bestowing nicknames on vessels was an old nautical habit. If *Agamemnon* could become Ham and Bacon, why should *Redgauntlet*, with her great clenched fist for a figurehead, not become *Old Fisty*? He was even less surprised that the varied collection of men aboard her, men who had been crimped, and then shouted at, hazed and bullied while aboard, were already beginning to think of themselves as a unit. He had seen the same with recruits to the Seventy-Third. Though they cursed and swore and grumbled at everything to do with the army, at the first sign of criticism of the regiment they banded together, prepared to fight and die for the very thing they professed to hate. Douglas presumed that a ship's crew, like a British Army regiment, was akin to an extended family. They would fight and squabble and complain amongst themselves, but unite against any outsider.

What did surprise him was that Tam said no more about deserting, even though *Charleston*, the ship to which he had claimed allegiance and signed articles, rode happily to anchor in Bressay Sound.

There was a crowd around the head of the pier on which they landed, seamen from half a dozen ports talking with a handful of fisherwomen with their unwieldy creels and distinctive dress. 'Women!' one of the Greenlandmen shouted, breaking into a shambling trot. He threw himself at the nearest one, took her face in his hands and landed a kiss. Barely a second later he was lying flat on the ground, on his face a look of surprise which changed to pain when the fisherwoman planted a solid kick to add to her punch.

'Get back to your home, smooth-mooth!' she yelled, kicking mightily as the Greenlandman scrambled along the ground.

'I didn't mean no harm! I thought you wouldn't mind!' The excuses were wasted: she swung her creel and knocked him flat again.

As two other women advanced, laughing Greenlandmen intervened. 'He's a first-voyager,' said Scrimmy. 'He doesn't yet know what he's doing.' He hauled the Greenman to his feet and cuffed him soundly. 'We'll take him out of your way.'

'Come on, Rab,' said Tam, 'I'll show you better sport than watching a Greenlandman make a fool of himself.' He ushered Douglas past the fishermen. 'You too, Scrimmy. Let's find the whisky.'

'Whisky, whisky, let's find the whisky,' Scrimmy chanted. 'Whisky, whisky, always makes you frisky.'

Lerwick seemed full of whaling-men erupting from every alc-house and filling every alley, singing, drinking, arguing and jesting. They mingled happily with the Shetlanders in their thick homespuns and broad knitted bonnets. One or two had their arms round the less moral of the island women, who shrieked with laughter and allowed their own hands to wander in a manner more intimate than respectable.

'Never mind the women.' Scrimmy threw his head back and bayed to a sky that was overcast with clouds of sombre grey. 'Find me whisky, whisky, find me some whisky.'

'We're finding, we're finding,' Tam told him. 'Just be patient.'

Once they had passed Commercial Street, the streets were like deep chasms which curved to minimise the impact of the eternal wind. The houses were stone-built, small-windowed and solid, the smells as familiar as those of the Overgate but overlaid with the tang of the sea. Stone dominated Lerwick; it was a town hewn from the land yet belonging to the ocean. Less concerned with architecture than the demands of their thirst, the whalers searched for a temple to their alcoholic faith.

'Whisky, whisky, let's find the whisky,' Scrimmy continued single-mindedly as Tam guided him through the low door of a cottage slightly outside the town. Sounds of revelry greeted them as they walked into the single room. Four fiddlers were playing a raucous reel for a group of dancers, who whooped as their feet drummed a sequence of complex steps in the centre of the floor. Other men watched from their places at the long, curving bar, or from the scattering of tables along the other three walls. More men, many more, ignored the dancers and bowed in worship to their one true god.

'Whisky, whisky!' cried Scrimmy. 'Tam's found me whisky!'

The first glass burned away the residue of salt from Douglas's throat. The second was warm and mellow until it exploded in liquid fire inside his stomach, while the third felt like a welcome from an old friend. By that time Douglas was quite prepared to accept the good fellowship of his shipmates, learning the words of the shanties they rattled out, and exchanging jokes with Tam and Scrimmy at the top of his voice. They were joined by a group of Greenlandmen from *Charleston*, rolling, laughing, boisterous men with bearded chins and faces as red as a sunset. They spoke of many things, from the beauties of a ship under full sail to the dangers of the sudden fogs off Cape Farewell, and Douglas listened when he could and sang when he could not. Linking arms with Scrimmy, he roared the words that he had learned from Paddy while they guarded an outpost near the Keiskamma.

A troop of the French cavalry came bravely charging down.
We were ordered, 'Form solid square,' and quickly was it done.
But when their Colonel came in sight, our numbers for to see,
He shouted, 'Retreat, mes braves, for them's the Seven And Three!'

The song ended in a wild shout in which Scrimmy, who had never been in any regiment, far less the Seventy-Third, joined with as much enthusiasm as Douglas, and even one of the *Charleston* men waved a bottle in the air to show his martial skills.

'So you're from that steam-kettle are you, soldier?' the Charleston asked. He was another of the stocky, clear-eyed men that the Greenland trade seemed to produce in such numbers.

'*Redgauntlet* – as good a ship as any I've sailed in.' Douglas was not sure if he was more proud of his ship or of his ability to speak without slurring his words. To drive his point home, he said, 'A fine ship. She won't explode on us, not like *Ivanhoe* did.'

'Explode? Who said *Ivanhoe* exploded?' The Charleston tossed back his whisky without noticeable effect.

'Everybody.' Douglas waved a hand around the room, which was now so full that even the tobacco and peat smoke seemed to squeeze into a corner. 'Everybody said so. She blew up on the thirteenth of July. Just ask anybody.'

'I don't say so,' said the Charleston quietly.

For a moment, Douglas clearly heard and saw Paddy: 'Listen to the man,' he advised, taking the stubby pipe from between his teeth. 'He's talking despite the drink, not because of it.'

Douglas met the seaman's level eyes, trying to fight off the effects of twelve straight drams of whisky. 'What do you say, then?' He knew that there was a stupid grin on his face, that Scrimmy was still chanting that wonderful song, that Tam was slumped in alcohol-fuelled melancholy, but those things were less important.

'I say that *Ivanhoe* did not blow up on the thirteenth. I saw her on the fourteenth.' He nodded to emphasise the fact. 'We were north of Hopeful Point and the lookout had seen a fall and sent out the boats. It was a nasty sea, choppy, with spume breaking over the smaller pieces of ice, and polar bears on the larger. We dodged about in the bergy bits for an hour or two, following the flag signals from the crow's nest, until a fog came down. You know what it's like up yonder: one minute it's clear as gin, the next it's pea soup, my boys, and damn you for a farmer.'

He drained another dram, stared into the bright flames of the fire and continued, 'Anyway, we'd drifted for a bit, listening for the ship's bell to guide us home, when the devil's emissary burst through the fog with a shower of sparks and smuts coming from her funnel. That was *Ivanhoe*. She was unmistakable with that profile, her great funnel for all the world like a pipe-stem and still carrying sail on her upper yards. She didn't see us, though, or she'd have picked us up.' His face darkened. 'That was a bad day, yon, for as soon as we broke the ice with our oars it froze again – it was like rowing through frozen porridge. Aye, we saw *Ivanhoe*, steaming away to the north and east, away from Hopeful Point, with that black and gold counter of hers gleaming above the ice and four of her boats inboard.'

'Her boats inboard?' Melancholy or not, Tam took a professional interest. 'Why were her boats inboard if there were fish around? And why was she steaming away?'

'How should I know? Ask her Master.' The Charleston indicated that he had no whisky, a serious matter which Douglas soon rectified. 'Anyway, she may have sunk in the ice – the devil knows it was bad enough – but if she did it wasn't on the thirteenth, for I saw her on the fourteenth of July, the day after you say she exploded.'

'Perhaps she blew up later that day?' Douglas suggested.

The Charleston shook his head. 'Out there, sound carries for ever. There is a hush on the ice so you can hear the pieces falling from a berg two miles away. You can hear the echo of a drowning man's thoughts. A ship exploding would have been heard ten, twenty miles away, more maybe. I tell you, *Ivanhoe* did not blow up on the thirteenth of July, nor on the fourteenth.'

'You're drunk, man.' Tam shook his head. 'Everyone knows *Ivanhoe* blew up on the thirteenth. You must have been dreaming.'

'What?' The mood changed so suddenly that Douglas blinked. The Charleston's hand curled round the neck of a whisky bottle.

'Hey, Ecky, are you dancing?' Another Charleston staggered past, with a girl on either arm and a grin splitting his bearded face. 'One of these lassies says she's never known a Greenlandman.'

'Never?' said Ecky in wonder, dropping his bottle and his aggression simultaneously. 'Bring her here and I'll soon change that.' He rose to his feet in one swift movement and, extending a hand as large as the paw of a polar bear, clamped it round the waist of the nearest woman. 'Right, my darling one, it's learning time for you.'

Tam grinned as the Charleston joined the stamping, roaring mob in the centre of the room. 'I was like that once,' he said.

'But then I got married.' He downed another glass of whisky in a single movement of hand and mouth and head. 'And now I may never see my Lizzie again. She doesn't even know where I am.'

'Write to her,' Douglas said. 'I take it we can get a pen and ink somewhere in Lerwick?' He spoke absently, his mind racing with the knowledge that *Ivanhoe* had not blown up on the thirteenth as Bully Houston had reported.

'I can't write to her,' Tam said glumly into his whisky. 'I'm no scholar.'

'Can she read?'

'Like the skelp-doup himself.' There was pride in Tam's voice. 'You should hear her read the paper to me. She knows all the words there is.'

'Well, then, I can write, if you tell me what to say.'

Tam's gloom dissipated. 'Would you do that for me?'

'We'll do it tomorrow,' Douglas promised.

Tam thrust out his hand. 'I'll never forget that. Nor will Lizzie.'

'You're drunk, man,' Douglas told him, but the eyes that met his were steady and sincere, if slightly sardonic.

'Drunk? Never.' Tam grinned. 'Come on, Rab, man, let's go and get our fortunes told. Buy some wind, eh?'

In accordance with a tradition which was probably old before the first Viking landed on the shores of Shetland, Tam and Scrimmy escorted Douglas to the spae-wife who sat in a corner of the alehouse.

She looked up with eyes that were intensely bright in a face composed of wrinkles. 'Four of you, then.' Her voice was as strong as her eyes.

'Only three,' Tam said.

'Three and the one that stands by the soldier's shoulder.' She pointed to Douglas, who glanced behind him. He felt the hairs rise on the back of his neck.

The old woman smiled. 'I can see him, even if you can't. Is it a favourable wind you want to buy? Sixpence for the wind, shipmates, and another threepence to hear your futures.'

They parted with their money.

Scrimmy sighed at the sight of such waste. 'That could have bought a lot of whisky.'

The spac-wife smiled. 'That still will buy a lot of whisky, but for me, not you. A seaman, you are, from a race that once bore the banner of freedom.' Her eyes were deep and clear and pitiless as she looked at him. 'A hard voyage lies ahead of you, seaman. You will have a fair wind when you need it and a foul wind you will curse, but there will be a good landfall at the end of it all.'

'And me?' Tam stepped forward. 'We're sailing on an unlucky ship. Will I see my wife again?'

'Again and again and yet again.' She spat on to the bench on which she sat and ran her nail through the foaming spittle. 'You will see death in your voyage, but return alive, and you will know betrayal, but not of you. I see you with money in your hand. Much money.'

'Oil-money, Tam, my boy,' said Scrimmy, nudging him. 'Plenty whales.' He ordered more whisky.

Douglas was last. When he looked into the spae-wife's eyes it was like looking into a deep tunnel, with brightness at the far end and the wind rushing in his ears. He said, 'Tell me about my voyage.'

'Heed the dead man who stands at your shoulder.' The old woman held his gaze. 'But you always have. I see a ship of fire and a ship of ice, danger from one you trust and friendship from one who despises you.' She looked away, grasped the coins with a hand with nails like talons and closed her eyes.

'Very cryptic,' Douglas said.

Scrimmy laughed. 'Not at all. Tam got told we'll catch plenty whales, I got told the weather will be bad but we'll get back safely, and you got told we're sailing in a ship which runs by fire and we'll be cold. What more is there to know?'

'The dead man at my shoulder and the danger from one I trust.' Douglas glanced behind him, as if he might see a corpse.

'You were a soldier, weren't you?' said Tam, helping Scrimmy with the whisky. 'So you'll have seen plenty dead men – that's likely what she meant.' He grinned. 'But I don't know why you should trust Bully Houston.'

They left Lerwick three days later, the crew augmented by ten Shetlanders who spoke of the sea as if it were their lover. All but the youngest had experience in whaling-ships and exchanged jests with the Greenlandmen about polar-bear hunting and angling for fulmar petrels, which they called 'mollies'. Two of the crimped Dundee men had tried to desert, but a woman had betrayed one and Houston dragged the other from his hiding-place in a stack of peat.

As soon as the pilot's boat turned back toward Lerwick, and *Redgauntlet* faced the Atlantic alone, Houston renewed the behaviour that had earned him the sobriquet of 'Bully'.

'So you think you're seamen because you've managed to limp from Dundee to Shetland?' The marline-spike he carried made him look even more formidable. 'I tell you, the German Ocean is a puddle compared to the North Atlantic. You'll meet storms where the waves are higher than the mainmast and winds that will blow you from the yardarms. You'll see fog so thick that you can cut it into blocks and use it for fuel, and rain so hard that it'll pierce your miserable hides. After that we'll round Cape Farewell and we'll hit really bad weather.'

'Careful now, Rab, don't trust him too much.' Tam's whisper was hardly audible, but it earned him an extra watch at the pumps.

Captain Fairweather nursed *Redgauntlet* into the Atlantic by sail alone while Houston cursed the crew and they in turn cursed everybody and everything as they sweated through labour that was harder by far than anything a convicted criminal was required to do. With every change of the wind,

Houston blasted the men up the ratlines, to the yards and tops and crosstrees, which were so high above the heaving deck they seemed to scrape the beard of God. As *Redgauntlet* fought the long Atlantic rollers, the gulf between seamen and Greenmen widened daily.

'I only signed on this steam-kettle because I thought she'd be easier to work than a real ship,' one of the Shetlanders grunted as he climbed past Douglas up the rigging.

'Keep it up, Rab!' shouted Tam encouragingly as he, too, sped upwards. 'You'll get there.'

'If he doesn't,' Houston roared, 'I'll tear the lungs from his body.' He boasted that he had such sharp ears that he could tell how taut every rope in the ship was by the sound of the wind in the rigging, and he proved it by eavesdropping on the men's conversations.

With the fore futtock-shrouds successfully negotiated and one hand gripping the foretopmast shrouds, Douglas stood on the foremast crosstrees and stared forward. He watched the great fist of *Redgauntlet*'s figurehead raise itself when she soared on a wave, then dip and punch into the sea, raising a cloud of spindrift which soaked him even at this height. Stretching ahead, a limitless expanse of waves moved and creased, folded in on themselves and broke with wicked crests of silver foam. Far beyond the visible horizon lay the domain of the whales, a ferocious place of bitter cold and winds which sliced through a man, of frost so keen that it turned a sailor black and great bears white. Astern was more sea, the creamy-white line of their wake, and no sign of Scotland.

This was the highest aloft he had ever been, for Captain Fairweather did not allow his Greenmen to be sacrificed to the masthead. Discipline, he claimed in that strangely cracked voice of his, was one thing, but losing terrified men before the voyage properly began was poor seamanship.

Houston was strong on discipline. He had the two deserters confined in irons on bread and water for three days, so they were chastened and shaking when he allowed them back into the daylight. He hazed the men from the blood-red glint of dawn until the night was agleam with stars, then started again. He rarely slept, rarely ate, and hounded the skulkers from below with fearsome oaths and the fists that had pounded the Carter into submission in less than fifteen minutes. Twice, men driven to desperation by his obscenity-laden abuse rounded on him, and each time he reduced the would-be attacker to a bloody pulp, then threw a bucket of salt water over the wreckage and ordered it back to work. Bleeding, bruised and broken, the men obeyed.

Once Houston mustered all the hands aft and railed at them for a full fifteen minutes, hardly stopping for breath. His words were rich with invective, colourful with oaths. It seemed the cook had complained that someone had broken into the small-stores and stolen bread, cheese and a jar of molasses. Houston promised that he would find the culprit and extract terrible retribution. A search followed, during which every man's bunk was turned over and every sea-chest was emptied on to the deck. Although no food was found, Houston justified his effort by confiscating all the sea-knives and grinding the points flat, 'Just in case one of you tries to stab me in the middle watch.'

As always, he took especial care to abuse Douglas, thrusting him against the bulkhead while he trampled his bedding underfoot. Picking up the blackthorn club that Douglas had hidden in case of emergency, he tested it with a short swing.

'Very pretty,' he sneered. 'Were you going to lie in wait for me, maybe? A wee ambush? Or did Mr Wyllie tell you just to keep watch on me this voyage?'

'Neither.' Douglas had proved his strength and courage in the army but Houston's power awed him. One-handed the mate lifted him until his feet were off the deck and his head pressed painfully against the solid beams above.

'I don't work for Wyllie,' Douglas managed to say.

'I'm watching you, boy.' Houston dropped Douglas upon his

face on the deck, then set one foot casually on his arm. 'If you take even one step over the line, I'll tear the living heart from your body and feed it to the gulls. Understand?'

Douglas understood. He watched Houston finish his search, and allowed Tam to help him back on his feet.

'He doesn't like you very much, does he?' observed Tam. 'Best do as he says. But mind that you don't trust him too much.' Obeying the unwritten Greenlandmen's law of discretion, he did not press for details of the relationship between Douglas, Wyllie and the mate, but changed the subject. 'Bread, cheese and molasses, eh? No wonder Bully thought the thief was a landsman. What sort of seaman would steal food when there's rum to hand?'

'It may be that rum was stolen, too.'

Tam shook his head. 'If it had been, you can be sure Bully would have mentioned it. It's not pleasant to know that there's a thief aboard, but hardly surprising considering where half the crew came from.'

'Mother Scott's, you mean?'

'Aye.' Tam suddenly shivered. 'Unless it was the ghost.'

At that, the men began to talk yet again of the ghost. It was generally accepted that it was the spinner's ghost that was stalking the ship. The tales had become greatly embellished in the telling, so that sober men swore they had seen a skeleton-like figure hunched near the storeroom, or had heard the rattle of a spinning-machine in the middle watch. One man even claimed that the ghost had approached him with an empty bowl in her extended arms.

Douglas was not persuaded. If ghosts, green or otherwise, were denizens of the spirit world, what need had they of bread and cheese? He shook his head. It was much more likely that a hungry crewman had stolen the food, but that was the mate's concern, not his. He closed his ears to the talk and replaced the blackthorn in its hiding-place.

As *Redgauntlet* slogged across the Atlantic, with the wind

seeming to coming from every quarter save the one she needed, Houston drove the crew until even the veterans were dropping with weariness.

'Why doesn't the Old Man use the engines?' asked Hughson, one of the Shetlanders. 'There's no point in having all that extra weight if we don't use the damned things.'

'He'll be scared of blowing us all up,' Tam told him, 'like *Ivanhoe*. Captain Fairweather seems a decent enough fellow. He'll not want to kill off his crew.'

'No? He'll let Bully Houston work us to death instead.' Hughson rubbed his back. 'It might be better to get blown to pieces.'

The Captain seemed to have heard Hughson's words. It was his habit to hold divine service on the Sunday, but even as he opened the hymnbook to sing, the wind altered and Houston bellowed for all hands to the braces.

'Belay that, Mr Houston.' Captain Fairweather always spoke as if he were on a Royal Navy vessel. 'There's no need to break the service for a breath of wind.' He raised his head so that all the crew could plainly hear him. 'The men deserve a rest on the Lord's day.'

Houston's anger showed in his face but the Master stood firm. He closed his hymnbook, keeping one finger in the required page.

Houston lowered his voice to a growl. 'We need the wind if we're to reach the fishing-grounds early. Either that or we must use the engines.'

'What we need, Mr Houston, is divine guidance, and we'll obtain it only through faith and worship.'

'The hands could alter the sails in fifteen minutes and then get back to the service.' Houston glanced at the unremittingly grey sky.

'You have been driving the men hard, Mr Houston. A short break will do them no harm at all.' Captain Fairweather opened his hymnbook again. 'Now, I suggest that you use that strong voice of yours to praise your Maker.'

'I'm only doing my duty,' Houston argued.

Fairweather nodded blandly. 'I have no doubt that you are doing your duty as you see it, Mr Houston. But your first duty on this ship is to obey my orders. Now sing, Mr Houston.'

When the rousing words of the hymn rose from *Redgauntlet*'s deck, Houston roared as if in competition with Nature herself.

'That's one in the eye for Bully Houston,' Scrimmy gloated.

'Maybe, aye,' Hughson said quietly, 'but give him his due, he's a good seaman. We could be at the edge of the ice in two weeks using the steam-kettle, but with these contrary winds . . . ?' He spread his hands in a gesture of helplessness. 'A month? Six weeks? And all the time eating stores we may need later.'

'As long as there's plenty rum,' Scrimmy said.

When the service finished and Captain Fairweather disappeared below – 'For his daily bottle,' Tam said – Houston stalked through the dispersing crew, blaspheming savagely. As he pushed between two of the crimped Greenmen, one winked and whistled a jaunty little tune, 'Villikins and his Dinah'. It was a harmless enough thing, possibly meant as a humorous reference to the strained relationship between Houston and the Captain, but Douglas felt rather than heard the sudden hush as the mate stopped dead.

'Who whistled?' Perhaps the conversational tone he used created a sense of security, for the Greenman at once owned up: 'It was me.'

'Was it?' Houston's smile was not unpleasant, but Douglas would have preferred a roar of anger. 'This is your first voyage, isn't it?'

The Greenman nodded. His shipmates backed slowly away.

'And have you ever heard a seaman whistle on this vessel? Ever, in all your time aboard?'

The Greenman looked around for support but found none. The crew lowered their heads rather than meet his eyes. One fingered the intricately carved piece of whalebone he wore as a good-luck charm, another put his hand to his brass earring, a third touched an amber button on his shirt.

'I don't know,' said the Greenman.

The sound of the waves slapping against the hull was suddenly very loud. Tam pulled Douglas back.

'You have not heard anybody whistle.' Houston kept his voice gentle. 'And do you know why not?'

'No.' The Greenman dropped his head.

'Because whistling calls up the wind. We cannot control the wind out here; we can only occasionally harness it. Look around you and tell me what you see. Look!'

The Greenman obeyed. 'The sea.'

'The sea, the whole sea and nothing but the sea. Million upon millions of gallons of bloody sea, waiting to be blown into waves you cannot imagine. Just pray to your God that your idiot whistling has not summoned a full gale.' Houston nodded once, as if to emphasise the point, then turned on his heel. He seemed to notice the circle of watching men. 'Well?' The roar was back, as biting and bitter as ever. 'What are you all standing about for like a gaggle of farmer's wives at market? If you've no work to do I'll find you some, by God. Shake out a reef in the topsail. You and you' – a thick forefinger stabbed at Douglas and Webster, another Greenman – 'find a couple of brushes and get this deck scrubbed.'

As the men scattered, Tam paused beside Douglas for a second and said, 'Houston let him off lightly. I'd have him keel-hauled for whistling like that. We'll pay for it, you'll see.'

Tam was right. After days of frustrating calms and flukey gusts, the wind rose. It started that evening with a faint moan from the north-east, accompanied by a belt of darker cloud, then the swell became longer, with curling grey breakers which smashed against *Redgauntlet*'s solid planking with enough force to make her shudder. Houston ordered the two men at the wheel to lash themselves securely to the mizzenmast, and he and Macmillan, the bosun, began a methodical check of all the sails and rigging. Only when the waves reared as high as the mizzencourse did he order sail to be reduced, bellowing orders from the deck as the seamen scurried aloft into the dark.

Full night brought a horizontal onslaught of rain, allied to a northerly wind which threatened to tear the men from the footropes.

'Look alive, you bloody farmers!' bellowed Houston, craning his head backwards to watch them. 'Get that canvas in!'

Sent to the starboard mainyard, Douglas fought the viciously whipping canvas, feeling his fingernails tear and his feet slide beneath him. The sail seemed huge and iron-hard; he punched into it, swearing in a monotone matched by the men on either side. He looked aloft to where the maintopgallant bulged rigid, and wondered how men could climb up there in conditions like this. *Redgauntlet* kicked and heeled, one minute saluting the sky with her fist, the next burying her forefoot in the sea so that tons of dark, ice-cold Atlantic water thundered aboard.

From Douglas's left, Scrimmy shouted, 'This is better than shooting Indians in Africa, eh? This is living.' Leaning far over the yard, he grabbed a handful of canvas and hauled it in. 'Come on, Rab, don't have a caulk there.'

As the mast gyrated wildly, writing an invisible message in the bitter night sky, Douglas cursed and worked, copying the seamen as best he could, until, miraculously, the sail was furled and he could get back down on deck. But the gale was only just beginning. It worked up all night, until the wind screamed a devil's cacophony in the rigging and the deck was under two feet of surging water.

For five days *Redgauntlet* fought the storm. Five days of pitiless wind and rain and muscle-tearing effort. For most of that time she was under close-reefed topsails and foresail, although Houston kept her under constant observation, never leaving the deck as he watched the ship and drove the crew. It took three men to control the wheel, and the mate had ordered that all three be lashed securely. He had also ordered lifelines rigged fore and aft and arthwartships, and food had been cooked when it was still possible to work in the galley. Occasionally he called, 'All hands! All hands!' and ordered them to some Herculean feat aloft that combined gymnastics and a supple, wiry strength. For twelve hours, as the gale reached its peak, *Redgauntlet* swung under bare poles, dragging a sea-anchor astern to keep her bows into the teeth of the dragon that poured its frozen breath on them from the north-east. The master appeared on deck once during that time; he exchanged a few words with Houston, then disappeared below.

'Look at him.' Scrimmy shook his head admiringly, ignoring the water pouring from his face and his raw, cold-reddened hands. 'The middle of an Atlantic gale and he doesn't care a damn. What a man!'

'Aye, and look at Bully Houston. Never off our backs, even at a time like this.' Tam put his head up and sniffed the wind. 'It's slacking, though. There's less salt in the air. We'll be up aloft within the hour.'

Again Tam was right. Houston must also have sensed the slight diminution of the wind, for he ordered the storm staysails set, and *Redgauntlet* was again a living thing, punching her fist time after time into the frenzied masses of water and shaking herself free.

'Cursed ship? Not this one. Not *Old Fisty*.' Scrimmy was jubilant as he stood his trick at the wheel, with Dunn, a boat-header from Dundee, at his side, and Douglas there to provide muscle. 'See the way she sails? Like a duck, all feathers and bill. There's no ill luck in *Old Fisty*, is there, my bonnie lass?'

The men at the wheel were relieved at regular intervals, but Bully Houston remained constantly on watch, red-eyed and haggard but caring for his ship, until the early morning of the sixth day. Only then, when the weather abated a little, did he entrust *Redgauntlet* to the quietly efficient Cargill, a very experienced helmsman.

'Dunn, you and the Greenman remain at your posts. Scrymgeour, you've done your trick. Wilson will take over.'

Tam grunted as he took Scrimmy's place. 'Here we go again.'

Cargill nodded at the sky. 'Keep alert, now. It's clearing, but we'll see a sting in her tail before the dawn's here.' Scorning the lifelines, he set himself foursquare on deck in front of the wheel and glanced aloft. 'We'll not be setting any more sail yet, either.'

Braced at the wheel, Tam spat over the leeward rail. 'This is what comes of whistling on board,' he said grimly. 'We'll be having words with that Greenman before long, mark my words.'

By two bells in the middle watch the sea had begun to moderate and *Redgauntlet* was running more easily. Houston appeared on deck, looked aloft and over to the starboard quarter, the weather side. 'More to come, Cargill?'

Cargill nodded. 'Aye. We're through the worst but there'll be a rough patch yet.'

'Tell me at once if anything changes.' To the men at the wheel he said, scowling, 'And you lot keep alert or I'll have your hides for a flying-jib.'

At four bells, two o'clock in the morning, the night was at its darkest and *Redgauntlet* was riding more smoothly than she had for a week. Advising Tam to keep a taut course, Cargill skimmed aloft to check the mizzentopmast shrouds.

'Different world when she's like this, isn't it?' Tam hardly braced his legs to steer in the quieter sea, and the night air was cool rather than sharp. 'This is what sailoring should be like.'

By now, Douglas had learned some of the hundreds of shipboard noises, so he could differentiate between the creak of a straining yard and the rustle of water under the counter. The sound he heard now was different, something that did not quite belong. He peered forward, past the three masts and the ugly, unused funnel. There was definitely a flicker of movement there, a dense blackness against the lesser black of the ship.

'Did you see that?' he asked.

'See what?' Tam was concentrating on the wheel, but Dunn peered forward. 'There's nothing there.'

'I'm sure I saw something.' Douglas had spent too long on piquet duty on the Cape Colony frontier to discount his suspicions.

'It was the ghost.' Tam's voice was suddenly hoarse. 'This is about the time it's normally seen. Keep close together, for God's sake.'

'You don't need me just now.' Douglas unfastened the ropes that bound him to the mizzenmast. 'I'll have a wee look.'

'You're mad. It's the ghost I tell you.' Tam's voice cracked with alarm.

'Tam's right,' the stolid Dunn advised. 'Best leave well alone.'

'I'll bell this cat.' Douglas had stalked the Gaika among the kloofs of the frontier, knowing that capture would mean hideous torture and death. He was confident that he could lay the seaborne ghost that robbed the small-stores for bread and cheese.

The principle of hunting was the same at sea as on land; keep low, keep quiet, keep patient and keep out of sight. He slid forward, hugging the shadows, using the creaks and groans of the ship to disguise the soft padding of his feet. He was convinced that his quarry was not a ghost but something as solid as he was, probably one of the crew searching for food. Whatever – or whoever – it was, it was unsettling the men and adding to the ship's bad reputation. Unmasking the ghost would be a small step towards ensuring a successful voyage.

The wind seemed to be rising again as Douglas moved forward. Spray spattered hollowly against the funnel, and he found it harder to keep his balance as the ship's motion increased. Cargill had said there would be a sting in the storm's tail, and here it came now. He staggered as a large sea broke over the bows, but there was definitely somebody ahead. He could make out the shape of a head, and there was colour there, too. Something green, briefly illuminated by the phosphorescence of a breaking wave. Douglas felt his heart start pounding; he was in an unfamiliar environment, and there was something inexplicable ahead of him.

He mouthed the first lines of the regimental song: 'Great Mars, the God of War/Did never see such men before.' He was of the Seventy-Third, was he not? What would Paddy McBride have done in his place? Laughed, probably, and shoved his bayonet clean through the ghost. But Paddy was a ghost himself now. 'If you're in heaven or hell, Paddy, my friend,' said Douglas silently, 'look after me now.' He thought of the Irishman's mocking eyes, the stolid courage that had carried him through every situation. Imagine that Paddy is at your side, Douglas told himself, and there's no ghost in the world can harm you.

Redgauntlet lurched again as two seas hit her simultaneously, and Douglas saw the thing emerge in a sudden turmoil of formless green: a head sparkling with phosphorescence and two skeletally thin arms. 'Stay at my shoulder now, Paddy,' he breathed, and heaved himself forward.

The thing shrieked, high-pitched, but rolled away with the motion of the ship. Douglas followed, grabbing the lifeline to stop himself going over the side. He saw the open mouth of a bony face, saw arms flailing as the ghost scrabbled for a hold on the smooth deck. *Redgauntlet* plunged her forefoot deep again and an avalanche of cold seawater roared over the deck, covering Douglas and the ghost.

Choking, blinded, Douglas clung desperately to the lifeline, but through the thunder of the water he heard a scream for help. Hanging on with his left hand, fighting the rush of water that wrenched at his feet and body, he reached forward – and

111

clutched something soft, something which tore beneath his fingers. The water was a solid weight on his body, cold and dark and wicked, while the muscles of his right arm felt as though they would tear with the strain of fighting the sea. The scream sounded again, shriller, more insistent, slightly further away.

'Hold on!' Douglas yelled. He forced himself to release the lifeline, and rolled closer to the side, over which the sea poured like a waterfall as *Redgauntlet* freed herself of its enormous weight. Through the water, clinging desperately to one slender iron stanchion of the rail, the green thing stared at him with eyes that were wide and black and terrified.

'Help me!' screamed Jimmy Gordon's widow. 'Please help me!'

Allowing the heel of *Redgauntlet*'s deck to roll him towards the woman, Douglas felt for the rail with his feet, but before he could move the sea thundered him forward. There was a second of sheer panic, then eye-watering agony as he crashed against the rail, with his legs either side of a stanchion. Biting off a yell, he reached upward, feeling his fingertips brush tantalisingly against the lifeline. He gasped as *Redgauntlet* heeled further, thrusting his groin harder against the stanchion. Bending one leg, he braced his foot against the stanchion and flung himself upwards, snatching desperately: he could have wept with relief as his hand closed round the lifeline.

Another wave bucked *Redgauntlet*, lifting Douglas from the deck and suspending his whole weight from the arm that held the rope. Chillingly cold Atlantic water engulfed him as the ship rolled back, and pain lanced through him as the stanchion again slammed into his groin. Overhead, the masts were tilting crazily, the mainmast yardarm nearly brushing the tops of the waves. The sea sucked at his legs, pulling him relentlessly towards the surging, frothing death beyond the rail.

Turning his head, Douglas saw Mrs Gordon: she was overboard, all but one arm, which was crooked round the next stanchion. The sea covered her up to her head. She was screaming, one word repeated over and over again: 'Jimmy! Jimmy! Jimmy!'

'Hold on!' Douglas shouted. He stretched his furthest; his fingers barely held the line, but it was enough to give him purchase. He hauled himself up. 'Put out your hand!'

Fighting the suction of the waves, his feet slithering on the streaming deck, he lunged sideways and clutched at the woman. He grabbed a handful of cloth. As *Redgauntlet* righted herself, he held on until the deck was nearly level, then released his grip on the line and hauled Mrs Gordon inboard.

She looked at him, mouth and eyes wide open, but now *Redgauntlet* had completed her roll and was heeling to port. Her bows dipped into waves that were black, edged with silver, and mountainous in the dark. Mrs Gordon shrieked and threw her arms round his neck in a powerful grip.

'Hold tight.' Douglas tried to sound encouraging, but her weight was choking him. She was still screaming, 'Jimmy! Jimmy! Jimmy!'

The water that thundered on to the deck was cold and heavy and malicious. It dragged at Douglas, hostile fingers pulling him away from the security of the ship. The woman's weight drained his weakened body, tore at his straining muscles. He felt the wound in his arm reopen, felt his strength drain until his hold on the lifeline weakened. His numb fingers slipped and Mrs Gordon screamed endlessly as they began to slide across the deck, towards the gaps in the rail. Douglas scrabbled uselessly at the smooth wood as the sea embraced them both, ushering them toward sucking death.

A shadowy figure staggered toward him, one hand outstretched, the other gripping the lifeline. Paddy McBride, come to welcome him to the next world. But Douglas could not go yet: he had solved the mystery of the ghost and he had to return to Dundee. 'Not yet, Paddy,' he gasped.

'Come out of that.' The accent was pure Dundee as Paddy lifted them both like children and threw them into the shelter of the funnel. 'Now come below with me, the pair of you.'

Douglas looked up into the glowering face of Bully Houston.

The North Atlantic, March–April 1860

Houston led Douglas and Mrs Gordon below and pushed open the door of a storeroom between the main coal-bunker and the engine-room. 'In, you.' He jerked a thumb to Douglas, but helped the woman with a rough courtesy.

'I think we've found our ghost,' Douglas said.

Houston silenced him with a grunt. 'She was never lost. The question is, what are we going to do with you?'

The store was surprisingly warm, with a storm-lantern hanging from a hook, casting weird shadows as it swung with the pitch and roll of the ship, and a straw donkey's-breakfast mattress in one corner. A half-empty biscuit-box lay on the floor. Houston noticed the direction of Douglas's eyes. 'Aye, she was the thief. Or rather I was.'

'You knew about her?'

'This is Mary Gordon. Her man, Jimmy Gordon, was the carpenter on *Ivanhoe*.'

Douglas nodded. Now that he saw her clearly, he was shocked by the change in her. The woman he'd seen in Dundee had been thin-faced; this woman was gaunt, her green eyes huge and black-shadowed and her soaked hair plastered to her head and across her face. But yes, it was indeed her.

Houston was still speaking. 'A bit of a queer fish, Jimmy; attended the Kirk, didn't even drink. But he was a shipmate of mine – not that you'd understand that.' He took up a square of canvas from the deck and rubbed the woman's hands and arms so vigorously that she protested. 'We'll leave you in peace now, Mary. Towel yourself dry and get your blood moving again.'

The surprising gentleness in his voice vanished, and he scowled at Douglas. 'You can leave me to deal with Wyllie's creature.'

'Wait.' She thrust herself free of the canvas towel. 'He saved my life, Willie, and nearly got himself drowned doing it.'

'Why?' Houston's scowl did not abate. 'Why should one of Wyllie's things save your life? What was he going to do with you afterwards?' His huge hands curled into fists. 'Don't you fret, now; I'll toss him overboard where he belongs.'

'No.' Mrs Gordon stopped his menacing advance with a single raised finger. 'I'm sure he meant no more than to help. See the blood on his arm, Willie? He hurt himself saving me.' And to Douglas, 'Who are you? What is your name?'

'My name is Robert Douglas, Mrs Gordon, and I don't work for Wyllie. I did for one day, the day of the prizefight, but I didn't like his methods, or his company. And it was Wyllie who had me crimped.'

Houston grunted again. 'Aye? Well, serves you glad for going to Ma Scott's. Mind you, I'm not surprised you were crimped. Horse Gilbride put round the word that he needed a crew for *Redgauntlet*, and Wyllie's the man for blood-money.' He shook his head. 'I've worked with poor crews in my time, but by the living Christ they don't come much poorer than this one. Hardly a seaman among the lot of you.' Some of the suspicion drained from his eyes. 'You're not Wyllie's agent aboard, then?'

'No,' said Douglas, puzzled. 'Why should he have an agent aboard?'

'To watch me. And that's all you're being told.' For an instant Houston had dropped his guard, but now the Bully returned. 'Now listen to me, whatever-your-name-is. I don't care if you were crimped or not. I don't care if you work for Wyllie or for the King of Delhi, but if you breathe one word about Mary's presence aboard this ship I'll kill you stone dead. Got that?'

'Of course.' Douglas nodded. 'But . . . but why *is* she aboard?'

'That's none of your bloody business,' Houston snapped. He took a step forward, but again Mrs Gordon stilled him with a gesture; it was remarkable the ease with which she controlled him.

'Willie, it's all right. Tell him the truth. It doesn't matter now, not now that he's seen me.' She gave her hair a brisk rub with the canvas. 'If you boys will leave the room for a minute, I'll change my clothes. You sailormen may not feel the cold and the wet, but we frail women do.'

When they returned she was wearing a seaman's costume, baggy white trousers turned up at the hem and a striped shirt that reached nearly to her knees. 'Right, boys,' she said briskly, 'Find a space on the floor and let's talk.'

They sat down on the deck, Houston positioning himself between Mrs Gordon and Douglas.

She said, 'Willie told you that I'm Jimmy Gordon's wife. What he didn't tell you is that he's my wee brother and that he was on *Ivanhoe*, too.' She squeezed his arm affectionately and leaned back against him. 'Ugh! You should have dried yourself, Willie. At least put something between us so I don't get wet again.' When he had obeyed, she continued, 'You're wondering why I'm here? Well, I don't believe Jimmy's dead. I can *feel* that he's alive. Willie doesn't agree, but he'll do as I say, won't you, Willie?'

Houston said nothing.

'I stowed away on *Redgauntlet* to get up to the ice. I want to find my man. He's up there, somewhere.'

Houston shook his head slowly. 'Don't raise your hopes, Mary. I was told that *Ivanhoe's* boiler exploded and everyone was killed.' He faced Douglas. 'I had a boat's crew out sealing at the time. When *Ivanhoe* disappeared we were alone in the ice. They all died, man after man.'

'Willie got frostbite. He lost two toes on each foot.' She sounded quite proud.

'Are you sure *Ivanhoe* blew up?' Douglas ignored Houston's

glare. He thought of what Ecky had said in Lerwick; but could he trust the word of a drunken man?

Houston shrugged. 'So people told me. I didn't see it.'

'Did anybody see it?' Douglas tried to sound casual.

'Only *Ivanhoe*'s surgeon. It was him that reported what happened.' Houston scowled again. 'You ask a lot of questions for a Greenman.'

'That's because I don't want to be blown up,' retorted Douglas. 'Anyway, I heard that you were the only survivor. How did the surgeon get back if *Ivanhoe* blew up?'

The scowl grew heavier. 'I think you've asked enough questions for one night, Mr Greenman.'

'The surgeon was rescued as well,' cut in Mrs Gordon, 'but I don't know how. Willie was the only known survivor of the crew.' Her smoky eyes were challenging as she looked at her brother. 'Jimmy's alive, too, I know he is. I can feel him.'

Houston and Douglas exchanged a glance but said nothing.

'So that's why I'm here. I'm going to find my husband. It surely won't be too difficult, for whaling-ships all fish in the same place.'

Houston shook his head. 'It's a huge area up there. We could be fishing hundreds of miles from where *Ivanhoe* was last seen.'

'I know. You've told me before,' she said dismissively, very much the elder sister correcting her wee brother. 'Now, Mr Douglas, you know all about us.' Her smoky eyes crystallised into something resembling green quartz. 'But if you tell anybody else that I'm here, Willie will throw you overboard.'

Houston lifted Douglas's arm. 'You report to the surgeon and get that cut attended to. And what's your excuse for deserting your post for so long?'

'I was hunting the ghost.'

'Time that ghost story was finished.' Houston shook his head. 'It unsettles the men and, God knows, they're afraid enough with all this "unlucky ship" nonsense.'

'The ghost was a stowaway who was lost overboard during

the gale,' Douglas said quickly. 'That should clear things up. It's a pity that *Redgauntlet* killed a woman when she was being launched, though. That seems to be the root of the trouble.'

'Aye. More nonsense. It's a pity the newspaper spread the story around.' Houston eyed Douglas narrowly. 'You seem to know about men. What did you say you were?'

'Sergeant in the Seventy-Third Foot.' Douglas displayed his tattoo. 'Which paper reported the launch? I'd like to see it when we get back.'

'I don't know, I never read the things. Mary?'

She thought for a second. 'The *North-East Gazette*, probably, but the Dundee paper would copy the reports. Does it matter?'

Douglas shook his head. 'Probably not. But the *Gazette's* an Aberdeen paper. Was *Redgauntlet* built there?'

'Aye, by Hall's – Gourlay's of Dundee built *Ivanhoe*. They have exactly the same specifications.' Houston shook his head. 'They were meant to be the first of a new breed of whaling-vessels combining steam with sail, so that they could go twice a year to the fishing-grounds.' Houston lifted his head and listened. 'Wind's getting up again – I'll have to go on deck soon. As I was saying, Horse Gilbride's idea was right. The ships were meant to steam to the Greenland Seas or New-foundland for the seal-hunting, bring the cargo back to Dundee and return for the whaling. The engines would make them faster and give them enough power to punch through the ice.

'Instead, what happens? *Redgauntlet* is branded an unlucky ship and *Ivanhoe* explodes. Now Old Man Fairweather is creeping along under canvas as if he doesn't want to get to the Straits at all. It's like the Waverley Company was cursed.' He rounded on Douglas. 'What the hell are you still here for? I ordered you to the surgeon. Fly, laddie, fly!'

Douglas flew.

That night, the name '*Davey*' tantalised Douglas anew as he lay in his bunk, trying to make sense of all that had happened.

Mrs Gordon was a new and astonishing complication. Given

how superstitious the Greenlandmen were, if they knew a woman was aboard it would be as bad as having a ghost. Douglas shook his head in grudging respect. She was a tough one, all right. He remembered what he'd said to Wyllie: he hoped Jimmy had appreciated her.

Until today he'd suspected Houston of being concerned in the loss of *Ivanhoe,* but the mate seemed genuine in his belief that she had blown up. The most important question, Douglas considered, was how she had been destroyed. If she'd exploded, it might have been because of a flaw in her design or building, in which case *Redgauntlet* was also at great risk. The only witness to the explosion had been the surgeon; he might have the answer.

But Ecky had insisted that he'd seen *Ivanhoe* the day after the supposed explosion. How was that possible? Could the surgeon have mistaken the date? And there were other questions. Why should Wyllie put someone on *Redgauntlet* to spy on Houston? And had that any connection with the loss of *Ivanhoe*? Then again . . . But at that point exhaustion claimed him and he fell asleep.

By the middle of April *Redgauntlet* was off Cape Farewell and preparing to enter the Davis Straits.

'This is the hunting-ground,' Tam told Douglas as they stood by the lee rail. 'Once we're round Farewell we might sight whales at any time, so we'll have to prepare. Watch how the specktioneer perks up now.' He snorted. 'Farewell, eh? What a name for a cape. Farewell to the Atlantic, farewell to safety and ease, and good day to ice and snow and a fog which freezes the blood in your veins.

'Aye,' chimed in Scrimmy, rubbing his hands together, his bearded face bright, 'and bid good day to the whales. Whales filled with oil we can turn into whisky. This is where we make the money, Rab, my boy.'

Douglas noticed a revived purpose about the ship. The

spektioneer, whose name was Gillespie, ordered the harpoons and flensing-knives sharpened, and the rasping of steel on iron grated through the half-deck as the blacksmith honed the points and barbs to a razor's sharpness. As the men went about their work, they boasted of the whales they would kill when they got among the ice.

Houston and Cargill supervised the bringing of the whale-boats up from the hold, where they had been stored to save them from damage from the Atlantic weather, to the main deck. The harpoons were spanned in, with one end of the foreganger rope spliced round the shank and the other spliced to the whale-line in the bottom of the boat. Then they were positioned carefully in the mik, a wooden crotch on the starboard side of the boat. Once the equipment had been checked, the boat was swung from greased davits, ready to be swung out as soon as a whale was sighted.

'You Greenmen,' ordered Houston, 'report to the slop-chest and draw some cold-weather gear – furs and mittens and a cap. Look lively, now. And if I find any of you working without your mittens I'll bloody keel-haul you.'

'That's kind of him. Free clothes,' said Smith, the Greenman who had whistled up the wind.

Tam laughed. 'Free be damned, man. It'll come out of your wages – and at sea-prices, too, double what it would cost you on land.'

Captain Fairweather sent one of the experienced men to the crow's nest, the barrel-shaped shelter high up on the mainmast; it was thickly lined with straw to keep its occupant from freezing in the bitter north. 'Keep a good lookout now, Gay, and sing out if you see anything.'

There was not even a suspicion of fog as they passed the notorious Cape Farewell and headed north, with the spectacular peaks of Greenland slashing the sky to starboard but with surprising splashes of green softening the ice-bound, rocky shore. Great flocks of birds besieged the ship, the heavy glaucous gulls that the Greenlandmen called burgomasters mixing with the mollies that chattered and swooped everywhere. One or two of the seamen scrounged pieces of fat from the cook, baited fishing-lines and threw them into the air to catch mollies.

'Seabird pie for the Captain,' Scrimmy said in triumph. 'We might get an extra tot o' grog for it.'

Tam nodded approval when Captain Fairweather and the surgeon shot at the circling loons. 'Good eating, them,' he said. 'Like roasted hare.'

Once they saw the beautiful white shape of a gyrfalcon hovering overhead, and twice an Arctic raven circled the mainmast.

'That's bad luck,' said Tam worriedly. 'Ravens are the devil's birds.'

'Nonsense.' Hughson nudged him with a sharp elbow. 'They're Odin's birds, come to bless the ship.'

At sixty-four degrees north an opaque white veil gradually hazed away the horizon. *Redgauntlet* sailed on until first her bowsprit and then her foc'sle vanished into mist which wrapped itself round them like a winding-sheet. A minute before, the sea had been bright and clear; now it was sluggish, leaden-grey and ugly as it broke noiselessly against the hull. The familiar shipboard sounds altered: even the creak of timber and the constant whine of wind in the ratlines were different.

As always when the weather changed, Houston appeared on deck. 'Sound the bell, one peal every minute,' he ordered, 'and fetch me the foghorn.' He looked aloft. 'Send word for Hughson; I want a good man aloft.' He looked at Douglas. 'You, go for'ard. If you see anything – anything at all – shout. Understand? I don't want to run foul of a growler or another ship in this muck. And pin your ears back, too: fog does queer things to sounds, and you might hear the ice before you can see it.'

Cloying and grey, the fog clasped *Redgauntlet* like a demon lover, streaming from the yards in long tendrils which snaked and changed and merged into each other, as deceptive as a whore's promise. Douglas peered for'ard over the bows, seeing nothing but a desolate damp mass into which the bowsprit probed and disappeared. The prospect of *Redgauntlet* ramming an iceberg while off Greenland lifted the hairs on the back of his neck.

The harsh bellow of the foghorn cleaved through the greyness from behind Douglas. He looked aft and saw two slim figures emerge from the shadow of the mainmast. One was tall and straight; the other was smaller and walked with the sway of a seaman.

'Anything for'ard?' shouted Houston.

'Nothing I can see.' Douglas returned his attention to his task.

'Keep alert. Trust your judgement.'

The sun was sultry hot. Douglas held the girl close. He could feel Paddy's amusement, and the disapproval of the men around. 'I trust you,' she said, and Douglas gave her a little squeeze before setting her down on the ground. It was good to be trusted, good even to be recognised as a human being. British soldiers were never the most popular guests in anybody's country, not even here on the Cape's north-east frontier.

'Don't trust him,' Major Donnachie mocked, pushing Douglas aside. 'He knows nothing.' But the girl's eyes followed Douglas as he marched away, with the smiling brown doll bouncing from his belt and the insects whining around his head.

Trust? Douglas shook away the phantoms and concentrated on trying to see through the fog. For a moment he was not sure if the blurred voices he could hear came from Africa or Greenland, but when he looked back along the starboard side he saw the doctor in conversation with Symbister, the youngest of the Shetlanders. The fog distorted their words, but the Shetlander sounded unhappy as the doctor guided him below. Douglas grinned; perhaps the lad had caught a dose of clap before he left home. Well, that was Dr Michie's job, and he was welcome to it.

The foghorn sounded again and then the bowsprit thrust into clear air and the sea sparkled ahead. There were no icebergs in sight, nothing ahead but a horizon which was hard and bright and beautiful, nothing to starboard but the distant mountains of Greenland.

'Douglas,' came the familiar bellow, 'stop skulking up for'ard there and get below to the pumps. Lively now, you lubber, and when I say lively I mean fly.'

The ship was more settled since Douglas had reported that the ghost had been washed overboard. Men spoke instead of the whale-fishing that lay just over the horizon. Each day the lookout reported other vessels in sight as the British whaling-fleet congregated in the hunting-grounds. The old hands recognised the ships by the set of their sails, or the shape of their hull. 'There's *Alert*,' Tam might say, or 'Yon's *Enterprise* of Fraserburgh, another unlucky ship,' or '*Abram* of Kirkcaldy'. Douglas realised that the names were a roll-call of glory and fame, much like the regimental roll-call of the British Army, and as much a witness to the slaughter of the enemy, if that term could be applied to a whale. Twice the lookout sighted seals, but Captain Fairweather was after larger game: *Redgauntlet* did not pause in her voyage up the Davis Strait.

The crew spent most of their leisure time discussing how much oil-money they would make and what they would spend it on.

'Women,' said Smith. The bruises the Lerwick fisherwomen had given him were healed now, so he was back to his habitual state of speculative lechery. 'As soon as we're paid off, I'm for Mother Scott's. That's where the women are.'

'I'll hire two whores and three fiddlers and buy four kegs of ale,' one of the youngsters said. He had been trying to grow a beard ever since leaving Dundee, but the wispy proof of his immaturity had earned him only coarse abuse. 'No, I'll buy *three* whores. I wore out two the night before we left Dundee and I was hungry for more.'

Scrimmy gave his unfailing answer. 'Whisky, whisky, I'll buy some whisky. Whisky, whisky, it always makes me frisky.'

Tam had been sitting in a corner with his head buried in his hands, but at this he looked up. 'What oil-money will you buy it with? We haven't caught a single seal yet, let alone a whale. And there's hardly enough real seamen here to crew one whaleboat, anyway.' He glared at the laughing men. 'And have you forgotten *Ivanhoe* so soon? Once the Captain fires up the boiler we'll all be dead, blown to fragments.'

'What's got into you, Tammy boy?' Scrimmy paused in his singing, his grin as wide as ever. 'Lizzie will wait for you, never fear.'

'You leave my wife out of this.' Tam shoved Scrimmy against the bulkhead and, hunch-shouldered, stalked out of the foc'sle. From somewhere to starboard came the melancholy call of a loon.

'What's the matter with him?' wondered Scrimmy, rubbing the back of his head. 'We've been shipmates for years and he's never acted like that before.'

'It's the curse,' said Smith. 'He's always on about *Redgauntlet* being an unlucky ship.'

Scrimmy nodded. 'Aye, you're a bit of a fool, Smithy, but you may be right this time. Tam's wrong, though; there's nothing unlucky about *Old Fisty*.'

'No?' Suddenly daring, Smith put in a challenge. 'How about the man Houston killed? Him that was washed off the bowsprit? And the stowaway Rab saw washed over the side? Or the spinner killed when she was launched? Tam's told me all about them. If that's not unlucky, what is?'

Scrimmy shook his head. 'I've sailed on bad ships, Smithy. You could feel the malice running through the fabric. *Fisty* isn't like that.'

'Yes, she is. The woman she killed cursed her – Tam told me so.'

'Then let's lift the curse.' Although Scrimmy was laughing as he rose to his feet, there was a serious edge to his voice. 'We know ways, don't we, lads?' He gestured to the old hands. 'Contribute, everybody,' he ordered, and each man handed over a small personal possession, a piece of clothing, a trinket from home, a piece of scrimshaw work.

'And the rest of you, too,' he told the watching Greenmen. 'A sacrifice to remove the curse.'

Douglas reached under his bed and handed over his length of blackthorn. 'Here. I was a soldier, so a weapon's significant. Anyway, I doubt I'll be using it.'

'Aye, it's too wee for killing seals, and as for whales . . .' Hughson led the laughter but there were a couple of raised eyebrows.

The young beard-grower boasted, 'If I'd known that was there, it's Houston would have been overboard.'

'That's a good thing to give, Rab, my boy,' said Scrimmy, weighing the blackthorn in one hand. 'Anybody else, now?'

'Yes, you, Smithy,' Hughson ordered. 'You're the jinx that brought the gale.'

'He should give more, then,' another Shetlander said. 'The bigger the fault, the greater the contribution.'

'What do you mean?' asked Smith.

'Something close to you,' Scrimmy said cheerfully, and he laughed as all the watching whalers leaped on top of the Greenman. There was a scrimmage of gasping bodies, and a few telling punches, then Smith was speadeagled on his back with a man holding each limb. 'Off with them,' Scrimmy said and Hughson bent close. There was a long wail from Smith, a few seconds' struggle and Hughson held up Smith's long woollen underwear up for inspection, crowing, 'That'll be a fitting sacrifice, won't it, Scrimmy?'

Douglas noted the anxiety on the Greenlandmen's faces as

126

they watched Scrimmy set to work. The life of every man depended on the ship. They believed that the success or failure of the voyage depended on Scrimmy removing the bad luck. Taut with concentration, Scrimmy fashioned all the oddments into a rough likeness of *Redgauntlet*, with three distinct masts and a piece of scrimshaw for the figurehead. Some of the Greenlandmen made suggestions as to shape or form, but Scrimmy ignored them all, just as he ignored their exhortations to hurry.

When he was satisfied, Scrimmy took up a storm-lantern and carried his model on deck, with the entire foc'sle crowd behind him. The Greenlandmen were grave-faced, the Greenmen curious, and Smith muttered in mingled anger and humiliation.

Hughson cuffed him gently. 'Shut up, Smithy, or we'll sacrifice you instead.'

'Find Tam, somebody,' Scrimmy said, 'so he can witness this. And bring another lantern.'

Redgauntlet cruised under topsails over a hazy sea as Hughson and two of the Greenmen escorted Tam to Scrimmy at the lee side of the funnel. Scrimmy raised the storm-lantern so that a yellow arc of light reflected on the sea.

'Right, Tam. We need something of yours, too – maybe that kerchief you wear, or perhaps your shirt?'

'Take his underwear, too,' Smith complained.

'He's no whistler,' Hughson said quietly. 'So keep quiet or it's overboard for you.'

Tam looked worried, but handed over his red neckerchief.

Scrimmy tied it to his model. 'O great god of the sea,' he cried, his voice carrying far in the hush, 'accept this sacrifice from your seamen and remove any curse upon this ship.' He set the model down on the deck, opened the front of the lantern, dripped some oil over the model and dipped a rag in the flame. Then he closed the lantern and handed it to Hughson.

'Are we ready, boys?' The words were quiet, but clearly

audible. The Greenlandmen nodded. 'Here we go, then. Say a prayer for the ship, lads.'

Lifting the model high, Scrimmy allowed the flames from his rag to play on the sails until they caught fire. Douglas saw the lips of many of the Greenlandmen moving silently as Scrimmy leaned over the rail and dropped the model into the sea, where it sparked and hissed amid the waves.

'Accept this sacrifice and burn away the curse.'

'Burn the curse. Burn the curse.' One by one, the Greenlandmen took up the chant. 'Burn the curse. Burn the curse.' There was something near desperation in their voices, and Douglas felt a quick twist of sadness. What would Miss Gilbride think of this display of paganism?

'You men,' Houston spoke in her place, his voice thundering through the ship like the wrath of Jehovah, 'you've had your little ceremony, now get back to where you're meant to be. If you've no work to do, I'll soon find you some. I've never seen the like.'

'That'll clear the bad luck away,' Scrimmy said reassuringly to Tam. 'You'll see.'

Perhaps the ceremony worked, for the weather turned bright the next day, allowing Houston to pile on sail. It was exhilarating to be scudding north in the clear coolness of the Davis Strait, with the sea breaking silver under the great fist of the figurehead and the canvas curved taut overhead. It was no hardship to work aloft, despite the cold that turned mittened fingers numb, and a pleasure to add his weight to the wheel when Hughson or Tam or Scrimmy steered ever northward. Even Houston seemed less unpleasant than normal.

'Best be careful,' Hughson warned. 'When a bully mate doesn't bite your head off, that means that he's planning something worse. Give him a wide berth.'

'Give me whisky, whisky, always give me whisky.' Scrimmy sang. 'I knew we could burn away the curse. Feel better now, don't you, Tam, me boy?'

Tam had taken to sleeping fully dressed and always carried a small gasket which held his essential dunnage. 'We're all going to go like the men on *Ivanhoe* did, Scrimmy. You stay close to me, will you? We've been shipmates for years and I wouldn't like you to die.'

Scrimmy put a wiry arm round his friend's neck. 'Well, Tam, we're all going to die one day, when our time comes, so I may as well go with you as with anybody else.'

There had been ice for some time, little pieces that the ship swept aside, but on the last day of April the lookout shouted, 'Iceberg! Iceberg dead ahead – and it's a big one!'

Before he had finished speaking Houston had launched himself up the ratlines. He elbowed the lookout aside and extended his telescope. After a minute he leaned over the side of the crow's nest and bellowed orders which had the helmsman sweating to alter course.

From his position on the yard, Douglas watched the iceberg pass. Even from a full mile away it was massive: a mountain of blue and white, banded near the waterline with black and green; mist wisped around the base. He had not known what to expect, but this thing, as large as Dundee Law, and seeming to possess a life of its own, awed him. The iceberg was quiet save for the splash of waves and the slight whistle of a breeze, yet seemed to carry a warning.

No longer was *Redgauntlet* sailing safely through the waves for which she had been designed. Now she was entering a new domain of ice-giants and deep, bitter frost. The prospect was suddenly frightening. Douglas did not envy Captain Fairweather and Houston their responsibility.

'Here we go, then.' Tam sounded almost relieved. 'That's us really among the ice now. If the Captain agrees, Neptune will be paying us a visit soon.' For the first time in weeks, he smiled. 'You'll see what I mean.'

Davis Strait, Spring 1860

There was always that fire and the horrors that surrounded it. The memory nagged at his conscience and his soul as soon as he closed his eyes, whether he was at a bush bivouac or in the barracks. Paddy tried to help with rough compassion and sound advice, but Paddy had not made the promise, Paddy had not broken the trust. He reached down, as so often before, and touched the hand, only to see it move away, rejecting his sorrow and refusing him forgiveness. 'I couldn't help it,' he said despairingly. 'I'm sorry.'

But a hand had no ears to hear, no voice to forgive, and the guilt remained, festering as a combination of self-doubt and self-loathing which ate away his self-respect and tore his heart inside out.

The blaring of a horn wakened Douglas and he groped for his rifle before he remembered where he was. The din echoed through every corner of the ship, joining the insistent clangour of the ship's bell, which was sounded every half-hour to mark the passage of the day. Unconsciously he counted the peals.

'Eight bells. Eight bells of the first watch.' Tam was wide awake and grinning at him over the edge of his bunk. 'That's midnight, in case you've forgotten, you landlubber.'

'What's that bloody noise?' Smith appeared, tousled-haired and angry. 'Not the bell, the other thing?'

'Neptune's horn.' Tam looked happier than he had all voyage. 'The great sea god hath summoned his own.' He lowered his voice. 'Now listen, Rab. Go forward early. Do

130

everything Neptune tells you to do, and at the right time give him this.' He pressed a small bottle into Douglas's hands. 'But keep it hidden for now.'

The horn blared again, louder this time, and chanting arose throughout the ship: 'He's coming. He's coming. He's coming.'

A score of oil-lamps cast their light on the deck so that there was not even a shadow in which to hide. About two-thirds of the crew were gathered in a semicircle round a canvas screen, the Greenmen separate from the rest.

'He's coming. He's coming. He's coming.'

Captain Fairweather was among the crowd, smiling with the rest, and even quiet Cargill looked amused.

'He's coming. He's coming. He's coming.'

'Who's coming?' Smith demanded, shaking off Hughson's hands. 'What's this all about?'

The horn grew louder yet, and a voice called, high above the blare, 'Permission to come aboard, Captain?'

'Granted with pleasure, Your Majesty,' Captain Fair-weather replied.

A strange procession emerged from behind the canvas screen: six figures, five with long white beards and hair of dripping seaweed. Their costumes would have resembled Roman togas had they not been made of Baxter's No 6 fine canvas. The sixth figure had long hair but no beard, and its face was painted in ludicrously bright colours. Douglas assumed that this was Mrs Neptune.

The smallest of the newcomers carried the foghorn and spoke in a voice which Douglas recognised as that of the spektioneer, Gillespie: 'I am Neptune, Monarch of the Ocean, and I demand to see these puny landsmen who wish to enter my kingdom.'

'Here they are. Here they are.' The crew pushed forward the Greenmen, who stood in an uncomfortable clump before His Majesty.

'God, what an ugly bunch!' Neptune shook his head in

131

disbelief. 'In my younger days we had men aboard ships, not creatures like these.'

'In your younger days, Jonah was still sitting in his whale,' riposted a Biblical scholar, to the obvious delight of the King's court.

With regal disdain, Neptune ignored the interruption. 'Some even have beards,' he said in shocked tones. 'And they stink.'

The crowd cheered again.

'Bring them.' Neptune waved his hand and his courtiers removed the screen, revealing a great canvas tank across which a plank was precariously balanced. The Greenmen were hustled forward amidst a chorus of jeers and laughter, but, Douglas noted with wry amusement, no whistles. 'Who dares sail into my kingdom?'

Remembering Tam's advice, Douglas stepped forward. 'I dare – with Your Majesty's permission, of course.'

Neptune stared at Douglas with eyes lined with age. His wife seemed to be having trouble with her wig; Douglas recognised her as the slim young Shetlander whom he had seen disappearing below with the surgeon, and wondered if his clap was cured yet.

Neptune pointed a trident which looked suspiciously like a harpoon. 'Sit him on the chair.'

The courtiers thumped Douglas astride the plank. One produced a basin containing a frothy mixture of tar, soap and more noxious substances, while another flourished a razor made from a rusty barrel-hoop.

'What is your name, landsman?'

'Robert Douglas, sire.' Douglas kept his chin up as the courtier smeared the stinking mixture liberally over his face. By accident or design, the brush entered his mouth as he spoke, but he had been expecting that, so showed no surprise. He had endured similar humiliation the first time he crossed the Equator.

'And are you willing to be one of my loyal subjects, Landsman Douglas?'

'Keep that brush from my mouth and I'll be the most loyal subject you've ever known.'

Grinning, the courtier rammed the brush right into his throat. The Greenlandmen cheered.

'Prove your loyalty, Landsman Douglas,' Neptune commanded.

Douglas reached inside his jacket and produced the bottle Tam had given him. 'Here is my tribute, O great Neptune.'

Neptune snatched the bottle, pulled the cork out with his teeth and took a long swallow. 'Shetland whisky.' He nodded appreciatively. 'You will make a good seaman. Introduce him to his new element.'

There was a loud cheer as the courtiers tipped the plank and Douglas fell backwards into the tank of water. He surfaced at once and, rather than cursing, had the sense to laugh along with the crew. Neptune's wife helped him out, and Neptune allowed him a small drink of the whisky.

'Well done, son of the sea. Next!'

Tam pushed Smith forward.

Scrimmy nudged Douglas and said, 'Put something dry on right away, Rab, or you'll be frostbitten before dawn.'

'Plank him down.'

'You're not ducking me!' But the courtiers ignored Smith's protests and thrust him on to the plank.

'Name?'

'None of your damned business!' As Smith swore, the courtier frothed his mixture and shoved the brush into his mouth. He kept it there, grinning, until the victim began to choke.

'Name?' Neptune asked when the brush was at last withdrawn.

'Benjamin Smith, damn you!'

'Let it be recorded that this landsman is henceforth known as Benjamin Smith Damnyou,' Neptune ordered, and the crew cheered. 'And can you prove your loyalty to me?'

'I'll not bribe you!' His mouthful of the mixture had not robbed Smith of his truculence.

'Wait.' Neptune stepped forward and inspected Smith closely. 'Is this not the landsman who summoned the wind?'

'It is, Your Majesty!' yelled the crew.

'Then shave the stupidity from him.'

The lather was plastered on so thickly that Smith's face could hardly be seen, then Neptune's assistant flourished the razor and roughly scraped off the mixture. Smith's curses changed to yells as the froth became red with blood, but the courtiers were ruthless, shaving heartily until his face was clear of froth.

'Now wash him.'

Again the plank was tipped and Smith fell into the tank. He emerged spluttering, but the courtiers pushed him under again and again, relenting only when Mrs Neptune took pity: 'Let him up. There's plenty more to duck yet.'

'Let me see that man.' Dr Michie pushed through the crowd. 'Come along to my cabin so I can examine you properly.' He glared at Mr and Mrs Neptune. 'We'll discuss this barbarity later.'

The remaining Greenmen had learned from Smith's example and did not struggle. They all paid tribute: one or two bottles of whisky or rum, some tobacco and bread. They all answered the questions respectfully and, although all were lathered and ducked, most escaped the shaving.

The more of the liquid tributes Neptune sampled, the more slurred his speech became. As the Arctic dawn lightened the horizon, he waved a bottle in the air. 'Welcome, new subjects.' He paused to adjust his wig, which had slid down over his face. 'Fiddlers, strike up a jig and let's raise the garland.'

At the beginning of the voyage every Greenlandman had brought a ribbon into the ship. Tradition demanded that married men buy their own, while the unmarried obtained theirs from their girl. Men who were unlucky enough to have neither wife nor sweetheart had snatched a ribbon from the bonnet of an unwary woman they chanced to meet. While off duty, they had spliced the ribbons into a garland which surrounded a carved model of *Redgauntlet*. Now, as dawn kissed the eastern sky, the garland was hoisted up the mainmast, to rousing cheers from the crew.

'That's the luck of the voyage, Rab, my boy.' Scrimmy passed around a bottle of whisky with as much liberality as Houston gave insults. 'We've burned away the bad luck, and now we're raising the good. You see,' and he leaned confidentially on Douglas, 'the women tied knots in the ribbons that they gave their men, and each knot stands for a whale we'll catch. I had a woman once, but she left me. Her name was Linda, I think. Can't remember. That's the drink for you. Anyway, I went to the spae-wife in Shetland and had her knot it for me.'

'How many knots did she put in?' Douglas asked.

'Oh, no, no, no.' Scrimmy shook his head portentously. 'We can't ask that. Counting the knots would take away the power. Here.' He thrust his bottle at Douglas. 'Have a drink.'

There were many men having a drink, and Bosun Macmillan produced a set of bagpipes, so that the complex music of the Gael competed with *Redgauntlet*'s two Shetland fiddlers in sweetening the bitter Arctic air. The decks vibrated with the pounding feet of more than forty men, and even Captain Fairweather joined in the celebrations. Douglas saw the surgeon smiling as he danced a waltz with Mrs Symbister Neptune, whose paint was nearly smeared from her face. Tam sat in the shelter of one of the whaleboats, watching. When the music lapsed, Symbister disappeared below decks.

'A fall! A fall!' came a shout from the crow's nest, where Houston had been keeping solitary watch. 'Come on, you useless lubbers! Hands off the bottles and on to the oars. There's whales to be caught.'

There was a moment of silence as the half-drunk men tried to comprehend his meaning. Some stared over the side, others looked blankly at Houston, who leaned down from the crow's nest, his face mottled with anger, and bellowed, '*Move*, you damned farmers. And when I say move, I mean *fly!*'

This time his words took effect. Houston had drilled his crew until each man knew exactly where he should be, but there was still pandemonium as men pushed one another aside in their haste to be first on the water. Everybody knew that there was extra money for the first boat to make fast to a whale.

Douglas slid into his boat as the greased davits lowered it on to the sea. He nodded to the crew. There was Gay, the harpooner, a lugubrious man from Crail; Robertson, the line-manager from Montrose; Dunn the boat-header from Broughty Ferry; the Shetlander Hughson, Scrimmy and Greig from Dundee, and himself. It was a good crew and pushed off from *Redgauntlet* only a few minutes after the bran-boat, the boat that had been on stand-by for a sighting.

Dunn was in charge until they reached the whale. He looked up at the crow's nest, where Houston had exchanged his speaking-trumpet for a pair of signal flags, and said, 'Right, lads, here we go. You, Greenman, just do what you're told and we'll be fine. We're after the fast-money and the oil-money, so pull like buggery when I say.'

With his greater range of vision in the crow's nest, Houston was in overall command of the hunt. He pointed one flag at Dunn's boat and the second at a point on the horizon, towards which the bran-boat was already racing. Fiercely ordering his crew to pull, Dunn hoisted the lugsail to catch the wind. Gay took the starboard bow oar, and pulled with such energy that the rest had hard work of it to keep time.

'We're catching her,' Hughson grunted as they neared the bran-boat. 'We'll be the fast-boat.'

'Save your breath and pull.' Gripping the long steering-oar in one hand, Dunn adjusted the set of the sail to catch the gusting wind. 'Come on, lads.'

Douglas was no expert oarsman, but as a hungry boy he had

borrowed skiffs to fish in the Tay. The family had depended on him for food, so he soon learned where to find the best catches. Memories of those days returned as he leaned into the oar, grunting with each stroke. It was hard work but exhilarating to see the boat's wake stream out astern, to hear the surge of the Arctic seas and to know that he was part of a team with a single object in mind.

'There she goes, lads.' Dunn took them so close to the ready-boat that they almost slithered past. He cast a critical eye over her crew, who looked to be suffering from the effects of Neptune's visit. 'They're a man short,' he said. 'Young Symbister's missing.'

'Their bad cess.' Despite the whisky he'd drunk, Scrimmy was pulling like a hero. 'We'll be the fast-boat – and that means oil-money, lads.'

'Save your breath. Pull!'

The waves had increased in size, and were clear green and smoothly surfaced until they broke under the impact of the oar-blades. Dunn opened the locker in the transom stern and handed each rower a piece of rag. 'Wrap it round your oar where it fits into the rowlock.'

Scrimmy showed Douglas how to do it. 'It masks the sound. Whales have good ears.'

'Everybody keep quiet now,' ordered Dunn, and a hush fell. He trimmed the sail again as the boat slid forward, the men pulling gently at the muffled oars. The lapping of the waves against the hull sounded very loud, but above it Douglas could hear another and most curious sound, something between a puffing and a snorting.

'Easy all,' whispered Dunn, hauling in the sail. 'Back water – quietly.'

The strange sound grew louder. As if in slow motion, Douglas saw Gay haul his oar inboard and take his place at the harpoon-gun that sat, squat and ugly, in the bows. Robertson checked the lines that ran aft from the neat coils on deck, between the legs of the oarsmen, to the open lockers in the stern. Dunn adjusted the steering-oar and braced himself against the thwarts.

'Would you look at that?' Scrimmy peered over his shoulder. 'Is that not a sight to tell your grandchildren of?'

Douglas looked and swallowed hard. About thirty yards away lay the whale. It was far bigger than he had imagined, a blue-black giant, encrusted with growths and gleaming with water. Little waves broke on the rounded back, while the great head bulged upward – whence its name of bowhead. A molly landed on its back, perched for an instant and flew off. The whale spouted again, and Douglas realised what had caused that strange sound.

For a second he felt a pang of sympathy for the immense creature he was about to help destroy. What reason had he to intrude on its territory, to attack and kill for profit? The reason of the hunter, he justified himself; the law of Nature that decreed that the strong would prey on the weak. It had always been like that and doubtless always would. Oil from this whale would power the lights that made the streets of Dundee safer for women to walk; would keep the jute factories running, thereby safeguarding hundreds of jobs – and without jute there would be no sacks or wagon-covers for the world. Bone from this whale would be used for stays in fashionable clothing and for chair-backs and carriage-springs, corsets and brush bristles, harps and whips. This whale had to die to maintain all the comforts of civilisation.

'It's a bloody shame, though.' Scrimmy must have caught an echo of his thoughts.

'Slowly, now.' Dunn guided the boat toward the whale. He kept behind it, out of its line of sight, and glanced frequently at the great tail that lay just under the surface of the water. One flick of those flukes could capsize the boat, or smash it into splinters.

They slid forward, losing way as the oarsmen eased up. Gay

squatted behind the gun, peering over open sights at the massive target ahead.

'Now,' Dunn said softly.

Gay fired. A second's silence followed the click of the trigger, and then the wickedly barbed iron harpoon arced across the water, the black streak of the line hissing in its wake. The men watched intently, and Douglas saw Scrimmy flinch at the muted thump of the harpoon embedding itself in the whale's back.

'Back water – quickly.' Dunn gave loud, rapid commands, the need for silence now gone. 'Hurry, for the love of God!'

A moment after the harpoon struck, the whale flailed its tail in agony. The massive flukes smashed down on the surface of the water, and the sea seemed to explode: green-silver water rose, hung for an instant in the air, then cascaded down, drenching the Greenlandmen as they frantically backed away. Gay hoisted a hand-harpoon from its mik and stood ready to strike. Robertson checked the line that hummed from the foreganger of the iron already fired.

As the whale dived, hauling the line behind it, Robertson calmly ducked out of the way, all his concentration upon the remaining four lengths of two-and-a-half-inch hempen line. At a hundred and twenty fathoms a line, that gave him a maximum of three-quarters of a mile between the boat and the whale, but the more line he paid out, the greater the chance of it snagging or curling back on itself.

'If that line should kink, Rab, my boy,' said Scrimmy, 'it would have your head off neat as a butcher's cleaver. But that's us that's got the first hook in. Fast-boat money, boys. That's whisky money for old Scrimmy.' He chuckled happily.

'We've got to land the fish first,' Hughson reminded him. 'Here we go.'

Still underwater, the whale was moving fast, towing the boat through brash-ice and white-flecked water. 'Up oars, boys,' Dunn commanded. 'Sit back and enjoy the ride.'

'And hold on, for God's own sake.' But the taciturn Greig's advice was wholly unnecessary.

After a few minutes the whale surfaced, still moving at some speed. Bows lifted high, the boat seemed to fly along in the great fish's wake. Gripping the gunwale to prevent himself sliding off the thwart, Douglas listened to Scrimmy's muttered commentary.

'That's the way, tire yourself out, Whaley . . . On you go, now . . . Tow away, but will you head in a circle, please, so we don't have so far to row to get back to *Fisty*? . . . And don't dive under the ice, please.'

Gay and Robertson stood in their allotted places, balancing effortlessly as the boat leaped and plunged. Gay still hoped to throw one of his three hand-harpoons. Robertson tended the line, watching for the fatal kinks that could mean disaster or dismemberment for any of the crew.

'She's tiring – not long now.' Gay watched intently as the whale's frantic dash eased into a steadier pull. The boat's bow dropped to the surface of the sea and the men relaxed a little. The whale stopped moving. Robertson coiled the suddenly slack line round the bollard-head, then jerked back as the whale plunged forward again. The line screamed out once more, smoking as the friction of its passage set it alight.

'Bugger.' Robertson emptied pannikins of seawater on the bollard-head.

The bows rose again as the whale raced away from *Redgauntlet*.

'Hughson, how long will this last?' asked Douglas.

'As long as it takes. Could be half an hour, could be five hours. Depends how strong the whale is.' He nodded astern. 'Here's help coming now, though.'

A second boat was approaching, its sail bellying in the wind and five oars dipping madly.

'That's the bran-boat at last. They're missing Symbister, though – see how they have to compensate for his oar? He'll get something to remember when they get back to *Old Fisty*.'

The bran-boat drew level, the men hauling at the oars and the harpooner squatting behind his gun. Douglas saw the puff of smoke, heard the flat report and saw the whale convulse as the barbs slammed home. Again there was the jerk, the surge forward, but the whale was weaker now, and had twice the weight to tow. When it slowed, Robertson coiled more of the line around the bollard-head, keeping it taut.

Dunn ordered them forward and said, 'Right, Gay, now – *now!*'

Gay stood in the bows holding the harpoon, three feet of barbed iron with a nine-foot wooden shaft, in both hands above his head. He paused for a second as the whale slowed, then thrust home, grunting with effort. The point thumped home a handspan behind the whale's hump and he twisted the barbs deeper into the immense body. This time the result was less galvanic, but Robertson was still kept busy with the line and pannikins of water as smoke and small flames rose from the bollard-head.

A third boat joined them, with the oarsmen gasping with exertion and Gillespie, the spektioneer and harpooner, still ludicrously dressed in Neptune's robes. A fourth harpoon plunged home: this time the whale only twitched.

'She's tiring, lads. Lances now.' Dunn steered the boat clear of the whale's tail, which was still lashing the water.

Gay took up the first of the four lances that lay in the bottom of the boat. Wickedly lethal, they had long heads which the spektioneer had honed to slice into the bulk of the whale. Dunn manoeuvred the boat to within a few yards of the animal, which heaved as it fought to breathe. Douglas's sympathy returned in full measure, along with a mad excitement at defeating such a vast adversary. Gay held his lance poised high a second, then stabbed it home with all his strength, aiming for the lungs. He twisted the shaft once, then reached for another.

'Her chimney's alight!' Greig pointed to the top of the whale, then cursed as he was suddenly covered in thick red and white froth.

Wiping the mess from his own face, Douglas looked over and saw that the whale was spouting mingled blood and water from its blowhole.

'Gay's got her lungs. She's a goner.' Scrimmy sat silent for a moment, resting his head on his arms. 'Hard luck, Whaley, but you had to die to feed a hundred Dundee bairns. And that's one for *Old Fisty*. Where's your unlucky ship now, then?'

Above them the mollies were already beginning to circle, sensing food.

But the hunt was not yet finished. The boat pulled slowly round to the whale's head and Gay lifted the slenderest of the lances, poised for a second and thrust it through the creature's great staring eye. When there was no response, the men cheered loud and long. They had killed their first whale of the season; *Redgauntlet*'s luck had returned, and there would be oil- and bone-money on their return to Dundee.

But first they had to get there; Douglas calmed his elation. Killing a whale would help to make the voyage a success, but it did not answer the many questions that plagued him. From Wyllie's involvement to seamen being warned off *Redgauntlet* to the letter summoning him to Ma Scott's, and above all the loss of *Ivanhoe*: how could all these things be covered by a single explanation? Perhaps this voyage would be a success, but he had not yet earned his pay.

'Here, Greenman – what's your name again? – Douglas. Stop daydreaming there and start working. We've a lot of work ahead of us yet.'

There was always a lot of work on a whaling-voyage. After the kill came the tow, with the whale's fins tied beneath its belly and towropes passed through holes bored in its tail. Tam told him that six boats could tow an average whale about one sea-mile in an hour. With three boats pulling and two miles to cover, the toil was torturous, but the men's spirits stayed high, and they sang an off-key and obscene version of 'Highland Laddie' which Douglas had not heard before.

Guided to *Redgauntlet* by the steady ringing of her bell, they all cheered when they pulled the whale alongside and eased the aching muscles of their arms and backs. But their work was still not done.

'We'll make the most of the good weather,' Houston decided. 'Hughson, get aloft and keep watch for more whales. The rest of you, get into your flensing-rig.'

Two of the boats were hoisted inboard and the third was put on bran. As spektioneer, Gillespie would be in charge of the flensing. The experienced men pulled on clothes which were already black with dried blood and blubber and began to sort through a selection of flensing-knives, savage weapons with handles four feet long and wicked, cleaver-like blades. Two of the harpooners attached great spurs to their boots and lowered themselves on to the whale's back to begin the flensing.

Gillespie ordered a long strip of meat to be cut from near the backbone.

'We'll eat that,' Tam told Douglas. He looked happier now, his eyes calm again and his hands no longer twitching as they had been. 'Now watch, for we'll all be busy shortly.'

The spurred harpooners hacked off the whale's head and hoisted it aboard, dripping blood, oil and water. That done, they used the flensing-knives to slice the blubber beneath the skin. Douglas had expected crude butchery, but the Greenlandmen were highly skilled, First, they removed from round the neck a collar of blubber. Then they put a wicked-looking hook into the flapping end of blubber still attached to the whale, which the whalers called the kant. They attached the hook to a windlass, which rotated the whale, enabling them to slice off the blubber evenly all round the carcass.

The process was systematic and thorough, interrupted only by the hundreds of mollies that flocked the ship, cackling hoarsely and flapping round the men's head in their frantic search for food. The men cursed them viciously, and swung their knives at them. A huge fish swam up, its gaping jaws showing an impressive array of teeth, and took an enormous bite out of the carcass.

'That's a shark, isn't it?' said Douglas.

Scrimmy glanced over from where he was chopping blubber into blocks and throwing it into the waist of the ship. 'Aye,' he said, 'Greenland shark. They often appear. It's all right though, soldier-boy, I've never known one to attack a man.'

'No?' Douglas recalled the evil shapes that had followed the troopships through tropical waters, and the dreadful tales of sharks attacking the survivors of *Birkenhead*. 'No wonder those lads wear spurs. I wouldn't fancy falling in with these brutes aside.'

Besides keeping an eye on the weather, Houston supervised the loading of the blubber as it was swung aboard by block and tackle. Now the unskilled men like Douglas were set to work, taking the great chunks of greasy blubber from the deck and thrusting them through the entry-holes of the iron storage-tanks. The whole ship was filled with the noise of the birds, the men's raucously cheeerful voices, and the stink of blood and whale, which seemed to penetrate into every pore of Douglas's body.

At last, after four laborious hours, all the useful blubber had been flensed and the great strips of baleen were hanging to dry in the chill wind. But there was still work to be done.

Houston ordered that the ship be thoroughly cleaned. 'That's only one whale. I want many more before this voyage is done. Get working, you lazy bastards.'

'And while you work, a dram for the crew, a dram for the ship.' Captain Fairweather smiled as he gave the order, which Macmillan, the bosun, obeyed with great alacrity.

'Man, Captain, you're the boy for me,' said Scrimmy with a grin, as the bosun handed him his gill of neat rum.

Even Tam looked pleased, though he drew Douglas's attention to Symbister, who, still in Mrs Neptune's costume, accepted his dram with tearstained face and shaking hands. 'Bairns, eh?' said Tam. 'They're always greeting at something or other. Somebody was probably getting on at him for missing his boat.'

Douglas was too busy with a hose and brush to pay much attention, or to wonder more than briefly what was the matter with the lad. He and the other Greenmen scrubbed and cleaned, scrubbed and cleaned, while *Redgauntlet* pushed on northward up the Davis Strait.

Next morning they found Symbister's naked body in the cable tier, his Mrs Neptune costume folded neatly at his side. The doctor said it was probably suicide.

Davis Strait, Summer 1860

'With Riff Koll Hill and Disco dipping/There you'll see the whale-fish skipping.' Scrimmy intoned the old whalers' rhyme as *Redgauntlet* eased into the Danish settlement of Godhavn on the island of Disco. There were other ships in the bay, whalers from Dundee and Peterhead and the last survivors of the once-mighty Hull fleet, as well as a trader from Denmark and a few light canoes – Hughson said they were called kayaks – which skiffed across the water like paper darts.

'That's the Yakkies.' Scrimmy pointed them out in case Douglas had been afflicted with sudden blindness. 'They live around here. Great people – do anything for you.'

'What are the women like?' Smith wondered. 'Do they like Scotsmen?'

'Too good for you, you whistling green landsman bastard.' Hughson cuffed him absently. 'Anyway, it's on sideways up here. The cold does that to them, so you'd have to be a contortionist, like in the circus.'

'What's on sideways?' Smith asked, and the Greenlandmen grinned at one another.

Scrimmy gestured to his groin. 'It is, you lubber. You have to lie athwart the woman's hawse up here. God, but you're stupid.'

'How do you do that?'

The Greenlandmen laughed again. They had caught another three whales on their voyage up the warm-water current that made the west coast of Greenland navigable, so they looked with some pride at the garland that fluttered at their masthead.

'Do we fish around here?' Douglas asked.

Hughson shook his head. 'No. The best fishing is in the West Water, across Melville Bay.'

'We're going there next, then?'

'If the ice lets us.' Hughson looked at the sky. 'And that depends on the wind.'

'The passage is known as the Breaking-Up Yard,' said Tam, 'because so many ships have been lost there. It's usually covered in ice, and we have to wait for a gap. Once we start sailing west, we have to keep going – there's no turning back – and if a north wind blows up we're in real trouble.'

'Why?' Douglas could guess the answer, but Tam enjoyed being the bearer of bad tidings.

'The wind blows ice down from the great northern fields, and *Redgauntlet* would get trapped.' He gestured to the western horizon. 'It's a ships' graveyard out there – and a sailors' graveyard, too. It'll be a miracle if we make it in *Old Fisty* with her jinx.'

Douglas thought of the seaman who had been washed overboard and the suicide of young Symbister. He pictured the scene again: the young man's naked body lying face down across a coil of rope, the blood on his legs where he must have cut himself, Mrs Neptune's costume neatly folded at his side. What despair had driven the boy to take his life?

'Aye, poor wee Symbister.' Scrimmy was suddenly sombre as he again caught Douglas's thoughts. 'His first voyage out, and his last.'

'Just like *Ivanhoe*.' Tam stepped back from the rail and faced west. 'And now we're sailing in her wake, out to the West Water and Hopeful Point. God have mercy on us all.'

'Maybe He will, but I won't.' Houston loomed over them, his rasping voice a reminder that some things never changed. 'You've got work to do.'

There was always work on *Redgauntlet*. There was work as she moved north, the crew gesticulating obscenely as they passed

Charleston. There was work when a sudden fog clamped down, deadening sounds so that every footfall was muffled and the hush of the sea was soft and sinister. There was work when they passed the hill that the experienced men called Kettle-Bottoms-Up, a name which made Dr Michie smile. There was work when they passed the Devil's Thumb, an isolated stack of rock which beckoned with sardonic humour to the whaling-ships sailing into danger.

Captain Fairweather had grown up and grown grey in the terrible beauties of the Arctic. He formed the crew along the deck as *Redgauntlet* passed barely a cable's length from the Thumb.

'Hats off, boys.' The order was unexpected, for the Captain habitually allowed Houston to take command. 'Pay respect to the Devil's Thumb.' Keeping their faces solemn, the crew removed their protective fur hats and saluted the rock. 'And may we be granted a successful voyage.'

'Tell that to Symbister,' Tam muttered.

'The man who spoke may remain at the masthead for the remainder of the day.' The Captain's voice was mild, but Tam moved at once.

Night in the Arctic was unimaginably different from anything Douglas had ever experienced. Years spent soldiering in the Southern Hemisphere had accustomed him to the clarity of the African air, but the Arctic stars pierced such brilliant apertures in the night that he felt scrutinised by God. Unusually, the engineer was on deck, cheerfully commenting that he was getting paid for doing nothing, when the northern sky exploded into life. First it was azure, then brilliant bands of green, red and yellow light flickered from horizon to horizon, wavering in an eerie silence which made Douglas wonder about the ships that had gone missing up here and the men who would never return.

' "What's that?" you ask.' The engineer used an oily thumb to stuff tobacco into his pipe. 'That's the smile of God. They call them the Northern Lights, or the Heavenly Dancers. Fascinating, aren't they?' He craned his head back. 'I've heard that they're caused by electricity, and if you concentrate you can nearly hear the electric in the air.'

They watched in silence as the lights merged into a vast curtain which encompassed the whole of the northern sky. Wavering beams of yellow arose in folds from the horizon to explode in vibrating flame, paling into near-invisible feathers through which bright stars glittered. The array of colours spread a strange peace over the stark seascape, so that even the immense expanse of chilled waves looked beautiful.

Douglas allowed his eyes to wander, noting the ratlines etched against the changing sky, the rise and fall of the bowsprit, the reflection of the sky in the ice that brushed against the side of the ship. He could not hear the electricity, only the wind breathing a celestial tune on the harp-strings of the rigging and the creak of wood on wood like the rubbing of branches in an enchanted forest.

'It's good up here.' The engineer smiled at Douglas, drawing on his pipe so the tobacco glowed red and warm and friendly in the night. 'I like the feeling of being on the fringe of the Great Unknown, with all the space in the world to ourselves.' He jerked his thumb aft, dismissing civilisation with a contempt which would have horrified his progressive peers. 'What is there back south? Dirt and disease and factories and crowds and machinery. How can a man live with that?'

'But you're an engineer,' Douglas pointed out. 'You're on the edge of progress, bringing light to darkness, educating the heathen.'

'Bugger all that.' The engineer shook his head. 'I'm an engineer because it pays well and it's a job with a future. Do you really think the heathen want to be educated into mill workers when they can walk into this vastness? Do you honestly believe that they would be better as the crippled wrecks you see limping from the factories to the pubs? I don't. They're happy, so we should leave well alone.'

Douglas thought of the natives of the Cape Frontier. They had been walking into vastness for millennia, until they were displaced by the Trekboer, the wandering Boers, and eventually had nowhere left to go. He thought of the few Bushmen he had seen, small people who melted into the land and seemed to live on nothing. 'Perhaps you're right.'

He looked again at the sky, and contemplated the beauty and the vastness. In the Arctic, as in Africa, beauty and danger co-existed, as if the edge of disaster spurred a zest for life. Fleetingly, he wished he had somebody to share that knowledge with, somebody who might understand on a deeper level than Scrimmy or Tam. The thought of Miss Gilbride came unbidden into his head but he pushed it roughly aside. She was of a class far above his; their worlds were as far apart as Dundee was from the Gaikas. There was also the letter, but he shied away from that question.

'Douglas, get below and get pumping. Do you think this is a pleasure cruise?' Houston was glaring at him and things had returned to normal. Even the Heavenly Dancers seemed suddenly dimmer.

Ice was frequent now, with bergs sometimes a mile wide, and two days after the Thumb they came to the ice-field.

'Welcome to Melville Bay and the Breaking-Up Yard,' Cargill said quietly.

Douglas stared at the panorama of unbroken ice that blocked their passage, an infinity of hummocky white that stretched to the horizon. Little waves splashed along the edge as the sea contested this frozen challenge to its dominion. 'Where does it all come from?'

'Ice builds up on the rocky islands on the north shore of Melville Bay.' Cargill nodded to starboard. 'The tide pushes the ice westwards, and the current takes it south, right across our path. What we want is a southerly wind to open a passage.'

He leaned back and sniffed the wind. 'Reckon there's one coming soon.'

Douglas nodded, accepting Cargill's judgement. He had learned that the old seamen could sense a coming change in the weather. They were constantly aware of the direction of the wind and the feel of the ship, unconsciously interpreting every sign Nature sent them. Scanning the frozen sea ahead, he saw a colony of seals watching the ship, while a dozen of the small black birds that the whalers knew as dovekies sat in a solemn row along the edge of the ice like a pew of Free Kirk ministers.

'They often sit like that,' Tam told him, 'just watching and waiting for us to die.'

For the first time since they had left Lerwick, Captain Fairweather ordered the engines to be started. *Redgauntlet* vibrated with new life as she probed for a passage to the West Water. She cruised first north and then south along the ice-rim, the black smoke from her funnel a reminder of the industry that had spawned her, while her crew whetted their killing-tools and dreamed of whales and money and their wives. There were sails astern as other whalers breasted the horizon, a gathering of predators coming to ravage the virginal purity of the North.

'There's *Enterprise* again, carrying her bad luck with her.' Tam pointed to a set of sails.

'Aye,' said Hughson, 'and that's *Charleston* astern of her. She seems to be watching over us.'

'I'm glad somebody is.' Tam nodded at the funnel with its *W* pierced by the quill. 'I'm expecting that thing to explode at any time.'

Snow showers were more frequent now, and Douglas spent every watch chipping ice from the spars and cables. 'This is where the steamship scores,' said Hughson, apparently happy to embrace new technology, 'for the heat from the funnel keeps the ice down. I've sailed on ships where the ice was a foot thick on deck and the frost formed on your blankets as you slept.'

As he worked, with the hammer blistering his hand and the

sweat freezing on his beard, Douglas wondered what he was doing there. His surroundings felt surreal after the bright colours of Africa, dead after the bustle of Dundee. Even more importantly, would he have a job when he returned, or had Mr Gilbride dispensed with his services as soon as he found out about the Chartist connection?

Chip, chip, chip at the shining ice. As he worked, slipping on the treacherous surface of the deck, Douglas recited to himself the old mariners' maxim of 'One hand for yourself and one for the ship.'

The work, though arduous, was monotonous and left his mind free to wander. The ugly suspicion returned that perhaps Miss Gilbride had intended to have him crimped. Might it be that she was working with Wyllie and had deliberately sent him into a trap? She might have recognised his tattoos, and resolved that no Chartist should work for her father.

There was also mystery over Symbister's death. The surgeon had pronounced it suicide, but why should the boy kill himself? And why strip naked first? Save for the dried blood on his thighs, there had been no obvious wound, so how had he died? Not by asphyxiation, for Douglas had seen hanged men: their faces were blackened, their tongues and eyes protruded, and their necks were twisted, bruised and torn. Nor had he died by knife or gun; perhaps it had been poison, then?

And then there was Mrs Gordon. Although there had been no sightings of the ghost for weeks, she remained a problem. There would be bad trouble if the superstitious Greenlandmen learned they had a woman on board.

Chip, chip, chip. This was as bad as manning the pumps, except that at least on deck he could see the world. There were polar bears on the ice, great white monsters which lumbered dangerously close to *Redgauntlet* as she slipped slowly through the water with her funnel belching smoke and her screw churning the sea.

Responding to a request from Houston, Captain Fairweather

allowed a party of men to hunt the seals that watched them through soft eyes. Douglas watched the resulting slaughter with mixed feelings. The sight of grown men bludgeoning animals to death with great clubs was not pretty. If the ladies of fashion knew the history of their fur coats they might not be so keen to buy them. On reflection, Douglas changed his mind. From what little he had seen of ladies of fashion, he doubted they would care, so long as they got what they wanted. Anyway, the pelts were not the Greenlandmen's main object. They were after the oil that would fuel the lights that made the streets safer for those fur-clad ladies.

The voice from the crow's nest rang out. 'Deck, there! A gap.'

As usual, Houston raced up the mast to see for himself. 'Call the Captain. Tell him there's a possible channel to the south-west.'

Houston could make alterations in course to save the ship from icebergs or storm, but only the Master had the authority to take her into the Breaking-Up Yard, where a shift of wind could trap a ship as securely as if she were entombed in solid rock. Nodding to the man at the wheel, Captain Fairweather slowly climbed to the crow's nest and squeezed in beside Houston. Every man on deck watched intently as he extended his telescope, for the success or failure of the voyage rested on his decision. The telescope moved from north to south, then slid in a great circle encompassing the entire horizon. Then he laughed, said something to Houston, returned to the deck and disappeared into his cabin. Only then did Houston give the orders that turned *Redgauntlet* to head south and west towards the channel in the ice.

'Here we go, then.' Tam looked dourly up at the sky, where white light gleamed round the edges of grey cloud. 'There's snow on the way and we're following *Ivanhoe* to Hopeful Point.'

'God save us all.' Robertson touched the lucky charm he wore round his neck, a scrimshaw whale. He had carved it himself on a successful voyage five years previously and claimed that it had kept him safe ever since.

'Amen to that.' Suddenly religious, Dunn took a deep breath. 'We could do with one of the Captain's sermon's now.'

Westward into the Breaking-Up Yard. A hundred and fifty miles of danger so extreme that in 1830 nineteen British whalers foundered and their crews, a thousand men in all, had followed custom and ransacked the ships, especially the spirits lockers; the ensuing carousal on the ice had become known, with biting humour, as Baffin Fair. Westward toward the whaling-grounds; westward into the ice, sailing over the graves of a hundred ships. Westward to find their fortune. Westward.

Houston ordered that the seamen should have their sea-chests packed in case of shipwreck. Most of the crew slept fully dressed and with a gasket of clothes to hand, and Tam exchanged bunks so that he was nearer the foc'sle hatch.

Douglas passed an entire watch carrying provisions from the hold to the deck. Once, Mary smiled at him from a dark corner of the hold. She did not offer to help, and neither of them spoke.

Once, when he reached the deck Scrimmy was waiting for him, grinning. 'Rab, lad, old Horse has put two years' supplies on this ship,' he said happily, as he stuffed a tin of Morton of Leith's Best Canister Meat inside his fur jacket. 'So me and you'll share some when we're off duty tonight.'

Douglas nodded. He dumped a boxful of tins on deck and lifted one. 'You take Morton's. I've already got two of these under my bunk – Robert Kinness's best. All the way from East Whale Lane.'

Scrimmy laughed. 'You're learning, my boy. Just don't let Houston catch you.'

Learning? Douglas thought of the times he had scrounged for loot or food, rummaging through native huts for a calabash of beer, or prodding his bayonet into the dirt floor of a Boer farmhouse in the hope of finding buried money. They had often found the native beer, but the Boer farmhouses had held only hand-made furniture and the family Bible. A sudden vision of Miss Gilbride's hazel-flecked brown eyes made him pause.

What would she think of a man who did such things? But then why should she think of him at all?

The channel was perhaps twice the width of *Redgauntlet*, ragged at the edges where ice had broken off, occasionally overlooked by precarious mountains of ice created by the wind piling up the floes one on top of another. Three times she was halted as the passage froze in front of her. Twice she was able to move astern, build up speed and ram her reinforced bows through the ice. The third time, however, even her seventy-horsepower engine was not enough, and Captain Fairweather ordered the men to carve out an anchorage.

'Here we go.' Tam took up the nine-foot ice-saw with both hands. 'We'll be stuck here for months now, unless the boiler blows up.'

'I'll blow up unless you get a move on, Wilson.' Houston jerked his thumb toward the ice. 'Fly.'

The Greenmen could only watch as the experienced men slithered over the side and literally sawed a sheltered anchorage out of the ice. Once again Captain Fairweather passed round rum to encourage the men, while the ever-attentive Dr Michie treated the blisters that formed on even the Greenlandmen's work-hardened hands.

'Man, Rab, this is the best voyage I've ever been on.' Scrimmy sat on the rail with his rum in one hand while the surgeon dressed the blisters on the other. 'The best of attention and plenty rum. Whaler's paradise, this.'

When, a little later, a northerly wind drove bitter snow into their faces and pressed the ice against *Redgauntlet* so that her reinforced hull creaked in protest, Tam reminded Scrimmy of his optimistic words. 'Some bloody paradise this, Scrimmy, man. If the wind pushes much harder we'll be out on the ice.'

'So much the better,' retorted Scrimmy. 'Then we'll have the run of the spirits locker.'

On the third day the wind veered east, then south, pushing back the ice so that the passage opened before them and

Houston's roar chivvied the men back to work. The great fist on *Redgauntlet*'s bow cast eerie shadows on the ice as she cleaved westward, with the mollies flocking hopefully and her crew alternately praying and blaspheming. After a ten-day passage which stretched the nerves of everyone aboard except Scrimmy, she steamed into clear water.

'We're through,' said Tam in astonishment. He stared astern, to where the sails of other whalers were visible. 'Is that *Charleston* there?'

Douglas shrugged. 'I don't know. One ship looks much alike another to me.'

'Aye, maybe so, but there's only one *Fisty*.' Scrimmy pointed aloft: a shaft of sunlight encircled the garland in a golden halo. 'And there's our luck, boys, guiding us to where the whalefishes blow.'

Scrimmy's words proved prophetic, for two whales were sighted the next day, and one was caught. The triumph was soured, though, when a sudden lash of the whale's tail rammed the steering-oar into Dunn's chest, smashing him face down across the thwarts and breaking a rib.

Scrimmy helped him to Dr Michie's cabin. 'You'll have a wee rest now, Dunny, while we catch the fishes for you. Just save some of the doctor's brandy for me.'

Two days later, with *Redgauntlet* pushing northward under easy sail and the gaunt black cliffs of Hopeful Point to port, the now familiar hail came from aloft: 'A fall. A fall! Two points to starboard and barely a mile away!'

'Thank you, *Fisty*.' Scrimmy patted the rail as he followed Douglas into the port whaleboat. 'You're nosing out the fishes this season.'

'We'll have less movement of your tongue and more of your hands,' Houston growled. 'I'm your new boat-header, so God help you if we're not first to this fish.' He snatched the steering-oar as though it was an enemy. 'I want this boat to fly!'

Scrimmy winked at Douglas and hauled on his oar. 'Here we go, then, fast-boat again.'

Unlike the earlier hunts, when the water had been clear and sunlight had glinted from the blades of their oars, now the sky was matt grey, banded with streaks of orange, while they pulled through brash-ice so thick that it felt like porridge, just as Ecky had said in Lerwick. They manoeuvred past small floes, some bright and clean and high in the water, others grim and leaden and ominous, with small waves splashing across the surface.

'These are washing-pieces,' Scrimmy said, 'because the sea washes over the top of them.'

'It'll be washing over the top of you unless you work harder.' Houston squinted astern to check his bearings from Cargill's signals in *Redgauntlet,* and steered the boat so close to a cottage-sized floe that the men had to raise their port oars to avoid a collision. 'Where's that lubber signalling us to go now? There's nothing here but icebergs. Back oars; that floe's got an under-water spur that'll rip our keel off.'

As he rowed, Douglas could see the ship's topmasts disappearing behind the bergs. Smoke lifted from the funnel, then merged with a smirr of snow which smeared across the grey sky. The number of icebergs increased, until Houston had to concentrate more on the boat's safety than on finding the whale. As he steered round a large, anvil-shaped berg, he looked astern again. 'Easy all. Let's look for this whale.'

The bight formed by the anvil sheltered them from an increasingly bitter north wind but left the view to the south open. As the boat slowed, a shaft of sunlight angled through a gap in the clouds so that Douglas could see melting water trickling down the lee side of the berg. Floes bobbed uneasily in the swell. One was shaped like a church, another was long and low and constantly turning with the waves, a third had a triumphal arch through which spray splashed. There was silence for a minute as everybody listened for the distinctive snort of a whale sounding.

'No trace here,' Gay reported, 'just the bergs.' His voice echoed strangely from the ice wall of the anvil.

'Maybe we'd best get back to the ship.' Greig looked inquiringly at Houston, only his eyes, nose and mouth visible between his beard and his fur cap.

'Might be an idea,' Robertson agreed. He stood up, balancing easily on the thwart. 'No, I can't see her, either. I'll shin up the mast.' He slid up quickly, and held on with his left arm, shading his eyes with his right hand as he tried to peer beyond the anvil. 'No good, I still can't see. Neither ship nor whale. We'll have to pull free of the bight.'

The wind had risen in the last few minutes, and outside the shelter of the berg the waves were long and grey, with crests that curled into wicked silver fangs. Two waves broke over the gunwale, sending gallons of bitter water surging around the men's feet and legs.

'Douglas and Greig, bale.' Houston jerked his thumb at the pannikin. 'Lively, now.'

The cross-currents created by the bergs threw waves against the boat from half a dozen directions. Within ten minutes it was obvious that they would be swamped.

Houston loosed a volley of oaths, then growled, 'Back to the bight, boys. We'll have to shelter there until the wind moderates.'

'That might not be for days,' Gay pointed out. As a privileged harpooner he could argue with Houston.

'Or even weeks,' Houston agreed, 'but we wouldn't last two hours in this.' As if to emphasise his point, another cross-wave caught the boat, sending her spinning crazily until he dug the steering-oar deep into the water. 'Nor would we find *Redgauntlet.*'

Douglas had never heard Houston explain an order before and guessed that he was worried.

The rising wind moaned round the mast, and bitter, slushy water washed shin-high in the bottom of the boat.

158

'We need to find shelter now,' said Houston, 'not in an hour's time.'

Despite its size, the iceberg had been pushed a good quarter-mile to the south since they left, and the men felt the strain of weary muscles before they eased thankfully into its shelter. The wind had increased further, shrieking across the top of the anvil, and breaking the crest of the clawing waves. Houston threw a running bowline over a spur of ice, sat in the stern and held the steering-oar like a sentinel caressing his rifle.

There was no let-up in the wind that long day. It pushed the berg further and further south, through brash-ice that became thicker as the afternoon progressed. Twice short showers of snow obscured the sky, and once a seal surfaced nearby, but the men were no longer interested in hunting. Everybody knew that they were being driven further from *Redgauntlet*, further from safety and deeper into the ice wastes. Only Scrimmy stayed cheerful, with the mate's curses barely subduing his snatches of song. The boat, like every other under Houston's orders, carried seven days' supply of food and fresh water, but that could not stave off the danger of the cold.

'All of you, move your legs, stamp some warmth into your feet,' said Houston harshly. 'I'll have no frostbite aboard this boat. The first man to get frostbitten will swim back to *Fisty*.'

There was little to do save keep baling, watch the sky and hope.

At some time in the early hours Douglas heard a man praying softly, the sound only just audible above the whine of wind round the sharp edges of the berg and the occasional loud splash as ice fell into the sea. Somewhere a loon called, bleak, eerie and unutterably lonely in the night.

A deep-red band in the east heralded the dawn. It revealed a panorama of unremitting bleakness. They were drifting into a vast field of ice, varying from the slushy brash, through which they could row, to great ridges, as wide as a house and six feet high, stretching from horizon to horizon.

'God save us all.' Robertson stared to the south. 'Listen for *Old Fisty*'s bell, everybody.'

'And watch for the smoke from her funnel,' said Greig, quartering the sky.

'Wind's dropped,' Houston said briskly. 'We can get back on the move again.'

Leaving Gay in command of the boat, he slithered and dragged himself to the summit of the anvil. 'No sign of *Redgauntlet*,' he reported when he returned, 'nor of anything else.'

'Except ice,' Greig said.

'Aye, there's always plenty of that.' Houston looked his crew over. 'We're in a bit of a hole here, men. We're in the middle of the ice and we don't know where *Redgauntlet* is, but we can be certain that they're searching for us as hard as they can. The Captain will know the wind's pushed us south, so he's likely steaming towards us right now, with every man aloft and the ship's bell ringing like buggery. *Fisty*'s got a signal-gun, too, remember, so listen for it while we pull to the north. When the wind alters, we can hoist the sail. There are other ships in this area, so even if *Fisty* doesn't find us, one of them will.' For the second time in Douglas's experience, Houston smiled. 'We'll all feast on a biscuit, then we're off.'

It was not easy for cold-weakened men to row through the brash-ice, and three times that morning they had to alter course to pull round drifts stretching for hundreds of yards. Twice they entered banks of fog which eroded visibility and distorted sounds so that their hails echoed mockingly back to them. Once a whale surfaced a bare cable's length to starboard, and the hunters quailed before its size and power. They rowed on, with Scrimmy singing snatches of sea shanties and Greig grumbling.

After his experiences adrift the previous year, Houston had ensured that every boat was supplied with a bell, which he rang every quarter-hour. At first the men listened eagerly for a return peal from *Redgauntlet,* but by noon they were too tired to do anything but row and, when they were spelled, gnaw another biscuit. An hour later Houston pulled in beside a berg and ordered them to run up the gentle slope to the pinnacled summit and back. When Greig refused, he spun him round and literally kicked him up the slope. 'I'm not losing any of you bastards to frostbite. Run! Use your legs – *fly*, God damn you!'

They ran, gasping, slithering, swearing, and hating Houston even as they felt the newly flowing blood prickle and cramp in their muscles. Douglas halted at the top for a moment, his arm around one of the slender pinnacles, and he gazed out over the ice: there was no sign of *Redgauntlet* or any other ship. After that it was back to the boat, rowing, sounding the bell, hailing and listening for the sounds of rescue that never came. Only the occasional whir of seabirds' wings and the soft surge of the sea augmented the moan of the Arctic wind. On Houston's command they once again pulled northward into nothingness.

By mid-afternoon even Scrimmy was quiet. The strained gasps of labouring men, the creak of oars in rowlocks and the dismal splash of oar-blades in the porridgy ice were the only sounds. By dusk they were tiring, their arms and back burning with pain, their buttocks rubbed sore on the rough thwarts, their legs numb with the cold that seeped up from feet which had long since lost all feeling.

'Stamp your feet,' Houston ordered. 'Keep the blood flowing. One at a time, though, or we'll have the bottom out of the boat. Stamp! You first, Gay, then the rest, one at a time so that I can hear you. Stamp. And yell, too.'

They stamped and shouted, the sounds echoing in the desolation. They stamped as the cold night descended again and Houston steered them into open water which lapped against the gunwales. They stamped as they passed an ice-floe from which a colony of seals watched them with soft, dispassionate eyes. They stamped in despair even as they listened for *Redgauntlet's* bell.

'Watches.' Houston gave rapid orders. 'Two men to sleep at a time, two to keep rowing so we don't lose the headway we've made, two men to bail, and everybody to listen for *Fisty*.'

'Even the men who are sleeping, Mr Houston?' asked Scrimmy.

'Especially the men who are sleeping.'

It was vilely uncomfortable crouching between the thwarts among the twitching legs of cramped men while the wind sliced through even the thickest furs. The night was clear, with brilliant stars hanging from a pale heaven.

Greig looked balefully up at them. 'Tam always says *Redgauntlet* was born under an ill star. I wonder which one it was?'

'The North Star.' Houston pointed it out. 'That's the star that leads to the Pole. And that's where she is now, up there searching for us.'

'Unless she's blown up, like *Ivanhoe*,' Greig said quietly.

'If she has,' said Robertson even more quietly, 'there's nobody looking for us, because nobody knows we're here.'

The night gripped them with frost that clawed into feet and hands and thighs, while shards of fear pierced their imaginations. The wind moaned like a man in agony, and the surge of the sea sounded like the sough of winter wind through the naked trees of a graveyard. Out to starboard, a seabird called eerily and the fall of a whale sounded in the gloom.

The day dawned bleakly. Douglas wondered who would be the first to die. He looked around at the crew, considering what he knew of each man. Houston, the man of iron. Scrimmy, a model seaman when sober but hopelessly addicted to whisky. Greig, possibly mentally the weakest of them. Robertson, tough, unemotional, with the weather-lined face of a fisherman. Gay, the harpooner, whose wiry body concealed great strength.

'Hey, has Mars seen such men before?' Paddy was grinning, and that devil-may-care look was in his eyes. 'The stars have. You're missing something here, Robert.' His shako was battered, the neck-flap hanging ragged over his neck, and his mocking face leathered by the sun. Insects hummed around him, bright butterflies hovered above his shoulder. 'You're not thinking, boy. What have I always taught you? A soldier fights with his mind as much as with his body. Never stop thinking, never stop looking.'

'What?' Douglas dragged himself back. He stared around again, seeing the tired, gaunt, chilled faces and the ice.

'You all right, Rab, boy?' Scrimmy touched his arm. 'You were talking in your sleep there.'

Douglas nodded. He was well aware that Paddy had not spoken to him, but something beyond his consciousness was offering advice. Doubt nagged inside his head. Something was wrong: he had missed something obvious. But what? There was certainly nothing wrong in the boat; these seamen knew their trade too well for that. So where? Up aloft? A paling sky, fading stars. Nothing out of the ordinary; there must be something in the ice.

There was an infinity of ice, floes of different shapes and sizes, long ridges where drifting ice had been forced together by wind and current, isolated icebergs in an immense variety of silhouettes. One nearby looked like a cathedral, complete with spires of glistening ice. Another, in the distance, looked like a Dundee mill, bulky and proud. Between them was a lumpy berg with three remarkably slender peaks and a protuberance which looked like a knight on horseback.

Douglas felt his blood quicken suddenly – he'd thank Paddy later. 'Mr Houston, do you see anything strange about that lumpy iceberg there?' He was surprised at the steadiness of his pointing hand.

'Strange?' Houston glowered at him. 'Has the cold shrunk your brain? It's a bloody iceberg, made of bloody ice.'

'Man, Rab, it's a Crusader.' Greig pulled back as far as he could. 'Look. It's a knight on horseback galloping over the ice. The pub's got a picture just like it.'

A shiver which had nothing to do with the cold ran through the boat.

163

'That's the ghost,' said Robertson flatly. '*Fisty*'s gone down and her ghost's come to haunt us.'

Greig began to gabble, Scrimmy laughed and Gay reached for a harpoon.

'Ghost be buggered.' There was strain in Houston's voice. 'That's *Ivanhoe*'s figurehead. It must have been blown here when she exploded.' Automatically, he steered toward the fragment of his old ship, keen curiosity on his face.

'I thought she blew up away to the north, somewhere off Hopeful Point.' Gay clutched his harpoon, ready to fight whatever was on the ice, be it Crusader, ghost or polar bear.

'Currents – look how far we were pushed in just one night.' Houston sounded subdued, but immediately reverted to his usual nature. 'Pull, you God-damned idle bastards. Once we've seen Ivor, it's back to searching for *Old Fisty*. Now pull.'

As they neared the figurehead, Douglas watched Houston's expression. His initial suspicions about the mate's escape from *Ivanhoe* had weakened as he witnessed Houston work harder than anybody to keep *Redgauntlet* afloat. They had disappeared completely when he watched Houston care for his sister. Whatever the man's secret might be, Douglas was certain it had nothing to do with the loss of *Ivanhoe*.

Houston began to swear in a fluent stream of obscenities which began in a monosyllable and ended in a tone of rising wonder. 'That's not just the figurehead, lads, that's the whole bastarding ship! That's *Ivan*, full and intact and with her hand stretched out to pluck us safe from the ice.'

'Jesus! We're saved.' Greig began to shake.

Closing his eyes, Douglas silently thanked Paddy McBride for his guidance.

'If that's *Ivan*,' Robertson said, 'how is it we were told she blew up?'

'More importantly', Scrimmy said, 'if that's *Ivan*,' where's her crew?'

Davis Strait, Summer 1860

The knight on his prancing horse greeted them with an upraised icicle-festooned lance, while the berg's slender pinnacles turned out to be the ice-encrusted masts.

'Ahoy, *Ivanhoe*, ahoy!' Houston's roar startled a flight of birds half a mile away but there was no visible reaction on the ship. 'They may be asleep – they were always a lazy set of lubbers. Ahoy! Wake up there!' He steered the boat round the iceberg.

'There's no smoke from the funnel,' said Douglas, 'but shouldn't they have the boilers working to keep her warm?'

'They'll have run out of coal months ago,' Houston told him. 'Probably they're all huddled together in one of the cabins.'

Ice completely encased *Ivanhoe*. It lay two feet thick on her deck, clung eight feet in depth around her hull and sheathed every mast and spar; it had created a beautiful, glistening tomb.

Houston was first aboard her, slithering on the ice-covered deck. 'Greig, guard the boat. The rest of you, come with me. Let's see what's happened here.'

The deck was deserted, a white emptiness which subdued even Scrimmy.

'You two, Douglas and Scrymgeour,' ordered Houston, 'check Captain Adamson's quarters. Robertson and Gay, go below to the half-deck, see if you can rouse the officers. I'll try the foc'sle.'

Douglas and Scrimmy made their way carefully aft, with Scrimmy trying to sound cheerful. 'Blown up, was she? Doesn't look blown up to me. Sound as the Law, she is. Wait till the lads see us – won't they be surprised?'

They used Scrimmy's sea-knife to break the ice that sealed the cabin door and pushed hopefully in. A narwhal-tusk paperweight held down the chart of Melville Bay that lay open on the desk, but there was no one there, only the smell of damp and the glitter of ice.

Douglas opened the logbook and read the last entry: 'Two miles ESE of Hopeful Point. Mate out with a boat. Surgeon reports two men sick. Weather closing in. Snow.' There were whales' tails decorating the margin of many of the previous pages, sure sign that *Ivanhoe* had had a successful voyage. 'Mate out with a boat': that corresponded exactly with Houston's story.

Scrimmy pulled his sleeve. 'There's nothing for us here, Rab. Let's see what the others have found.'

Houston was leaning against the mainmast, his face drawn and white. He pointed silently to the foc'sle hatch, then slumped to his knees in the lee of the funnel.

'You look after the mate,' Douglas ordered, instinctively a sergeant again. 'I'll go below.'

He descended the slippery companionway to the foc'sle, which was identical to *Redgauntlet*'s. There were men in the bunks, some face down, some on their side and one sprawled across the sea-chests that served as a table. Ten men. All were dead. Their faces were whitened by frost or blackened by the ice, and a loathsome green mould tinged the hollows of their sunken cheeks. Some had their eyes open, and Douglas had the uneasy feeling that their stare challenged this living man who intruded into their quiet world.

Douglas had seen death in many of its forms along the Cape Colony frontier and in India, but he had never before seen a roomful of frozen men. Breathing softly, he checked each body, hoping against hope to feel a pulse, a flicker of breath. He found nothing.

Gently, he touched the shoulder of the nearest man. 'Sorry, boys, but there's nothing that I can do for you.' He eased the door closed behind him, and went back on deck.

'They're all dead,' said Robertson, staring at him in horror; his mouth was a black hole round which his beard was white-rimmed with frost. 'Down below, they're all dead.'

Douglas nodded. 'I know. I've just checked.'

'The bosun, Erchie, the second mate, Chippy, the carpenter, Three-Fingered Shug – all of them.'

Douglas realised that he meant different men. 'Where?' he asked.

'Below, in the half-deck.' Robertson shook his head, trying to dispel the horryfing sight. 'I knew them all. I've served with them, drunk with them. Jesus, man, I still owe Chippy five shillings; he'll not see it now.'

Patting the line-manager's arm in wordless sympathy, Douglas swung below. He found a scene like that in the foc'sle: the men lay frozen on the deck. Most looked peaceful, as though they had died in their sleep, but one or two appeared to have struggled before succumbing. There was a raised hand here, a clenched fist there, but resistance had not helped. All were dead, with the same vile green tinge on their cheeks.

While he waited on deck for Houston's next order, Douglas leaned against the foremast and pondered. A crew of frozen men on a ship which had been reported destroyed a year ago. Whaling-men were used to losses: hardly a season passed without one or more ships going down, while the loss of individual men, or the occasional boat's crew, was accepted as part of the job. Even so, there was something uncanny about *Ivanhoe*. Ecky's tale of her steaming away the day after she was said to have exploded, the fact that she was entire and un-damaged in the ice . . . Nothing made sense. As Paddy had told him, he was missing something.

On the thought, Douglas realised that no orders had yet come from Houston. He looked aft. The mate was still on his knees by the funnel, shoulders hunched, head hanging; he looked beaten. Douglas stepped away from the mast and straightened his shoulders. He had stood on the sidelines long enough; it was time he took part in this deadly game.

'They're frozen to death.' Douglas had gathered the whale-boat's crew in Captain Adamson's cabin. 'There's no one but us alive on the ship.'

Shocked faces stared silently back at him. Even Houston said nothing.

'Now,' Douglas ordered, 'I want a thorough inspection. Mr Houston, you know the crew. I want you to make a list of them. Write down the name of every man aboard *Ivanhoe* and we'll see if they're all accounted for – perhaps somebody else managed to escape. Scrimmy, you and Greig see if there's any food left. We could all do with a meal, something hot.' It was difficult to talk with his facial muscles half frozen: warmth and food were vital for them all.

'Something hot?' Gay glared at him through reddened eyes. 'If there was any fuel left, don't you think the crew would have used it? That's why they're all dead, man. This steam-kettle burned all the fuel so fast that they didn't last the winter.'

Douglas tapped the Captain's desk. 'This is wood – it'll burn. So will the cabin fittings, the spare spars, the canvas. There's plenty fuel. Go to the galley and make us something hot. And Scrimmy, keep clear of the rum.'

Houston came slowly back to life. 'You cold-blooded bastard,' he said, thrusting his great head across the desk. '*Ivanhoe*'s full of my shipmates – dead shipmates – and all you can think of is your belly. What sort of man are you?'

'The sort who's doing your job for you.' Douglas felt his own anger rising. After years of giving orders as a sergeant, it had been difficult to endure the mate's hazing. Now he would endure it no longer. 'I can't bring your shipmates back to life, but if we work together we might just pull through. Make that list, Mr Houston, while I try and save the lives of your men.'

'What?' Houston stared at him, the shock and horror changing to predictable rage. 'You cheeky bastard! I've always had my suspicions about you. Too cocky by half – and a creature of Wyllie's.'

Douglas rounded on him, exulting in the knowledge of what was to come. 'You're the one who fought for Wyllie. I didn't.'

Houston's fists bunched. He far outmatched Douglas in strength and weight, but Douglas had taken part in scores of bloody encounters with rival regiments, Indian sepoys and hostile tribesmen. He dodged the blow, ducked inside the mate's guard and smashed an elbow into his groin. As Houston grunted, Douglas followed up with a backward head-butt to the jaw, hooked his leg behind Houston's knee and thrust all his weight against the mate's chest.

Houston fell heavily, mouthing incoherent obscenities, and Douglas leaped on him and slammed his forehead against the bridge of the big man's nose. There was an immediate rush of blood. Douglas stood up and landed two solid kicks in Houston's ribs.

'When you get up, you can write me that list,' Douglas continued; he was surprised how calm his voice sounded. 'I want to know the name of every single man who should be aboard this ship.' He looked at the others. 'I'm going to see how many more bodies there are. Robertson, bring that storm lantern and come with me. Gay, you help Scrimmy and Greig. Keep busy, keep warm, keep alive.'

'And who are you to tell us what to do?' demanded Gay. As a harpooner, he was one of the elite, and he was not inclined to take orders from a Greenman.

'Robert Douglas, lately a sergeant in the Seventy-Third Foot.' He hoped he could placate Gay, because he would need the harpooner's cooperation. 'Listen, you men are seamen and you know what to do in a storm at sea. But this sort of thing is what I'm trained for, what I'm used to. Surely we can work together for our survival?'

Gay looked as if he wanted to argue, but a glance at Houston, who was heaving himself to his feet, blood still streaming from his nose, dissuaded him. He nodded and said, 'We'll find enough fuel to keep us warm.'

The other men took their cue from him, and dispersed to begin work.

They found Captain Adamson in the coal-bunker, face down with a shovel in his hand, as dead as all his crew. While Robertson held the lantern, Douglas turned the body over, looked at the sunken eyes and saw only desperation.

The lantern cast long, flickering shadows among the whitened mounds in the coal-bunker. Using the heel of his boot, Douglas kicked the nearest mound until something skittered free. He picked it up, rubbed off the frost and raised it to the light: coal. Black, dirty, life-saving coal. He threw it back on the heap, his mind wrestling with a new mystery. There must be hundreds of tons here, more than enough to power the boilers, many times more than enough to have warmed the ship for months. So why, in God's name why, had her crew died of cold?

As they left the bunker, Douglas noticed something lying in the angle between the companionway and the bulkhead. He picked it up and rubbed away the covering of frost. It was a piece of smooth green stone, expertly carved into the likeness of a bear. He automatically put it in his pocket, and then hurried back to the Captain's cabin.

There he found that Scrimmy had lit the stove and Houston had thawed enough of the ink on the desk to write out the crew-list. Heat from the stove had spread around the cabin, freeing the books on the shelf from their prison of ice and exposing the fine panelling of the bulkheads. Small tears of water slid from the furniture and fell heavily and steadily on to the thawing carpet. The face of the chronometer on the wall could be seen again: it had stopped at three o'clock.

The warmth was ecstasy after so long in the unheated whaleboat, and Douglas told Robertson to go and fetch all the other men. While he waited for them, he studied the crew-list. There had been forty-eight men on *Ivanhoe*, but only twenty-eight bodies had been found. Houston and his boat's crew had been out hunting seals, and the ship's surgeon had survived, which meant that twelve men were still unaccounted for. Why? What had become of them?

When the rest of the crew arrived, they looked numb, as if they refused to accept the truth. Douglas had seen expressions like that before, in the aftermath of battle, or when a frontier patrol returned from the site of a massacre. They needed somebody to take charge.

'Listen, lads. I haven't been quite straight with you. I was a sergeant, that's true, but now I work for Mr Gilbride as his Personal Assistant.' He watched for a reaction but most of the men seemed too stunned to care. Gay looked sideways at him. Houston curled a blood-smeared lip.

'And what does that mean?' Houston mouthed the question through swollen lips.

'It means that although you have charge of the ship, Mr Houston, I am taking charge here. Got that?' There was no reply. Douglas continued, 'There are mysteries about *Ivanhoe*, and two vital questions which must be answered. First, why did most of her crew freeze to death in a ship full of coal? Second, twelve men are not among the dead but are missing. What has become of them?'

Only Houston, Gay and Scrimmy responded. They shook their heads blankly.

'Then have we have a Flying Dutchman here? An insoluble mystery?'

At once, fear began to tinge the faces before him as superstition, the curse of Greenland men, replaced shock.

Douglas toyed with the carved bear in his pocket, hoping for some help. 'Well, what do you think? There must be something that you seamen can see but I can't.'

'Maybe it was mutiny.' Gay avoided looking at Houston. 'Maybe the Captain was a tyrant and the mate was a bully, and the men mutinied and killed each other.'

171

'Adamson a tyrant?' Houston barked a laugh. 'He was even softer than Fairweather. And the mate was me. I'm no bully – as you all know. Firm but fair, that's me. Mutiny? I'd soon have sniffed that out, by God. There were no mutineers aboard *Ivanhoe*.'

Douglas nodded. To give the man his due, he was always keenly aware of the temper of his crew. He would indeed have sensed a mutiny. 'Any other ideas?

'There are three boats missing.' Trust Houston to notice that. 'I was out in one, so that leaves two. Two boats, two crews – twelve men. Maybe they were out after a whale and couldn't get back.'

Douglas nodded. 'That seems the most likely explanation. *Ivanhoe* was seen steaming away from Hopeful Point, so perhaps the men had to be abandoned for some reason.'

'Can't think why.' Robertson was resting his chin in his hands as he sat half slumped across the Captain's desk. 'Why abandon men in the ice? And how did the crew die? There was no reason for them to freeze to death.'

'And they were all green.' Greig sounded close to breaking-point. 'All their faces were green – like the ghost.'

'No, it was the cold that made them green; I've seen the like before. And we found the ghost, remember?' Even now, grieving for his shipmates and nursing the bruises of his fight with Douglas, Houston was quick to protect his sister. 'It was a stowaway. And there was never a ghost on *Ivanhoe*.'

'I heard stories about one,' argued Greig.

A lump of melting ice slapped on to the bookshelf, and only Houston did not jump or flinch.

'I served on her and I know,' he said flatly. 'There was no ghost. Nor did she blow up. I think somebody's been spreading tales, Mr Personal Assistant Douglas.'

Douglas nodded. He put the carved bear on the desk in front of him. 'I believe you're right, Mr Houston. But why? And who? And has that anything to do with the death of the crew?'

The mate shrugged. 'Damned if I know, and damned if I care much. All that matters is that there are twelve men missing. When I left Ivan she had a full crew. I was told she blew up and I believed it.'

'Mrs Gordon didn't,' Douglas reminded him. 'She said she knows her man's still alive.'

Houston narrowed his eyes warningly. 'I want to find out what happened to these men far more than you do. I knew them. They were my shipmates. But even so, I think we have more important matters to deal with. We have to keep ourselves alive.'

Douglas flicked the stone bear with his finger so that it rolled across the desk; Scrimmy caught it instinctively. He met Houston's eyes and went on, 'Maybe these men thought the same. Maybe there is something in this ship that killed them. I've heard that blubber sometimes causes poisonous fumes.'

'Aye, it does,' Houston agreed, 'but that's when men are stuck in the hold with casks of blubber. Ivan's designed so that the men are never *in* the blubber tanks. Anyway, these men died all over the bloody ship.'

'Not the blubber, then. Could it have been fumes from the funnel or the stoves? Poisonous coal?'

Greig instantly shifted away from the stove, but Houston merely kicked it and said contemptuously, 'Poisonous coal, my arse. These men died of the cold. I've seen it before. I was in a whaleboat full of men dying of the cold. Believe me, that's what killed these men, too.'

'So the question,' Douglas said, 'is why? Why didn't they light a stove?'

'Maybe there was somebody else here,' suggested Scrimmy. He held up the bear. 'Where did you find this, Rab?'

'Below, near the main coal-bunker.'

'Show me that.' Houston snatched the bear and looked closely at it. 'This is Yak work. They barter stuff like this for metal tools – knives, axes, things they can't make themselves.'

'Yak?' asked Douglas.

'Esquimaux,' said Gay, 'native people. We saw them in Disco Bay, remember?' He reached for the bear. 'It probably belonged to one of the crew, and he dropped it.'

'By the coal-bunker? This was the engineer's first whaling trip.' Houston shook his head. 'The firemen, too – I remember them at the ice ceremony.'

'He could have got it from another of the crew,' Gay said stubbornly.

'He could have got it from up his breech but he didn't. There's been a Yak on board, probably more than one.' Houston set the bear very carefully on the desk.

'Maybe the Yaks killed the crew.' Robertson shot a quick glance at the cabin door. 'They could be here now, waiting for us.'

Houston shook his head. 'Nonsense. How did they do it? Hold our men down until they froze to death? Well, freezing's what we'll do ourselves unless we do more than just talk. Any ideas, Mister Personal Assistant Douglas?'

For a moment Douglas could think of none. They seemed to have talked in a circle, airing their fears but resolving nothing. Yaks, poisonous fumes, mutiny: none of those theories made sense. Houston was right: the crew had frozen to death in a ship whose bunker was full of coal. He pulled himself together and told himself sharply that the men were looking to him for leadership.

'Ideas?' he said. 'Yes, I have some. First, we'll put the bodies together in the foc's'le until we can bury them properly, then we'll get under way. I want to find *Redgauntlet* as soon as possible.'

'Is that all?' sneered Houston. '*Ivanhoe* carries a crew of forty-eight. To sail her it takes seventeen mariners, an engineer and firemen, plus the Master and at least one mate. There are six of us here, and at sea you're just a bloody liability, Mr Personal Assistant, sir.'

'We'll all have to work extra hard, then, won't we, Mr Mate, sir?' Douglas held Houston's gaze until the latter looked away.

'But she's frozen in,' Gay reminded him, 'frozen solid. We can't release her. Even if we chip at the ice for a month we won't get her free. We're trapped here as surely as her crew.'

'Isn't there a signal-gun aboard?' Douglas asked.

'Of course there's a God-damned signal-gun,' snapped Houston. 'What sort of God-damned fool question is that?'

'If there's a gun, there'll be gunpowder. We'll blast her free.'

Davis Strait, Summer 1860

Gilbride had provided ample gunpowder for the signal-gun and the harpoon-guns. There was a stack of canvas bags stored for'ard for signalling, and a further two hundred pounds in reserve. That was enough for a small battle, Douglas reflected, but unfortunately a winter in the ice had allowed dampness to set in and the entire outer layer was ruined. A single spark could still blow the ship to pieces, however, so Douglas levered the bags apart with a wooden marline-spike.

He examined the results. 'Not too bad. We have about fifty pounds of powder here, and perhaps three times that amount below. That ought to be enough if we use it properly. Let's try, anyway.'

Scrimmy chuckled. 'Whatever you say, Rab. You can't do any harm, because *Ivanhoe*'s already been blown up.' Nothing ever seemed to get Scrimmy down.

Douglas set Houston and Robertson to work on the engine, and Gay and Greig to light every stove in the ship. 'The more warmth we generate, the better,' he explained.

Ever the pessimist, Greig said, 'Won't we run out of coal? If we do, we'll freeze in the winter – this is summer, remember.'

'We shan't be here in the winter,' said Douglas firmly. 'If the mate can get the engines turning over, we should be able to force our way out.' He hefted one of the bags of powder. 'Scrimmy and I will blast away as much of the ice as we can. And if we do have to overwinter, well, we've hundreds of tons of coal and I'll burn every piece of timber in *Ivanhoe* if need be.'

'The owners won't like that,' Scrimmy said, smiling.

'The owners think she's sunk already. Anything we salvage for them is a bonus. We're going to set her free, Scrimmy, and then we're going home.'

An investigation proved that *Ivanhoe* was central to her own berg. That meant that there was no large body of ice from which to detach her. She was drifting nearly broadside on, with the ice thickest along her port quarter, which faced north. Her starboard side, in her lee, was much less affected, while her bowsprit and figurehead were free save for their hanging icicles.

'What do you reckon, Rab?' Scrimmy asked. 'Do you think we can do it?'

'Maybe. If Houston can get the engines to start, we have a chance.'

But when he asked the mate 'What progress?' the response was not encouraging.

'No chance.' Houston shook his great head. The sweat on his face was already freezing into his beard. 'She's frozen solid. I don't know much about engines, but I do know that it needs to turn the screw, and the shaft between the screw and the engine is one solid block of ice. If the screw can't turn, we can't move.'

'What if we could unfreeze the shaft? Would that help?'

'Even then,' grunted Houston, 'the screw's outside so it'll be iced over. If the shaft was free and the screw was also free, we might have a chance, but they're not.'

'Not yet. I want every lantern, everything that can generate heat, brought into the engine-room. Fuel up the boilers, too, but be careful they don't blow up. I want this place as hot as the hob of Hades, and I want you to find a long rod, maybe the slenderest of the whale-lances, and poke away at the shaft.'

'And what will you be doing in the meantime?' Houston was already moving lamps and lanterns. 'Enjoying the Arctic scenery?'

'Freeing the screw from the outside.' It felt good to make

decisions after weeks of obeying orders. 'You may hear a bit of a bang, but don't worry about it. Come on, Scrimmy.'

Douglas and Scrimmy took picks from *Ivanhoe*'s stores, climbed down on to the ice and began to hack at the solid-packed ice around her stern. Every blow jarred their arms horribly, but they persevered, and eventually they made a tunnel twice as long as a human head and sloping towards the rudder.

'That'll have to do,' Douglas said. He placed five pounds of gunpowder in the centre of the hole. 'Gunpowder explodes upwards, so it should loosen the ice above it.'

He laid a long trail of the coarse-grained powder on a strip of sailcloth, bent over the top and applied a light. The flame sputtered a little, then took hold and fizzed along the trail. A thin black smoke rose to the clear sky. When the flame disappeared into the hole, Douglas pulled Scrimmy back, but the explosion disappointed him: it dislodged less than a handful of ice.

'We'll try again,' Douglas decided. 'This ice must be harder than granite.'

'What the hell are you up to?' Houston leaned over the taffrail, twenty feet above their heads. 'It was like the devil's orchestra in there, then the whole ship shook. Greig nearly pissed in his breeches!'

'Tell Greig to use the heads. The next bang will be much bigger.' Using the strongest lance, Douglas burrowed the tunnel deeper and placed twice the amount of powder, before again laying a fuse-trail to a place of safety.

'How long will this take?' asked Scrimmy. He pointed at the sky. 'That looks like snow.'

'It always looks like snow. We'll be as long as it needs.' Douglas applied the light and again watched the flame hiss and splutter along the canvas. This time the explosion was much more satisfactory: chunks of ice were blown skyward and powdered ice and snow formed a hazy cloud over *Ivanhoe*'s stern.

'It's cracking,' said Scrimmy excitedly.

He was right. The ice was starred by a zigzag pattern radiating out from the point of the explosion.

'More pick-work,' said Douglas.

He attacked the ice again, raising hand-sized pieces which Scrimmy levered off and pushed aside. As they neared the stern of the ship, he could see the tip of the ice-encased screw and hacked desperately toward it. 'Pray that the screw hasn't been damaged, Scrimmy.'

Above them, *Ivanhoe*'s bulk loomed darkly, a creature of wood and steel which could take them to safety or crush them in an instant. The light was fading to the evening dim, and the storm-lantern in their depression provided only a glimmer of consolation.

'More gunpowder than before?' Scrimmy was grinning as usual. 'It would save us a lot of effort.'

'Why not? A last charge for the night.'

Ten pounds this time, and the explosion rattled from the hull. When the smoke and shattered ice cleared, the top half of the screw was in the open air and the bottom half in dark, clear water.

'That was easy enough,' said Douglas, matching Scrimmy's grin. 'Now all we have to do is free the rest of her.'

They rested for an hour while Greig fed them all on Morton of Leith's preserved meat and steaming hot coffee.

Houston raised his mug. 'Enjoy this lads – it's duty-free.'

After the meal, Douglas followed the mate down to the engine-room. With half a dozen lanterns adding their heat to that of the boiler, this was the warmest place in the ship. Houston had succeeded in removing the ice from three feet of the propeller-shaft, and had Robertson and Gay working as stokers. 'I think there's a safety-valve for this machine,' he said, slapping the engine resoundingly, 'but I don't know where. The heat's helping, anyway. As soon as we get the shaft free, I'll try the thing out.'

'Have you any idea how it works?' Douglas looked curiously at the gleaming monster of brass and steel and paint.

'Not yet, but if an engineer can do it, so can I. It's only a glorified steam-kettle, after all.'

'Well, good luck. It's back to the ice and the gunpowder for us.'

Even with cloud masking the sky, the Arctic night was more grey than black, but Douglas and Scrimmy still needed four storm-lanterns for enough light as they placed the charges. Armoured with experience, they worked to a system, tamping the charge home before withdrawing, lighting the fuse-trail and watching from a safe distance. The explosions battered through the dull night, echoing across the frozen wasteland, while the flash of powder reflected in myriad colours from the surrounding floes.

'You'll upset the neighbours,' Scrimmy warned. 'The polar bears will be complaining.'

'As long as they don't get aggressive.' Douglas glanced behind him. Tam had warned him about the size and power of the great white bears.

By midnight there was dark water visible from the stern to the mizzenmast on the port quarter, but they had used about a third of their store of powder.

'And this is the easy side,' said Douglas. 'I think we should shift to the weather side.'

'We'll have to soon,' Scrimmy agreed. 'If we carry on here, we'll float away from the ship.'

The ice on the starboard side was much thicker, so Douglas used more gunpowder. Again they worked forward from the stern as they tried to free the working section of the ship. They could hear the throb of the engine and the clatter of Houston working.

'Let's hope he knows what he's doing down there,' Scrimmy said. A terrible scream sounded above them, and they both jumped. 'God save us all! What's that?'

It was like nothing they had heard before, a high-pitched, continuous squeal which seemed to come from the very heart of *Ivanhoe*, as if she was in agony. Douglas crouched, covering his ears. The sound continued, not varying in pitch, tone or volume, until eventually Douglas realised that it was mechanical rather than human or supernatural. Sensing movement, he looked up. The funnel was emitting a steady jet of white steam which brought the upperworks of the ship into stark silhouette. Douglas let out his breath in a long, shuddering moan; it eased his taut nerves.

Nudging Scrimmy with his boot, he smiled with relief and said, 'It's the safety-valve for the boiler, like they use in railway trains. It lets the excess steam escape.'

Scrimmy was swearing, but then he began to laugh. 'Man, Rab, I thought it was the ghost coming for us in person. Just steam, eh? Man, I need a drink. Just one wee bottle of whisky would set me up fine for the night.' He shook his head in wonder as he watched the white clouds that enveloped the masts and spars. 'Steam, eh? If we could direct it down here it would help melt the ice.'

At some time in the small hours the screaming ended as the last of the excess steam was expelled, but the two men worked on, hacking out holes, placing powder charges, assessing the results of the explosions. A pale sun was easing through the eastern sky as they blasted away the last of the gunpowder, and Douglas walked round *Ivanhoe* to check their handiwork. A channel of clear dark water extended from the stern two-thirds the length of the ship. Only a short section on either side of the bow was still encased in ice.

'Not bad,' he conceded. 'Not bad at all.'

'Good enough for a wee dram?' asked Scrimmy hopefully.

Douglas shook his head. 'You're a good man when you're sober, but you're a danger to yourself and everybody else with a drink in you.' He touched Scrimmy's shoulder. 'Sorry, son.'

Scrimmy shrugged. 'Just thought I'd try.'

181

Tired, hungry and filthy with powder-smoke, they returned to the ship.

Houston was still working. 'See?' He led Douglas round the engine, as proud as if it were his own invention. 'I think this is how it works.'

Douglas listened to Houston's explanation for only a few minutes. 'Can you make it go?'

'I think so.'

'Then do. Scrimmy and I have freed the screw and most of the hull. We're depending on you to do the rest before she freezes in again.'

Houston gestured around the engine-room, where the remainder of the crew was lying in varying stages of exhaustion. 'Give them a couple of hours. Let the lads have a bit of a caulk.'

Douglas was about to condemn the mate for his misplaced charity, but caught the words back. He was right: they would need all their energy to keep *Ivanhoe* afloat. It would be better to let everybody rest and hope that the water did not freeze again. 'You're right, Mr Houston. I think we could all do with some sleep.' He looked uncertainly at the engine; it was his responsibility now, since he had taken control. 'Will that be all right without us?'

'Och, yes. I'll load the boiler up high and let it burn slow. The heat will do Ivan good.'

Douglas, Scrimmy and the mate squeezed themselves into empty spaces on the deck, and before long the only sound was that of a man snoring.

Douglas awoke to hear footsteps padding around him. At first he thought he was back on the frontier and groped for his rifle, but the throbbing of the deck brought him back to reality. He sat up with a jerk just as Houston began to curse. The engine-room was full of smallish, squat, fur-clad figures with swarthy faces and almond-shaped eyes. Douglas tried to move but one of the intruders leaned over him, jabbering in some strange language.

'What?' Douglas stared into the expressionless face. Then he understood. These must be Esquimaux, Yaks, perhaps the Yaks who had left the soapstone bear – and might have murdered *Ivanhoe*'s crew. 'No!' Douglas struggled to his feet and aimed a punch at the nearest man, who threw back her hood, smiled at him and held out something that looked like a twig. The punch became a wave as Douglas saw what was happening.

The raiding-party were chattering happily, prodding one another and allowing their children to run around the engine-room as if it were their playground. None carried weapons.

'What the hell's going on, Scrimmy?' he demanded.

'Yaks.' Scrimmy was holding hands with two of the children. 'They heard the noise we were making and came along to investigate.' He raised his voice. 'Any whisky for the Yaks, Mr Houston? Cheer them up a bit, like?'

'Can they speak English?' Douglas asked, and addressed the room: 'Can anybody here speak English?'

The woman he had nearly punched stepped forward. 'I can. Some.'

'Some's good enough for me. More than I can speak Yakkish, anyway,' Douglas said. 'Who taught you? Never mind. What are you doing here?'

'Fetching you,' she said, and pointed a stubby finger at him. 'Captain?'

Douglas shook his head. 'No, not me.' He indicated Houston. 'That's the mate over there. Mr Houston.'

The woman grimaced. 'Bully Houston dead in ice.'

'No, I'm bloody not.' Houston pushed through the crowd of Esquimaux and Greenlandmen, who looked as if they were about to have a party. 'Who says I'm dead in the ice?'

She looked at him. 'Bully Houston dead in ice.'

Scrimmy came over, carrying a small child in his arms and chewing something. 'Who's the lady?' He held out his hand. 'I'm Peter Scrymgeour but everybody calls me Scrimmy.'

She took his hand, pulled him close and rubbed his nose with her own. 'Good morning. I am Nataraq.'

Scrimmy bowed. 'Good morning, Nataraq. Thank you for coming to see us.'

'Fetching you. Good morning.' She pulled Scrimmy's sleeve. 'Captain?'

'I'm not the Captain,' he said, with something like alarm. 'Tell her, Mr Houston, tell her who you are.'

'Bully Houston dead in ice.' It was obvious that Nataraq had only a handful of phrases. She pulled Scrimmy's sleeve harder. 'Fetching you. Jimmy Gordon.'

'What?' Houston grabbed her by the shoulders. 'What did you say?'

'Good morning, Captain.'

'She said Jimmy Gordon,' Douglas confirmed. The image of Mary Gordon's smoky green eyes returned to him. 'He's one of the missing men.'

'I know fine who Jimmy Gordon is, damn you.' Houston put his face close to Nataraq's. 'What do you know about him? About Jimmy Gordon?'

'Jimmy Gordon. Fetching Captain.'

One of the other Esquimaux, a long-haired man with a moustache that descended to his chin, pulled Houston's hand away from Nataraq. He called the Esquimaux together and pointed at the door. 'Jimmy Gordon. Wally Taylor. Willie Syme.'

Douglas checked his list. 'They're all among the missing men.'

'I know their bloody names. Wally Taylor was the engineer.' Houston watched, frowning, as the Esquimaux began to file out of the engine-room. 'I think they've come to take us to the others.'

Nataraq turned in the doorway. 'Jimmy Gordon,' she said. 'Qallunaat.* Fetch.' She pointed to Scrimmy, who had passed the child to the moustached man. 'Scrimmy. Fetch.' Smiling broadly, she followed her companions.

---

* White man.

184

'After them,' Houston ordered, but by the time the Green-landmen reached the deck the Esquimaux were already pad-dling away in a small flotilla of kayaks. 'Stop!' Houston's roar echoed across the Arctic. 'Come back!' But the Esquimaux paddled on, skimming past ice-floes with apparent unconcern, until they vanished behind a large berg.

'Another mystery, then.' Douglas leaned over the taffrail: there was already a film of ice over the water they had blasted clear. 'But I'd say they've been aboard before. They knew about you being lost in the ice, and some of the names of the crew.'

'Maybe they did kill them. Maybe they were the murderers.' Gay looked haggard, his beard streaked with grey hairs which Douglas had not noticed before.

Douglas thought for a moment. 'Maybe, but I doubt it. After all, they could easily have killed us this morning, rather than waking us up.' He sighed. 'It's a nice morning: let's not waste it. Something to eat first, then we'll try and free *Ivanhoe*.'

'What about the old crew?' asked Houston in a low voice, as if he felt guilty about revealing weakness. He jerked a thumb toward the foc'sle. 'I don't want to share a ship with a lot of dead men. Besides, once Ivan heats up they'll start to stink.'

Douglas considered. 'We'll give them a decent burial when we get into clearer water.'

'Aye. And the Esquimaux? They knew about Jimmy Gordon and the others.' Again there was that hint of guilt.

Douglas looked at the chilled sea that stretched all around them. 'We can either search for *Redgauntlet* or search for Jimmy Gordon. We can't do both.' He realised what the guilt was: Houston wanted him to make the decision.

'Perhaps not. Let's get *Ivanhoe* free first.'

Getting power to the screw proved much more difficult than starting the engine, for no one had even a rudimentary knowl-edge of machinery. The crew pushed every lever and turned every knob that they could find, but the screw remained

185

obstinately still. They spent the rest of the day in increasingly frustrated toil, until Gay resorted to kicking the solid casing of the engine and Houston to swearing in four languages. Greig buried his head in his hands and sobbed silently.

'Bit of a bugger, eh?' said Scrimmy. 'I reckon it's time for a tot of rum. That usually helps.'

With his knuckles torn and bleeding from violent contact with various mechanical protuberances, Douglas's resistance was low. He nodded unthinkingly and Scrimmy fled aft. He returned with his breath smelling of rum and with a small keg under his arm. 'Thought I'd better bring enough for every-body.' He grinned as Houston swore even more loudly than usual and raised a spanner to hit the boiler. 'I'd leave off that, if I were you, Mr Houston. Wally Taylor won't like it if you damage his engine.'

Grabbing the keg, Houston took a long draught. 'If you can find me Wally Taylor, I'll give you a five-gallon cask to yourself.'

Scrimmy chuckled gleefully. 'Thanks, Mr Houston. I'll go and get it – Nataraq's just bringing him aboard.'

'Stay where you are, you lying, lubberly, drunken bastard!' Houston's temper finally cracked. Hurling the spanner into the far corner of the engine-room, he grabbed Scrimmy and raised a huge fist.

Scrimmy cringed. 'Mr Houston, don't hit me. Look!'

In walked a smiling Nataraq. 'Fetch qallunaat. Good morn-ing.'

Behind her came a group of fur-clad people, one of whom, a large man with a thick black beard, said loudly, 'What the hell are you doing to my engine, Willie?'

Davis Strait, Summer 1860

'I said, Willie, what the hell are you doing to my engine?' repeated the bearded man, and he shoved Houston aside. 'You'll blow the damned thing up.'

'Wally? Wally Taylor?' Mouth agape, Houston let Scrimmy drop to the deck. 'Where have you come from?'

'Never mind that now.' Taylor was already busy with the engine, and as he worked the vibrations dropped markedly. 'What the devil were you trying to do here? She's running far too fast.'

Douglas stared in disbelief as more men pushed into the engine-room. 'Are you all from *Ivanhoe*?' he asked.

There were six of them, and they seemed as astounded he was. They were all smiling hugely, and one had unashamed tears in his eyes as he shook hands with Scrimmy and the other Redgauntlets. They all talked without pause as they introduced themselves and the equally animated Esquimaux who had brought them.

Douglas ticked the names off his list: Wally Taylor, engineer; Willie Syme, line-manager; Alex Dodds, mariner; Robert Watson, mariner; Alex Ogilvie, boat-steerer, Jimmy Gordon, carpenter. Jimmy Gordon . . . 'Not a tall man, but well-made,' Mrs Gordon had said of him. He looked small now, with a face the colour of walnut and bright, sharp eyes. Douglas wondered if he should tell him his wife was aboard *Redgauntlet*.

All the Ivanhoes were weather-beaten and gaunt, with prominent cheekbones and great beards that could not have felt the edge of a razor for months. Most clung to the Red-

187

gauntlets or stared around the engine-room as though seeing the gates of Heaven. The rum-keg was already halfway round the crowd, with the Esquimaux sharing the load manfully. Indeed, they were drinking more than the Ivanhoes, who were being surprisingly moderate for British seamen.

Douglas moved to Houston's side and shouted for silence. There was a very small reduction in the noise, but it took Houston's Atlantic roar to bring a hush.

'My name is Robert Douglas, and I work for Mr Gilbride. We were trying to get Ivan moving again. With you lads' help it should be easy, and then we'll find *Old Fisty* and go home to Dundee.'

There was a second's silence, then cheer after cheer exploded round the engine-room. The strength of the rescued men's emotion was obvious. Even Wally Taylor furtively wiped away a tear while big Houston solemnly patted his shoulder.

When the noise had subsided, Douglas continued, 'We've only got a skeleton crew, so we'll all have to work twice as hard as normal.' This time the cheering was more subdued. 'But before we start, Mr Houston and I would like to know what happened to *Ivanhoe*. If you'll come one at a time to the Captain's cabin, we'll listen to what you have to say.' He turned to Scrimmy. 'Sorry, Scrimmy, you can't open your keg yet. We need you too much.'

'Too late, Rab. I already have.' Scrimmy held up the evidence. 'But don't worry; the Yakkies will help drink it.'

The Ivanhoes all told similar stories. The ship had been cruising around Hopeful Point under easy sail, with Houston and a boat's crew on bran. When the lookout sighted seals Houston had rowed to investigate, then fog descended. The next thing any of the men remembered was an Esquimau bending over them. The Esquimaux had taken them ashore and looked after them all winter.

'They saved our lives,' said Jimmy Gordon. 'I'll never forget that.'

'So you don't know what happened? You all just collapsed?' asked Douglas, deeply puzzled.

'That's how it was – there was nothing at all unusual.' Gordon's eyes were intelligent. 'We had our dinner, the rum went round, and then the second mate made our watch check the running rigging. I remember feeling a bit tired – relaxed, like – when I woke up, Natarq was on board. They don't like being called Yaks by the way. They're Innuit.'

'Innuit. I'll remember that,' said Douglas. Names had been very important to the tribesmen on the Cape frontier; no doubt the Innuit were the same. With the thought came a flash of memory. One of the colonials had accused Paddy of being an English rooineck. Paddy hit him. '*Irish* rooineck,' he told the prostrate man. 'Irish rooineck of the Seventy-Third Foot, and don't you forget it.'

'There was one thing,' Gordon said. 'When we woke up Ivan was under power, but we'd had her under sail. You don't steam in the fishing-grounds, because it scares the fish.'

Douglas nodded. Ecky, from *Charleston*, had said *Ivanhoe* was under power when he saw her.

Wally Taylor said that he'd shut off the engine before leaving with the Innuit. 'I hoped to come back, but we never got the chance. You see, she'd run into a berg and was tearing her engine to bits, otherwise the Innuit couldn't have boarded her. We were only six men, not enough to man her, so I thought it best to stay with the Innuit.'

'Only six? What about the other survivors?'

Taylor shook his head. 'There weren't any – we checked the whole ship. Everybody else was dead.'

'Did you count them? Check to make sure everybody was there?' Douglas ran an eye down his list. There were still six men unaccounted for.

'No. Why should we do that? Where would they go?'

'That's just what I want to know. I want to find all the missing men, and find out what happened on the ship.'

189

The engineer shook his head. 'We've been trying to work that out ever since we left, but we're no further forward. We had our dinner, and then we got a tot of rum. I'm not a drinking man, so when I'd had a sip I gave mine away. Then the Innuit woke us up. Simple as that.'

Again Douglas consulted his list. 'Did you notice the doctor or any of these men?' and he read out the names.

Taylor shook his head. 'They might have been there, but I can't say for certain.'

Houston spoke up. 'We know the surgeon, Dr Michie, is still alive. He's serving aboard *Redgauntlet*.'

'What?' Douglas stared at him. 'Dr Michie was the surgeon on *Ivanhoe*? Why didn't you tell me?'

'I thought you knew.' He shrugged. 'Does it matter? As long as you can score him off your list.'

'I'll speak to him when we get back to *Redgauntlet*. It's a pity I wasn't told earlier. He might be able confirm that it was poisonous fumes that made everybody collapse. '

'I didn't notice any fumes,' the engineer said, then suddenly grinned, showing startlingly white teeth behind his black beard. 'Unless it was the fumes from the rum.'

So the conscientious Dr Michie had been the other survivor. Douglas could not imagine that thin, almost frail man struggling through the Arctic ice while the tough Greenlandmen died on *Ivanhoe*. However, as a medical man he would be the most likely person to understand what had happened to the crew.

For the next few hours Douglas was too busy to worry about reasons and motives. While Taylor and Robertson laboured over the engines, the crew dealt with their dead comrades. It was a painful task removing their possessions and putting the bodies in the foc'sle for later burial. The Innuit were not permitted to help. This was a deeply personal matter, a wordless last service the Greenlandmen performed for their shipmates. By mutual if unspoken consent, the men had quartered themselves in the half-deck, the space once occupied by the specialists. The foc'sle was left to the dead.

When the bodies had been moved, Houston ordered a double tot of rum all round, Scrimmy cheerfully accepting the quota of three Ivanhoes who had signed the temperance pledge. As Douglas admired their resolution he had a sudden vision of Ellen Gilbride's serious, concerned face. She would have nodded gravely, he thought, folded her arms and demanded that Douglas should also abstain. And perhaps—

'Ahoy, Mr Personal Assistant!' Houston's bellow travelled the full length of the ship. 'Stop day-dreaming for a moment and lend a hand here. *Move*, you useless lubber! Get your idle farmer's body across where I can use it. We're going to roll her clear.'

Rolling the ship was a simple process. All the men save the engineer gathered on one side and then, on Houston's word, dashed across to the opposite side.

'If we can roll her enough, she'll break free of the ice,' Scrimmy said. 'It sometimes works.'

There was no movement for the first dozen attempts, but when Taylor got the screw turning, they felt a slight shift. Looking over the stern, Douglas saw a churned-up soup of brash-ice and seawater, and he felt the strain as *Ivanhoe* tried to pull ahead.

'Port side,' ordered Houston. 'Run!'

They ran back and forth, Greenlandmen and Innuit together, with Scrimmy carrying an Innuit child as if it were his own and Nataraq screaming with laughter. There were loud creaks from the ice, a groaning shudder from the ship, and pieces of ice fell from the spars to explode in vicious fragments on the deck.

'Ignore that. Run!' The mate led from the front; the ship rocked under the weight of galloping people. 'She's moving! Did you feel that?' The ferocious Bully Houston sounded as excited as a boy in a sweetshop. 'We're doing it!'

With a screech that set their teeth on edge, *Ivanhoe* pulled clear; great lumps of ice from her hull crashed deafeningly into the water alongside. The Greenlandmen cheered and the Innuit clapped their hands and grinned at the happiness of their qallunaat friends.

'She's alive again.' Houston put his arms round the solid pine of the mainmast and hugged it. 'We're back in control.' Laughing, he lifted Nataraq high in the air and gave her a resounding kiss which had the Innuit giggling loudly and the Greenlandmen nudging each other. 'And we could not have done it without your help. You saved my men, my little Yakky – Esquimau – Innuit – whatever you call yourself. What can I give you in return?'

'Rum,' said Scrimmy instantly. 'You can give them rum, and metal tools and things like that.'

'Come on, then, my Yakkidy-yak friends. Come with me and choose what you want.' And he led them below to the storerooms.

Douglas retreated to the stern. There was always a lot to think about and never enough time. Every turn and twist of this voyage revealed a new mystery, and every discovery led to further confusion. How had these six men survived when all the others had died? Also, how had the surgeon managed to escape? Obviously a ship must have picked him up, but how? Had he rowed alone in the missing boat? Or had he left with a full boat's crew, who had all died except him?

The Ivanhoes were emotional as they said farewell to their Innuit hosts. Remembering a frontier village where the Fingoes had entertained his company of the Seventy-Third for a week, Douglas understood how they felt. The combined crew lined the rail and waved when the Innuit returned to their kayaks. Scrimmy had been reluctant to part with the child, but the mother had consoled him with one of the many bottles of rum she had accepted from the stores. *Ivanhoe* seemed the poorer for the loss of the Innuit, and Douglas felt a touch of loneliness in the sharp brightness of another Arctic morning.

'What course, Mr Personal Assistant?' Houston was only half mocking. 'It seems you've put yourself in charge, so it's for you to set the course.' His eyes were as bleak as ever, but there was a new expression there, too. Wariness, perhaps, or even respect.

'You know I'm no seaman, Mr Houston. Where do you think *Redgauntlet* will be?'

'We've drifted quite a bit south.' He made rapid mental calculations. 'We'll head north by north-east, and put up lots of smoke so we can be seen from as far away as possible. I'll post one man aloft. The rest will be needed to work the ship.' His smile made him look more like a gargoyle than a seaman. 'Including you. And now that the ship's heating up, the melted ice is flooding her. That means pump-work, Mr Douglas, your favourite.'

Douglas grimaced. 'There are more mysteries than ever now that we've found *Ivanhoe*.'

'Aye. Strange that she didn't blow up. I wonder who started that rumour?' His eyes widened with the sudden shock of knowledge. 'It must have been the doctor. Maybe he heard a berg calving and thought it was the ship.'

'Perhaps.' Douglas nodded, but that solution sounded too simple. He resolved to pay a lot of attention to Dr Michie when they next met. 'We'll ask him later, once you've found *Old Fisty*.'

Working a two-shift system, four hours on and four hours off, they steered north by north-east into a day of brilliant clarity. Although her seventy-horsepower engine pushed *Ivanhoe* at a steady six knots, the crew was still busy aloft. A year in the Arctic had rotted much of the canvas, so Houston aired the remains of their sails on the deck, and hoisted every stitch the ship could take. Even if the sadly flapping sails hardly increased her speed, they did make her more easily visible.

'We look like washday in the Overgate!' Greig tripped over one of the sails that Houston had draped over the boats.

193

'I didn't know they did washing in the Overgate,' Alex Dodds said cheerfully.

'Och, Doddsie, you've just forgotten how to wash after your time in Yakland. But what if we see a whale?' wondered Willie Syme.

'Our tanks are full.' Houston jerked a thumb to the hatches. 'Ivan had a very prosperous voyage until the time I left. Once we find *Fisty* we'll make our way back to Dundee.' He smiled for a second time that day. 'Won't that make Horse Gilbride sit up and take notice?'

When they reached the area where they had left *Redgauntlet*, Houston steered in gradually increasing circles, sounding the bell every ten minutes. 'We can't stay more than a few days,' he told Douglas, 'because we'll have to cross the Atlantic before summer ends. I wouldn't like to face an October storm with a skeleton crew.'

On the third day Scrimmy, who was lookout, saw topmasts thrusting up beyond a low berg. 'Sail ho!' he yelled. 'And it's *Old Fisty*! I'd know her anywhere!'

'Sound the bell.' Houston was already halfway up the ratlines as he shouted. 'Sound everything that makes a noise. Douglas, get below and tell Taylor to throw everything on to his blasted fire. Tell him I want this ship to fly. Gay, steer directly for *Redgauntlet*. If you lose her I'll have you broken to landsman and you'll be scrubbing the heads until we sight the Inchcape light. The rest of you, blow! Blow into the sails.'

From his position right for'ard, Douglas watched the figure-head rise and dip as *Ivanhoe* thrust herself through the brash-ice, saw the reinforced bows, powered by the strength of seventy horses, cleave through the crust of ice. After twenty minutes he saw *Old Fisty*'s topmasts appear. Ten minutes later she was in clear sight, only a few cable-lengths away, with her fist rising and falling lazily, and half her sails flapping on the yards.

'Poor seamanship.' There was more than mere annoyance in Houston's voice. 'They've got lazy without me. Well, I'll soon

194

see to that.' He raised his voice to a roar which caused half a dozen dovekies to shoot up from their perch on an ice-floe. '*Redgauntlet* ahoy! Are any of you lubbers awake this morning?'

There was a pause, then a faint answering hail and somebody waved from the stern.

'Steer to close her,' he ordered. 'She's dead in the water. Close with her . . . Full astern . . . Stop engines. Dammit to hell and gone, what's wrong with that ship?'

'Look!' Jimmy Gordon pointed incredulously at a figure at *Redgauntlet*'s stern. 'That's Mary! That's my wife!' Balancing on top of the rail, he waved both hands, laughing madly. 'Mary! Mary, it's me, Jimmy! It's Jimmy.'

'But where are the others?' Suddenly Houston sounded very old.

Davis Strait and the North Atlantic, Summer 1860

'Jimmy! Oh, my dear, I knew you weren't dead!' Mary Gordon's voice was high and strained as it floated across to them. 'But hurry, please. Everybody here's dead.'

Leaving Greig and Scrimmy to make the ships fast, Douglas followed Houston and Gordon aboard *Redgauntlet*. Mary burst into tears of joy and threw herself at her husband in an embrace which ended only when Houston pulled them apart and said urgently, 'Mary, what's happened here? Where's Captain Fairweather?'

'They're all dead. All except me.' Mary clung to her husband's arm, and ignored the wondering comments of the other men. 'You'll have to do something, Willie.'

Douglas had a feeling of déjà vu when he entered the foc'sle, and saw Hughson lying on top of a confusion of bodies. He leaned across the Shetlander and felt nearly sick with relief when he heard his steady breathing. The other men were the same, in a deep slumber but still alive. There was no fire in the small stove, and ice had formed on the deck and bulkheads.

'They're alive,' Douglas reported to Houston.

The mate nodded grimly. 'So are most of mine. Pitlethan and Brown are dead – knifed by the look of it. The others are in a deep sleep, so deep that I couldn't rouse them. The steam-launch is missing, too. It's exactly the same as on *Ivanhoe*.'

Douglas felt a spasm twist his stomach. 'Exactly the same, as you say. The foc'sle stove was out, too. Were the half-deck stoves still lit?'

Houston's brow creased in thought. 'No, no, they were doused, all of them. And the hatch-covers were open, which is strange.'

'Very,' Douglas agreed. 'Unless we get some heat into the ship, these men will all die of the cold – again, exactly like on *Ivanhoe*. I think some sort of miasmic gas must have knocked them out.'

'Damned steam-kettles!' Houston kicked the funnel hard. 'Two ships. Two good crews lost, or nearly lost. Obviously steam-ships are no good in the Arctic. It must be the combination of coal power and the cold that's killing the men. We'll ask the doctor what he thinks.'

Douglas nodded slowly. 'Do that. If you can find him.'

'What? He'll be asleep in his cabin like the rest.'

'He may be, but I doubt it. In fact, I very much doubt that Dr Michie is aboard at all.' Walking to the bulwark, Douglas looked over the sea, with its grim beauty of ice-floes and majestic bergs. 'I think he's out there in the steam-launch.'

'Why?' Houston stared piercingly at him.

'I have no idea, Mr Houston, but he escaped from *Ivanhoe* and I believe he has also escaped from *Redgauntlet*. Perhaps your sister can tell us, if she's been conscious all through what happened.'

The surgeon was not the only man missing. A check revealed five others: Captain Fairweather, Tam Wilson and three Greenmen who had been crimped from Mother Scott's.

'Not the men I'd choose to take with me in a small boat, steam-powered or not,' said Houston grimly. 'Wilson's a steady man, but the other three are a waste of rations – most Greenmen are.'

Douglas scratched his head. Now there were yet more mysteries on a voyage of unanswered questions. What could have induced the Captain leave his ship? Why had he left his men to die? And what part did the doctor play in all this?

He asked, 'How many men have we now, from both ships?'

Houston made his calculations aloud. 'When we left Shetland we had forty-eight. We lost one in an accident, and young Symbister killed himself. That left forty-six. With six missing and two murdered, there are now thirty-eight, plus the six from *Ivanhoe*. That makes forty-four.'

'Enough to crew both ships?'

'Plenty, if all these lazy buggers work when they wake up.'

'What about navigation?'

'I can navigate. So can Cargill.'

'He'd better take charge of *Ivanhoe*, then.' Douglas looked out to sea again. 'We have another decision to make, Mr Houston: shall we search for the Captain? I wish I knew how long ago he left.' He sighed, wishing yet again that Paddy was at his side. 'We'll see what Mrs Gordon knows. Where is she?'

'Where would you be if you hadn't seen your husband for over a year?' Once more Houston revealed a surprising humanity. 'Give them an hour together first, then we'll talk in my cabin.'

Mary Gordon's face was still tear-streaked but full of joy when they gathered. She sat on Houston's chair while the men squeezed on to the bunk or sat on the deck. Jimmy Gordon squatted at his wife's feet. The brass chronometer on the wall was silent, its hands static and useless.

'Well, Mary, tell us what happened,' said Houston.

'I don't know. I've no idea at all. I was in my wee room and there was a sudden noise upstairs. I hid, of course – I hid a lot after you went missing, Willie.'

'It would have been a hard time for you,' he agreed.

'What sort of noise?' asked Douglas.

'Footsteps, like people running. And there was shouting – an argument. I listened for a while, until there were no more footsteps. Then the engine started. I listened for hours, but there was no noise except the engine, so in the end I came out, and I found everybody sleeping. I couldn't wake them.' She shivered, remembering. 'I thought they were dead.'

'What time did it go quiet?' Douglas asked.

'I haven't got a clock, but it must have been about noon, just after dinner and grog were served.' She smiled. 'I always knew when it was time for the grog because the men would be singing.' The smile broadened. 'Some of their songs were rather . . . rude, but I didn't mind that. Except Brown and Pitlethan's songs. They didn't drink anything so they had nothing to be happy about. They just sang hymns.' Smoky green eyes expressed contempt for hymn-singers.

'Aye? Well, they won't be singing any more hymns,' said Houston shortly. 'They're both dead.'

For an instant Douglas saw Paddy pointing at Mary, but the image disappeared when he shook his head. 'Sometimes I think Tam Wilson was right and *Redgauntlet* was unlucky from the Friday she was launched. Maybe that spinner really did put a curse on her.'

'What spinner?' asked Jimmy.

'The spinner the ship crushed when she was launched.'

Mary smiled wrily. 'There wasn't anybody killed at *Redgauntlet*'s launch, was there, Jimmy?'

Jimmy shook his head. 'No, and we were there, Mr Douglas – I'm from Aberdeen, you see. Nobody was killed. And the launch wasn't on a Friday, either, because that's unlucky. It was on a Saturday.'

Douglas was bemused. 'But the papers said it was a Friday and that a spinner fell under her keel and was crushed.'

'The papers would,' said Jimmy scornfully. 'They like their wee stories.'

'Indeed they do,' agreed his wife. 'That's why people read them – that's why I read them – and they believe what they read. I tried to tell people in Dundee the truth, but they believed the papers, not me. They said I was half-crazed with grief for Jimmy, and that the papers wouldn't have printed the story if it wasn't true. In the end I gave up.'

'There are a lot of wee stories about these ships,' Douglas said. 'We were told *Redgauntlet* was unlucky, we were told *Ivanhoe* had blown up, and we were told there was a ghost on each of them.'

Douglas again glimpsed Paddy standing over Mary; he realised he was missing something. He cast his mind back to what she had said. *Ivanhoe*'s launch? No, not that. Before they talked about the launch, what had she said? That Brown and Pitlethan sang hymns. But many people sang hymns. There must be something else.

He said, 'Mrs Gordon, tell us more about Brown and Pitlethan.'

'Why? They were very quiet men. They thought they were better than everybody else because they went to the Kirk and didn't drink or swear.' Her smile was brief and cynical. 'Little good did it do them. They're both dead.'

'You three can talk all night, but I've got two ships to command.' Houston rose to his feet. 'I'm going to check the men again.'

'Very well, Mr Houston. As soon as they wake we can start to search for the Captain. Keep in close touch with *Ivanhoe*.' Douglas spoke absently, his mind still wrestling with the problem of Brown and Pitlethan. He knew he was missing something.

'Aye,' grunted the mate. 'I'll wager they're just dead drunk. The Captain was always liberal with the grog. Sore heads the day.'

Douglas smiled automatically, but something in those words jarred. Dead drunk? He said, 'Wait, Mr Houston. Mrs Gordon told us that the men got their dinner and rum and then collapsed. Brown and Pitlethan didn't drink. I presume they ate, though?'

'As far as I'm aware.'

'And *Ivanhoe*'s engineer, Wally Taylor, he doesn't drink much, either, does he? He hardly touched the rum that Scrimmy handed round.' Douglas was on his feet. 'It's the rum.' He had a sudden vivid image of Scrimmy and the Innuit pouring rum into their mouths. 'God, Houston! We must stop the men drinking or they'll all die!'

Houston was already at the door, roaring orders to leave the rum alone.

His sister watched him with a mixture of concern and amusement in her eyes. 'It can't be the rum, Willie. I've been drinking it, too, and I'm all right.'

'We've all been drinking it,' he replied, 'right from the start of the voyage.'

Douglas nodded. 'That's true.' He saw this theory drift away. 'Unless something was added to the rum . . . Yes, that must be it! The crew was drugged, and that's why Brown and Pitlethan were killed. They didn't drink, so they had to be got rid of – that was the shouting Mrs Gordon heard. Then, when the men were unconscious, the stoves were doused and the hatches opened so that they'd die of cold like the Ivanhoes.'

'But why? And who in God's name would do such a thing?' Houston was a hard, foul-mouthed man who controlled a recalcitrant crew by sheer lungpower and disciplined the dregs of Dundee by the force of his fists. But he was shocked to his soul at the calculated murder that had been planned here. 'It must have been one of the missing men. Who are they again?'

'The three Greenmen, Tam Wilson, Dr Michie and the Captain.'

'Impossible,' declared the mate. 'It can't be any of them. The Greenmen haven't the knowledge, Tam Wilson was crimped, just like you, I've known Captain Fairweather for years and I don't believe it was the doctor. He's an educated man, for God's sake, a respectable gentleman.'

Douglas sighed. 'You're right about Tam and the Greenmen – I think we can discount them. That leaves the Captain and the doctor.' He drummed his fingers on the desk. 'The more I think about it, Mr Houston, the more I suspect Dr Michie. Listen.' He ticked off the points on his fingers. 'The doctor would know how to drug the crew. He could have put something in the rum, and when the Captain saw that most of the men were dead he might have taken whoever was still alive and abandoned ship. Everything points to Dr Michie. So we've worked out who, and perhaps how, but' – Douglas thought of the slender, dapper doctor and shook his head – 'we don't know why.'

'He must be mad,' said Mrs Gordon. 'That's the only answer.'

'We'll search for the boat for a couple of days yet,' Douglas decided. 'I don't like to think of Tam and the Captain in the company of a murderous madman.'

'Aye, and not only them,' said Houston. 'I don't like to think of any of my lads out there in the ice. You feed the stoves and I'll look *Old Fisty* over. When the lads wake up we'll start searching.'

The crew awoke by ones and twos throughout the day, suffering from nausea, lethargy and a thumping head. Douglas questioned each man closely but learned nothing new. All had eaten their dinner, all had drunk a large tot of rum, and none could remember anything else. Nobody had seen Captain Fairweather leave the ship.

The rest of the day was taken up by the melancholy task of burying the dead, for the crew were adamant that the Ivanhoes should be given a decent send-off. Houston read the service and the bodies, sewn up in sailcloth and heavily weighted, were slid overboard. Each sullen splash seemed to tear something from the heart of *Ivanhoe*, as if the ship herself grieved for the loss of her crew. Ogilvie and Syme seemed especially moved, while Taylor insisted on saying a last goodbye to his firemen. Mrs Gordon held her husband's hand tightly throughout the service, shuddering as each body slipped into the uncaring sea.

When the last ripple from the last splash had lapped the two ships' hulls, Houston had a keg of whisky opened and ordered everyone a double tot, but it was still a sombre gathering that watched the Northern Lights wave a flickering farewell to the men of *Ivanhoe*. The crew listened respectfully as Macmillan, the piper, slow-marched the length of her deck and the strains of *Flowers of the Forest* flowed out across the sea.

'Goodbye, lads.' Scrimmy stood at the taffrail. Forcing the bung from his keg of rum, he poured what remained into the sea. 'Safe voyage.'

'The lads aren't happy about leaving Tam and the Captain out here,' Houston told Douglas. 'I told them we'd be searching.'

'Yes, for two days,' Douglas agreed, 'perhaps a little more if we have enough fuel. Then we'll have to steer for Dundee.'

Houston lifted his voice. 'Right, you lubbers. We can't do anything more for these lads, but we can find the Captain. Mr Cargill, you take *Ivanhoe* and half the men. Keep my topsails in sight at all times. I don't know what other madness will happen on these ships, so signal me if you see anything.'

'Aye.' Cargill nodded briefly and glanced at his new command. 'If we lose you in foul weather, I'll wait for you at the mouth of the Tay.'

Douglas looked astern, trying to identify the patch of sea where the bodies of *Ivanhoe*'s crew had been deposited, but he could not. Nothing of the dead men remained, save in their comrades' memories.

It was ferociously hot on the day when the patrol stopped at the frontier farm. Nearly blinded with sweat, Douglas accepted a pitcher of water from the farmer's wife and emptied it at one draught. She smiled at him, and introduced her husband and children. It was not normal for redcoats to be made so welcome, but these settlers understood and were glad that the soldiers were there to defend them. Life on the frontier was precarious at all times, and never more than when the tribes were out.

203

The little daughter was especially friendly, laughing as she ran from soldier to soldier, despite her father's admonitions. She came to Douglas, her smile showing white teeth in a face which had been browned by the sun despite the large white poke-bonnet that seemed to be worn by every European female in Africa.

'You won't let the tribesmen kill us, will you, Mr Soldier?'

Douglas shook his head. 'No, I certainly won't.'

'Do you promise?' The smile was full of sweetness, the eyes clear and blue.

'I promise.'

She smiled again, and pushed her cloth doll into his hand. 'Here you are. You take Milly for a while. Bring her back next time you come, and she can tell me about all your adventures.' The child looked so small and innocent amidst the savagery of Africa that Douglas lifted her and held her warm little body close.

'I know you'll help us,' she said. 'I trust you.'

The patrol marched away, into the brown dust of Africa, Douglas holding the doll with a self-consciousness that betrayed his youth.

Paddy nudged him with a hard elbow. 'Shouldn't make promises you can't keep, young Robert.'

'I'll know if they're in trouble,' Douglas said, 'and I'll run back to rescue them.'

When they returned to the farm three days later, all they found of the girl was her hands and feet and part of her skull. The rest of her had been burned to ashes by the fire the tribesmen had lit on her belly. The mutilated bodies of her father and brother were there, black with flies, but they could find no trace of her mother.

Douglas buried the doll with what he could retrieve of the girl's body. He resolved never to make promises again, for he now knew himself to be a man whom it was unsafe to trust. And he swore never again to leave anybody alone in danger if he could prevent it.

They searched not for two days but for five. Five days of scouring the ice for signs of a small boat; five days during which the weather remained settled, with light winds and cool, crisp days; five days during which Houston rotated the men in the crow's nest so that none endured the bone-chilling cold for more than an hour. Twice the lookout sighted whale-spouts, but there was no longer any interest in profit. Eight times they saw seals, and always there were the birds. Douglas grew to hate the mollies that circled and called, waiting to feast on the corpse of a whale.

One evening they saw the topsails of another ship. There was intense excitement, and both *Ivanhoe* and *Redgauntlet* sounded their bells, but neither could get close before nightfall. In the morning the sea was empty. Douglas felt sick. He did not want to leave men alone in the Arctic.

In growing frustration, Douglas questioned the survivors again, but they all gave the same story as before: they had had dinner, they had had an extra tot of rum and they had fallen asleep. Nobody had seen the Captain leave, nobody had seen the doctor or Tam Wilson, and nobody had seen the three Greenmen.

Superstition raised its head again, and Hughson spoke for many of the men when he blamed Mrs Gordon for some of the ill luck. 'Should never have a woman aboard a ship,' he said. 'It always causes trouble.'

Scrimmy laughed at him. 'Trouble? She probably saved your life. I'd have my wife aboard any time, if I knew where she was – she'd make a better sailor than half the crew.'

Although he was acting as master, Houston had refused to move into the Captain's quarters. Now he sat in his cabin and stared at Douglas with the sullenness of a man who resented failure. He said, 'We've been five days searching without a sign.

Even if they're still afloat, they'll be dead of frostbite and hunger by now.'

Douglas knew he ought to agree: he had found it hard enough on the whaleboat after just two days, and Captain Fairweather had been out twice as long. But he said doggedly, 'We mustn't give up hope. They might have been picked up by somebody else.'

'We've seen only one other sail.' Houston spread his hands wide. 'But, as you say, we can hope.'

'Another two days,' Douglas insisted. 'We can surely spend two more days searching.'

'We're already on watch and watch,' Houston reminded him, 'and we've two half-crews, many of them raw Greenmen. I'd like to get them all home safely.'

'Two more days, just.'

'One,' said Houston with finality. 'Then we're heading back.' He lowered his voice. 'They were my shipmates too, Douglas, but I don't want to kill this crew by trying to save men who are likely already dead.'

Perhaps it was the long, cold winter it had endured, or the rough treatment that Houston had subjected it to, but that night *Ivanhoe*'s engine sputtered and died. Houston manoeuvred *Redgauntlet* as close as he could and transferred his own engineer to help Wally Taylor, but despite all their combined skill, and all the prayers and curses of the crew, *Ivanhoe* remained obstinately powerless.

'She's shot.' Taylor wiped his oily hands on a rag which looked even oilier. 'Seized up solid. There's no way she'll run again without a major overhaul. It's wind and canvas for us, I'm afraid.'

When the news was brought to Houston, he cursed for a full three minutes without a single repetition. 'We haven't the men to sail her – all we've got is a crew of God-damned landsmen and drunks.' As if in agreement, *Ivanhoe* bobbed her figurehead, the ice on the long lance glittering in the evening sun. 'We've no

206

choice now, Douglas. We'll have to head for home. I'll send five of my decent seamen into *Ivanhoe* to help with the sails, and we'll use steam-power alone. With luck we might reach Dundee before the worst of the weather comes.'

Houston unrolled a chart on his desk, using books to weight the corners, and jabbed one leg of a pair of dividers down upon it. 'This is our position, Mr Douglas, about twenty miles south-east of Hopeful Point, with the cold current pushing us south down Baffin Island towards the coast of Labrador. To reach home we must survive the Breaking-Up Yard, round Cape Farewell and then cross the Atlantic. We've less than one full crew between two ships, one of which is crippled, and we have few experienced hands. We also have only one navigator on each ship, and the men are already tired and frightened.'

The lantern above their head swung to and fro with the movement of the ship, sending the shadows leaping across the chart. Houston went to the port-hole and looked out. 'And now the sea is rising.'

Douglas nodded. It would be stupid to remain in the Arctic any longer. 'You may be right.'

The wind rose during the night, driving both ships astern. From *Redgauntlet*'s deck, Douglas watched the insect-like figures of *Ivanhoe*'s crew balancing on the slender footropes as they battled with recalcitrant canvas. Great green seas exploded against *Ivanhoe*'s bow, but then Houston was calling for all hands and he was too busy to care about the sister ship as fierce waves hurled *Redgauntlet* into her own mad dance.

They were two days battling that squall, two days when nobody got an instant's sleep, when even the most superstitious blessed Mrs Gordon for carrying hot coffee to every man on the ship. When a block spun from above, bounced heavily on the deck and gashed Dunn's leg, it was she who helped him below to the surgeon's cabin, she who cut away his trouser-leg and sewed up the ragged wound with stitches that were surprisingly neat considering the ship's gyrations.

When she had done, she surveyed her handiwork with a critical eye. 'It will hold,' she said, 'but you won't be working for a while.'

Dunn nodded his thanks, and was back aloft within the hour, one leg encased in canvas trousers, the other bulky with already bloodstained bandages.

'Men!' said his surgeon exasperatedly. 'No wonder they're always hurting themselves.'

On the third day the storm abated. Douglas was surprised that *Ivanhoe* was still in sight, her topmasts thrusting from the southern horizon; but the wind rose again that afternoon and shrieked through *Old Fisty*'s bare rigging like the soul of an abandoned seaman.

Gently pushing her husband aside, Mrs Gordon took his place at the wheel, in support of Douglas and Hughson. 'Jimmy, you go aloft,' she said. 'You're needed there more than here.'

On the fourth day the wind altered to the north-east so that *Redgauntlet* was driven towards the jagged coast of Baffin Island. Houston forcibly removed his sister from the wheel and fastened a cable round himself and the other two helmsmen. 'There's worse to come.' His bellow was almost lost in the shrieking wind. 'Get below, Mary, damn your hide.'

'I'm needed here.' She was every whit as obstinate as her brother.

'You're needed alive.'

'Damn you, too, Willie Houston,' she shouted, her mouth an inch from his ear.

'I was damned long ago! Now for God's own sake, woman, get below!'

She stared at him for a second, with intense regret in those smoky green eyes. 'Yes, Willie.'

On the fifth morning the wind moderated. Houston untied himself and began a meticulous inspection of the ship. To Douglas's knowledge, he had not slept since the storm started, and he was haggard and red-eyed, but he was as indomitable as ever.

'Is there any sign of *Ivanhoe*?' Douglas asked.

'Not yet. It's still too dark.' But the mate raised his telescope anyway. 'I'll stand half the men down so they can get some sleep. You get some, too.'

'When I know *Ivanhoe*'s safe.'

There was no sight of her that day, nor the next. The atmosphere on *Redgauntlet* was tense. The seamen well knew how easy it was to part company with a ship in a storm, but they had only recently re-found comrades they had believed dead, and the thought of losing them again was unbearable. One or two began to murmur about unlucky ships and the presence of a woman on board, but Dunn gestured to his bandaged leg and swore to fight anybody who said anything against his surgeon.

'Cargill's a good seaman – he'll see her through.' Scrimmy grinned, revealing a gap in his teeth where a parting line had struck him.

Houston was busy with his chart and dividers. '*Ivanhoe* will have been pushed further south than we have, so we'll cast back for her.'

They found her two days later, heading north and east under staysails and royals, and the two crews cheered each other as they met. There was another celebration that day, with whisky and rum sweetening the exhaustion of Arctic sailing.

The next morning *Ivanhoe* lost her mainmast.

Davis Strait and the North Atlantic, Summer 1860

Douglas watched in horror as first *Ivanhoe*'s maintopgallant mast swayed, and then her maintopgallant stay parted with a report like fifty rifle-shots. As the mast scythed down in a great arc, its weight snapped the maintopmast stay, and spars, sails and rigging blocks all crashed to the deck. Only the elasticity of the mainsail prevented the maintopgallant yard from also arrowing downward.

'Please God, we might be able to salvage something,' a Shetlander murmured devoutly, but the next moment the tough canvas tore with a rip like a thousand saws working.

For a moment Douglas thought the yard would plummet right through the deck, but the mainsail diverted its course slightly and it plunged into the sea, raising a tumult of water whose droplets reached even to *Redgauntlet*. The lower topmast cap was next to fall, but that shock was dwarfed by the screeching crack of the mainmast splitting a dozen feet above the deck. *Ivanhoe* slewed helplessly to port as the whole confusion of spars, canvas and rigging slithered over the low bulwark.

'God have mercy,' breathed Scrimmy, awed. 'What a mess.'

The noise was still echoing between the two ships as *Ivanhoe* slowly settled into a heavy list and the waves and ripples gradually subsided.

'Steer for her.' The strain in Houston's voice was evident. 'She'll need our help.'

'Aye.' Scrimmy shifted a quid of tobacco from one side of his mouth to the other and ejected a brown stream into the spittoon that was thoughtfully placed beside the wheel. 'Ours and the dockyard we have in our hold.'

'Watch your damned mouth, Scrymgeour.' The words were characteristic, but Houston's customary fire was lacking and he swayed with fatigue as *Redgauntlet* approached the crippled *Ivanhoe*.

'The storm must have weakened her,' Douglas said, 'that or her winter in the ice.'

'Either way it's a dockyard job,' said Scrimmy as he surveyed her. 'Where's the nearest port?'

Douglas cast his mind over the chart that Houston had shown him. 'St John's, Newfoundland, or perhaps Godhaven.'

'There's nothing at Godhaven.'

'Stow your gab, you two,' barked Houston. 'We've got to save her first.'

He steered *Redgauntlet* alongside *Ivanhoe* and called for the engines to be stopped. 'Mr Douglas, you and Gay take over here. I'll ferry over as many men as we can spare and help clear off that rubbish.'

He led his men in a fierce assault on the mass of blocks, tackle, spars and cordage that littered *Ivanhoe*'s deck. There was the flash of axes in the weak sun and the mighty swings of determined men, but still it was more than two hours before she was cut free. Even then she would not remain on an even keel. Lacking her mainmast, she rolled so heavily that each time she nearly dipped her gunwales under water and threatened to shake loose more of her spars.

Gay glanced skyward. 'God grant us a spell of decent weather. She won't live through another storm like the last one.'

Houston drove his men far into the night, and Douglas left Gay in charge of *Redgauntlet* and took hot food across to *Ivanhoe*. Mrs Gordon accompanied him, armed with bandages and potions from the doctor's surgery to dress the numerous cuts and grazes that were the natural result of tired men working with jagged wood and sharp axes.

211

'Mr Douglas, I thought I told you to remain in charge of *Redgauntlet*.' Houston looked bleaker than ever in the flickering lights of the storm-lanterns. 'However, now that you're here you can make yourself useful. Find Wally Taylor and do whatever he tells you.'

By daybreak Houston had *Ivanhoe* stable, and by the next day he had created a jury-mast by fishing the largest spare spar from the stores on to what of the mainmast still stood. The new mast sat clumsily between fore and mizzen, an ugly, stumpy contraption which held mere scraps of canvas.

'Can she sail?' Douglas wondered.

Houston shook his head. 'Hardly at all. She'll make no speed through the water.'

'Will she reach St John's?'

Houston's glare came through eyes so tired that they looked as if they had been painted red. 'St John's? Have you the money to pay for a dockyard job? No? I thought not. Neither have I. And I doubt that either of us has the authority to plead credit on behalf of Mr Gilbride.'

Douglas looked at the crazy rig that was all the power *Ivanhoe* now possessed. She looked like a ship scrawled on the pavement by a three-year-old child. 'No. So what do you suggest we do?'

Houston grinned savagely. 'We sail home, Mr Personal Assistant Douglas. We sail home to Dundee where we belong.'

'Is there no alternative?'

'No. If we go into St John's we could well rot there for months, maybe even a year, while letters about the costs pass over the Atlantic to Scotland and back. Have you ever seen dockyard prices? Unbelievable. And the blubber would be spoiled, so there'd be no profit for the company. And remember, Mr Douglas, *Ivanhoe* is already sunk. Would they believe she's floating again?'

'We could leave her in St John's and carry all the men home in *Redgauntlet*,' Douglas suggested.

'No.' Houston slammed his fist down on the bulwark – Douglas wondered which was the harder. 'I've left my ship behind once already. I won't do it again. We sail both ships home together, Mr Douglas, or I stay in *Ivan* and you can get *Old Fisty* back by yourself.'

It was another two days before *Ivanhoe* was ready to sail. Even then she could make no more than two knots, and when the wind veered she barely made steerage-way. Houston was like a sheepdog with a wayward lamb, constantly steering *Redgauntlet* round her stricken, crazy-rigged sister ship, constantly shouting orders, advice and encouragement across the gap.

Eventually Douglas blocked the bell of the speaking-trumpet with his hand. 'Go below and get some rest, Mr Houston. You'll wear yourself out else.'

'And then you'll have me to deal with,' chimed in Mrs Gordon, appearing behind her brother as if by magic. She surveyed him with worry-clouded eyes and said more gently, 'Come below, Willie. Your ship's in good hands.'

'Good hands?' Houston swayed as he spoke. 'Douglas here is a blasted soldier and the others are drunks and whorehouse-men. I won't leave this deck until we're safe in Dundee and . . .' Douglas caught him as he fell.

Douglas and Scrimmy carried Houston below to his cabin and helped Mrs Gordon remove his boots and tuck him into his cot. It was a full day and a night before he awoke.

Until then, *Redgauntlet* continued her voyage without either master or mate, under the command of an erstwhile sergeant of the Seventy-Third Foot advised by a motley, argumentative but forcibly sober collection of mariners and harpooners. Douglas held her speed down so as not to lose *Ivanhoe*. The latter limped painfully on, her crew running themselves ragged every time the wind altered.

On the third day after Houston had reappeared on deck, *Ivanhoe*'s foretopsail ripped right across. 'I'm surprised it lasted this long,' Houston said resignedly. 'It was half rotted after a season in the ice. We picked the best, but even Baxter's canvas can't endure for ever.'

They spent another day moving *Redgauntlet*'s spare canvas over to *Ivanhoe*, and more than a day replacing the most decayed of *Ivanhoe*'s sails.

Blind Sandy, *Redgauntlet*'s sailmaker, sat at his bench in the half-deck, stitching with needle and palm. 'This old stuff won't last long,' he prophesied, dipping his needle into the sheep's-horn of lard that he wore round his neck – 'Helps the needle go through,' he explained to Douglas. 'See this sail?' and he held it up. 'This is meant to be number three canvas, so it should be quite stiff, but feel it.' He held it out for Douglas to try. 'It's like paper. Thin as charity. Rotted to pieces by the damp.' He shook his head in sorrow. 'It's a crime to dress a fine ship in rubbish like this. We'll pay for it; mark my words, we'll pay later.'

Douglas watched and listened with interest, as Blind Sandy told him the names and uses of things he'd never heard of: the sail-pricker and the sail-stabber, the seam-rubber and the pegging-awl, the stitch-mallet, and the fid-stool with its collection of bone and wooden fids, the small marline-spikes for puncturing stiff canvas. The sailmaker was a skilled man, a master of his trade, and Douglas wondered what would have happened if he himself had been apprenticed to a trade rather than forced to march behind the drum. He might be a craftsman now, with respectability, a nice house and a wife, rather than hoping for a job which might last a week or a month or a year. He touched the rough tattoo on his arm and sighed. What had happened had happened and could not be changed.

The weather thickened as they neared Cape Farewell. There was not one star in the sky to guide Hughson at the wheel, and a thick sleet came out of the south and drove stingingly into their faces. Houston ordered the maintopsail close-reefed and the maintrysail balance-reefed. 'And reef the main staysail with double sheets – rove ready to set, mind, if you know what that means, you damned useless buggers.' And then, quietly, 'How is she, Mr Douglas?'

For all the mate's care of *Redgauntlet*, Douglas knew that 'she' meant *Ivanhoe*. He looked astern. 'Still there, still sailing.'

Houston had ordered that both vessels carry lights, and now *Ivanhoe*'s canvas glowed with a strange phosphorescence, which some seamen claimed foretold a death but which acted as a beacon on such a filthy night.

'So are we,' Hughson said. 'God send we pass Farewell safely. After that we can just steer for Scotland.' He cursed as the wind blasted a hatful of sleet into his face.

'The North Atlantic can be a bitch, too, mind.' Houston took a spoke of the wheel from Hughson. 'Watch your steering, damn you.'

A thick flurry temporarily blinded them, but when they emerged *Ivanhoe* was still there, battling as valiantly as the proud knight at her bow.

'Hughson, it's not a hay-cart you're steering.' Houston swore again, and landed a roundhouse thump on the unfortunate helmsman's shoulders. 'Get below and leave *Old Fisty* to me.'

'There's nothing wrong with my steering.' With the sleet running from his fur cap on to his face and dripping from his chin on to the gleaming oilskins that covered his clothes, Hughson stood his ground.

'Get below, you bloody lubber. You're relieved.'

Swearing foully, Hughson left, keeping a tight hold on the lifelines as he negotiated the dangerous passage to the foc'sle hatch.

'Good seaman, that,' said Houston. 'We could do with more like him.'

Douglas nodded. 'Aye, we could. So why relieve him?'

'So I can tell you something.' The mate's eyes slid away, then he lifted his chin and glowered straight into Douglas's face. 'When I came on this voyage I wasn't meant to return in *Fisty*. I was meant to leave her and get myself picked up by another ship.'

Douglas hid his surprise. 'Go on.'

'I was to get her to the Breaking-Up Yard and leave her there. She'd blow up like *Ivan*, and then I'd be free.'

'Free of what?'

Houston's glare was poisonous. 'Are you totally bloody stupid? I'm up Tick River, man.' He shook his massive head. 'I'm in debt, like half of Dundee. Gambling debts.'

'In debt to whom?'

'To that fornicating bastard Wyllie, of course – the Serpent. That's why I was prizefighting, to pay some of it off. I owe hundreds. He said that if I left *Old Fisty* and her crew of cripples and fools in Melville Bay, he'd release me. If I didn't, he'd take my sister into one of his hells.'

'*What?*' Douglas was speechless for a moment. When he found his voice he said, 'But she's here.'

'I know.' Houston's grin was suddenly cheerful. 'I could have hugged her when I saw that she was the stowaway. If she's with me, Wyllie hasn't got her, but I couldn't leave with her on board, could I? She saved you all, did Mary.'

'Would you have done it?'

A sudden squall sent a succession of waves exploding over the bow, so that both men were too busy to speak for a few minutes. As soon as they could they both looked anxiously astern: it seemed an age before *Ivanhoe* emerged safely from the squall.

Houston showed no sign of replying to the last question, so Douglas asked another. 'Did you have anything to do with what happened to *Ivanhoe* last year?' He had to put his mouth nearly in Houston's ear to be heard above the scream of the wind.

'No.' The reply was emphatic.

'Were you going to help murder the crew of *Redgauntlet*?'

'If I was, I wouldn't tell you,' Houston replied, 'but I give you my word that I knew nothing about it.'

There was a sudden lull in the wind, an eerie calm which left the two men breathless as they faced each other across the spokes of the wheel.

'So why tell me now?' asked Douglas.

'Why not? At first I thought you'd been sent by Wyllie to watch me – I'd seen you working for him at the prizefight, remember – and I was going to kill you. But the way you've acted since, I know you're not Wyllie's man.'

'Not now, not ever.' Douglas looked astern again. Again he saw *Ivanhoe* there, battling bravely along with her staysails straining and her shortened mainmast bending under the pressure of the wind. 'There's a lot I still don't understand, Mr Houston. Why should Wyllie want you to leave *Redgauntlet* in Melville Bay? And what would have happened to you then?'

Houston shrugged. 'I'd have been all right. *Charleston* was following our smoke, and she'd have picked me up.'

'*Charleston?*'

'Yes. She hugged our stern all the way from Disco.' Houston smiled. 'I made sure her master heard about the rich fishing-ground *Ivanhoe* had discovered. He'd guess *Redgauntlet* was heading that way, so he simply followed us.'

'And Wyllie? Do you think he had anything to do with what happened on both ships?' Douglas remembered the sunken eyes and the frozen bodies, the green mould in the recessed cheeks. He also remembered Wyllie's smooth smile and languid movements. Wyllie had threatened him; Wyllie had been present when he was crimped; Wyllie had threatened to make a whore of Houston's sister.

'Of course, but I don't know how. Or why.'

'I was thinking the same.' Douglas looked pensively at the mate's huge frame. 'Perhaps we should pay a wee visit to Mr Wyllie and ask him some questions when we get back.'

Douglas had once seen a lion give the same sort of yawning smile as Houston produced – but the lion had not been gripping a marlin-spike in a paw that would have done justice to a polar bear.

'I'd like that, Mr Douglas. After what he threatened to do to Mary, I'd like that very much indeed.' The broad face darkened. 'But I still owe him a lot of money, and he's always got a small army to protect him.'

Douglas raised his eyebrows. 'I'm sure we could handle a bruiser or two.'

Houston looked him up and down, nodding slowly. 'We could,' he agreed, 'but maybe not nine or ten. And there's the money I owe him.'

'Mr Gilbride might help there.'

'Mr Gilbride's a businessman, not a benevolent society.'

'If we return him two ships full of blubber and bone he'll be a much richer businessman,' Douglas said, 'and therefore more inclined to benevolence.' And perhaps to overlooking having a Chartist as a Personal Assistant. 'So perhaps we should tell him about Wyllie.'

'Tell him what?' Houston asked quickly. 'That Wyllie wanted me to desert my ship at sea and I agreed? I'd get no more appointments as a mate – in fact, I'd be lucky if I got ten years' hard labour. At the very least it'll be a debtor's court, for Wyllie isn't the man to forgive and forget.'

The storm moderated as soon they weathered Cape Farewell. The sister ships kept in company across five hundred miles of the North Atlantic while the wind blew kindly from the west and the men prayed to a suddenly benign God. Three times in that period Houston rowed across to *Ivanhoe* to help with minor problems, and twice they changed the crews to give the exhausted Ivanhoes a rest.

Wally Taylor, Willie Syme and Jimmy Gordon refused to leave their ship, so Mrs Gordon left *Redgauntlet* to be with her man. Many of the Greenlandmen had been superstitiously worried about having a female on board, but now, perversely, they missed her. She had been the confidante of every man aboard, as well as a nurse for the injured and a hard worker in galley and foc'sle.

When they reached mid-Atlantic the next storm screamed down from the north. And *Ivanhoe* lost her mizzenmast.

North Atlantic, Summer 1860

'God damn and blast it all to Hell and gone!' Houston leaned over the taffrail and watched in impotent rage as *Ivanhoe*'s upperworks were once again reduced to a tangle of splintered wood and flailing cordage. 'How in the name of Creation are we to get her to Dundee in that condition?' For a moment he looked skyward, as if seeking divine help, then he spoke again in a voice weary with resignation. 'Get the boat out, lads, and let's have a look at her.'

This time Houston made *Redgauntlet* fast alongside *Ivanhoe* and had every man save the engineer work until the wreckage was cleared away and a jury-mizzenmast rigged. It was another five days of muscle-tearing labour before the mate was satisfied, and the ship that emerged was ugly enough to give a seaman nightmares. There was no spar taller than her foremast, and that was shortened by the loss of the foretopgallant mast, which was now fished to the stump of her mizzen. Macmillan, the boatswain, had contrived a cats-cradle of cables and ropes to keep the jury-rig in place and, if *Ivanhoe* could barely make steerage-way, at least she was afloat, upright and stable.

'If she can't make her own way, we'll tow her,' Houston promised. 'And if that doesn't work I'll throw all you buggers in the water and you'll bloody well push her to Dundee. I'm damned if I'll lose her now.'

Douglas looked at the makeshift rig on *Ivanhoe* and thought of the thousands of miles of sea that still lay between them and home. 'We'll do that,' he promised quietly. 'We'll get both ships to Dundee, and spit in the eye of Wyllie and all his plans.'

Houston looked down at him from his six foot odd of muscle and bone, still formidable despite the exhaustion that lined his face and dragged the proud shoulders down. 'A few days ago you said we should deal with Wyllie ourselves, remember?'

'I remember.'

'Does that mean you'll stand by me?' Fatigue and hard labour had forced the intemperance coarseness out of Houston so that the hidden hesitation was exposed. Douglas thought that, for the first time, he was seeing the true man.

'Jimmy Gordon might come along, too – he has a score to settle for what he's suffered.'

'No, keep the family out of this. Just you and me.' Houston held out his hand. 'But don't let me down.'

For an instant Douglas was back on the frontier with that smoking homestead and the remains of a little child. He closed his eyes and shook away the memory. 'I can't make a promise it might be impossible to keep, but if it's humanly possible I'll stand by you against Wyllie. Is that good enough?'

The hand remained outstretched, so Douglas grasped it.

The mate nodded once, gravely. 'It's good enough.'

They held the grip for upwards of a minute, while the two vessels moved together in the high swells of the Atlantic. Douglas had shaken hands with many men, from the friendly Fingo tribesmen of the frontier to the bedraggled Chartists who stood in failure at Forfar, but he had never experienced such an intense stare as Houston subjected him to now. It felt as if the mate was trying to see deep into his soul.

'Let's go home, Rab.' That rare grin appeared, cutting through the dour mask of weariness. 'Hell or Dundee, eh?'

Two days later *Ivanhoe*'s jury-rig collapsed in a riot of cordage and spars. Houston made good his promise to tow her. Douglas and the other Greenmen could do little more than admire the mate's seamanship as he organised a towing hawser, but they did contribute to the sweat and toil involved. At last, *Redgauntlet* gradually built up enough power to pull her wounded sister through the sea. The dense smoke pouring from her funnel smeared greasily over both ships, tribute to the technology that might yet save them all.

Houston surveyed the few scraps of canvas that *Ivanhoe*'s ramshackle masts could bear. 'Two thousand miles to go. If she loses anything else aloft, I'll have the men stand on each other's shoulders and hold their shirts up to catch the wind.'

'Can we tow her all the way to Dundee?' Douglas asked.

'If the coal lasts. But by the look of that smoke we're using it up fast. Pray for a gentle westerly breeze to push Ivan along without knocking down any more spars.'

Given favourable weather, an auxiliary-powered whaling-ship like *Redgauntlet* could expect to cross the Atlantic in fourteen days. Towing the crippled *Ivanhoe*, however, the passage from Cape Farewell to the tenth degree of longitude, just west of the Hebrides, took her six weeks. They were six weeks of finger-gnawing tension as the crews watched *Ivanhoe*'s fragile spars with mounting anxiety; six weeks of worry as Houston and Douglas regularly checked the coal-bunkers. Twice they hove to and transferred boatloads of coal from *Ivanhoe* to *Redgauntlet*. Both times there were angry exchanges as tired men vented their frustration on their crewmates, but the labour gave *Redgauntlet* enough fuel to continue towing.

As they neared home waters, Houston called the Shetlanders together. They gathered around him, weather-beaten, work-weary and proud, seamen in their natural element.

'I'm not going to call at Lerwick, I'm going to sail straight up the Tay to Dundee with both ships and both crews.' He waited for a reaction, but the Shetlanders said nothing. '*Old Fisty* needs all the hands she can get. You men are among the best there are. Are you willing to stay aboard?'

The Shetlanders murmured together for a few minutes, then Hughson, their unofficial spokesman, nodded and said, 'For *Old Fisty*, then.'

They used the last of the coal as they rounded Rattray Head.

Douglas led the men in scavenging for anything which would burn, and by the time they passed Buddon Ness they were reduced to throwing the cabin fittings into the boiler.

Despite their fatigue, the crews had been busy during their little free time. As they passed the Abertay Spit, a deputation led by Scrimmy approached Houston on deck.

'If you please, Mr Houston, sir,' said Scrimmy, the humility of the words at odds with the broad grin on his face, 'we – that is, the lads and I – thought we might hang a banner from the mast, sir. A welcome home, like. If you don't mind, sir.'

'What?' Houston had hardly slept for weeks. He had lost a lot of weight and his eyes were sunk deep into their sockets as he glared at Scrimmy. 'You God-damned lubber, we've got enough to do without decorating the ship with banners.'

'Aye, sir,' Scrimmy agreed. 'Here's what it says, sir.' He held out a piece of paper. 'And there's one for Ivan, too.'

When Houston read it, there was almost the hint of a smile in his eyes. 'Aye, all right, then. But don't let this nonsense get in the way of your work.'

The distinctive shape of the Law welcomed them home, the square reassurance of the Old Steeple a reminder of familiar hymns and staid Sunday Mornings. A trio of oystercatchers winged parallel to *Redgauntlet*, undeterred by the foul fumes her funnel belched to the mauve-banded grey sky. The banners fluttered boldly aloft as they slid past Marine Parade in the middle of an October morning. '*The luckiest ship in the world*', the banner from *Ivanhoe* proclaimed, while *Redgauntlet* advertised herself as '*The second luckiest ship in the world*'.

An amazed and excited crowd gathered on the Parade to watch the smoke-spuming *Redgauntlet* tow her crazy-rigged consort home. Incredulous fingers were pointed at *Ivanhoe*, and Douglas smiled to himself as he thought how soon the news of her resurrection would spread through the town.

'Whatever happens next,' he told Houston, 'we've got them both home.'

'And not a man lost under my command.' There was pride in Houston's voice. 'That's a better record than Captain Fairweather had.' He surveyed the crews. 'Look at them. Outward bound from the Tay we had a crew of farmers and whining lubbers who didn't know the bobstay from a bollard. Now look at them. They're seamen – my seamen.'

Those seamen were working furiously hard to bring their ships into the docks. Some were aloft, others were hauling on lines and yards under the orders of Cargill or the bosun. They worked in disciplined silence, despite the fact that the homes of most of them were only a seagull's call away. The skinny, drink-sodden human debris that had been dredged from Mother Scott's was now wiry and weather-beaten, while the Greenlandmen, once so contemptuous of their green colleagues, acted like the veterans they were.

'You've made them into a fine crew, Mr Houston.' Douglas raised his voice: 'Come on, my lads. Let's hear a cheer for *Old Fisty*.'

The result was a lusty roar which easily carried across the water to the Ivanhoes. They cheered back, waving their free hands.

'Again ' Houston lifted the speaking-trumpet, and his bellow could be heard across half of Dundee. 'Cheer for *Fisty*. Cheer for Ivan. No, lads, cheer for yourselves. We've made it home, boys.' He winked at Douglas and added quietly, 'And girl.'

The crews responded with an even more enthusiastic cheer. They lined the rails and watched the crowds stare and yell and point at the bold banners. Douglas wondered how many were *Ivanhoe* widows who had prayed for the return of their men. There would be renewed hope when they saw the ship limp in, and sick disappointment when they learned how few of their men had lived. Perhaps they would not think *Ivanhoe* so lucky.

Individual voices carried high above the general roar.

'I'm Hettie Matheson. Is my man safe?'

'You were dead, and you've come back!'

'Daddy. Is my daddy there?'

'How many fish? I said, how many whales?'

There was a sudden surge as a two-horse dray ploughed through the crowd, its tall wheels scattering the watchers.

'That's Horse Gilbride come to check his profits.' Houston had reverted to the sardonic bully mate. 'Or to give the both of us to the bluebottles.'

Douglas was too weary, both mentally and physically, to care about the future. He had done everything he could and it was time to let fate take care of the rest. 'Why Horse Gilbride? Why that name?'

'Horse? His name is George Gilbride, so his initials are G. G.' For the first time in weeks, Houston lit his pipe, sending sweet tobacco smoke to blend with the acrid fumes from the funnel. 'Geegee, the same as bairns call horses.'

'Of course.' Douglas nodded. He wondered absently if anybody ever had called Mr Gilbride 'the Wizard'.

Mr Gilbride was even larger and more imposing than Douglas remembered him being. He swung aboard *Redgauntlet* with a newspaper under his arm, pointed his narwhal-tusk walking-stick at Houston and Douglas, and said abruptly, 'You two have much to explain. Come with me to the Captain's cabin.'

Mr Gilbride's eyes were everywhere, examining the condition of the ship, and before he went below he stared at *Ivanhoe*, at the crazy assortment of spars and ropes that constituted her upperworks.

Houston raised his eyebrows and followed Mr Gilbride through the main hatch. Douglas also followed, wondering if he would still have a job when he emerged into daylight again.

'It's stuffy in here.' Mr Gilbride thrust open the bull's eye ports, allowing fresh air to blast in from the harbour.

'I haven't used it since the Captain disappeared,' Houston explained.

Having dusted the seat of the Captain's chair with his

handkerchief, Mr Gilbride sat down and laid the newspaper and his walking-stick on the desk. The carved face on the stick's handle rolled to face Douglas, and Sir Walter Scott stared sightlessly at him.

'You've kept the ship's books up to date, Houston?' The mate nodded. 'Good. The customs people are already aboard, and they'll want to examine everything. But before they do, give me a brief account of the voyage. I want to hear all the salient points.'

Houston left out nothing of significance, mentioning the loss of the crewman on the bowsprit, the suicide of young Symbister, the discovery of *Ivanhoe*, the mysterious collapse of *Redgauntlet*'s crew, the disappearance of Captain Fairweather, and the gruelling voyage home.

Mr Gilbride listened intently, occasionally touching his walking-stick, as if seeking inspiration from Sir Walter. When the tale was done, he looked from Houston to Douglas and back again. 'You have had an interesting time,' he said ironically. 'Has either of you formed a theory as to the reason for it all?'

'Well, sir . . .' Douglas hesitated. He was deeply reluctant to accuse a man against whom he had no evidence, nothing but curious coincidences. But he had to speak, he knew that. 'It is possible that Dr Michie may be concerned in some way. He survived aboard both *Ivanhoe* and *Redgauntlet*, and it seems that in both cases the crews collapsed after a rum ration was issued. I think he may have put something in the rum.'

'Why should he do that?' demanded Mr Gilbride. 'Dr Michie is a respected practitioner, a graduate of Edinburgh University. What possible reason could he have?'

In the silence that followed, the sounds of shipboard life came to them as the customs officers cleared the crew off *Redgauntlet*. Whalers often tried to smuggle duty-free tobacco and spirits ashore. With two whalers arriving simultaneously, the excisemen would be busy for the next few days, and until the blubber was unloaded into the boiling-yards, there would be a constant official presence on board. Douglas could understand why men like Houston hated to see their ships in port, preferring the dangers of the sea to the frustrations and confinements of life in dock.

Eventually Douglas said, 'I cannot tell, sir.' He looked at Houston for support, but the mate only shrugged. Though a master of seamanship, he was obviously uneasy in the presence of land-based authority. 'I suspect, sir,' Douglas went on, 'that Mr Wyllie may be involved, but I don't know how.'

'Mr Wyllie, too?' Mr Gilbride touched his stick again. 'He offered you a job, if I recall aright.'

'Yes, sir.'

'But you took my offer instead.' Gilbride looked at Douglas from beneath his brows. 'I received your letter from Lerwick. We had to resort to a boarding-master to raise a crew, and unfortunately you were caught in the net.' There was a pause, during which Douglas heard a woman laugh hysterically somewhere nearby. 'The day after you disappeared, somebody sent me an anonymous letter. Shall I tell you what it said?'

Douglas shook his head. 'I think I can guess, sir.'

'It said that the magistrates at Forfar had sentenced you to join the army for being a Chartist and that respectable employers should have no truck with you.'

'Yes, sir.' Douglas readied himself to leave the cabin. He would again have to seek a job of any kind he could get.

Mr Gilbride smiled. 'I threw it away, of course. I never pay heed to anonymous communications.'

Douglas closed his eyes as relief washed through him: he was still employed. 'Thank you, sir,' he said with deep gratitude.

'Good. That resolves the matter. Was it Wyllie who sent the letter?'

'He told me he would, sir.'

'Very good.' Reaching forward, Mr Gilbride flicked open the newspaper and tapped a marked article with his forefinger. 'Now read that, the pair of you.'

Terrible Loss of Another Waverley Steam-Powered Whaler
The whale-ship Charleston *of Dundee has called in at Aberdeen*
bearing the Master, Surgeon and one member of the crew of the Dundee
auxiliary-steam-powered whale-ship Redgauntlet. *The surgeon told*
a terrible tale. Miasmic fumes had escaped from the engine-room of
Redgauntlet *and, mingling with the poisonous gases from the stored*
blubber, formed a noxious cloud which overcame nearly the entire crew.

It was in vain that he attempted to revive the stricken men, but he
pulled the master, Captain Adam Fairweather, and one of the crew to a
small boat and rowed away. Before Charleston, *of the Eastern*
Sealing and Whaling Company, rescued him, the surgeon, Dr Michie,
heard a loud explosion, which he suspected was Redgauntlet's *boilers*
bursting.

This is the second successive season that a steam-powered vessel of
the Waverley Company has been lost with nearly all her hands, and this
journal must ask why the Company continues to send its brave men to
sea in vessels so obviously unsuited to the task.

Mr Gilbride smiled grimly. 'So Dr Michie is regarded as a hero,
and you have brought most of my crew back from the dead. I
believe congratulations are in order.'

'Thank you, sir. I'm glad to learn that Captain Fairweather
survived, but do you know the crewman's name?'

Mr Gilbride produced a small notebook from his pocket and
scanned the pages. 'Ah . . . Thomas Wilson, a common mariner. Do you know him?'

'Very well, sir.' Douglas could not prevent a grin from
spreading across his face. 'He and I were crimped together.'

'Indeed? Tell me, Mr Douglas, why were you in Mother
Scott's? It is . . . that is to say, it carries a rather unsavoury
reputation.' He looked slightly embarrassed.

'Somebody sent me a note telling me a man I was looking for
might be there.' And that, thought Douglas, was more un-
finished business.

'I see. Who was the man?'

'A bruiser called Peter Williamson. He is the man who scared people off signing on *Redgauntlet*, and he works at Mother Scott's as well as for Wyllie.'

'Indeed?' Mr Gilbride raised his eyebrows. 'This situation becomes more tangled by the minute. Did you find him?'

'Oh yes, sir, and he found me. He helped crimp me, after I had been drugged.'

'Laudanum,' Houston said calmly. 'It's what Lucy Scott always uses. The charming smile, the flattering attention, then a few drops of laudanum in the drink and another seaman is caught.'

'Are you certain of that?' asked Douglas. He found it hard to reconcile the mate's words with the friendly young woman behind the bar.

'Oh yes, she's well known for it. But she normally catches men for long-haul voyages which don't attract the best crews.'

'Laudanum in the drink.' Douglas shook his head wonderingly. 'How simple. That's what the doctor must have done on *Ivanhoe* and *Redgauntlet*. Laudanum is made from opium, isn't it? They use it in all sorts of things.'

'Including rum, apparently.' Mr Gilbride's face hardened. 'And the abstainers were murdered out of hand, you say?'

'Yes, sir.'

'I'll have Dr Michie questioned at once. We'll get to the bottom of this.'

Douglas had another thought. 'Sir, who wrote this newspaper account?'

'I've no idea. Why?'

'This is the *North-East Gazette*, the same paper that carried a report of *Ivanhoe*'s launch. That was also wholly inaccurate.'

Mr Gilbride waved a dismissive hand. 'Perhaps they need better staff. Of course, they can only report what they were told, and doubtless Dr Michie told them about the loss of *Redgauntlet*. They may feel a little foolish when they learn that both ships are safe, and their cargoes, too.'

He stood up and lifted his walking-stick from the table. 'Mr Houston, you have work to do. Mr Douglas, so have we.' He went to the cabin door, then turned, smiling. 'Mr Mate, I believe you must present yourself for a Master's Certificate, for I wish you to command *Redgauntlet* again next season. Now, Mr Douglas, let us first have some conversation with the police and then pay a call on Dr Michie.'

Dundee, Autumn 1860

From its site in Laurel Bank, on the slopes of the Law, the doctor's house commanded a fine prospect of the Tay. Standing four-square and solid within its garden, it had iron railings to separate it from the public street and iron bars securing the lower windows.

Mr Gilbride remained in his carriage. Douglas and two blue-uniformed police officers strode up the path to the front door. The police sergeant, a tall, broad-shouldered man made larger by his hat and air of authority, rapped smartly.

The young manservant who answered looked with something like awe at the burly representatives of authority who confronted him. 'Good morning, gentlemen. Do you wish to see the doctor?' His smile was as pleasant as his voice.

'We do indeed. Is he at home?' The sergeant spoke slowly, but Douglas had experience of searching for deserters in the army and knew that speed was more important than politeness.

He pushed into the house, shouting, 'Dr Michie, where are you?' He opened each ground-floor door he came to, upsetting an elderly cook so that she nearly dropped the pot she was holding. He found nothing untoward so, still shouting, he sprinted upstairs, followed more slowly by the sergeant and leaving the astonished manservant and constable standing in the hall.

The doctor emerged from a small room on the upper floor, and closed the door behind him. 'What is the meaning of this hubbub?' he demanded angrily. Then his expression changed, anger giving way to recognition and then shock. 'I know you!'

'Yes, Doctor, you do. I'm the ghost of all the men you murdered on *Ivanhoe*.' Douglas's rage got the better of him and he leaped forward and seized the doctor by the throat. 'You killed dozens of men, Dr Michie, and you're going to tell me why.'

'Now, sir, that's not the way to do it.' The sergeant sounded as calm as if he were advising a carter not to park across an alleyway. He laid a large hand on Douglas's shoulder. 'Come along, sir, and we'll have all this cleared up by tea-time.'

'All this?' echoed Dr Michie. 'What do you mean?'

'There seems to have been a misunderstanding, sir,' said the sergeant. 'A ship was reported lost but she's turned up again, and men who were dead are now alive.'

Douglas let his hands drop from the doctor's throat. ''Two ships, Doctor, *Ivanhoe* and *Redgauntlet*. Do you recognise the names?'

'Of course I do,' said Michie, and he smiled. 'You say they've been found? And the crews? But that's splendid news. All the men are alive and well, I hope?'

'Some,' replied Douglas through gritted teeth. 'Enough to see you dangling from a rope, anyway.'

'Now, now, sir, there's no call for that sort of talk,' said the sergeant disapprovingly. 'Please come along with us, Doctor, and we'll get to the bottom of this affair.'

Dr Michie smiled again, running a hand over his little moustache. 'With pleasure, sergeant. That is very good news indeed – the best, in fact. If you'll permit me to fetch my things from my bedchamber . . . ?' He indicated the room he had come from.

'Of course, sir. We'll wait downstairs until you're ready.' The sergeant took Douglas's arm in a firm grip and led him downstairs. 'If you act in that manner again, sir, I shall be obliged to arrest you.'

'But he's a murderer!'

'He may be, or he may not be. Whatever the truth, it is not your place to dispense justice.'

They waited in the hall for several minutes. The policemen stared stolidly at the wood-panelled wall opposite, but Douglas was prickling with impatience. Through the ticking of the long-case clock in the corner, he thought he heard the murmur of voices upstairs.

He beckoned to the manservant, who was hovering uncertainly at the back of the hall, and asked, 'Is there anybody else upstairs?'

'No, sir, only the master.'

'Then what's going on?' asked the sergeant as the murmurs upstairs became shouts.

Forgetting his dignity he leaped up the stairs with Douglas hard on his heels. There was a scream from the doctor's bedchamber. The sergeant smashed open the door and Douglas hurled himself inside.

Dr Michie lay across the bed, one hand at his throat and blood spreading down his chest. Across the room, a lithe, blue-coated figure was in the act of slithering out of the window.

'Here! Stop, you!' The sergeant hesitated, torn between caring for the doctor and following the attacker.

Douglas had no such qualms. He dashed to the window and looked out, just in time to see the blue-coated man jump down from the wall into the shrubbery below, race across the garden and clamber over the iron railings.

'We need help here,' the sergeant said, but Douglas was already through the window. He leapt the twelve feet to the grass below, recovered and ran toward the railings. As he vaulted over the spiked tops, he saw the man speeding down the hill, head down and legs pumping madly.

Douglas raced off in pursuit. He leaped the stone wall of another garden, ignoring the shouts of a frock-coated man who was probably the householder, and saw the flicker of a blue coat in front. He followed it across a neat lawn and over another wall, closing all the time, but realised he could not continue for long: shipboard life was not the best preparation for running.

There was another wall ahead, higher and topped with broken glass. The man threw himself upwards, scrabbling for handholds on the rough stone. Gasping for breath, Douglas dived at the man's feet but missed, and the few seconds it took him to regain his balance allowed the fellow to get clear. Even as he in turn scaled the wall, Douglas was fleetingly aware of something familiar about the man, his size, the way he held his head and—Damn! The glass atop the wall had sliced his outstretched hand. Blood spurted from his fingers as he stood on the wall and looked out into the maze that was the Hilltown.

There was movement to his left, a hint of blue. Douglas leaped down from the wall. In ugly contrast to the wealth and refinement of Laurel Bank, before him lay a warren of dirty streets and mean alleyways bordered by rotting tenements. Gaunt-faced people gaped at him and bare-foot children stared with the bitter eyes of old age. Filth squelched underfoot where an open sewer had spilled its nauseating contents. There came an amused cackle from an old woman sitting nursing a gin-bottle, and a black and brown dog barked at him, then, when he took a step towards it, tucked its tail between its hind legs and sniffed the ground.

The blue jacket disappeared into one of the tenements. Douglas followed, with blood still dripping from his hand and the breath rasping harsh and hot in his chest. He emerged from the close into an enclosed courtyard from which a dozen doors opened. There was no sign of the man in the blue coat.

The next morning, after a much-enjoyed night's rest, Douglas was summoned to the office in Dock Street. As usual, Mr Gilbride was seated behind his desk, the familiar bust of Sir Walter Scott at his back and the steady ticking of the clock a reminder of all the time that had passed since Douglas was last here. The lady's hazel eyes smiled down upon him from the portrait.

'So the doctor is dead,' said Mr Gilbride thoughtfully.

'Yes, sir.' Despite the bandage and Mrs Sturrock's careful attention, Douglas's hand was throbbing painfully, but he made himself ignore it. 'However, we now know there's somebody else involved.'

'As you say. Mr Douglas, let us go through everything we know and try to unravel some of the mystery.' He extracted a sheet of foolscap from the chaos of his desk and, dipping his pen into a pot of ink, began to speak and write at the same time.

'Item one: Dr Michie drugged the crew of *Ivanhoe* and left them to freeze to death.

'Item two: Dr Michie and Mr Houston were the only survivors. Captain Fairweather in *Charleston* rescued the doctor.

'Item three: Dr Michie tried to drug *Redgauntlet's* crew, but failed because of you, Mr Houston and a stowaway.' He paused and looked up at Douglas. 'Is all correct so far?'

'Yes, sir. I did not know Captain Fairweather rescued Michie last time.'

'No?' Mr Gilbride raised an eyebrow. 'Oh yes. I'm sure I told you that I poached him from the Eastern Company.'

He leaned over the paper again. 'Item four: Dr Michie was murdered by an unknown man in Dundee.

'Item five: Peter Williamson, one of Wyllie's bruisers, tried to prevent men from signing on *Redgauntlet*, and he was at Mother Scott's when you were crimped.' Gilbride looked up. 'Now, tell me who advised you to go there.'

Douglas swallowed hard. 'Sir, it was . . . It was your daughter, sir, Miss Gilbride.'

'My daughter?' said Mr Gilbride, narrowing his eyes. 'And how, Mr Douglas, could she know of the existence of such a place?'

'I cannot say, sir, but she sent me a note in which she said that one of her unfortunates had told her the man who stabbed me in the Merchants' Arms public house worked there.'

'Sent you a note?' Mr Gilbride's voice rose an octave. 'I've never known her to be anything but direct. If she wanted you to know something, she would tell you herself. Did you keep the note?'

Douglas nodded. He had stored it beneath the mattress in his lodgings.

'Oh?' Fatherly protectiveness battled with anger and incredulity in Mr Gilbride's face. 'Bring it to my house and we will show it to Ellen. I should like to hear what she has to say about this.'

Dundee, Autumn 1860

It took Douglas some time to persuade the gatekeeper to allow him to enter the grounds of Mr Gilbride's estate at Westferry. The house was not visible from the gate; unsure what to expect, Douglas set off up the long, tree-lined drive. Not until he reached the final curve of the drive did he see the house, and its magnificence made his mouth fall open.

David Bryce had designed Waverley House in the Scottish baronial style, creating a controlled riot of bartizans and corbelled windows; corbie-step gables drew the eye to a central tower whose tall windows must, Douglas thought, afford a view from the Abertay Spit to the Bay of Invergowrie. He had seen many fine houses, from those in Bedford Square and Russell Square, which arose amid the squalor of London, to the gabled Dutch beauties of Cape Town to the exquisitely carved palaces of India. But never had he seen a building which so proudly proclaimed itself to be a blend of romance, nationality and modernity.

A servant escorted him from the great hall through the archway into the inner hall, from where a banistered stairway swept upwards to a landing dominated, Douglas was unsurprised to see, by another bust of Scott. Broad doors opened from the landing, their brass handles reflecting the light from the chandelier. The stairs continued up to another landing, and then upward again to the topmost floor of the tower, where Mr Gilbride had his study.

Despite the impressive view from the great windows, it was the interior that caught Douglas's attention. Between the windows, which allowed all the light of Tayside to enter, bookcases stretched from ornately plastered ceiling to carpeted floor, while a long brass telescope was positioned to allow observation of the shipping on the Tay. In the centre of the room stood a desk whose flanks were carved with faces – Douglas hazarded a guess that they were those of characters from Scott's novels – while two glass cases held models of *Redgauntlet* and *Ivanhoe*. A newspaper lay open on the desk.

Mr Gilbride rose and came to meet him, smiling, hand outstretched. 'Mr Douglas, you are welcome to my home. Do you like it? A shrine to the Wizard of the North, and a sanctuary from the troubles of the world.'

'A very fine house, sir. Indeed, I doubt I've ever seen a finer.'

The smile grew. Mr Gilbride rang a small bell and, when a neat parlourmaid appeared, said, 'Morag, we should like some tea.

'Sit down, Mr Douglas,' he went on, gesturing to a leather-bottomed chair whose legs and back were carved with images of mounted knights and a lady with long hair. 'That's the *Ivanhoe* chair. It is reserved for visitors – I use the *Redgauntlet* chair myself. And now that you have so ably demonstrated the success of my auxiliary-powered vessels, I am about to order the *Talisman* and *Antiquary* chairs to be carved.' The smile became conspiratorial. 'As no doubt you are aware, those are two more of Sir Walter's novels, and soon they will also be well-known ships of the Waverley fleet.'

'I see. May I offer my congratulations, sir?' Douglas looked around the room and could not help but compare its trappings of fantasy and comfort to conditions in the Arctic: the squalor, the stench and the bitter cold. He heard movement behind him as the tea was brought in. 'But I should make clear that Mr Houston was as much involved in the success as I was – indeed, more so.'

'Mr Houston did his duty admirably.' Mr Gilbride looked over to the tea-bearer. 'Put the tray on the desk, my dear. Thank you. Now, will you not join us?'

Douglas blinked: had Mr Gilbride really called his parlour-maid 'my dear'? Then he turned his head and saw Ellen Gilbride standing by the desk. He rose hastily to his feet and bowed clumsily.

As when he had seen her before, her dress was that of someone indifferent to the dictates of fashion: rather than a billowing circular crinoline, she wore a skirt which fitted closely round her hips but was full enough to accommodate her free-striding walk. Light from the tall windows brought out the hazel flecks in her eyes, which were surveying him with some interest.

He moved aside, and invited her to take the *Ivanhoe* chair.

'What is this tale of a letter, Mr Douglas?' she asked when she was seated. 'I did not send you one.'

Reaching into the inside pocket of his jacket, Douglas produced the note, now sadly crumpled. 'This is what I received. You will see it is signed with your name.'

Miss Gilbride dismissed the note with a single glance. 'My name, perhaps, but not my signature.'

Douglas did not understand why, but he felt a wave of relief at her words.

Mr Gilbride held out his hand. 'May I see it?' He took it and examined the writing closely. 'A fine hand, and one which accurately captures your turn of phrase. I know of no one else who calls the destitute "unfortunates".'

'Which means that whoever sent it knows Miss Gilbride well.' Douglas took back the note and replaced it in his pocket. It had lost much of its former importance. Now it was only an aid to solving a mystery.

'Perhaps,' she conceded. She went to the desk and took up the newspaper. 'May I, Father?' At his nod, she began to turn the pages. 'But perhaps not.' She held it up and with a slender finger indicated a small advertisement.

Mr Gilbride and Douglas joined her at the desk and bent their heads to read.

Miss Ellen Gilbride seeks ladies of breeding, intelligence, Christianity and compassion to assist in relieving the distress of the poor. Miss Gilbride has already opened one establishment in Dundee for helping these unfortunates and intends to open more. Apply to the offices of this newspaper for details.

Douglas sighed. 'I take your meaning. Since you use the word "unfortunates" here, anybody who reads the Dundee newspaper would know of it.'

'Not only this newspaper, for I placed a similar advertisement in the *North-East Gazette*.' The hazel lights in her eyes had dimmed a little.

'Oh? That may have been unfortunate.' Douglas dropped his guard for a minute. 'The *Gazette*'s reporting is so far from accurate that it may well call you a follower of the Hindu religion.'

'Indeed it will not,' she said hotly. 'Mrs Sturrock recommended that newspaper – she says she is acquainted with one of the proprietors. He lodged with her many years ago, before his business became so successful.'

Douglas judged it advisable to withdraw a step. 'Mrs Sturrock? There can be no better recommendation. I stand corrected.' He ignored the amusement on Mr Gilbride's face and went on, 'Then perhaps, sir, Miss Gilbride can help me in another matter?'

Miss Gilbride stiffened instantly and a dangerous sparkle came into her eyes, but before she could speak, Mr Gilbride intervened: 'My daughter has the will of a man, Mr Douglas. It has been many years since I could compel her to do anything of which she disapproved. You do not need my permission to address her.'

'You have received some medical training, ma'am. Do you help your father to select the surgeons for his whalers?'

The fierceness of her expression would have done credit to Bully Houston. 'It has been many years since I could compel

239

my father to do anything of which he disapproved. He does not need my permission to select underlings for his ships.' Her eyes were haughty, and the hazel had expanded once more into the brown. 'Mr Douglas, I have no dealings with the men my father employs. In fact, I doubt I could tell you the name of any of them.'

Douglas had been unmoved by the tantrums of army officers, and by Bully Houston's hazing, but he found himself almost helpless in the face of the scorn of a girl five years his junior – he could almost hear Paddy laughing. He pulled himself sharply together and found his voice. 'Do you recall ever having heard the name Dr Michie, ma'am?'

She shook her head. 'It means nothing to me. From which medical school did he graduate, and when? Who were his colleagues? You do not know? No, I supposed you would not. If you knew more than his name I might be able to help you, for I am acquainted with some of the doctors at the new Infirmary.'

Mr Gilbride rang the bell on his desk. When the parlourmaid came into the room, he said, 'I wish a message to be taken to my clerk. He is to send me all the files on the crew of *Ivanhoe* and *Redgauntlet,* and everything about the surgeons. Tell him the matter is urgent.'

Miss Gilbride said she had household duties to attend to but would return when the files arrived. Without so much as a glance at Douglas, she left the room.

'While we wait,' said Mr Gilbride, 'would you care to try my telescope?' Having settled Douglas by the window, he cleared his throat and continued, with a note of constraint in his voice, 'Her mother died some years ago, but she and Alice cope impeccably. They have lacked their mother's guidance in matters of feminine decorum, perhaps, but both have developed alternative attributes.' He paused for a second. 'Ellen especially. I call them fair Ellen, from *Lochinvar*, and Lady Alice, from the *Ballad of Alice Brand*, two of Scott's poems – but pray don't repeat that, for, as you may perhaps have noticed, Ellen can be a little quick-tempered.' He sighed. 'Yet she has taken charge of the household and organises everything most capably – and me, too, I dare say. Alice is the opposite of her sister. She's a wild, flighty creature, forever going riding or shooting. I own that she is a fine shot, but that will not help her find a husband.' He sighed again. 'Have you children, Mr Douglas? Or a wife?'

Douglas turned from the telescope and shook his head. 'No, sir. I have not been fortunate enough to meet the right woman.'

'No? Ah well, perhaps you're lucky. They're a worry, a constant worry.' He looked around the luxurious room. 'You may think me a successful man, Mr Douglas, but money does not solve one's problems: it merely brings problems of a different nature. Men come courting, but they're as often after my inheritance as after my daughters, and I will not permit the kind of marriage in which my girls would be stifled and controlled for their money.'

'Indeed not, sir.' But Douglas could not imagine Ellen Gilbride being controlled by anybody.

The parlourmaid entered, carrying the files.

'Thank you, Morag,' said Mr Gilbride, taking them from her. 'Pray ask Miss Gilbride to join us directly.' When the door had closed behind the maid, he went on, 'I am glad you asked for her help. I'd like her to help me in the running of the company, but she refuses. Sometimes,' he said wistfully, 'I wish I had a son.'

When Miss Gilbride rejoined them, he set the files on the desk. There were three, one each for *Ivanhoe* and *Redgauntlet* and a separate, thinner one for Dr Michie. Simpson had sent an accompanying note assuring Gilbride of his best attention at all times, which Ellen pushed to one side.

'Here we are,' said Mr Gilbride. 'Dr Michie graduated from Edinburgh University in 1857, worked in Dundee Infirmary in

1858, but sought a challenge. Served as surgeon on *Ivanhoe* in 1859 and *Redgauntlet* in 1860.'

'Dr Michie? I was at the Infirmary two years ago, and I don't remember a doctor of that name.' She studied the file over her father's shoulder. 'What is he like, Mr Douglas? Describe him.'

Douglas considered for a minute. 'Dapper, quite young, very thorough. He had a wee moustache which he was always touching.'

'Dapper, young and with a moustache . . .' Miss Gilbride looked up from the file. 'Was he thin, with dark hair?' When Douglas nodded she frowned. 'That does sound like one of the Infirmary doctors, but his name was Morgan, not Michie.'

'It must be a different man, then,' Douglas said.

'Dr Morgan was asked to leave.' She looked thoughtfully at her father, as if wondering how much she should tell him. When she spoke again her voice had hardened. 'He was a practitioner of unnatural vice.'

'Unnatural vice?' Douglas held her eyes, which were now an expressionless dark brown. 'Will you explain that a little, ma'am?' His satisfaction at the colour that rose into Miss Gilbride's pale face turned instantly to self-disgust, but she straightened her back and continued, 'Dr Morgan preferred the company of young men to that of women.'

'Nothing wrong with that,' Mr Gilbride protested. 'Lots of chaps prefer business and hunting to holding girls' hands in the moonlight.'

She turned all the force of her eyes on him. 'Father, he used young men as if they were women.'

'What? Good God!' He gazed at his daughter, aghast. 'How the devil do you know of such things? You should be ashamed of yourself!'

Fearing a renewal of her anger, Douglas said quickly, 'Sir, if I may use your pen I may be able to resolve the matter of the doctor's identity.'

In the army, he had often sketched the terrain and positions he had scouted: perhaps that skill would serve his purpose now. On Mr Gilbride's nod, he turned over the note the clerk had sent with the files and set to work on the back of it. Within a short time he had produced a rough likeness of Dr Michie. He held it out to Miss Gilbride and asked, 'Is this anything like the man, ma'am?

'Why, yes, that's Dr Morgan. A horrible little man.' She wrinkled her nose in distaste and suddenly she looked like a young woman rather than a dedicated medical practitioner.

'Good God!' Mr Gilbride said again. 'And I employed him as a surgeon! I hope he did not indulge in his wicked practices on *Redgauntlet*.'

'No, sir, all he did was try to murder everybody.' Douglas could not keep the sarcasm from his voice.

A vision of Paddy McBride came to him, Paddy carrying a slim young man in his arms; the youth was naked save for a wig of seaweed which was somewhat askew. Paddy lifted his burden's head and Symbister gazed into the room from sightless blue eyes. When Douglas shook his head the vision disappeared but the message was clear.

'Jesus,' he said softly, and immediately apologised to Miss Gilbride. 'Sir, I think he did do those wicked things, with a young Shetlander called Symbister.'

'The boy who killed himself,' Mr Gilbride said at once. 'Do you think that is why?'

'It may be, sir. Or the doctor may have killed him so that he could not talk.' Douglas thought back. Symbister had been missing from the fast-boat, and had been upset on the night when he was found dead. And then there was the care with which the surgeon had examined each crewman. He said, 'I believe Dr Michie and Dr Morgan were indeed one and the same, but that does not tell us why he murdered so many men.'

'You told us yourself,' Mr Gilbride pointed out. 'If he killed Symbister to stop him revealing his filthy secret, that may also be why he killed the Ivanhoes.'

'All of them? And then put to sea in a small boat at the back edge of nowhere in the hope that a ship would pick him up? It's unlikely.' Douglas began to pace the room as the thoughts flowed through his mind. 'No, sir, Dr Michie cannot have been working alone. I believe that Symbister was a mistake, and had nothing to do with the drugging of the crew. I believe the doctor went aboard *Redgauntlet* knowing what he intended to do, and knowing he would be rescued afterwards – by *Charleston*.'

'But how could he know she would be there?' Miss Gilbride sounded excited.

Douglas remembered what Houston had told him. 'This was planned well in advance. All *Redgauntlet's* crew knew that *Charleston's* captain was following her, hoping to find the good fishing-grounds. Michie must have known, too, and—' He broke off as a terrible thought struck him.

'And?' she prompted.

'And so did Captain Fairweather,' he said quietly.

Mr Gilbride looked stricken, but he took Douglas's meaning. 'Captain Fairweather was *Charleston's* Master when she rescued Dr Michie after the loss of *Ivanhoe* – as I told you, Mr Douglas, he was for a time employed by the Eastern Sealing and Whaling Company – and he also survived the supposed loss of *Redgauntlet*.'

Douglas nodded. The pieces were beginning to click into place. The jovial Captain Fairweather had often ordered a double ration of rum for the men, doubtless so that they would later unquestioningly accept the grog laced with laudanum. And he had refused to use the engines on the outward crossing of the Atlantic, which meant that *Redgauntlet* was in company with the other sail-powered whaling-ships when they made landfall at Disco. The engines had, however, been used in the Breaking-Up Yard, which would have enabled *Charleston* to follow the smoke. It seemed that Fairweather had drawn *Charleston* along like a dog on a lead, so that she would be close by when he took the steam-launch and deserted his ship.

'Yes, sir,' he said, 'I believe Captain Fairweather is the link. But why? Why kill so many men – all the Ivanhoes who froze to death, and the Redgauntlets who abstained from drink? And where does Wyllie fit into this strange pattern?'

'The Lord will reveal all in His own time.' Miss Gilbride's face and voice were grave.

'Yes, ma'am, but in the meantime I think we should interview the Captain.' He looked again at his likeness of Dr Michie. 'I only wish that the surgeon was still alive so we could interview him as well.' Paddy nudged his arm so he looked more closely at both sides of the paper. 'Good God, sir, look at this.' He laid the sheet of paper, the sketch downmost, beside the note purporting to be from Miss Gilbride. 'It's the same handwriting.'

There was a long silence while Mr Gilbride studied them, with his daughter peering over his shoulder.

At last he said wearily, 'You are right, Mr Douglas. That is Simpson's writing. My clerk's in this too. Fairweather and Simpson.' Anger replaced the weariness. 'How many more, for God's sake?'

'There's no need for blasphemy, Father,' his daughter chided him.

'Perhaps not, ma'am, but there is great need for speed.' Douglas tapped the files. 'By now everybody knows your ships are back, and Simpson knows you are reading these files. It may be that he and Captain Fairweather are working together. Or it may be merely that he took a dislike to me and therefore arranged for me to be crimped.'

'No.' Gilbride shook his head. 'Simpson has no initiative. He can only follow orders. I think it more likely that he's being used to spy on me.'

'If you're right, Father,' said Miss Gilbride quietly but with some intensity, 'when he learns some important information he will take it to his employer.'

'That's obvious, child.'

'If we knew what information Simpson wanted, we could feed it to him and follow him, to discover where he goes.' It might have been significant that she looked at Douglas as well as her father. 'Then we will know if Captain Fairweather is indeed his employer.'

Mr Gilbride nodded. 'But we don't know what they want.'

'No, sir, but I think we may be able to guess.' Douglas was pacing the room again. 'We know somebody spread rumours to stop men signing on *Redgauntlet*. Wyllie was involved, but we don't know why. We also suspect that Dr Michie murdered the crews on the orders of these same people, who later murdered *him*, presumably to stop him revealing who they are. From that, we can surmise that these people want the Waverley Company to fail in its business.' He wondered if he should say anything about Houston, but decided to let sleeping seadogs lie. Mr Gilbride knew of Wyllie's involvement; it would not help to reveal that the mate had been blackmailed.

'Yes, yes,' said Mr Gilbride testily, 'we do indeed know all that. Get to the point, sir, for God's sake.'

Ignoring the minatory look Miss Gilbride gave her father, Douglas continued, 'If we let Simpson have information about the company, something he can use – perhaps something about your new ships, *Talisman* and *Antiquary* – he'll be eager to pass it on as soon as possible. I'll follow him and then we'll know. I think he'll go to Wyllie.'

'You tried to follow the man who killed Dr Michie,' Miss Gilbride pointed out acidly, 'but you lost him in the Hilltown.'

Douglas remembered a handshake on *Old Fisty*'s deck. 'I might enlist some help.'

'Just in case you don't succeed, we'll make it false informa- tion.' Gilbride began scribbling notes. 'Now, I don't know who to trust any more, so we must keep the details secret.' He glanced up at Douglas. 'This help you mentioned, don't tell him too much.'

'It's Mr Houston, sir. I believe I can trust him.' He was surprised at the gentle expression on Miss Gilbride's face when she looked at him.

'It seems, Mr Douglas, that we are putting a lot of trust in you.' Her tone was acid, but in her eyes the hazel was steadily replacing the brown.

Dundee, Autumn 1860

Douglas felt the reassuring bulge under his jacket for the fifth time in half an hour as he waited in the slithering mist that softened the outlines of the Dock Street tenements. It was well over a year since he had carried a firearm, but Gilbride had insisted, even accompanying him to the newly established firm of Gows in Union Street to help select it; Douglas had chosen an English-made Tranter revolver, which had been the favourite weapon of Major Donnachie, and it was now thrust into the waist of his peg-top trousers. He stood outside a ship's chandler's, puffing on his pipe and with his square cap firmly pulled over his eyes. With his dark braces and tarred canvas shirt, he could have been any recently discharged seaman.

Mr Gilbride allowed his clerk an hour's break for lunch, and at exactly five past twelve Simpson appeared. He looked taller than he had in the office, perhaps because he was clad in a long black overcoat. He glanced surreptitiously to right and left while he buttoned his coat, then set off along Dock Street, head down and shoulders bowed. He kept to the middle of the pavement, and strode unheeding past the seamen and their women, the purposeful businessmen and the swearing carters with their overworked horses. Two fishwives with massive creels and broad, work-worn faces argued forcefully as he lunged past, automatically nodding to a man in the tattered red coat of a soldier, who perhaps remembered past hardships and hoped for a better future.

From Dock Street Simpson turned left and headed toward the teeming ancient tenements and crumbling wynds that made up the district known as the Vaults. Douglas followed, determined not to lose him, determined to atone for his previous failure. At the entrance to one of the narrow wynds, the clerk paused, looked back again, then slid into the wynd.

As soon as Douglas turned in to the wynd, he felt claustrophobia set in as the thick, damp air of the wynd wrapped itself round him. Not the salty dampness of *Redgauntlet*'s foc'sle but the clammy, mouldy dankness of generations of neglect, dry rot and crumbling stonework. The ground beneath his feet was foul with mud and human excrement. Doorways opened to left and right, black entrances gaping into the homes of the hopeless poor. There was a baby crying somewhere, and a woman mumbling drunkenly in Gaelic. A bottle rattled at Simpson's feet and then they were out of the wynd and into a courtyard where a sign proclaimed there were lodgings to be had and a pig nosed busily in a rotting pile of effluent.

Simpson entered one of the doorways that opened off the courtyard. His footsteps clattered as he climbed the staircase within its external tower. Douglas followed, past two platties, but slipped into the deep shadows of a recessed doorway as Simpson mounted a flight of wooden steps that stretched up to an attic room.

Douglas touched the Tranter's smooth handle for reassurance. He could either follow and chance what happened, or report back to Mr Gilbride and have the police deal with whatever was up there. Moving forward slightly, he glanced into the courtyard, and felt a rush of relief when he saw the huge figure of Houston standing motionless in the shadows. He steeled himself to burst into the attic, but at that moment the door opened.

Peter Williamson stood there; his yellow waistcoat was stained and his face unshaven. There was a woman at his side, naked arms draped around his neck and a mass of black hair descending to her waist. She laughed and whispered something in Williamson's ear as he spoke to Simpson. Her hands loo-

249

sened, slipped lingeringly down Williamson's body as he stepped outside, then she disappeared back inside in a flicker of linen shift and bare limbs.

Douglas shrank back into the doorway as Williamson and Simpson passed. The door behind him opened quietly and a neatly and cleanly dressed woman stepped out. She smiled shyly and began to scrub the plattie with a hard brush.

Douglas followed the two men down the stairs and, after a pause to let them get a little ahead, across the courtyard. He peered round into the wynd and saw that they had turned towards the Vaults. Douglas set off after them, grateful for Williamson's yellow waistcoat, which was easy to pick out in the crowds.

Twice they stopped and looked back, but each time Douglas was able to slide into shelter. They passed the docks: the tang of salt air twisted a pang of memory, and the cry of seagulls seemed the call of the mariners lost in the ice-fields of the north. As they went further the crowds thinned somewhat, and Douglas dropped back and crossed the road so as to be out of his quarry's direct sight.

The area was shockingly familiar: they crossed an iron railway-bridge and struck out into the forgotten land between the railway and the Tay. The stench of blubber from the Eastern Company's boiling-yard assaulted Douglas's nose as he watched Simpson and Williamson walk straight into Mother Scott's. He had done enough; he had established a definite link between Simpson and the Crossover, and he could report back to Mr Gilbride.

'Rab. Rab Douglas!' The voice sounded from behind him. 'I've been looking for you.' Tam Wilson advanced, hand outstretched in greeting and a broad smile on his face.

'Tam!' Douglas grasped the hand with relief and pleasure. 'I was worried about you – we searched for you for days.' The Personal Assistant took over. 'You'll have to report to Mr Gilbride, though, and tell him what happened.'

'So I will, Rab, but not just yet.' Tam's honest face was weathered, his eyes warm and friendly. 'Come away into the Crossover and we'll sink a dram or three.' His hand was insistent on Douglas's arm. 'I heard that *Old Fisty* towed *Ivanhoe* from Cape Farewell to the Tay, with half the crew dead and it blowing a hurricane the whole time.' His laughter was infectious.

Douglas shook his head. 'Not the Crossover. I've bad memories of that place.'

'Me too, and I intend to drink them all away.' The hand tightened on Douglas's arm, and Tam said in a hard voice, 'Away in you come, Rab, and we'll talk.'

It was easy to escape from Tam's grip, but he instantly gave a shrill whistle and three men came running out of the Crossover. Douglas's quick punch disposed of the first, but the second slammed him into an armlock.

The third was Williamson. 'Afternoon, Mr Sergeant. I thought I saw you skulking in the Vaults. Did you enjoy your trip to Polar Bear land?'

'Tam! What's happening here? Lend a hand.' But Tam shook his head, still smiling, and followed the struggling men into the dark doorway of Mother Scott's.

The place was even more ramshackle than Douglas remembered, an establishment of many apartments, where crooked stairs coiled into hidden neuks and padded doors opened into secret rooms. The three men bundled him past the low bar at the entrance, through a heavy door and down a flight of stairs. Another door, heavily studded, and then complete blackness. Somebody lit a storm-lantern and Douglas saw he was in a stone-slabbed cellar furnished with a wooden chair and a long bench of rough planks. There were three lanterns mounted on the walls, and green slime oozed down between them.

'This is our domain.' Williamson sounded proud. 'This is where Tam and I do some of our best work.'

'Tam?' Douglas pulled one arm free and tried to swing a

251

punch at Williamson, who sidestepped with ease. 'Tam, what's all this?'

'Tam, what's all this?' Tam mimicked, laughing. 'This is where you answer questions, Rab.' He waited until Douglas had been thrust down on to the chair and securely bound to it, then continued, 'This is where you tell us who you really are and tell us everything about Horse Gilbride.'

'But you know about me! I was a sergeant in the army and I was crimped into *Redgauntlet*. You were there, Tam – you were crimped, too.'

'Don't you understand yet, Rab?' Tam knelt at his side. 'I wasn't crimped. Think about it: why would I be in a place like this when Eliza was with child?' He laughed. 'I was paid very good money to be on *Redgauntlet*, far better than I'd ever earn as an ordinary crewman.'

Douglas glared at him. 'Good money? Who paid you? Wyllie? Tam, listen. We think he's involved in murdering the Ivanhoes and drugging the boys on *Redgauntlet*. Him and Dr Michie.'

Tam raised his eyebrows. 'Oh, is that so? I didn't know that.' He laughed again, and spat in Douglas's face. 'Mr Wyllie's given me a new house, Rab, rent-free for a year. What's Horse Gilbride given you?'

'Self-respect.' Douglas felt the spittle running warm down his face. He looked into Tam's eyes, still unable to believe the truth. 'Did you know about the murders on *Redgauntlet*?'

Tam shook his head. 'Robert, Robert, when will you understand? I work for Mr Wyllie. I was on *Redgauntlet* to make sure the doctor did his job. The men drank their laced rum, collapsed and should have died of the cold, like the Ivanhoes did. There were a couple of temperance men, but I cut their throats.'

'*You* did?' Douglas fought against the ropes that held him.

Tam, honest, frightened, superstitious Tam, smiled at him. 'I did, the same as I cut Dr Morgan's throat when he became a liability, the same as I'll cut yours when you've answered our questions. Unless you decide to join us.'

Douglas recalled the blue-jacketed man scrambling over the railings of the doctor's garden. He should have recognised Tam then. Perhaps he had, but had not been able to believe what he saw.

Tam drew the seaman's knife from his belt. 'It was amusing when Bully Houston accused you of being sent by Mr Wyllie to spy on him, when all the time I was spying on the doctor.'

'Why?' Douglas refused to flinch as Tam laid the knife-point against his cheek. 'Why did Dr Michie kill all those men?'

'Because Mr Wyllie told him to, and what Mr Wyllie wants Mr Wyllie gets.' Tam pressed harder, until the knife-point pierced Douglas's skin. 'And because if he didn't do as he was told the whole world would know about his liking for handsome young men.' He twisted the knife a little and slowly pulled it down Douglas's face. Douglas pulled back his head as far as he could, but still Tam slowly cut his face open.

Douglas's mind was racing. So that was how Wyllie worked: he found a weakness in a man or a secret from his past and used the knowledge as a lever. Wyllie had manipulated Houston through his gambling debts, and had tried to do the same to Douglas through his Chartist connections. He had given Tam financial security for his wife and child.

'Now, Sergeant Douglas. I believe Horse Gilbride is planning to add another ship to his fleet. Name? Type? Where will she be built?'

Douglas thought quickly. It was no secret that Gilbride named his vessels after Scott's novels. What had Gilbride told Simpson? Douglas tried to recall the details of this trap. '*Rob Roy* – she's going to be *Rob Roy*.'

Tam withdrew the knife. 'Good boy. That's what Horse told Simpson. Now tell me the rest.'

The cut stung and blood ran warm into Douglas's mouth. 'You said I might be able to join you.'

'Did I? Why should you want to do that?' Tam signalled to Williamson, whose casual backhanded slap rocked Douglas back in the chair. 'After all, you've already turned down one chance to work for Mr Wyllie.'

Douglas felt for loose teeth with his tongue. 'So I did, but it would be better working for Wyllie than being knifed.'

'Don't trust him, Tam.' Williamson slapped Douglas again.

'No, don't ever trust him.' Douglas had not heard the door open behind him, but Lucy Scott was in the room, her voice immediately calming the tension. She walked gracefully across the squalid room, her lilac skirt rustling softly and the light catching her golden curls. 'I know Robert Douglas, formerly Sergeant Douglas of the Seventy-Third Foot and now Personal Assistant to Mr Gilbride.'

She stood beside Tam, a smile in her clear blue eyes. 'He's a very dangerous man. It's mainly because of him that *Ivanhoe* and *Redgauntlet* came back.' She held up a hand as Douglas protested. 'No, no, Mr Douglas, there's no need to be modest. We're well aware that Bully Houston provided the seamanship, but we also know that you told him what to do. You spoiled our plans, Robert.' She laid an elegant finger on his chest, shaking her head in disapproval.

'Will I just kill him, then, Lucy?' Tam jerked Douglas's head back and put his knife to the taut throat.

'Don't be hasty, Tam,' she said, gently pushing the knife away. 'Have we found out everything he knows about Mr Gilbride's business?'

'Not yet.'

'You had better tell us, you know, Robert.' Lifting her skirt from the knee, Lucy knelt beside Douglas. 'I liked you the minute I saw you. You're strong, brave, and obviously resourceful. Quite handsome, too, with that long jaw of yours and the devil-damn-you look in your eyes. Unfortunately, I think you're also loyal. Loyal to your regiment in the wars and loyal to George Gilbride.' She shook her head, sadness in those expressive eyes. 'I think you're too loyal to Gilbride to help us willingly, so we'll have to persuade you.' Leaning forward, she laid a soft hand on his cheek and kissed him on the mouth. 'I'm sorry, Robert.'

She stood up. 'Strip him, boys, and put him on the bench – and let us have a little more light to work by.'

Tam lit two of the wall-lanterns while, under Lucy's watchful eye, the bruisers untied Douglas. They held him expertly while Tam ripped the clothes from his body.

'What's this?' Tam held up the revolver. 'My, my, look what the soldier-boy was carrying.'

'A very dangerous man,' Lucy repeated softly. She slid a finger from Douglas's chin down to his navel, and patted him gently. 'On to the bench with him and make him secure.'

Douglas jerked his head back, catching Williamson on the bridge of the nose, but Tam landed a sharp blow to the groin which doubled him up and followed it with a kidney-punch. Momentarily helpless with pain, Douglas gritted his teeth as he was rolled face up on to the wooden bench. He fought fiercely, but Williamson and one of the bruisers lay on top of him while Tam tied his ankles and wrists to the corners of the bench.

'That's better,' said Lucy approvingly. 'I feel much safer with you like that.' One of the bruisers brought the chair over and she sat down, a slim hand resting on his upper thigh. He caught a faint waft of her perfume; it was delicate, like the scent of primroses.

'Now, Robert, I'm going to ask you a lot of questions, and I want you to answer them all. If you do, I'll be pleased. If you don't, we shall hurt you. Do you understand?'

Douglas nodded, and his heart began to thud rapidly.

'Good.' Lucy patted him. 'Please answer truthfully, for I don't wish to hurt you.'

'You could let me go,' Douglas said, but she only shook her head, with compassion in her eyes.

'No, Robert. I'm sorry but I can't do that.' Her lips parted, revealing a tiny gap between her top front teeth. 'I do hope you'll cooperate. That would please me.'

The door opened and Simpson came in, accompanied by a huge man whose mountainous form was silhouetted against the lamps in the passageway outside. Then Williamson lifted one of the storm-lanterns down from the wall, and Douglas had eyes for no one else.

'Hot whale-oil, Sergeant. Nasty stuff if it spills on you.' Williamson came and stood beside the bench, opposite Lucy. He placed the lantern on Douglas's stomach.

'Now, Robert.' Lucy caressed his face with her hands and voice. 'Now you can help me. Where does Mr Gilbride intend to build his new ship?' Her mouth remained open, pink tongue darting to touch the gap in her teeth.

Douglas filled his lungs and roared as loud as he could. '*Fisty! Old Fisty!*'

Simpson staggered as his companion shoved him aside. Tam turned, knife in hand, but was flicked aside by one swipe from Houston's massively muscled arm. Williamson flung the storm-lantern at Houston, who ducked, swerved and threw a punch which lifted Williamson clear off his feet. The other two bruisers dived at Houston, one wielding a leather cosh, the other a length of heavy chain. Lucy sat calmly watching, her hand still light on Douglas's thigh.

The chain wrapped itself round Houston's head, and the cosh landed once, twice, three times on his upper arm. Houston staggered, roaring, and Tam moved in, knife held underhand for the groin stroke. Douglas fought savagely against the ropes, but to no avail.

'*Fisty! Old Fisty!*'

Shouting men poured into the cellar; seeing their familiar faces, Douglas nearly laughed. Scrimmy was there, howling his whisky song as he wrestled the chain-wielder to the ground. Jimmy Gordon, thin-faced and hard-eyed, tackled the man with the cosh. Robertson and Gay threw themselves at Tam.

And still the Redgauntlets came. The cellar became a crowded confusion of bodies.

'Back away, boys.' Lucy Scott's voice was soft but clear, and it was somehow audible through the noise of the fight. She stood up and walked calmly towards the door. The Greenlandmen parted like brash-ice before *Redgauntlet*'s reinforced bows. Not even Houston tried to stop her.

When she reached the doorway she turned. 'Good-bye, Robert, for now. In a way I am glad we were interrupted. I really do like you, you see.'

To Douglas's amazement, Scrimmy opened the door for her. 'Stop her, Scrimmy,' he said urgently. 'That's Mother Scott.' Not a man moved. Lucy went out and Scrimmy closed the door behind her.

'Well, at least cut me free, then.'

'Leave him be,' ordered Houston, 'until these others are safe. Nearly didn't find you, Mr Douglas – this place is a warren.'

Knife slashing wildly, Tam made a dash for escape, but Greig tripped him neatly, then kicked him savagely in the ribs. 'Murdering . . . bastard. Dirty . . . murdering . . . bastard.' Each word was accompanied by another kick.

The mood had changed abruptly. Douglas had witnessed the like before, when a carefree brawl changed to something much more serious and what started as an affair of belt-buckles, black eyes and bloody noses ended in drawn bayonets.

'Cut me free,' he repeated. This time Houston obliged, and Douglas pulled Greig off the cowering figure of Tam. 'No murder, Greig. We're not as bad as they are.'

Only Williamson continued to show resistance, swearing foully as he stood with his back in a corner. He had knuckle-dusters on his left fist and a long metal bar in his right. 'Come on, then, you Greenland scum. Fight me.'

Houston stepped forward, but Douglas pushed in front of him and said, 'He's mine. Hear that, Williamson? You're mine.' Stooping, he picked up the length of chain, swung it

257

once to test the weight, then threw it at Williamson's legs. Taken by surprise, Williamson tried to sidestep, but Douglas had expected that. His first punch took Williamson in the throat, the second landed in his groin; as the knuckle-dusters flailed weakly, Douglas slammed his doubled fists into Williamson's kidneys.

'And that's done for you.' Douglas kicked away the metal bar, wrestled off the knuckle-dusters and, unable to restrain himself, stood on the prostrate man's head before turning to the Greenlandmen. 'I didn't expect to see you lads here.'

The men grinned at him, one or two looking sheepish. 'Well,' said Robertson, 'Mr Houston said there was to be a fight, like, and we're all shipmates, Fisties.'

'Besides,' said Scrimmy, 'it's a grog-shop, right? So there might be some whisky for the boys.'

There were more grins, and approving laughter.

'Couldn't let you down, Rab,' came Willie Syme's quiet voice, 'nor Mr Houston there, not after you rescued us from the ice.'

To cover his feelings, Douglas took his time picking up his revolver from where it had fallen. People had delighted in telling him that the Greenlandmen were a drunken, quarrelsome bunch of troublemakers, riddled with superstition and always ready to scream for their rights. That might be true, but they had another side. These were good men, real men, prepared to risk their lives to help a shipmate in need. As he looked at them he felt a flood of affection, not far removed from what he had felt so often for the men of the Seventy-Third.

He swallowed and said, 'You're fools, the lot of you – thank God!' He had expected the subdued chuckle that followed, and responded by taking command again. 'As long as you're here, though, let's get this adder's nest cleaned up.'

'Aye, Rab.' Scrimmy's grin was even wider than usual. 'But you'd better put some clothes on first. You might shock the ladies.'

While he dragged on his torn clothes, Douglas told Gay and Greig to go to Mr Gilbride and tell him what had happened. 'Tell him we're searching for evidence.'

'Evidence, aye.' Greig gave Tam a casual kick. 'But we'll be back, so leave some whisky for us.'

Douglas led the Redgauntlets through the corridors and dark chambers of Mother Scott's. There were private rooms where painted young women, some still in their early teens, looked at them through ancient eyes, and other rooms adorned with paintings which would have shocked Nero. There was the public room Douglas had been in, where half-dressed women danced attendance on witless men. There was a room where one man filled bottles with turpentine, a second added flavouring and colour from an assortment of tins, and a child who could not have been more than eight years old pasted on bright labels.

They found a room whose walls and ceiling were composed entirely of mirrors; the next was filled with pipes, the scent of opium, and supine, dead-eyed men; while yet another was furnished with furs and exquisite carpets and quilts from the East.

In a room full of whips, belts and birches, an old woman looked up. 'Don't you be making a mess, now,' she said crossly. 'I've just got this place clean after the last lot.' She had a bucket of pink liquid at her side and a duster in her hand.

Twice they entered rooms where intense men were gambling, seated at tables covered with green baize. Both times the burly watchers withdrew hastily before a rush of shouting Greenlandmen.

'Gambling hells.' Houston curled his hands into fists. 'Places I know too well.' He took a step forward.

Douglas caught him by the arm and said, 'Come with me to find the office – let the others tear the place apart. We need paperwork, addresses, proof that Wyllie and Mother Scott were behind the deaths on *Ivanhoe*.'

'Tam will tell us all he knows – that should be enough.' Houston looked uneasy. Like Douglas, he was only too aware that an establishment like Mother Scott's was a nearly irresistible temptation for the Greenlandmen: already a couple had disappeared to try the contents of a bottle or the warm welcome of a woman. 'Maybe we should get out now.'

'Tam probably will tell us all he knows,' Douglas agreed, 'but how much is that? He's at the bottom of the pile, a common mariner. I want the admiral.'

Scrimmy staggered past, singing, a bottle of bright orange liquid in his hand. Alex Dodds kicked open a door and slipped inside, reappearing with a small, rounded woman at his side. 'Here, Jimmy, just like the Innuit girls.'

Jimmy Gordon looked and spat. 'No comparison, Doddsie.'

'Near enough for me.' Dodds withdrew into the room again.

Gordon kicked open another door. 'Mr Douglas, there's more stairs through here.'

For a second Douglas thought he saw a shadow in the doorway, a rangy man in a red coat: Paddy McBride, shaking a warning finger. He took the revolver from his pocket, ducked though the low doorway, and began to climb the stairs, Houston thumping along behind him, carrying a lantern. There were sounds of fighting below, the thud of blows, somebody shouting hoarsely, a woman's scream. Douglas hesitated: the Greenlandmen were his responsibility. But they were grown men, well able to look after themselves, and he must shut his mind to everything but the task in hand.

Fifteen steep steps, twenty and a small landing opened up before them. There was one door of polished pine, its brass handle gleaming in the light of Houston's lamp.

Douglas turned the handle, pushed. 'It's locked.'

'Bugger that! I've taught you all I know and still you know nothing. Out of the way.' Houston lifted his boot to the height of the lock, braced himself and kicked. The door burst open and Douglas looked inside.

The room was small, square and simple, its floor covered by a plain red carpet. Four candlesticks gleamed on the marble mantelpiece above the fireplace in the opposite wall, and a grandmother clock ticked softly in the far corner. In the centre of the room, facing a multi-paned window, stood a leather-topped desk on which there were an inkwell, a pipe and a sealskin tobacco-pouch.

The desk drawers were locked, but Houston wrenched them open, spilling papers on to the floor.

'Ah, this may be what we want.' Replacing the revolver in his pocket, Douglas began to sift through the assortment of handwritten and printed forms. Most he discarded as of no immediate interest: 'Receipt . . . bond . . . receipt.' There was a bundle of letters tied with a red ribbon and addressed to Maurice Scott by Lucinda Wyllie. They were dated some thirty years previously. 'Who's Maurice Scott?' he wondered.

Houston shrugged. 'No idea. Maybe Mother Scott's husband.'

'Lucy Scott's husband? I doubt she was born thirty years ago.' Douglas put the letters aside and began to rummage through the next drawer.

'Could be her father, then.' There was a yell downstairs, followed by the crash of breaking glass, and Houston shifted uneasily. 'Hurry up, will you? I'm a wee bit worried about the lads. They're capable of anything if I'm not there to look after them.'

'Wait, here's something.' Douglas ran his eye down the document. 'It's a deed for the Eastern Sealing and Whaling Company. A share document.'

'Eastern? That's the company that owns *Charleston*. Keep looking.' The noise from downstairs grew even louder.

'Aye. And here's another. More shares – thirty-two in *Charleston*, twenty in *Dudhope*, twenty in *Coldside*, thirty-two in *Gowrie*. It loooks as though Wyllie owns shares in all of them.'

'And they're all Eastern Company ships.' Houston went to

261

the door and peered down the stairs. 'I think Williamson and his lot are free again.'

'There's more here, something from Captain Fairweather.' Douglas read it quickly. 'It's a partnership agreement between him, Wyllie and Lucinda Scott. They own the entire Eastern Company.'

'Fairweather, Wyllie and who? Lucinda Scott? That must be Lucy Scott's full name.'

'Must be,' Douglas agreed, 'and she's a central part of the whole thing.' Folding the agreement, he tucked it inside his jacket. 'So now we know. Let's finish here and pay Captain Fairweather a visit.'

'Mr Houston?' Scrimmy's voice sounded from below. 'Wyllie's here with a bunch of men. And I think Jimmy's dead.'

Dundee, Autumn 1860

'Jimmy!' Houston's roar echoed through the building. 'I'm coming, lads!' Taking the stairs four at a time, he thundered down to where Scrimmy stood. 'Where away? Where's Jimmy?'

'Down that way.' Scrimmy waved a vague hand. 'We were looking for papers, like, and maybe a bottle, and this smart-looking fellow appeared and Jimmy told me it was Wyllie. Then the fellow poked his stick at him, but it wasn't a stick, it was more like a sword, and Jimmy went down.'

'He's mine.' Houston spoke more softly than Douglas had ever heard him. 'Wyllie's mine. I'll swing for the bastard if I have to.'

In his yellow waistcoat Williamson stood out among the men trying to push the Greenlandmen back into the cellars. Douglas saw Wally Taylor slumped on the ground holding his head, and Robertson was leaning against a wall wrapping a strip of linen round his arm, which was bleeding profusely. A large man was holding Greig while Tam punched him, again and again and again. It was not a one-sided contest – both sides had suffered casualties – but surprise and local knowledge had helped Wyllie's bruisers against the scattered Redgauntlets.

The arrival of Houston and Douglas at the rear was a fully equal surprise.

Heedless of anything except revenge, Houston hurled himself at Wyllie's men, knocking two down without breaking stride.

'Wyllie,' he roared, 'I want you! You're mine!'

Wyllie stood aside, smiling slightly and flicking his swordstick to and fro. 'So here you are, Mr Houston. Come to pay off some

263

of the debt you owe, have you?' He flexed his wrist and the long blade glinted in the lamplight. 'Come and pay in blood.'

Even Houston paused before the menace of that deadly steel.

'Not so brash now, eh, Mr Bully Mate? Where are all your threats? Are you sure I'm yours, or are you *mine*?' On the last word, Wyllie lunged: Houston only just sidestepped in time. The blade flicked again, slicing through a fold of Houston's jacket. 'What, no more boasts, Mr Bully? Are you a coward as well as a gambler, a debtor and a ranter?' The sword whirled in little glittering arcs, driving Houston back and further back until he was hard against the wall. 'When you're gone, Mr Mate, who will look after green-eyed Mary, now that I've spitted Jimmy like a rat? Think on that for a second.'

Paddy was there, standing beside Houston, sighting along his rifle-barrel. He cocked an eyebrow at Douglas.

Douglas raised his revolver and shot Wyllie through his sword-arm. The report echoed along the corridor like an iceberg splitting in Melville Bay.

Wyllie dropped his sword and looked at the blood spurting from his arm. 'You shot me,' he said. 'Me!' Then he screamed, high-pitched, again and again and again, until Houston knocked him unconscious.

Douglas looked around, and saw that the fight was going against the Greenlandmen. Wyllie must have pulled in every tough and bruiser from his establishments the length and breadth of Dundee, and they were experienced in dealing with brawling sailormen. Scrimmy was reeling under the assault of two squat and muscular creatures who grunted with the force of each blow they landed. Dodds was on the floor, curled up against a hail of kicks from another bruiser.

'*Fisty!*' Douglas shouted. He slipped a punch, smashed the barrel of his revolver across the teeth of a one-eyed man, and gasped as a cosh bounced from his shoulder. The cut on his face had opened again; fresh blood rolled down his face.

Astonishingly, Lucy Scott was there, in the midst of the

melee, rallying her troops with calm advice and reassurance. She pointed to Douglas. 'That one. Put him down and we've won half the battle.' Meeting his eye, she smiled and blew a kiss across the press of battling bodies. 'Hello, Robert.'

A bruised Williamson led the rush toward Douglas, bowling aside a bemused Willie Syme. Douglas ducked the downward swing of a lead-weighted cosh, threw the first man over his shoulder and jabbed an elbow into the throat of another, but then Williamson was on him, growling. From the corner of his eye Douglas saw Houston rising from a press of bodies, fists battering like the pistons of *Redgauntlet*'s engine; then something smashed against his temple and he staggered back, blocked a kick to his groin, gasped as white agony seared his left arm. Fresh blood soaked through his shirt and dripped from his fingers. There was a roaring in his ears and he could feel his strength ebbing.

'Seventy-Third!' His yell became a croak as the weighted cosh slammed into his kidneys. 'To me! *Fisty! Old Fisty!*'

The floor was rising toward him, its security a welcome release from the pain. There was Paddy, marching toward him in the Bengal heat, and there were the colours, flitting in the distance, oh so pretty, reds and greens and blues, as the women gathered behind Paddy, shrieking. Douglas smiled. When had the Seventh-Third recruited all these women?

'Where is he?' The shriek was piercing, edged with determination as the women mobbed along the corridor. 'Where's my man, Wyllie?'

As Paddy came closer, Douglas saw him metamorphose into a woman whose thin face and smoky green eyes were as familiar as the ice on *Redgauntlet*'s rigging. That was Mary, Jimmy's wife, come to rescue him from the Arctic. Douglas lurched towards the wall, hugging the agony of his arm, head and kidney. No! This was no way for a sergeant of the Seventy-Third to act. His men trusted him.

'Seventy-Third!' No, that wasn't right. '*Old Fisty!*' Using the wall as a lever, he pushed himself upright in time to see Mary Gordon lead the *Ivanhoe* widows and a group of other women in a kicking, scratching, biting rush which took Wyllie's men wholly by surprise. It could not last long, though, for with all their anger and determination the women were no match for the bruisers.

'Ivanhoes, help your wives! Redgauntlets, to me!' Houston's roar gave his men heart. He rose tall again, his great fists smashing the face before him to a bloody pulp, and rallied them. Even the wounded Greenlandmen took up the battle-cry: 'Ivan! *Old Fisty!*'

Taken on two fronts, Wyllie's men tried to run, but there was nowhere to go. First one dropped his weapon and begged for mercy, then another, until all the fighting had ceased. Some of the women were not inclined to mercy: Douglas saw one man surrender and then be felled by a shrewd kick in the groin, which left him moaning and cowering on the ground; while a group of women exacted summary vengeance on another bruiser.

'Well done, boys.' Lucy Scott was as calm as ever. 'You're a remarkable man, Robert. I thought I had done for you this time.' She walked up to him, laid her hand gently on his wounded cheek and smiled, her blue eyes as gentle as a lover's. 'This isn't the end, Robert. You and I working together could do great things.'

With the slow swing of her hips mesmerising every man, Lucy once more walked through the ranks of the Greenland-men. She had a smile for every man she passed; she touched Houston with the tips of her fingers and stepped daintily over one of her own fallen.

'Please allow me to pass.' She waited for the *Ivanhoe* widows to stand aside.

'You murderous bitch!' Mary Gordon's roundhouse punch landed square on Lucy's face, and in an instant half a dozen screaming women surrounded her. They dragged her to the ground and beat and kicked her with a fury which attracted the admiration even of Bully Houston.

'Now there's something,' he said as his sister seized Lucy by the hair and pounded her face on the floor. 'I didn't think Mary had it in her.'

'Willie.' Jimmy Gordon stood swaying in the doorway, grey as a ghost and with his whole chest and belly covered in blood.

'Jimmy!' This time the scream was a joyous one, and Mary Gordon fairly leaped across the room to her husband. She caught him in her arms and gently lowered him to the ground, supporting him against her shoulder. Houston hurried over and knelt beside them.

'The Captain . . . and a woman . . . that way.' Jimmy raised a wavering hand and pointed through the doorway. 'Down . . . third staircase.'

'Captain Fairweather?' Houston rose at once. 'I'll get him.'

'I'll come too.' Repressing his pain, Douglas stepped over Wyllie and joined him.

'You're hurt.' Houston was already moving. 'You'll slow me down.'

'Stop talking and keep moving.' Douglas handed his revolver to a bruised Robertson, told him to guard Wyllie's men with it, and hurried after the mate. At the head of the stairs he overtook him and descended into a blackness which stank of rotted seaweed and salt water. He remembered the place, although on his last visit Wyllie's bruisers had been dragging his barely conscious body. 'This is the way to the sea.'

'Aye.' Houston pushed ahead of him. 'So there'll be a boat down here.'

Dry steps led to others which were slippery with seaweed. Then there was water lapping coldly at their feet. They were in a cellar, with a stone roof arching above and an arc of light showing ahead. Between them and the light was a boat, with two men rowing mightily and two figures huddled in the sternsheets.

'God damn and blast it to buggery and gone!' Furiously, Houston threw a handful of seaweed after the retreating boat. 'We'll never catch them now. Mr Douglas, use your gun. Shoot them.'

'I gave it to Robertson.' Douglas strained in the dark to see who was with Fairweather.

'Can you see another boat?' Houston peered along the edge of the water. 'There – what's that?' A square-nosed, flat-bottomed miniature lighter, barely fifteen feet long, was moored to an iron ring, with a long pole leaning against her stern.

'I think this was a wine-cellar once,' said Douglas. 'The ships must have unloaded at low tide and the men punted the cargo inside.'

Houston nodded. 'Probably at night to beat the excisemen.' He stepped into the lighter. 'Right, on you come and we'll catch them.'

'In that?' Douglas surveyed the boat. Even in the gloom of the cellar it looked unsteady. He could not imagine how it would react to the fast current and chops of the Tay.

'It's all there is. Come on.'

Douglas stepped aboard, fell to his knees and grabbed the low gunwale. There was a faint smell of rotting wood. 'Is this safe?' He thought of the frozen men on *Ivanhoe*, of young Symbister dying naked and alone, of the grief of the widows at the dockside. 'Push off, Mr Houston.'

Houston's muscles bunched and the lighter rocked crazily, with water surging aboard. 'Bail. Bail, you useless lubber!'

Douglas cupped his hands and bailed, throwing the water overboard in a constant stream that did nothing to lower the water-level. 'I think we're leaking.'

'Of course we're bloody leaking. Half the planks are stove in. Bail like buggery or we'll sink. Can you swim?'

'Swim? Yes.'

'Well I can't, so don't stop baili—*Duck!*'

The stone arch was only an inch or so clear of Douglas's head. There was a second of deep darkness, a drip-drip of green slime, then the lighter rose alarmingly with the swell of the Tay: Douglas bailed frantically. Houston changed his stance and used the pole to scull them onward. The rowing-boat was only about twenty yards ahead, but the oarsmen knew their business and the gap increased even as they watched.

Captain Fairweather turned and looked back at them, then turned away again, leaned forward, and began to step the mast.

'If they get a sail up we'll never catch them.' Houston was panting with the effort of sculling. 'Can you see who else is in the boat?'

'I think Tam's one of the oarsmen. I can't make out who the woman is.'

Despite Houston's desperate efforts with the pole, the gap was still growing. A larger wave hissed along the lighter, cascading cold clear water around their legs. 'We'll never do it.' Houston did not stop sculling. 'I wish you'd brought your gun.'

The river was busy, with the Fife ferry puffing slowly across to Ferryport on Craig, a dozen shrimp-boats competing with the undecked Broughty herring-boats and two brigs coming from the Baltic. There was also a steam-launch which looked set to pass between the lighter and the shore.

'Look at the God-damned wake from that God-damned launch,' panted Houston, still sculling. 'He'll capsize us if he's not careful.'

The launch came closer and a tall man stepped out of her cabin.

'What are you doing out here?' Mr Gilbride grinned at them, obviously well pleased with himself. 'Come aboard and explain yourselves.' Then he saw the dried and crusted blood on Douglas's face, and his expression changed at once. 'Good God, man, you're hurt!'

Douglas allowed Mr Gilbride to help him aboard. Cargill,

quiet and efficient as ever, was steering the launch. At his side was a solitary policeman, who looked as if he was enjoying the novelty of a cruise on the river. Mr Gilbridge ushered Douglas into the small cabin, followed by Houston, and there, not greatly to Douglas's surprise, was Miss Gilbride, sitting in an easy chair. He looked around the cabin, and saw painted in large white letters above the portholes the word '*Redgauntlet*'.

Mr Gilbride had followed his look. 'Yes, Mr Douglas, it's *Redgauntlet*'s steam-launch, which the master of *Charleston* returned after picking up our men. As we thought, he was following *Redgauntlet* to find the whales.' He glanced at Houston. 'He had nothing whatever to do with the murders. But your wounds must be tended to at once. Ellen, my dear . . . ?'

Miss Gilbride hurried to fetch warm water and bandages, and upon her return her father continued, 'We sent Gay to lead Inspector Murdoch and a dozen men to Mother Scott's, and then we remembered the sea-gate, so we thought we'd see what we could see – Ellen's idea, of course.'

She ripped open Douglas's shirt-sleeve. 'Alice used to bring me sailing here before the devil led her into attending prize-fights.' She tilted her head and surveyed the wound. 'What a mess you've made of your arm. See, it's scored right through your tattoo.' For a second she met his eyes. 'Now that the Chartist hive has been split, where will the bees live, Mr Douglas?'

Houston had gone back on deck and forcibly replaced Cargill at the wheel. He was steering for Fairweather's boat, but the wind was coming off the land and it was a close contest. 'Mr Gilbride, sir,' he called, 'can we get any more speed out of her?'

'She wasn't designed for racing,' Mr Gilbride called back.

Miss Gilbride tied the last knot in Douglas's bandage. 'There, sir, your arm will do now. But I don't know what can be done for your face.' Her smile seemed to mock him.

Douglas thanked her, then suggested they all go on deck to watch the chase. Both Gilbrides agreed with alacrity.

As they emerged on deck, a flurry of wind blew smoke from the narrow funnel into Mr Gilbride's face. He coughed and said, 'By God, what a foul contraption!'

'Don't blaspheme, Father,' said Miss Gilbride at once, but her severity was a little marred when the wind teased several tendrils of hair free of their hairpins and blew them over her face. She brushed them away crossly.

'He's getting away – this damned wind.' Houston looked round. 'Beg pardon, Miss Gilbride.'

'I should think so indeed.'

'Where does he think he's running to?' asked Douglas. 'He surely can't be planning a long voyage in that wee thing. He must be going to land somewhere further down the coast.'

Mr Gilbride shook his head. 'There's an Eastern ship sitting just off the Mouth of Tay. I was watching her this morning through my telescope. I believe Fairweather intends to get aboard and sail away.'

'We must keep steam up, then,' said Houston, 'and – look, sir! Look at Fairweather's boat. The wind's veering and he'll have to tack.' He was jubilant. 'We can steer a straight course and cut her off.'

Douglas did some calculations in his head. Houston was right. Fairweather's boat was faster than the steam-launch but, as soon as the wind shifted, the launch could subtend the angle to catch her.

Again Fairweather turned round, this time with something in his hand. A flat crack sounded across the water.

'He's shooting at us,' said Cargill calmly.

'Is he, by God?' Mr Gilbride took a couple of strides forward. 'Never let it be said that I hid away from danger. I feel like Rob Roy.'

'Oh Father, don't be foolish.' Miss Gilbride pulled him back. 'Mr Douglas, will you tell my father to be sensible?'

Douglas realised that father and daughter were enjoying themselves immensely. All the rest of Miss Gilbride's hair had now worked loose and was whipping madly around her head, while her face was scoured bright by the wind of their passage. There was a sparkle in her eye that he had never seen before.

'Leave Mr Douglas alone, Ellen.' Gilbride was grinning like a boy. 'How are we doing, Mr Houston?'

'Duck, sir!' Houston shouted. On the instant there was another crack and something punched a neat round hole in the bulkhead beside Douglas. 'We're getting very close.'

With an apologetic glance at Miss Gilbride, Douglas vaulted on to the small foredeck. Fairweather's boat was only a few yards away, jinking to and fro in the fitful the wind. The Captain was standing erect, resting the pistol on the crook of his arm as he fired, aiming each shot with great deliberation.

'Stand by.' Houston eased the wheel round, so that the launch's bow nosed closer to the boat.

Fairweather squeezed off another shot, which flew high, then turned away to work the sail. Houston spun the spokes of the wheel, but again Fairweather manoeuvred away. Spindrift spattered Douglas's face as he crouched, waiting for a chance to jump the gap. The woman in the sternsheets hunched down still further, pulling the hood of her heavy cloak over her head.

As the launch closed, Tam lifted a boathook menacingly. The woman leaned towards Fairweather and shouted in his ear.

In the nick of time, Douglas realised that the Captain was drawing a bead on him.

'Duck, Robert!' It was the first time Miss Gilbride had ever used his given name, but Douglas ignored her. He poised himself on the tiny foredeck and, when Houston again spun the wheel, threw himself at Fairweather's boat. For an agonising moment he hung in mid-air, the launch sliding with a dipping wave and the boat rising sickeningly to meet him.

With a jarring thump he landed on the gunwale. A second of

wild panic as Fairweather thrust the pistol at his head, and then he was rolling inboard, kicking out with both feet. He felt the satisfying shock of solid contact, and then Tam was looming over him, teeth bared and the wicked barb of the boathook poised above his belly.

Douglas twisted away and reached up – he felt the wound on his arm tear open again. He seized the shaft of the boathook and pushed backward, matching Tam's strength with his own. There was a pair of feet to his right, so he raised his head and bit deeply into the calf of the nearer leg; the owner screamed and jerked away. But Tam was pushing down on the boathook, grimacing with effort, pressing the steel point against Douglas's stomach.

There was a sudden heavy lurch and somebody shrieked. Tam overbalanced, releasing the boathook. The mast of the little boat cracked, splintered and slewed overboard. Then Cargill was standing astride Douglas and Houston's great roar sounded, followed by the solid *whump!* sound of a hard punch. Douglas struggled up on one elbow and looked about him. A lively scene met his eyes. Houston had rammed Fairweather's boat and driven it up on to one of the Tay's many sandbanks. The policeman had the second oarsman in a headlock, Houston was wrestling Fairweather to the deck, and Cargill had his hands round Tam's throat and looked set to strangle him.

The woman was swearing fluently. She scrabbled in the tilted bottom of the boat, came up holding Fairweather's revolver and aimed it. 'I'll kill you, too, *Mister* Gilbride,' she hissed.

Douglas lunged upwards, but he was forestalled by Miss Gilbride, who jumped at the woman, forced her arm down and held it tight until Douglas reached out and removed the gun.

'By God, Miss Gilbride,' he said, 'that was a near thing.'

'By God, Robert, so it was.' She smiled brilliantly and brushed the wild hair from her face.

Their eyes met, held; then both looked away.

Douglas got to his feet, tucked the pistol into his belt and turned to see the face of the woman he held.

Mrs Sturrock spat in his face.

Dundee, Autumn 1860

They sat in the warmth of the drawing-room at Waverley House, with the fire crackling cheerfully in the hearth, while Morag served tea and cake. As the door closed behind her, the clock whirred softly and began to chime. Douglas had forcibly to prevent himself from converting the ten chimes into two bells of the first watch.

Mr Gilbride set his teacup down and leaned back comfortably in his leather armchair. 'Well, that was an interesting day.'

'Indeed, sir.' Douglas knew that he should not have felt so much at ease in his employer's house, but he did not care. He relaxed and allowed the fire's warmth to ease the nagging pain of his wounds. Even after Ellen's most careful ministrations the cut on his forearm still seeped blood, and his face ached from Tam's knife. He closed his eyes and was instantly back in the cellar, speadeagled on the bench with Lucy Scott sitting warm and perfumed at his side while her tongue dripped poisoned honey into his soul.

'So Mrs Sturrock was behind it all the time. Who would ever have thought it?' Mr Gilbride lit a cigarette, fixed it into a long ivory holder and allowed the smoke to curl up towards the ceiling. 'Have you been able to learn the whole story, Mr Douglas?'

'No, sir. I believe I have managed to fit most of the pieces together, but there may be gaps.'

'Ellen will tell you, then. She is much better at that sort of thing than I am.' Gilbride waved his cigarette toward his daughter, who sat primly on a hard-backed chair contemplating the religious sampler she was embroidering.

'It's really quite simple, Mr Douglas.' Her eyes were nearly all hazel and her creamy complexion was still tinged with colour from her excursion on the Tay. 'Mrs Sturrock – Mrs Lucinda Sturrock – has been married three times. Her first husband was one Mr Jonathan Wyllie, who owned a number of public houses in Dundee. You shot their son, I believe.'

'I did. I thought he was the one behind all the trouble.'

'Indeed he was not. He was only managing some of his mother's concerns.' She lifted her teacup and took a sip. 'Well, Mr Wyllie died of what was thought to be disease, possibly cholera, though I think it more likely to have been of poison – but of course we cannot know now. Mrs Wyllie then courted and married Maurice Scott, owner of the Crossover Inn. Unfortunately, the inn lost much of its usual respectable custom when the Arbroath Railway opened, so the Scotts made it into a house of ill repute – gambling, kill-me-deadly whisky, loose women, dancing, even a place where seamen could be crimped by unscrupulous ship-owners and masters. The devil's own place.'

'I agree with that, ma'am.'

'And so you should, Mr Douglas. But Mr Maurice and his wife had a baby girl, the beautiful Lucy, whom you know.'

Douglas remembered her presence more than her features, her aura of charm and seduction. If Mrs Sturrock had had the same allure when she was a young woman, it was no wonder that she had been able to marry where she wished. He nodded. 'I met her.'

'And she met all of you, I hear.' Miss Gilbride's look was severe, with just a hint of brown creeping into the hazel. 'Anyway, Mr Scott conveniently died, leaving his business to his wife. Then came husband number three, Mr Sturrock, property-owner and tenement landlord.'

'And what happened to him?' Douglas found that he was

276

fascinated by the play of light in her eyes. He already knew that they changed colour according to her mood, but he had not realised how rapidly that change took place.

She screwed up her nose. 'He fell through the rotted stairs of one of his own tenements. It may be that the fall was not an accident, but again we cannot know now. Like his predecessors he left his property to his wife, who was by now a rich woman.' She took another sip of tea. 'So Mrs Sturrock was now the owner not only of residential property in the Overgate and the Hilltown but also of three public houses and the Crossover Inn. She was also the mother of a fine upstanding young man, whom she sent to the High School of Dundee and the University of St Andrews, and mother of the beautiful Lucy.' Her eyes met Douglas's. 'Whom you know.'

'Indeed.' Douglas waited expectantly for the rest of the story, but Miss Gilbride seemed to be contemplating the subject of Lucy Scott. Eventually he asked, 'How did Captain Fair-weather become embroiled in Mrs Sturrock's schemes?'

'He was to be husband number four. He already owned shares in half a dozen ships, and he knew Wyllie. It seems that he fell under Mrs Sturrock's spell, and she offered him her money and her hand, provided he fell in with her plans to enter the whaling-fishing industry. She realised that whale-oil would become more and more lucrative in the growing jute trade and, being the woman she was, wanted to control the whole market, which meant removing the opposition.'

'In other words, the Waverley Company?' Douglas looked at Mr Gilbride, who nodded.

'Precisely,' said Miss Gilbride 'Once my father's company had been destroyed, Mrs Sturrock would have been able to set her own price for whale-oil with the jute merchants. The Captain was her pawn, another step on her way to . . .' She screwed up her nose again. 'To I'm not sure what.'

'And the doctor?'

'Dr Morgan-Michie.' For a second she looked almost guilty.

'I fear that I am partly to blame for that. Mrs Sturrock was one of the benefactors of the Infirmary. She gave hundreds of pounds, and often visited to make sure her money was being used correctly. I met her there, and foolishly told her of my concerns about Dr Morgan's predilections. She must have welcomed the chance of having a doctor whom she could control, and she recommended to Captain Fairweather that Morgan should join *Ivanhoe*. I was grateful to her for removing him from the Infirmary, so' – a shake of the head and a rueful sigh – 'when she asked if she could assist in my work with my unfortunates, and asked me about Father's business, I told her perhaps more than I should have.'

Douglas said, 'I think there's more yet. It was Mrs Sturrock who showed me Mr Gilbride's advertisement for a Personal Assistant, and she strongly encouraged me to apply. She was delighted when I was appointed, and every time I returned to my room she asked me about my new job and listened closely to every detail I told her.'

Mr Gilbride smiled at him. 'You must not blame yourself for that, Mr Douglas, for how could you have guessed what she was at? Speaking of the advertisement, you recall that she recommended you to advertise in the *Gazette*, Ellen? Indeed, she told you that she knew one of the proprietors.' The cigarette described an airy gesture. 'That was Mr Laurence Forbes, who is in fact sole proprietor of the *North-East Gazette* – hence the reports that damned the Waverley Company.

'And one last thing. You'll remember that damned—So sorry, Ellen, my dear, a slip of the tongue. I should say, that wretched business of the curse and the spinner to whom I paid compensation? Well, as the entire story was a fabrication, I'll wager that Simpson simply slipped my twenty pounds into his own pocket. Never did like the man. Nitpicking scoundrel!'

There was a faint click as Miss Gilbride replaced her cup and saucer on the tray. 'Well, well. You certainly are a wizard,

Father. Mrs Sturrock spun a fine web of deceit, did she not? Was Mr Forbes to be her fifth husband, I wonder?'

'Possibly.' Mr Gilbride went to the fire and stirred it with the poker so that bright sparks flew up. 'But a matter of more direct importance is where Mr Douglas is to live, now that his landlady is in prison and likely to remain there.'

'I'm sure I don't know,' said Miss Gilbride demurely, 'but no doubt he'll find somewhere more suitable than a room in the Overgate. Perhaps you could rent him one of your houses, Father?'

'That is an excellent suggestion,' he said. 'That is, if you wish to continue in my employ, Mr Douglas? Perhaps your first experiences have made you wish to work elsewhere?'

'Mr Douglas is a man of principle.' Miss Gilbride looked sternly at Douglas, as if challenging him to dispute the fact. 'He's not a man to be put off by a little difficulty. Of course he will stay.'

'That's settled, then.' Mr Gilbride turned as the door opened and a young lady entered. 'Ah, Alice, my dear, I'm glad you have joined us. I don't think you have met my Personal Assistant, Mr Douglas, who has just saved my company from bankruptcy and kept us all out of the gutter?'

Miss Alice Gilbride bounced in, smiling, and held out a frank hand. 'How do you do, sir?'

Although of the same parentage as Miss Gilbride, she could hardly have been more different. Whereas her sister was reserved, almost stern, Miss Alice smiled as freely as a puppy wagged its tail. Whereas Miss Gilbride dressed in sombre colours and her hair was nearly always controlled, Miss Alice looked as if she had pulled on the first things that came to hand, and half her hair was loose so that it cascaded over her elfin face – the very same elfin face that Douglas had seen laughing from a carriage during the prizefight.

He took her hand as if it were made of glass. 'A pleasure to meet you, ma'am.'

Miss Alice laughed as readily as she smiled. 'Ma'am? That's what the servants call me when Father is listening. My name is Alice.'

'I think Mr Douglas is very well aware who you are.' Miss Gilbride's eyes were nearly black. She rose from her seat and the two young ladies stared frostily at each other.

Mr Gilbride winked at Douglas. 'They're like a pair of cats sometimes, these two – all that hissing and posturing.' He crossed the room to a fine mahogany cabinet and took out a decanter. 'Brandy, Mr Douglas? Or whisky if you prefer.' He smiled. 'I can guarantee that there's nothing added.'

Miss Alice took the decanter from her father's hand. 'Let me pour, Father.' Her ready smile excluded her sister. 'After listening to Ellen's preaching I am sure Mr Douglas will need a large glass. Is that not so, Mr Douglas?'

The clock's ticking sounded loud in the pause that followed.

Ellen stepped up to Douglas and laid a hand on his uninjured arm. 'After seeing the trouble it can cause, Mr Douglas has decided to stop drinking.' With a single, appealing glance to her father, she reached up, drew Douglas's head down, and kissed him, very gently, on the chin. 'Is that not correct, Mr Douglas?'

Douglas was aware that the question had nothing to do with drinking. He had to make a decision now: allow himself to trust and allow this woman to put her trust in him, or else walk away. The faded red jacket and rangy form of Paddy McBride appeared beside Gilbride, but this time Paddy held a little girl by the hand. The girl was smiling.

'Indeed it is not. But I will drink only if you join me, Ellen.' He looked down into eyes of pure hazel.

Historical Note

Although the characters in *Whales for the Wizard* are all fictitious, many of the incidents are based on historical fact. Dundee in 1860 was undergoing a period of considerable industrial success, often at the expense of poor living conditions for the inhabitants. The city was also at the forefront of British whaling. In 1858 Gourlay's shipbuilders of Dundee installed a steam engine in the wooden whaling ship *Tay*. The experiment was a success and for the next fifty years the auxiliary powered whalers of Dundee were to dominate British Arctic whaling.

Boarding masters, or crimps, were one of the more unpleasant factors of maritime life in the closing decades of the nineteenth century and the opening decade of the twentieth. They were particularly ferocious in the western seaboard of the United States and South America, but Britain had its infamous quota. Among the worst was Mother Symrden of Liverpool, one of a handful of motherly women who turned a fine profit by doctoring the grog of seamen and accepting the blood money payment from a captain desperate for a crew.

The case of *Ivanhoe* being recovered after a season in the Arctic is not unique. In 1826 *Active* of Peterhead was abandoned in the ice with her cargo of seven whales. Next season she was recovered and brought home. Twenty-eight years later, in May 1854, the whaler *Resolute* was abandoned at 76 degrees north 94 west, only to be recovered in September of 1855, having drifted 1,200 unseen and lonely miles in the interval.

In 1879 the Dundee steam whaler *Arctic* carried a five-ton steam launch across the Atlantic to be used in the Bay of St John's in Newfoundland. Mr Gilbride stole a march on history by a few years, but he was obviously a progressive man.

Malcolm Archibald
Dundee, 2004

POLYGON is an imprint of Birlinn Limited. Our list includes titles by Alexander McCall Smith, Liz Lochhead, Kenneth White, Robin Jenkins and other critically acclaimed authors. Should you wish to be put on our catalogue mailing list **contact**:

Catalogue Request
Polygon
West Newington House
10 Newington Road
Edinburgh EH9 1QS
Scotland, UK

Tel: +44 (0) 131 668 4371
Fax: +44 (0) 131 668 4466
e-mail: info@birlinn.co.uk

Postage and packing is free within the UK. For overseas orders, postage and packing (airmail) will be charged at 30% of the total order value.

Our complete list can be viewed on our website. Go to **www.birlinn.co.uk** and click on the Polygon logo at the top of the home page.